Praise for #1 *New York Times* bestselling author Susan Mallery

"If you want a story that will both tug on your heartstrings and tickle your funny bone, [Susan] Mallery is the author for you!"
—*RT Book Reviews* on *Only His*

"Mallery...excels at creating varied, well-developed characters and an emotion-packed story gently infused with her trademark wit and humor."
—*Booklist* on *Only Mine*

"Mallery's prose is luscious and provocative."
—*Publishers Weekly*

Praise for *USA TODAY* bestselling author Sarah Morgan

"[Sarah] Morgan's brilliant talent never ceases to amaze."
—*RT Book Reviews*

"Each book of hers that I discover is a treat."
—*Smart Bitches, Trashy Books*

#1 *New York Times* bestselling author **Susan Mallery** has won the hearts of millions of readers around the world with books described as "immensely entertaining, intensely emotional" (*RT Book Reviews*), "hilarious" (*Fort Worth Star-Telegram*) and "heartwarming" (*Publishers Weekly*). One major retailer recently described her as "the queen of romantic fiction." While she deeply appreciates the accolades of critics and booksellers, Mallery is even more honored by the enthusiasm of her readers and the word of mouth that catapults her toward the top of the bestseller lists time and again.

Mallery lives in not-so-sunny Seattle with her husband and a toy poodle who makes her laugh every day and who's not even a little bit impressed by her growing fame. Visit Susan online at www.susanmallery.com.

USA TODAY bestselling author **Sarah Morgan** writes hot, happy contemporary romance. Her trademark humor and sensuality have gained her fans across the globe and two RITA® Awards from the Romance Writers of America. Sarah lives near London with her family. Visit her at sarahmorgan.com.

#1 *New York Times* Bestselling Author

SUSAN MALLERY

THE GIRL
OF HIS DREAMS

⟨H⟩**HARLEQUIN**® BESTSELLING AUTHOR COLLECTION

ISBN-13: 978-0-373-01177-3

The Girl of His Dreams

Copyright © 2016 by Harlequin Books S.A.

The publisher acknowledges the copyright holders of the individual works as follows:

The Girl of His Dreams
Copyright © 1997 by Susan Mallery, Inc.

Playing by the Greek's Rules
First North American Publication 2015
Copyright © 2015 by Sarah Morgan

Recycling programs for this product may not exist in your area.

HARLEQUIN®
www.Harlequin.com

Printed in U.S.A.

CONTENTS

THE GIRL OF HIS DREAMS

Susan Mallery

CHAPTER ONE

"But Mr. Cookie has never spent the night away from home," the woman in the waiting room wailed.

Kayla Bedford overheard the conversation and rolled her eyes. "Mr. Cookie needs to get out more," she said to herself as she turned on the water and began rinsing the large, soapy sheepdog in front of her.

Duchess endured the bathing stoically, staring mournfully at Kayla, as if silently asking how someone who claimed to love animals could stoop so low as to *bathe* them.

Kayla tilted the dog's nose up so she could rinse her forehead without getting soap in her eyes. "Don't give me that sad little look," she said. "You smell bad. If you'd stop rolling in the mud, your owners would stop bringing you in for a bath. It's your own fault."

Duchess accepted her responsibility in the matter with a sharp bark and a swipe at Kayla's nose. Kayla laughed and ducked back to avoid the pink tongue, not to mention the dog's breath.

"You've got to start flossing, kid," she said.

She finished rinsing Duchess and unhooked the short metal leash that kept her charge in the tub while she worked. She grabbed an oversize towel from a rack on the wall and stepped back. Duchess liked to give herself a good shake before submitting to drying.

"But I haven't seen *all* the facility," Mr. Cookie's owner said. "What's in there?"

"Our dog-grooming facility. But you shouldn't go in there. Kayla is working with a—"

Kayla heard her boss speak, but it took her a couple of seconds to react. Unfortunately, that was one second too long. The door opened, and a woman stepped into the room. Her clothing obviously cost more than Kayla made in a month. Mr. Cookie's owner had perfectly groomed hair, perfectly done makeup, and enough jewelry to support a family of four about two years.

Mr. Cookie wasn't too bad himself. He was a tiny Yorkshire terrier with a blue bow between his ears.

"Wet dog," Kayla said quickly, positioning herself between the well-to-do customer and Duchess.

She was too late. Mr. Cookie spotted Duchess and barked. The huge sheepdog pricked up her ears. Doggie eyes met. If it wasn't love at first sight, it was something darn close. Mr. Cookie jumped out of his mistress's arms at the same moment Duchess leaped from the tub.

"That hideous creature is going to hurt Mr. Cookie!" the woman shrieked.

Patrick Walcott, Kayla's boss, took the woman's arm. "Mrs. Kane, there's nothing to worry about. Duchess is a well-behaved dog. Mr. Cookie is fine. See?" He pointed at the two dogs, who were sniffing noses. The terrier made low sounds in his throat, as if the moment were too much for him.

"Your dog is going to be fine, Mrs. Kane," Kayla

said quickly, "but you're not. Please step back before Duchess decides to—"

Suddenly Duchess braced herself on four stiff legs and shook. Water flew everywhere. It was like getting caught in a rainstorm. Blast that thick coat, Kayla thought as the spray soaked through her smock and T-shirt, down to her skin.

Mrs. Kane yelped and jumped into the foyer. Her high heels narrowly missed Patrick's right foot.

Mr. Cookie endured the downpour, and when Duchess bent her head low to sniff his face, he swiped at her with his tongue. Duchess returned his affection, her long lick nearly knocking him off his feet.

She eyed the smitten couple and shook her head. "Just like Romeo and Juliet. You guys are doomed."

Abruptly Mrs. Kane swept into the room, bent down and picked up her soaked dog.

"Mr. Cookie is a purebred terrier," she announced in the same tone British broadcasters used to point out the queen. "I can't believe you would let a mutt like that roam free in this establishment. This will never do at all. I'm taking Mr. Cookie on vacation with me."

With that, she turned and walked away.

Kayla stared after her and tried to suppress a laugh as Mr. Cookie struggled in his owner's arms. Obviously, a life of luxury was nothing when compared with Duchess's earthier charms. The dog yipped in protest as he was carried from the building.

Kayla cleared her throat and tried to look suitably regretful. "I'm really sorry, Patrick," she said. "If I'd known she was going to open the door, I would have kept Duchess on her leash."

"It's okay, Kayla. I warned her not to come in. She didn't want to listen." He winked. "Frankly, I wouldn't want to be responsible for Mr. Cookie."

"Oh, it wouldn't be a problem. We would ask the Andersons if Duchess could spend the weekend, then we'd put them in a cage together. They would have a wonderful time."

He touched the tip of her nose. "Wicked child. Don't you know Mr. Cookie is a purebred?"

Kayla crouched on the floor and wrapped a towel around Duchess. "So is she. She even has papers. Don't you, sweet girl?"

Duchess licked her cheek.

Kayla grinned at Patrick. "The dog really needs to start flossing regularly. I've told her, but she doesn't listen. I think you should give her the 'healthy gums and teeth' lecture."

"It works better if I tell it to the owners."

A petite blonde walked toward them. "Dr. Walcott, your next patient is ready." She handed him a chart.

He took it and thanked her, then turned back to Kayla. "What time are you going to Sunshine Village?"

She glanced at the clock on the wall. "In about forty minutes."

"I want to come with you. Their resident cat needs to be vaccinated."

"Of course, you wouldn't think of telling them to bring the animal in here."

"Of course not."

"You don't bill them, either, do you?"

He raised his eyebrows. "Are you angling for an accounting job?"

"Smooth way of telling me to mind my own business, Doc."

Patrick waved and headed for the examining rooms. Kayla stared after him for a minute. She'd known Patrick since she was a freshman in college, seven years ago. He was by far the nicest man she'd ever known. And not bad-looking, she thought, leaning out the door and watching his long-legged stride. His cotton lab coat covered his behind, but she'd seen him in jeans enough to know it was pretty impressive. She'd teased him once that there were probably women who had shrines to his butt hidden away in their closets. He'd brushed her comment off with a self-deprecating wave.

So why wasn't he married? she wondered. In the time she'd known him, he'd dated a lot of women, but no one seriously. What was his problem?

"So what's your problem?" she asked nearly an hour later as they sped down the freeway toward Sunshine Village. The late-afternoon sun drifted toward the horizon, making the ocean glitter as if dusted with golden sparkles.

Patrick drove the van with an easy confidence. He'd abandoned his lab coat and now wore a dark blue T-shirt tucked into jeans. One elbow rested on the open driver's-side window. His skin was tanned.

He glanced at her, his blue eyes nearly as dark as the T-shirt. He had nice eyes, she decided. They were the best part of his face. Well, except maybe for his mouth. He had a good mouth. Firm, well-shaped lips that nearly always curved up into a smile.

"My problem?" he asked.

"How old are you? Thirty-one, right?" She didn't wait for a response. "I've known you seven years. In all that time, you've never dated a woman more than a couple of months. Why is that?"

"Gee, Kayla, stop being subtle and get to the point."

"So I shouldn't have asked?"

"Why do you want to know?" *His* question neatly avoided both of hers.

She leaned back in the seat and pointed to their exit, which was coming up. "I'm not going to be here much longer," she said. "Two months, sixteen days. Then you'll be on your own. I worry about you. Maybe you should rent my apartment to someone really cute."

"There's something to think about," he said easily. "I've always been partial to redheads."

Kayla frowned. Although she wanted Patrick to find somebody wonderful and be happy, she wasn't thrilled with the idea of a dazzling redhead taking over her apartment. Kayla rented the one-bedroom unit above Patrick's two-car garage. It was small, but suited her needs. She'd had it since she graduated from college.

"What if I want to keep renting my place?" she asked. "You know, as a temporary home when I'm between travels."

"No problem. Just let me know what you decide."

"I hate it when you're agreeable," she muttered.

"Why?"

"Then I come off as the cranky one, and I'm not."

He gave her a slow, knowing smile.

They pulled into the parking lot at Sunshine Village. The two-story building looked more like a collection of villas than a retirement home. Red tile roofs and gleaming white stucco contrasted with lots of grass and trees. In back was a huge garden tended by several residents. In addition to flowers, they grew vegetables.

Kayla jumped down and went to the rear of the van. Three large dog cages sat in the back. She opened each cage and clipped a leash on the occupant. Patrick collected his medical bag and joined her.

"I'll get Trudi," he said, taking the dalmatian's leash. Barely two years old, the black-and-white dog still acted like a puppy. After trying to leap up and lick Patrick's face, she danced at the end of her lead, barking with excitement as they moved toward the building.

Elizabeth, a seven-year-old collie, followed more sedately. "Always a lady," Kayla said. She carried Rip, a small black poodle, in her arms.

They walked into the large gathering room downstairs. Several of the residents were already waiting for their arrival. The animals were greeted by name. Patrick handed her Trudi's leash and went in search of the oversize tabby who made her home there.

"You trap that boy yet?" Mrs. Grisham asked as Kayla led Trudi to the large, dark-haired woman sitting on the edge of the sofa.

"Not yet," Kayla said, grinning at the familiar question. "I've tried seducing Patrick, but he's immune to my charms," she teased.

"Then you're not trying hard enough," Mr. Peters said, and wiggled his eyebrows. "A lovely young lady like you? Why, in my day—"

Mrs. Grisham cut him off with a wave of her hand. "We've heard about all your days too many times already. I think Kayla's playing hard-to-get."

"Patrick and I are good friends. I swear. I've known him for years."

"Uh-huh. Who are you trying to convince with that sorry tale?" Mrs. Grisham said.

Kayla laughed. "But it's true."

She moved closer with the dogs. The dalmatian recognized Mrs. Grisham and strained to get closer. Kayla held her off and commanded her to sit.

"Oh, don't worry. Trudi jumps a little, but I'm used to it." Mrs. Grisham petted the dog's smooth head. "How's my pretty girl?" Trudi wriggled with excitement. Mrs. Grisham took her leash.

Once Trudi was settled, Kayla released Elizabeth. The collie was well behaved. She circled the room, stopping at each resident's side. Some were favorites, but she tried hard to play fair.

Kayla left the two dogs and headed for the stairs. Once on the second floor, she walked to a suite of rooms at the back. The door was partially open, and she knocked as she entered.

Sarah looked up from the book she was reading and smiled. "Kayla, what a surprise."

Kayla kissed the older woman's wrinkled cheek and set Rip on the bed next to her. The tiny poodle stepped carefully onto Sarah's lap and stared at her happily.

"I've missed you, scamp," Sarah said, petting the small dog. She held out her free hand to Kayla. "And you." She squeezed Kayla's fingers. "Pull up a chair. My daughter sent me the scrapbook."

Kayla dragged over a lightweight metal chair and settled next to Sarah. "She found it, then?"

"Yes, right where I told her it would be." She pulled

open her nightstand drawer. A faded, dusty book sat on top. "You get it, dear."

Kayla drew it out of the drawer. The pages were twelve inches square and bound with ribbon. The cover was plain except for the word *Memories* scripted in tarnished gold. She set the book between Sarah's hip and the edge of the bed.

Sarah turned to the first page. Grainy black-and-white photos showed a young couple ready to board an old-fashioned plane.

"I wasn't much older than you are now," Sarah said. "Danny, my husband, wanted me to see Paris. It was 1950 and he'd spent some time there during the war."

"Great hat," Kayla said, leaning close to study the picture. Sarah had been wearing a wool dress and a small, stylish hat. Her hair had been dark then, falling to her shoulders in smooth waves. The young man at her side was dapper in a pin-striped suit. His grin embraced the world, and he held his wife as if she were the most precious part of his life.

She sighed. "You look very much in love."

"We were. Oh, there were bad times, of course. But I loved Danny with all my heart. I still do."

Kayla knew Sarah's husband had passed away nearly ten years ago. She touched the older woman's arm. "That's what I want. Love to last a lifetime."

"You'll find it."

"I hope so. I'm nearly twenty-five."

"How long?"

Kayla chuckled. "I'll turn twenty-five in two months and sixteen days. Then the money from the trust fund will be released and I'm off to Paris."

"We stayed at a lovely hotel near the Seine." Sarah flipped through the album. She found a postcard of the building and pointed. "I wonder if it's still there."

Rip flopped over on his back, begging for attention. Sarah gathered him up in her arms and stroked his soft fur. "Aren't you a love?" she said, then nodded at the book. "You look through it, Kayla. Paris has changed in the past forty-something years, but it will give you some ideas about what to expect."

Kayla flipped the pages, stopping at photos of churches and museums. She studied the streets of the city, wondering what it would look like now.

"I'm very excited," she said. "I've wanted to go to Paris since I was twelve."

"And meet a handsome Frenchman?" Sarah teased.

"Actually, I was thinking I might meet a prince."

"Quite right. You're pretty enough to tempt a prince."

Kayla glanced down at her faded T-shirt. There were an assortment of stains from a day spent washing dogs. Her jeans showed white at the seams, and her athletic shoes were so old that if they were tires they would be considered bald.

"Ever glamorous. That's me. Why, just today I was telling Patrick we ought to start serving latte in the waiting room."

"Oh, stop, child." Sarah gave the back of her hand a slight tap. "You *are* a pretty girl. It has nothing to do with what you're wearing. It's in your face and the way you carry yourself. If you don't believe me, ask Patrick."

Kayla closed the photo album and set it back in the drawer. "Patrick sees me as a dependable employee and a good friend. Pretty doesn't enter into it."

"And you've never noticed that he's handsome?"

Kayla glanced toward the door to make sure no one was listening, then leaned toward the other woman and spoke in a whisper. "Not only is he extremely good-looking, but his rear end is perfect. It's all that jogging he does."

"So?" Sarah arched her eyebrows. "Why are you going off to find a prince, when you have one right here at home?"

"Patrick?" She shook her head. "That's silly. He's just...himself."

Patrick? Never, she thought. He was her friend. He'd let her cry on his shoulder when a young man broke her heart her junior year of college. She talked to him about her plans for the future, helped him write his grant proposals.

"If there was any kind of a spark, it would have already flared by now, Sarah," she continued. "You're going to have to accept the fact that I'm going to marry a prince. But don't worry. I'll invite you to the wedding."

Sarah patted her nearly useless legs. "I'll be there. Even if I have to crawl."

Kayla waved the words away. "Never. We'll send the royal jet for you. Maybe one or two young men to rub your feet on the way, too."

Sarah laughed. "You are a love. I'll miss you when you're gone."

Kayla leaned forward and hugged her. "I'll miss you, too. That's the only bad part about leaving."

"Oh, I almost forgot." Sarah put on her reading glasses and picked up a letter on the nightstand. "I've written to my friend Marie. I told you about her. Danny and I met her when we visited Paris. She's answered me and says she would be delighted to introduce you to her granddaughter, who is only a couple of years older than you." She smiled. "You'll have friends when you arrive."

"Thank you."

They chatted for a few more minutes, then Kayla collected Rip and promised to return at the end of the week. Downstairs, she found Patrick talking to Mrs. Grisham. Mr. Peters caught her eye and motioned to Patrick, then winked. Patrick turned and caught the gesture. He glanced at Kayla and shrugged, as if to say, "What can we do?"

"Did you vaccinate the cat?" she asked, walking toward Patrick.

"Whiskers is the picture of health, and safe for another year," he said.

She remembered his attempt to vaccinate Whiskers last year. "Did she scratch you?"

He held up his left hand. A long red welt curved across the back, from his little finger to his wrist.

She winced. "At least it's not as bad as last time."

"Small comfort."

"You could have asked me to help."

He looked insulted. "I can handle an eighteen-pound cat on my own."

"It must be tough being so macho."

He reached around her and tugged on the end of her braid. "I'll write you up for insubordination."

"Go ahead. I'm friendly with the boss, and I'll appeal."

Kayla realized all the residents were listening intently. Mrs. Grisham caught her gaze and nodded encouragingly.

Perfect, she thought, then called Elizabeth to her side. "We'd better be going," she said cheerfully, determined to ignore the not-so-subtle matchmaking. "I'll be back on Friday."

Patrick picked up Trudi's leash, and they said their goodbyes as they left the building.

"Are they always that bad?" Patrick asked as he stowed his medical bag behind the driver's seat.

"About getting me in a relationship?" She nodded. "Yeah, they are. It's worse when you're with me. Then they want to turn us into a couple. When you're not around, I'm usually bombarded with pictures of grandsons, nephews, or told to check out the guy cleaning the pool." She secured the latch on Rip's cage.

"Have you told them about your plans to seduce a prince?"

She grinned. "Only Sarah. I don't think the rest of them would approve. I suppose it's sweet of them to care about me."

"Why wouldn't they? You care about them. You started this program two years ago, and they've never had to miss a visit. If you weren't around, you made sure someone else was. They appreciate that." He slammed the rear door of the van. "You're not going to be easy to replace."

She moved toward him and wrapped her arms around his waist. She was five foot seven, but Patrick towered over her by six inches. When he hugged her back, she rested her head on his shoulder and inhaled his familiar scent.

"I'm going to miss you," she said.

"Compared to your rich prince, I'm pretty forgettable."

She smiled up at him. "No way. I bet he can't cook as good as you. And he would probably be very upset to know that I would like to encourage a romance between Duchess and Mr. Cookie."

"*I'm* very upset to hear that. They're both purebred animals. Besides, have you thought about how the pups would look?"

She stepped back. "Not to mention the logistical difficulties of Mr. Cookie trying to—"

"Kayla." He growled her name in mock anger.

She laughed and went around to climb into the passenger's seat.

"What are we doing tonight?" she asked as he pulled out of the driveway.

"We aren't doing anything. I have a date."

Kayla's throat closed unexpectedly, and she found it difficult to ask, "Anyone I know?"

"Maybe."

Usually, his teasing made her laugh. Today she felt a tightness in her chest. She couldn't explain the reaction, and it made her uncomfortable.

"Have a wonderful time," she said, relieved that her voice sounded completely normal. What on earth was wrong with her? "Don't forget we have a lot of work to do in the living room before I leave." They were stripping off old wallpaper and replacing it with something less floral. "Of course, if the relationship works out, you can get her to help you," she added.

"Gotcha," he said.

She turned toward him. "What? You *don't* have a date?"

He normally wore his hair brushed back off his forehead. By the end of the day, a few strands always tumbled forward. He pushed them away. "You deserved it, telling me I was getting old and should get married."

"I never said you were old. I said in the seven years I'd known you, you'd never been involved in a serious relationship." She folded her arms over her chest and looked out the window. "I hate it when you're difficult," she muttered.

"I thought you hated it when I was agreeable."

"That, too."

"So are you coming over to help me tonight?"

"I shouldn't. I should let you finish on your own."

"But you won't."

"Are you cooking?"

"Grilled chicken and a salad. I thought I could cajole you into fixing rice."

"Did you make your secret barbecue sauce?"

"Does Mr. Cookie want Duchess?"

She laughed, her good humor restored. "Okay, yes, I'll be there."

As she watched the familiar scenery slip by, her world righted itself. Next to her two sisters, Patrick was her best friend. She needed things to be okay between them. She couldn't wait to tell him about Sarah's photo album. He would understand what those old pictures meant to her. He always understood.

CHAPTER TWO

ALTHOUGH THE SUN had long since set, light spilled onto the back patio from the kitchen window and the malibu lights set around the garden. Warmth lingered from the sunny day, although by ten the temperature would drop into the low sixties. Patrick pushed against the concrete deck and sent the swing rocking.

Kayla sighed and rested her head against the soft cushions. "I could spend the rest of the night right here."

She reclined on the swing, her back supported by the swing's right arm and a throw pillow she'd brought out from the living room. She rested her bare feet in Patrick's lap. He rested one hand on her ankles. With his other hand, he stroked the delicate arch pressing against his thigh.

"You're just trying to get out of doing the dishes," he said.

She opened one eye and gazed at him. "But I cooked dinner."

She was the picture of innocence and contentment. All an act, he thought, and grinned. Inside, she had the heart of a pirate. "You cooked the rice and set the table. I did everything else."

"I kept you company by the barbecue. That was work."

He grabbed her feet and tugged, pulling her down so that she lay flat on the swing seat. She tried to giggle and yelp at the same time, the noise she made sounding like a seal.

"Patrick, no," she said breathlessly. "Don't."

"Too late. You're trying to weasel out of the dishes."

"No, no, I'll do them. I'll do all of them. I'll even wash the floor."

"Cheap talk."

He wrapped his arm around her ankles to hold her still. Then, with his free hand, he brought his thumb and forefinger together like a crab's pincer.

"Patrick, don't!" She gasped with laughter as he moved his fingers closer to her feet bottoms. She tried to sit up, but she was laughing too much. "I give. I give!"

He released her. "Let that be a lesson to you."

She collapsed back on the swing. Her jean-clad legs fell across his lap. "I swear I'll do the dishes," she said, and inhaled deeply. "Just give me a minute to catch my breath."

"Lightweight."

She tucked her arm under her head and gazed at him. "We can't all get by on six hours of sleep and running five miles a day. Some of us like to conserve our energy for other things."

"Like what?"

"Like sleep."

He rested one hand on her shin, the other just above her knee. "You need energy to sleep?"

"Sure. If it's done right."

He raised his eyebrows. Kayla had interesting theories on almost everything in life. He wasn't sure he wanted to hear this one.

When he didn't speak, she blinked flirtatiously. "You're not going to bite?"

"Nope."

"It's a great explanation."

"Thank you, no."

"Fine. Be a toad. See if I care." She pouted.

He didn't respond. She was silent for about ten seconds, then poked his thigh. "You always win," she said. "Why is that?"

"I'm a naturally superior being."

That took a heartbeat for her to register. Kayla didn't disappoint him. She sprang up and grabbed his hand, trying to twist it behind his back. He let her tug and grunt, but his arm didn't budge.

"You're not strong enough," he said mildly.

"I hate that." She gave up on his arm and settled for squeezing his fingers together as hard as she could. She generated enough pressure to make him notice, but not enough to really hurt.

A strand of hair drifted onto her face. She released him and brushed it away impatiently. Settling back on her knees, she said, "I've got to start working out. When I'm strong enough, I'm going to kick butt."

He touched her cheek. "I'm a runner, Kayla. You're going to have to catch me first."

"Figures." She smiled. "I swear, you're not winning this one. If I have to, I'll *hire* someone to kick butt."

"Just like I always say. You have the heart of a pirate. When did you get to be so bloodthirsty?"

She twisted around and sat next to him. He dropped his arm around her shoulders and she rested her head on his chest. "It's part of my charm. You love it." She snuggled closer. "Any news on the grant?"

"Nothing yet. I'm hoping to hear in the next few weeks."

"I know the wait's the worst part, but it's going to work out. They have to give you the money. You're the best candidate. I just know it."

Her faith touched him. "Thanks, Kayla. You were a great help to me. I couldn't have finished the proposals without you."

While Patrick's private veterinary practice was successful, in the past couple of years he'd found himself growing restless. In college, he'd spent as much time as possible working in the research lab studying disease in house pets. His goal had always been to return there.

"Is the lot you were looking at still for sale?" she asked.

"It was the last time I drove by." He squeezed her shoulders. "Don't get your hopes up too much. This is a very ambitious project. Not only does it require building an entire six-story building, but then it has to be staffed. We're talking about millions of dollars."

"What about the clinic?" she asked. "Will you still work there?"

"I'm not sure. I think I'd prefer to focus on the research for the first couple of years. Of course, it's going to take some time to get the building constructed. I'll hire a couple of vets and ease them into the practice."

"A couple? You think you work that hard?" Her voice teased.

As she stared up at him, he saw the light from the window reflected in her green eyes. Cat eyes, he thought. All-knowing and beautiful. She'd showered before she came over. She rarely bothered with perfume, so her sweet scent came from soap, shampoo and her smooth skin. Her hair hung loose down her back, the natural curls teasing his forearms.

He remembered her as a slightly awkward, shy eighteen-year-old. Over the past few years, she'd become an attractive woman. While they'd never been a couple, they were good friends. He was going to miss her when she was gone.

"You're going to need two replacements, as well," he said.

Her mouth straightened. "You think so?"

He nodded. "I'll get a part-timer in to take care of the grooming. The more difficult problem is finding someone to take over the visitations to Sunshine Village."

She ducked her head and leaned against his chest again. "I know. I've been worrying about that, too. We're going to have to find someone who really cares about the people there. I think I'll start asking around. Maybe someone at one of the colleges, or a stay-at-home mom looking for something different to do while her kids are in school. I'll make sure it's right before I leave."

"Are you going to find me a new best friend, too?" he asked, only partly kidding.

She wrapped her arm around his waist and squeezed. "Oh, Patrick, it's not like we'll never see each other again. I'll be back, and we'll stay in touch."

"I know, kid. It'll be fine."

He heard the smile in her voice as she said, "I'm not a kid anymore."

"I know."

He could feel her breast pressing into his midsection. Reminding himself that Kayla was just a friend didn't stop a sliver of interest from sparking to life. He ignored the sensation. He'd felt the occasional spark before and done nothing about it. He preferred Kayla in his life as his friend. That way, there were never any scenes, angry words or false expectations, and there was no risk of breaking up.

If he was going to be completely honest with himself, he didn't want her to go. But not wanting her to leave him wasn't enough to convince him to ask her to stay. Kayla had spent years planning this trip. Her whole dream in life was to travel. She wanted to see the world. He'd grown up moving from one military base to another. What was the old cliché? She wanted wings, and he wanted roots.

He cared enough about her to wish her well on her journey. When she was gone, maybe he would take her up on her suggestion that he start dating. That would distract him from the hole her absence would create in his life.

He pulled his arm free of her and stood up. "You're trying to make me forget that there are dishes to be done. Don't think I'm going to let you get out of your duty."

She grumbled under her breath, then held out her hands. He pulled her to her feet. "All right, Mr. Tyrant. I'm coming. Maybe you should chain me to the sink so I can't escape."

He lightly kissed the top of her head. "Whine, whine, whine. And here I was going to be nice and let you dry."

She darted in front of him and spun until they were facing each other. Her eyes crinkled at the corners as she laughed. "Yes, Patrick. Please let me dry. You know I hate washing."

Ten minutes later, he was up to his elbows in soapy water. Kayla sat on the counter next to him, holding a dish towel and waiting for the next glass.

"I'm sorry I got so weird when you said you had a date tonight," she told him. "It just sort of caught me off guard. With so little time before I leave, I guess I selfishly want you to spend your free time with me."

He smiled, remembering her cranky expression. "No problem."

She took the glass he offered and began to dry it. The overhead light reflected off Kayla's hair, turning blonde into spun gold. She wore a plain white T-shirt tucked into clean, worn jeans. Her feet were still bare. Loafers rested by the front door. The first thing she did upon entering her home or his was to kick off her shoes.

"Do you ever think about getting married?" she asked.

He rinsed a plate, then handed it to her. "Sometimes. I don't think I'm ready yet."

"You're thirty-one."

"So you reminded me earlier today."

"What aren't you ready for?"

He shrugged. Marriage was a big step. "I've avoided long-term entanglements," he said. "Much as you have."

She tossed her head and flipped her hair over her shoulder. "I'm saving myself for my prince. What's your excuse?"

He reached for the pot she'd used to cook rice and pushed it under the water. The bay window in front of him wasn't curtained, so the glass acted as a mirror, reflecting his image and the room behind him. He stared at the reflection for a couple of seconds.

"I don't have one," he admitted at last.

Kayla leaned toward him and touched his shoulder. "It's your dad, isn't it?"

"Yeah. I guess. According to what everyone told me, my folks were really in love."

"But that's a *good* thing. You should want that, too."

He shrugged. "I don't have a memory of it. She died when I was two. What I do remember is my dad mourning her. It was as if he'd lost a leg and was forever cursed to walk with a limp. Except the missing part of him was his heart. He lived another twenty years, and there wasn't a day that he didn't pray for her to return."

Patrick remembered coming home from school early once. He must have been nine or ten. He hadn't known his dad was in the house, so he'd let himself in the front door, using the key he wore around his neck. He'd found his father in the dining room. The older man had sat at the table, the wedding album open in front of him. Silent tears had poured down his face. He hadn't made a sound as he turned pages and wept.

The memory was as clear today as it had been then. He'd felt his father's pain. The depth of the wound had terrified him. As a child, he'd feared being abandoned by his only living parent. He'd crept out of the room without letting his father know he'd seen him.

"I don't want to love like he did," Patrick said softly. He picked up the pot and began scrubbing it. "It was tragic."

"It's wonderful and romantic. That's what I want."

Patrick shook his head. "Too much pain. I respect and admire my dad, but I think he was weak. He could have recovered. He chose not to. I don't want any emotion controlling me that much."

Kayla looked at him. "You might not get a choice in the matter."

"There's always a choice."

She eyed him speculatively. "You need a good woman to snap you out of this funk."

"I'm not in a funk."

She ignored him. "A woman. But what kind?" Her brow furrowed. "Someone who likes animals and is patient. Someone you can really talk to." She tilted her head toward the living room. "Someone who won't mind the fact that half your walls are being stripped of wallpaper and the other half need to be."

"A redhead," he put in.

Her sniff was the only reply. "Pretty, smart, funny," she went on. "In short, me!"

Patrick was pleased he was only washing a pot, because her words caused him to let go and the metal container clattered into the sink.

He stared at her. She met his gaze and grinned.

"Well?" she asked. "Are you speechless?"

"Yes."

"Good. I adore being in control." She batted her lashes.

"Kayla, I—" He paused, not sure what to say.

"We'd be perfect together. We get along, we like each other. I'm charming, you're sensible."

He sensed she was teasing him, but he couldn't respond. It was as if he couldn't catch his breath. He looked at her, trying to figure out her game. There had to be one. Him and Kayla? After all this time? No way.

But once the seed was planted, he realized it wasn't as shocking as he'd first thought. Kayla and him? Was it possible she'd been harboring some romantic feelings for him? He didn't think so. Surely he would have sensed something.

"We're friends," he said at last.

"Agreed. But we do have enough in common to be a great couple."

Her expression was happy, her eyes were bright with humor. She didn't look lovesick. There was a piece missing. There had to be.

"We want different things in life," he said, deciding to play along and see where she was going. "You want to travel, I want to settle in one place."

"We share the same values," she said. "We care about each other. We have mutual respect. Isn't that important?"

It was, but he didn't want to answer her. "What are you getting at?" he asked.

She gave an exaggerated sigh. "Okay, here's the deal. I think you really do need to be with a woman, and I have one in mind."

"You want to set me up?"

"Don't sound like you're getting vaccinated against some tropical disease. You'll adore her. I promise."

"I've heard that before."

He reached for the pot and rinsed it off. She wasn't declaring undying love, she just wanted to set him up. Good, he told himself, and ignored the tiniest flicker of disappointment. Better for both of them. They *were* great friends, but they would never make it as a couple. He couldn't imagine caring for her that way.

Kayla jumped off the counter and touched his arm. "I'm not kidding. You'll adore her. And here's the best part. She looks just like me."

He opened his mouth, but she gave him a warning look. "Don't even think about saying anything tacky, Patrick. I'm holding a wet towel, and I'll make you pay."

He winked. "Whip me, beat me, tie me up—"

"Patrick!" She cut him off with a shriek. "Be serious. I'm going to call my sister Elissa and invite her out for a weekend. You guys can meet. She might be the woman of your dreams."

He sobered quickly. He didn't want to meet the woman of his dreams. He'd given up on dreams of love a long time ago. The price was too high.

Kayla waited, shifting her weight from foot to foot. She was obviously impatient to have him approve of her plan. He had no interest in meeting her sister, but he wouldn't hurt her feelings by telling her that. She would enjoy having one of her sisters spend the weekend with her. He could meet the lady, talk politely, then be on his way. Elissa's visit wouldn't change anything.

"Do your worst, kid," he said.

She gave him a quick hug. "You're going to love her," she said. "I promise."

"That's what you told me about sushi."

"Elissa is much nicer than sushi."

"She'd better be."

"Have I ever been wrong?" she asked, then wrinkled her nose. "Okay, don't answer that. But I'm not wrong this time. You'll see."

CHAPTER THREE

"QUELLE HEURE EST-IL?" the voice intoned through her headphones.

"Kell err a teal," Kayla repeated dutifully over the yapping of dogs in the kennels. Her alcove of an office was right off the boarding area, which normally didn't bother her, but today she was trying to learn French.

"You guys aren't helping me," she called over her shoulder. "I'm trying to ask the time." The volume of the barking increased. She turned up the volume on the app. "Apple what? Oh, forget it." She turned off her phone. "I'll listen to it tonight."

She rose to her feet and headed into the kennels. At the sight of her, most of the dogs quieted, with whimpers of pleasure replacing the barking. Kayla paused and greeted them all. She took a few extra minutes with the dogs being boarded. Although pets had a good time going on walks and playing with other residents, they missed their families. Kayla stepped into a kennel and knelt in front of a large, gentle golden Labrador. Big brown eyes met hers but the dog didn't raise his head from where it rested on his paws.

"Come on, Sammy. Don't be sad. They're coming back today."

Sammy's expression didn't change. Kayla glanced over her shoulder to make sure no one was around. The staff would tease her unmercifully if they knew what she was about to do.

Easing against the concrete wall of the kennel, she sat on the floor. To her left was a doggie door that led to a twenty-by-eight foot outdoor area. Each dog had its own run. On her right was a raised, padded platform that served as a bed. Sammy's toys were scattered around, although he hadn't played with them much.

She stretched her legs out in front of her and patted her lap. The large dog slowly lumbered to his feet. He moved closer, then cautiously stepped onto her thighs. Kayla tried not to wince as the sixty-five-pound animal sat on her lap and leaned heavily against her chest. She wrapped her arms around Sammy and began to softly sing about the purchase price of a dog in a store display.

She continued the song, rocking Sammy, rubbing his back and head. He sighed heavily. After a few minutes, his tail started thumping against the ground. By the time she'd completed the song for the fourth time, he'd shifted off her and picked up one of his chew toys.

They wrestled with the toys for a while. A dog in the next kennel barked, challenging Sammy to a race. The Labrador took off out the doggie door, racing to the back fence. Kayla smiled as she let herself out.

"Mission accomplished," she said as she walked toward the exit. She checked bowls as she went, making sure they all had water. Although the kennel wasn't her responsibility, she didn't mind looking things over when she was back here.

At the door, she paused and counted empty kennels. Just three. Only about half the residents were paying boarders. The rest of the dogs either came with her to Sunshine Village or were strays.

A familiar feeling of guilt tightened in her chest. Word had gotten out that Kayla took in strays, so there was a steady stream of them. Placement wasn't too difficult, although sometimes it took a while. Unwanted dogs were treated, fed, housed, all for free. Patrick never complained, never hinted that the strays cost him a lot of money, not just for their food and medicine, but in what he could be making if he was able to take in more paying boarders.

Patrick understood why she cared about the strays. He understood everything. There was a strength about Patrick. Solid—that was how she would describe him.

She pulled the door open and found the object of her thoughts standing in her alcove.

She laughed. "Patrick. I was just standing in the kennel thinking about how wonderful you are. And here I could have told you to your face."

He didn't return her smile. His expression was grim.

"What's wrong?" she asked. "Is there an emergency?"

"A lady has brought in a stray," he said curtly. "Is there room in the kennel?"

She nodded. Patrick only got angry about strays if they'd been mistreated. "How bad?"

He shrugged. "I haven't examined her yet. Skinny, scared. About what you'd expect. Everyone else is tied up. Can you help me with the examination?"

"Sure."

She followed him to the waiting room.

A small woman with pale skin and short, graying hair sat on the bench against the wall. Her face was drawn, and dark shadows had taken up permanent residence under her eyes. Next to her was a little mixed-breed dog. Shaggy hair, big eyes. A shudder rippled through the dog every few seconds. Kayla had a bad feeling that when she picked the animal up she would be able to feel all its ribs.

"Mrs. Francis?" Patrick asked.

The woman nodded.

"I'm Dr. Patrick Walcott. This is Kayla." He settled next to the woman and gestured for Kayla to sit by the dog. Patrick pulled a pen out of his lab coat and adjusted his clipboard. "Tell me about the dog."

"Don't know much," Mrs. Francis said, and shrugged. "Been around the neighborhood a year, maybe two. Sweet dog. Gentle, loves kids. Never bitten anyone, not that some of the boys in the neighborhood haven't tried her patience. I've rescued her a time or two myself." Mrs. Francis twisted her hands together.

Patrick's voice was low and soothing. "That's very good of you. Most people don't bother."

The older woman smiled. "I like animals."

"When was she abandoned?"

"I can't rightly say. Been close to a month, I think. Her owners, I never knew them well, just moved. Left her behind."

"You don't think she got left behind by accident?"

Mrs. Francis's mouth twisted down. "I heard things about her family, and they weren't nice. They didn't forget her." She placed her hand on the dog's back, stroking it. "I wanted to keep her myself, but it didn't work out." Color crept onto her cheeks. "Sometimes there's barely enough food for my children, but I've been making it work. Then I got a promotion. I work full-time now. There's going to be more money for all of us, but I won't be home during the day. I can't leave her out in the yard. Not with those boys around. It's not safe. So I hoped if I brought her here you could find a place for her with some nice people."

Patrick asked a few more questions and made notes. Kayla had to swallow the lump in her throat. She reached out her hand and let the little dog sniff her fingers. A fuzzy tail thumped against the plastic cushions on the bench.

"Pretty girl," Kayla said quietly, and received a pleading look from big, sad eyes.

"Does she have a name?" Patrick asked.

"Not that I know of. My middle girl says she looks like that dog that used to be on TV. You know the one."

"Benji," Kayla filled in.

"That's it." Mrs. Francis offered a wan smile. "I was afraid I couldn't keep her, so I didn't let my kids name her. I figured naming her would make it too hard to let her go."

Patrick rose to his feet. "Mrs. Francis, I appreciate all you've been through. You've obviously grown attached to the dog, and I suspect it's going to be hard for you to give her up, too."

The older woman stood up. "Maybe," she said, casting a glance at the little dog. "But I want to do what's right."

Patrick placed his hand on her shoulder. "We'll take care of her. Kayla is in charge of finding homes for our dogs, and she'll make sure this dog gets a good one. I promise."

Mrs. Francis blinked several times. "Maybe one with children."

"Of course," Kayla said. "A loving family with a big fenced yard. She'll be very happy."

Patrick walked to the desk and said something to the receptionist. She reached into a drawer and handed him a slip of paper. He returned to Mrs. Francis's side.

"One of the grocery store chains in the area has been very supportive of our attempts to place strays. They've offered to offset the cost of feeding and caring for an animal when good people like you take the time and trouble to rescue them." He handed her a gift certificate. "You can use this at any of their stores."

Mrs. Francis stared at the certificate. "A hundred dollars?" she breathed, then glanced at him. "I didn't spend anywhere near that much. She doesn't eat but a little."

He smiled. "I know, but you had to get here, didn't you? And you've rescued her more than once. You deserve it, Mrs. Francis. Please accept it, and tell your children thank-you."

Kayla picked up the little dog. As she'd feared, she could easily count the ribs. She held her close and felt her shiver.

The woman touched his arm. "Thank you, Dr. Walcott. You're a good man." She kissed the dog on the top of her head, then walked out into the parking lot.

Kayla blinked several times.

Patrick glanced at her. "You gonna cry, kid?"

"I hope not. This kind of stuff always gets to me."

"Yeah. Me, too." He took the dog from her arms and held it expertly. "Come on, little girl. Let's see how you're doing."

Fifteen minutes later, Patrick had completed the exam. Kayla assisted. The little dog didn't squirm or try to get away. She lay still, completely docile.

"I can't decide if she knows we're trying to help her or if she's given up," Kayla said, knowing he would hear the worry in her voice.

"I see some life in her. I think she's going to be fine. Aren't you, sweetie?" He stroked the dog's head. "There's obvious malnutrition, and fleas. We'll have to test her for worms. She's probably never had any shots, but I want to wait a couple of days to start her on that." He glanced at the clock. "Jo should be here."

He walked to the phone attached to the wall just outside the examining room. After picking up the receiver, he punched a couple of buttons, and then his voice came over the loudspeakers. "Jo, please come up to examining room three."

Less than a minute later a black-haired nineteen-year-old burst into the room. "Yes, Dr. Walcott?" she asked.

"We've got a new resident." He gestured to the dog. "She's in pretty good shape, except for a few fixable things. Get her a basket and some soft blankets." He frowned. "Are you on tonight?"

Jo nodded. "Until 6:00 a.m." The teenager hurried to the little dog and gathered her up. "Oh, what a pretty little girl." She cuddled the dog close. "Does she have a name?"

"Not that we know of," Patrick said.

"I suppose Muffin is out of the question."

"Absolutely."

Kayla smiled. Jo had been trying to name strays Muffin ever since she started working here, nearly a year before. Patrick had never agreed.

"Mix up some of that special feed," Patrick continued. "Small servings. No more than half a cup. But feed her every couple of hours, all night. Lots of water. See if she'll go for a walk with you. You know where the extra leashes are. Use flea powder for now. I don't want to shock her by giving her a bath. That can wait. Oh, and I'll need a sample to test for worms."

"Done," Jo said, and carried the dog from the room.

Kayla stared after them. "Gee, and I was going to offer to take her home with me."

Patrick walked to the sink and washed his hands. "I know," he said over the sound of the water. "I could see it in your eyes. If Jo hadn't been on duty tonight, I would have encouraged you. But she's the best."

Someone was on duty at the clinic every night. There was a small room in the back with a comfy cot, a desk with an office chair and good light. When Kayla first worked for Patrick, she'd spent her share of nights at the clinic. Some of the ill animals required medication or postoperative treatments every couple of hours, but apart from that it was easy duty. She remembered getting a lot of studying done. Of course, more than once she'd brought one of her favorite dogs into the room with her. She'd often awakened to find a bemused Patrick shaking his head in disgust while a large canine took up more than half the cot and used her legs for a pillow.

"Next Thursday I'm scheduled to speak at a children's center downtown," Patrick said. "If our new guest turns out to be as calm and good-natured as she seems, then I'd like you to come along and bathe her. I want the kids to see how to do it right. Maybe they can even give her a name."

"Not Muffin," she teased.

He grabbed a paper towel and dried his hands. "No Muffins, no Buffys."

"What about Mr. Cookie?"

"I refuse to even comment on that one."

"I happen to like pet names. You want all of them to have people names."

"Of course."

She laughed. "Why?"

He put his arm around her shoulders. "I don't have to answer to you."

They headed for her alcove. "I know why," she said. "You think dogs are people, too."

He ignored her and moved to her littered desk. After pushing aside a couple of folders, he found her desk calendar and wrote down the appointment for the children's center.

"You don't trust me to remember?" she asked, trying to work up some irritation.

"I know you."

Her emotions weren't in the mood to bubble and boil. Probably because Patrick was right. She did sometimes forget appointments.

She crossed to the calendar on the wall. The picture

on top showed the Seine and the Left Bank of Paris after a storm. Everything was wet, all grays and dark browns, except for a spray of bright yellow and pink flowers resting on a table by the river. A black marking pen hung from a string next to the calendar. Kayla glanced at the clock and saw it was after five.

"Another day closer," she said, and made a big X in the box with today's date.

Patrick looked at the calendar, but didn't say anything. What did he think about her leaving? she wondered. She knew he would miss her. But how much?

"Any news on the grant?" she asked.

"Nothing." He shoved his hands in his lab-coat pockets. "It'll be a while, so stop asking."

"I want them to hurry. I want to know what's going to happen, and I don't want to find out after I leave."

He smiled and lines fanned out from the corners of his blue eyes. "I'll call them up and tell them they have to let me know by July first."

Several months ago, Kayla had thought her birthday would never arrive. Now it was just around the corner. "I'm not leaving that day. How long will it take to start construction?"

He leaned against the edge of her desk. The overhead light made his short light brown hair gleam. "I've already picked the construction company. I suppose they can break ground as soon as the check clears."

She sat in her chair. "This is going to be an exciting project. I'm thrilled for you."

"I hope it all works out. I haven't done any serious research since college. I've been keeping current on what's going on, but that's not the same as being in the middle of it. People lose pets to diseases that should already have a cure. And we never know what part of our animal research is going to spill over and help humans."

She tilted her head and studied him. "You're a good man, Patrick Walcott. One of the last nice guys."

He frowned. "Gee, thanks. All men want to be told they're nice."

"Okay, you're nice, good-looking and sexy. Is that better?"

"Nice try, but I don't believe you."

She stiffened in her chair. "But I'm telling the truth."

"If I was so good-looking and sexy, how come you didn't have a crush on me when you first came to work for me? Jo does."

Kayla tried to keep calm. She didn't want to start blushing. She'd had a crush on Patrick when she started at the clinic. Thinking about him had kept her up more than one night. But she'd been terrified to let him know. She'd been just a kid, and he an older, mature man. Now the age difference was no big deal, but at eighteen, seven and a half years had felt like a lifetime.

The phone on her desk rang. Kayla picked it up. The voice at the other end asked for Patrick, and she gladly handed over the receiver.

While he was busy talking, she made her escape. How odd of him to bring up the subject of crushes. Thank goodness he didn't know about hers; he would tease her unmercifully. Although it had been a long time ago. Why should she be so sensitive about it now?

She didn't have an answer. All she knew for sure was that she would do almost anything to keep Patrick from knowing how she'd once felt about him.

* * *

"Remember," Patrick said. "You know your pet best. If you think something is wrong, then bring the animal in."

He glanced around the crowded room. The Children's Community Center had been built almost entirely with donations. It sat in a poor section of the city, nearly dwarfed by large office buildings. Traffic sounds spilled in from outside, but in here was a haven for children.

The center served as an after-school day-care facility for children ages six to thirteen. It stayed open through the summer, offering different programs for kids whose parents had to work. Patrick had been coming here since he first opened his practice.

"Anybody here ever get vaccinated?" he asked.

A little girl in blond pigtails pulled her fingers out of her mouth long enough to ask, "What's that?"

"Shots," an older boy announced. "You got 'em when you were a baby. They're so you don't get sick."

"That's right," Patrick said. "What's your name, son?"

The boy, maybe eleven or twelve, sat a little straighter. "Jackson."

"Jackson, should pets get vaccinated, too?"

The boy thought for a second. "Sure. They get sick, just like us. And if you don't, they're gonna get rabies, then everybody dies."

Several children gasped.

Patrick held up his hands. "Wait a minute. Jackson's half-right. Your dogs and cats need vaccinations to keep them from getting sick. One of the vaccines is against rabies. But very few domestic animals get rabies these days, and even if a rabid animal bites you, you're not going to die."

Kayla stood next to him. "They're not going to like the cure much, though," she said in a soft voice.

He smiled at her. "I wasn't planning to tell them what it was."

"Good thinking."

He returned his attention to the children. "My clinic is open on the second and fourth Saturday of the month. You can bring your dogs and cats to me, and I'll vaccinate them for you. You don't have to remember my name or the days I'm there. I put up a flier on the bulletin board." He pointed to the bright yellow sheet of paper.

Jackson eyed him cautiously. "Shots cost money. Sometimes there's not even enough for dog food."

"I know," Patrick said. He'd dealt with this question several times before. "If your pet needs shots, bring it in. We'll worry about paying for it later. Also—" he addressed the whole room "—if your pet is sick, don't wait for those two Saturdays. Call the office and tell them you need to come. Any other questions?"

Kayla leaned close. "You're going to be swamped with work from this."

He shook his head. "I've made the offer before. Only a couple take me up on it. Most of these kids can't afford to have a dog or cat. I wish it was different. I would rather worry about my bottom line and have their lives enriched by a pet."

"Just like I said. One of the good guys."

"As long as you don't call me nice."

"Yes, boss."

When he answered the children's questions, he'd moved aside to let Kayla take his place. She set their latest stray on the portable table he'd brought with them. He spoke to Mrs. James, one of the volunteers who worked at the center. She showed him where to fill the tub with warm water, then offered several pitchers so they could rinse the dog.

"Someone brought her into the office," Kayla was saying when he returned. The children had left their seats and gathered around the table. "A family moved away and left her behind."

A beautiful girl with expressive brown eyes and coffee-colored skin petted the dog. "On purpose?" she asked.

"I'm afraid so. Sometimes people do that."

He set the tub in front of Kayla. She smiled her thanks, then returned her attention to the children. She handled their new charge gently, soothing the animal with continuous touches.

They'd only had the dog six days, but already she'd started to gain weight. Her eyes were clear, her expression was interested. She'd stopped shaking a couple of days ago.

Kayla worked quickly and efficiently. She told the children that the dog didn't have a name. Would they like to pick one?

"Benji!" someone called.

"Benji's a good name," Kayla agreed, "but this little dog's a girl."

They argued over names for a couple of minutes, and then Jackson stepped forward. "How about Rhonda?"

The girl in pigtails nodded. "Rhonda was nice. She used to work here, then she moved away."

Kayla glanced at their faces. "Everyone agree?"

The kids nodded.

"Rhonda it is." She looked over her shoulder at him. "That okay?"

"Anything but Muffin."

She grinned.

Kayla finished rinsing the dog, then wrapped her in a fluffy towel. Patrick watched the proceedings. Kayla talked to the children as if they were intelligent adults. They responded to her attention and practically glowed when she favored them with a smile. He knew what that felt like. Sometimes when she turned her smile on him he felt—

He frowned. He wasn't sure what he felt. He shouldn't feel anything. They were friends.

She finished towel-drying Rhonda and released the little dog. The animal approached the children slowly, interested but cautious. Kayla urged them to sit on the floor and be very still. They did as she asked. In a matter of minutes, Rhonda was racing from kid to kid, yapping happily, her whole body vibrating from the vigorous sweep of her tail.

Kayla looked on, obviously pleased. Her full lips turned up at the corner. Odd that he'd never noticed how smooth her skin appeared, or the slender line of her neck. She wore a baggy T-shirt tucked into worn jeans. A uniform he'd seen her in a hundred times before. Yet today he admired the curve of her hips and the tempting roundness of her behind.

It didn't matter that she'd only been teasing him,

trying to set him up with her sister. One sentence had changed everything.

We'd be perfect together.

He couldn't forget or let it go, and he didn't know why. Was he attracted to her, specifically, or to the idea of having a relationship with someone? If it was the latter, then he was fine. It meant he was ready to look around and maybe take a chance on caring. Not love— that was way too risky for him—but affection. Respect. Mutual understanding. If it was the former, if he was attracted to Kayla, then he was in trouble.

Kayla stood up and walked toward him. When she reached his side, she wrapped her arms around his waist and sighed. "You're doing a good thing here." She nodded toward the kids, who were playing tag with Rhonda. The little dog raced around small feet, ducked under chairs, and had them all laughing.

"But I'm not nice, right?"

She laughed. "You were nice to me. You took in a lonely, homesick eighteen-year-old and gave her something that mattered. I wouldn't have made it through college if it hadn't been for my job at your clinic."

He remembered that time. She'd missed her sisters desperately. "I never understood why the three of you didn't go to the same college. You'd been together all your lives. It must have been hard for all of you."

"It was," she agreed. "But we wanted to do it. We'd always been the Bedford triplets. It was time to learn how to be ourselves." She looked up at him. "So, nearly seven years after the fact, thank you."

Her earnest expression made him uncomfortable. "I didn't hire you as a charity case."

"Why did you?"

He smiled. "Do you remember our interview?"

"Not really."

"I was examining a particularly uncooperative hundred-and-ten-pound Doberman named Thor. You were earnestly trying to sell me on your meager qualifications. The more nervous you got, the more you patted the dog. By the time the interview was over, he was licking your hand and didn't even flinch when I gave him his shots. I knew then you were a natural."

"So it worked out," she said.

"Agreed." But why hadn't it worked out romantically?

The question came from inside his head, and he didn't know how to answer it. Before he could try to figure out what that meant, Mrs. James approached them.

The woman was about his age, pretty, with soft brown hair. She smiled at him, then turned her attention to Kayla. "I know you take dogs to visit senior citizens. Do you work much with children?"

"I can," Kayla said, and stepped away from Patrick. "What did you have in mind?"

"I heard about a girl through a friend of mine. Her name is Allison, and she's about nine, I think. She was in a horrible accident. She's in a body cast at a rehab center. She's not supposed to move at all. Of course, she's very upset, and not responding to anyone. I thought if you had time, you might visit her."

Kayla didn't hesitate. "I'd love to."

Mrs. James smiled. "Let me get the address and phone number. I don't think she can have visitors other than family until next week, but I'd like to be able to call her mother and tell her you're coming."

"Please do."

While the woman went off to get the information, Kayla sighed. "I know exactly how that girl feels," Kayla said.

Patrick remembered Kayla talking about a similar situation when she was twelve. A car accident had put her in the hospital for close to a year.

He leaned close and kissed the top of her head.

"What's that for?" she asked.

"Because you're one of the nice guys, too."

She smiled. "And I'm more understanding. Being called nice doesn't offend me."

He studied her familiar face.

"Why are you suddenly looking so serious?" she asked.

"I hope this prince of yours appreciates what he's getting when he falls for you."

CHAPTER FOUR

KAYLA POURED HERSELF a cup of coffee and glanced at the clock. Two minutes until nine. She still had time. She added milk and sugar, picked up her plate of toast and moved to the sofa in the living area.

Saturday morning had dawned bright and clear. The temperature would warm into the high seventies. She'd heard a lot of other places described as paradise, but as far as she was concerned, San Diego had the best weather in the world. She couldn't imagine living anywhere else.

She stared out her large window. Her second-story west-facing view provided her with just a hint of the ocean. If she stood on tiptoe, she could see a sliver of blue. This morning she didn't bother checking. It was enough to know the water was there.

Promptly at nine, her phone rang. Kayla picked it up and heard two other voices already chatting. Her sisters paused long enough to welcome her to the conversation.

"How are you, baby sister?" Fallon asked.

Kayla grinned at the familiar greeting. Fallon was the oldest. Elissa had been born exactly six minutes later, with Kayla a full twelve minutes after Elissa. "I'm fine. What about you guys?"

"We're switching computer systems," Elissa said, then groaned. "I can't tell you how many hours I've been working. They swear it will be done on Monday, but I know they're lying. I figure Wednesday, maybe Thursday. At least it will be over this week."

"Tell me about it," Fallon said. "The school is putting on a summer festival just before school gets out. Ten-year-old boys do *not* want to dress up as any kind of plant, especially not flowers."

"Gee, my job is going great," Kayla said. "I have no horror stories to share."

The three women continued to chat. Kayla listened as her sisters brought her up to date, and then she told them what was going on with her. There were people who said that in addition to looking exactly alike, the triplets sounded the same, especially on the phone. Kayla didn't agree. She could always tell who was talking, although she was willing to admit that much of that came from context, as well as sound.

Elissa changed the subject. "Has anyone been out on a date recently?"

Silence filled the line.

Kayla laughed. "I guess that's a no, huh?"

"I don't get a lot of single guys coming through my classroom door," Fallon stated. "What's your excuse, Elissa? Don't tell me there aren't some gorgeous doctors at the hospital."

"You've been watching too many television dramas. Of course there are single doctors. At least I assume there are. But I work in administration. I don't get to spend a lot of time hovering around the surgery unit."

"I, of course, have an excuse," Kayla reminded them.

"That's right. You're going to marry a rich prince." Fallon hummed a couple of bars of the "Wedding March."

"Have you identified a candidate?"

"Of course not. I don't want to start stalking someone and have him think I'm crazy."

"The implication being you're completely sane?" Elissa teased.

"Mock me all you want, ladies. You're just jealous because I have a plan. When our trust-fund money is released, I'm going to make changes in my life, and neither of you can say the same."

"I have plans." Fallon sounded superior. "Sensible plans."

"What? Buy a couple of savings bonds and put a fresh coat of wax on your car?" Kayla sipped her coffee. "Fallon, you've got to get over being so darn sensible. Live a little."

"I do live. Just because I don't want to run off to Europe and fall in love with a stranger doesn't make me a stick-in-the-mud."

Kayla retreated. She didn't want to argue with her sister. Especially not on such a perfect day. "What about you, Elissa? Any plans?"

The line was silent so long, Kayla asked, "Elissa? Are you still there?"

"Of course." Her sister's voice sounded strained. "I've been thinking about a few things I'd like to do. Nothing is settled yet. Are you leaving on our birthday?"

"No. I thought we'd spend it together," Kayla said. "Isn't that what we've planned?"

Fallon cut in. "Of course it is."

"I think it will take me a week or so after that to get ready," Kayla continued. "I haven't bought my tickets yet."

"Don't forget our Christmas plans," Fallon said. "You'll be back for that, won't you?"

"Are you kidding? Christmas in the Caribbean… I wouldn't miss it for anything." Kayla smiled at the thought. She and her sisters had been planning a holiday in the tropics for years.

"Fallon, I think you should go ahead and pick out a hotel," Elissa said. "I don't mind where we stay."

"As long as it's nice," Kayla put in. "Five stars for sure."

"I'm happy to. My class is studying the history of the area, so I have a lot of research material. Something quiet and secluded."

"With warm sand and blue ocean," Elissa said dreamily.

"And cute pool boys," Kayla added, chuckling.

"What about your prince?" Fallon asked.

"Oh, royal weddings take a long time to put together."

"How convenient. Okay, I'll take care of it." Fallon paused. "This is going to be different from our campouts."

"I know," Kayla told her. "I can't wait. You remember the one we took during our junior year of college? Boy, the tents were getting ratty."

"Hey, we were traveling on a budget."

"I remember." Kayla frowned. She also remembered

how their mother hadn't been interested in the triplets anymore. Once they stopped cooperating with her plans to have a show-business career, she'd emotionally abandoned them. So the three girls had clung to each other. They'd worked part-time jobs in high school, saving enough money to buy some camping gear. After that, they'd spent as much time as possible away from home. Even though they went to different colleges, they'd managed to spend long weekends together.

"Didn't we invite some guys to that campout?" Fallon asked.

This memory was more pleasant than thinking about their mother. Kayla grinned. "Yes, we did. I distinctly recall having a serious talk with them, explaining that there absolutely would be separate tents."

"Why didn't they believe us?" Fallon sighed. "Never mind. I know the answer. They're guys."

"One of them—gosh, I can't even remember his name—got so bad, I had to push him in the lake."

Fallon chuckled. "Didn't he leave after that?"

"Can you blame him?" Kayla shook her head. "What fun we had." She had the fleeting thought that it would have been nice to invite Patrick along. But back then she'd been all of twenty, and he'd been her boss. They had always gotten along, but they hadn't been friends like they were now. She would have been too intimidated to ask him to join them.

"What do you remember, Elissa?" Fallon asked.

Their middle triplet cleared her throat. "I didn't go. I'd already left college."

Her voice sounded sad. Kayla wondered if Elissa was ever going to let her past go.

"Oh, that's right." Fallon quickly changed the subject. "I'll let you two know what I find out about the hotel. Are we still talking about staying from the twenty-second of December through the twenty-ninth?"

"Sounds good to me," Kayla said.

"Fine," Elissa answered.

"Okay, great. Look, I've got to run. I've got tons of errands, and it looks like it might rain. Talk to you guys next week. I love you."

"Love you, too," Kayla called, and Elissa joined in.

There was a click on the line as Fallon hung up. Kayla stared out the window and tried to decide if it was appropriate to talk about Elissa's past.

"Are you all right?" she asked.

"Of course," Elissa answered quickly. "Why?"

"You sounded sad for a minute."

"I'm not sad. It's just with our birthday coming up so quickly, and the trust money being released, I have a lot to think about. Some of it is serious."

Kayla understood completely. Elissa had gone down a different road from either of her sisters. "I'm here for you," she said. "If you want to talk or anything."

"I appreciate that."

Kayla drummed her fingers on the arm of the sofa. "I've been thinking. Why don't you come down here for a long weekend? We haven't seen each other in a while, and it would be fun."

She didn't bother mentioning her plans to fix up Elissa with Patrick. Maybe some quality time with one of the good guys would cheer up her sister.

"Are you sure?" Elissa asked. "You're going to be

busy getting ready for your trip. I wouldn't want to intrude."

"Come on. You're never in the way. We always have a good time. I think it's what we both need."

Elissa laughed. "You're right. I've got plenty of vacation days. I've already carried over a week from last year. I'll do it. The computer program will keep me busy for about three weeks. When's convenient after that?"

They quickly settled on a date. "Bring something sexy to wear," Kayla said. "We're going out on the town."

"Kayla, what are you planning?"

"You'll just have to wait and see. But I promise, you'll love it."

Kayla had nearly finished washing her kitchen floor when someone started pounding on her front door. She straightened and leaned the mop against the wall.

"I'm coming," she called as she stripped off her yellow rubber gloves and dropped them on the floor.

As she headed for the door, she crossed her fingers, hoping her visitor was Patrick. After the phone call with her sisters, she'd decided her apartment needed a thorough cleaning. She'd been at it for a couple of hours. She was sweaty, not wearing a speck of makeup, her ponytail was coming undone, and she wore cut off shorts and a shirt that should have been tossed six months ago. Patrick was used to seeing her looking scruffy; any other neighbor would be shocked.

The pounding continued. She pulled open the door. Patrick stood beaming on her front porch. "Where's the fire?" she asked.

His grin broadened. "I got it!"

She stared at him, not sure she understood. "Got what?"

He waved a multicolored overnight-mail envelope. "The grant." He stepped into the apartment and tossed the package in the air. "I got it!"

She screamed his name, then opened her arms wide. "You did it! I knew you would!"

He swept her close and swung her around the room. She held on tight, laughing with him. Joy filled her. "This is so perfect," she said.

"Tell me about it." He lowered her to the ground and took her hands in his. "They gave me all the money I'd asked for. Enough for the building, the equipment, everything. I can hire the scientists and the staff."

"I'm so happy for you."

She couldn't stop smiling. She figured she was probably glowing as much as Patrick. His irises glittered with excitement. A lock of light brown hair tumbled onto his forehead, and she brushed it back.

He hugged her again. She squeezed his muscled body. "You've worked so hard," she said. "This is great. I'm thrilled and proud."

"Hey, I couldn't have done it without you. We both spent a lot of hours on those grants. I owe you."

She chuckled into his chest. "No, now we're even. You've done a lot for me, Patrick. I helped because of that, and because I wanted to."

She pulled back slightly. He looked down at her. "Okay, we're even. That means the glory belongs to both of us."

Her hands rested on his sides. She could feel his strength. "I'm always willing to accept the glory."

"This time, you earned it. Thank you."

He raised a hand to her cheek. He cupped her face gently, then bent down and kissed her.

Kayla raised herself up on tiptoe to meet him halfway. For that split second before their lips touched, she didn't think anything of it. She and Patrick had kissed lots of times. Pecks on the cheek, brief brotherly-sisterly kinds of greetings. They'd tickled each other, given back rubs, cuddled when it was cold, clung together during scary movies.

She didn't notice anything different when his lips first brushed against hers. Without thinking, she slid her hands up his chest to his shoulders. His fingers touched her waist.

She started to smile in anticipation of what she would say next. But the words disappeared as Patrick's mouth lingered against hers.

Confusion blossomed first, then a faint tingling that started at the tips of her fingers before skittering down her arms. Heat came next. Surprising heat that stole her breath and made her want to cling to him.

His lips moved gently, softly, sweetly. Her world spun suddenly, nearly knocking her off balance. His grip on her waist tightened, and she found herself leaning into him, wanting her aching breasts to press against his chest.

She'd been kissed before. Short kisses, long kisses, kisses that felt as if the guy were trying to perform a medical procedure. But she'd never been kissed by Patrick. Not a real kiss.

Her breath caught in her throat as she waited for him to deepen the pressure, to touch his tongue to her lips and let her invite him in. He did neither. Just when she was ready to surrender, he pulled back and released her.

"This is going to be great," he announced, ruffling her bangs as if she were a ten-year-old. "We're both going to get what we want."

"Huh?" The tingling lingered, and her mouth ached so much, she couldn't form words.

"You're going off to Paris, and I'm going to build a research center."

"Oh. That. Um, sure. It's going to be wonderful."

Kayla stared at him, searching his face for some proof that he had also been affected by the kiss. But Patrick looked the same as ever. No fire darkened his eyes, no passion tightened his body. His lips barely looked damp. Was *she* crazy? Hadn't he felt the fire between them? Or hadn't it happened at all? Had it just been her imagination?

She stepped back and moved to the window. For once, the familiar view didn't comfort her.

The measles, she thought quickly. A relapse, like with malaria. Or she was getting that flu everyone had been talking about.

There had to be a perfectly logical explanation for her reaction to his kiss. She wasn't attracted to Patrick; she couldn't be. He was her friend, and it would be wrong to feel that way about him. Besides, she was leaving. She had places to go, people to meet, including a prince.

Fortunately, Patrick didn't seem to notice her preoccupation. He moved next to her and touched her arm. "I've got to get to the office," he said. "Someone is bringing in a pregnant cocker spaniel and wants me to supervise the birth." He ran his hand through his hair. "There's so much work to do. I've got to start interviewing replacements."

He bent down and kissed her on the cheek. Much to her amazement, the tingling started up again.

Before she could protest or examine what was happening to her, he'd stepped back and headed for the door. "We're celebrating tonight," he announced. "Steaks and champagne. I won't even make you cook anything. Say seven?"

"Ah, fine," she murmured, unable to do anything but stare at him. As the door closed behind him, she continued to look at the place where he'd stood and wonder what was wrong with her.

When she heard his car backing down the driveway, she shook her head and tried to break the spell. She glanced at the clock. She had nearly six hours to figure out her strange reaction and what had caused it. Then came the tricky part. She needed either an antidote or a way to make sure it didn't happen again.

CHAPTER FIVE

PATRICK FLIPPED CHANNELS and listened to the splashing sounds coming from the kitchen.

"I hope you appreciate this," Kayla called. "You know how I hate to do the dishes."

"I wish I could get grant funding every day."

She laughed. "Then it wouldn't be special, so we wouldn't have to celebrate. Therefore *I* wouldn't have to do the dishes."

"I knew you'd try to weasel out of it."

"I'm here, aren't I?"

That she was. She'd arrived on time, bringing him a huge plant and a bottle of his favorite Scotch. She'd even dressed for the occasion, replacing worn jeans with newer ones, and her ancient T-shirt with a long-sleeved white blouse that buttoned down the front.

He returned his attention to the television, but nothing looked interesting. He glanced at the clock. It was nearly nine. Maybe there was something good coming on. He checked the channel listings and read through the offerings. One of the all-family networks had a special Saturday-night feature. He chuckled, then turned to that channel.

"Kayla, come out here."

"Just a sec. I'm nearly finished." Several cupboards banged shut as she put the pots and pans away. There was a moment of silence, and then the refrigerator door opened. "You want more champagne?"

"Sure."

She came out of the kitchen carrying her glass and the half-full bottle. As she walked toward the sofa, he increased the volume on the television. The sound of children singing filled the room.

Kayla stopped in her tracks, stared at the TV, then at him. "Turn that off this instant."

He grinned. "No way, kid. Come on." He patted the sofa cushion next to his. "You can take it."

She shuddered visibly. "I haven't seen one of these for years. And I would prefer to keep it that way. Tell me it's just one episode."

"Sorry. A four-hour marathon, until well after midnight." He patted the sofa again. "You're here for the duration, so make yourself comfy."

She plopped down with a groan and handed him the champagne bottle. After setting her glass on the light oak coffee table in front of her, she pulled her knees up to her chest and buried her face. "I can't stand it."

Patrick glanced at the television. The credits finished, and the first scene opened. Several children played in a courtyard. Girls jumped rope, while the boys were involved in a game of baseball. A pretty eight- or nine-year-old skipped onto the screen. Her hair was a mass of gold ringlets, her eyes were bright green. A yellow-and-white gingham dress flared out to her knees, and she wore black and white oxfords.

She walked up to the pitcher and smiled prettily. "Let me play, Billy," she said.

The older boy dismissed her with a wave. "Get out of here, Sally. Baseball is just for guys. Girls aren't smart enough or good enough to play."

"Boys against the girls," Patrick said. "Let me guess. Sally rallies the girls to form their own team, there's a play-off game and the girls kick butt."

Kayla rocked slightly and moaned. "I can't believe you're making me watch this."

"Is it really that awful?"

She raised her head and glanced at the TV. "I guess not." She studied the screen for a minute. "At least that's not me. I think it's Elissa."

She relaxed a little, letting her feet slide to the floor. Patrick leaned back against the sofa and shifted his weight. Then he cursed silently. For the first time since buying the couch four years ago, he noticed the damn thing had a high back. Too high for his purposes. The top of his head barely cleared the top. There was no way he could casually rest his arm along the back.

He tried to picture another way of making it work, then had to hold in a laugh when he realized he was acting as desperate as he had on his first date in high school. Back then, getting his arm around Christina's shoulders had been paramount. He vaguely recalled succeeding, because he could remember her gazing up at him, as if inviting him to kiss her. Of course, he'd been too scared to try. He'd left that for their second date.

This isn't high school, he reminded himself. He wasn't a nervous sixteen-year-old. He was a grown man, and he'd known Kayla for years. If he wanted to put his arm around her, he could. He'd done it countless times.

But tonight was different, and he had no one to blame but himself. It was that kiss. He hadn't been able to forget it all day.

Had it really happened the way he remembered it? Had that incredible passion been real? All through the afternoon, when he should have been thinking about his grant and the new research facility, not to mention a pregnant cocker spaniel, he'd thought about Kayla. She'd haunted him. He'd heard her laugh, seen her smile, imagined the shape of her body. He'd relived the kiss until his body heated with desire.

He didn't have any answers. He just knew that if he didn't touch her soon, he would go mad.

Casually, he let the remote control slip from his hand. Instead of just bending over to pick it up, he rose and poured them both more champagne. Then he picked up the remote. But when he sat back down, he moved closer to her. Close enough that their arms were almost touching.

Kayla winced at the show. "Some of this dialogue is really bad. Or maybe it was just the delivery."

A commercial came on, and Patrick muted the volume. "How long did you and your sisters appear on 'The Sally McGuire Show'?"

"We started just after our eighth birthday and completed four seasons. At first it was fun, but after a year or so, we were ready to get out." She brushed her hair off her shoulder. "None of us wanted to be Hollywood kids. It was unfortunate, because that's all our parents wanted from us."

The show came back on. He increased the volume. Sure enough, Sally had organized the girls into a rival baseball team. They had cute pink-and-white uniforms. Even their mascot, a little white poodle, wore a matching coat and cap.

Kayla pointed to the girl on the pitcher's mound. "That's Fallon. She was the best pitcher of the three of us."

"How can you tell?" In his eyes, all the Sallys on the show looked exactly the same.

"I don't know. I just can. I recognize her, of course, but I also remember shooting most of the episodes."

When Sally came up to bat, Kayla laughed. "That's me. I even run the bases. Elissa had started out with this scene, but she fell and skinned her knee. They didn't want that showing, so she isn't in much of the baseball-game show."

"I've never met your sisters."

"Really? I guess not. The few times they've visited me here, you've been gone. But Elissa is coming out for a weekend, and you'll meet her."

He turned to Kayla and frowned. "You're *not* going to set us up. Understand?"

"Why not?"

Because right now he couldn't think of anything but how to get his arm around her. "I can find my own women."

"I haven't seen any hiding out here. Apparently you're not doing a great job."

"Kayla." His voice was a low growl.

"All right. I won't fix you up. I'll just introduce you. If you like her, ask her out yourself. If you don't, no harm done. I didn't tell her about you. Don't get all in a snit."

"I don't do snits."

She rolled her eyes. "Of course you don't, Patrick. You are the most even-tempered, perfect—" She glanced at the screen. "Oh, look."

A commercial came on for a popular children's shampoo. A beautiful young mother sat with her daughter, and they were watching "The Sally McGuire Show." The show went into a commercial, and it showed the triplets talking about how much better their hair was since they'd started using the new brand.

"Commercials, too?"

She nodded glumly. "I'd wondered why we were getting residual checks. Now I know. They're using part of an old commercial in the new one."

"Did you three work all the time?"

She shifted toward him, resting one knee on the sofa and sitting on her foot. "Sometimes it felt like that. Mom put us in commercials when we were babies. Because we were perfectly identical, we could be interchanged at will, thereby allowing the commercials to be shot faster. There are restrictions when working with children. We had a few parts in some forgettable movies, then the series started when we were eight." Her green eyes darkened with emotion.

"You don't like that part of your life, do you?" he asked.

She shook her head. "We just wanted to be normal kids. When we weren't working, we went to this upscale private school. But we weren't ever there long enough to make friends. So it was just the three of us. At least we had each other. I feel sorry for the kids who have to go through that alone."

He tried to imagine her childhood, but it was completely foreign to him. Over the years she'd told him bits and pieces, but this was the first time he'd heard the whole story. "Did you explain to your parents that you were unhappy?"

She shrugged. "We were too scared. We knew what would happen. Then I was in that bad car accident just before our twelfth birthday. I was in the hospital for weeks, then in rehab for almost a year. Fallon and Elissa refused to continue the show without me. No triplets, no Sally McGuire. They talked about bringing another character in, but some viewer polls showed that the audience wouldn't accept that. There was a movie of the week in the fall after my accident. Elissa and Fallon handled the part alone. Sally and her friends were all adopted, and the orphanage closed down. Everybody was happy."

He knew her well enough to figure out there was more to the story. "Including your parents?"

She wrinkled her nose. "Oh, let's say they would have preferred a different ending. They were furious at my sisters, but there was nothing they could do." She leaned her shoulder against the back of the sofa. "My parents ended up fighting so much, they got a divorce. Then it really got ugly."

He touched the back of her hand. "You don't have to tell me any more of this."

"I don't mind." She squeezed his fingers, but didn't meet his gaze. "I know we've talked about this before, but I guess I never told you details because I was embarrassed."

"About what?"

"I don't know. I was never a big star or anything, but people get weird when they find out about the show."

"Why would that matter?"

She glanced at him. "I know it wouldn't *now,* but when I first met you, well, I was afraid you would think I didn't really need the job. Then, after I'd kept the secret for a while, there didn't seem to be a good time to tell you. Are you mad?"

Their fingers entwined. "No, Kayla, I'm not mad. I understand it must have been difficult for you. What happened after the divorce?"

"My parents were very bitter about the money," she said. "The judge was afraid they would spend it all, so she set up a trust for us. We were allowed to withdraw funds for college tuition and board. Nothing else until we turned twenty-five. Then it's released to us. In college, we all had to work part-time to pay for books, gas for the car, spending money, that sort of thing. So I did need my job with you."

Her eyes were huge pools, nearly as clear as emeralds, with a faintly haunted expression tugging at the corners. Lamplight reflected the gold in her hair and made her skin look pale and smooth. Why had he never noticed that she was so much more than pretty?

"At least now your trust fund makes sense," he said. "I'd always wondered where it came from."

"Now you know."

"You did the right thing," he continued. "Look at where you are now. You're all grown, with a terrific future planned."

"Thanks," she said, smiling shyly before turning her attention back to the screen. The first show had ended, and another one had started. "Oh, my." She pointed. "This one is awful. Just as filming started, we all came down with chicken pox. And do I mean all of us—every kid on the set. Worse, I recovered first, and I had to do most of the acting."

"Why is that so bad?"

She shuddered. "Because I have so little talent. There's a very heartfelt speech in this show. I practiced and practiced. It still came out horrible."

"I can't tell the difference when you're on the screen."

"You're being very kind."

She faced front and started to watch the show. Patrick kept his attention on her. They weren't holding hands anymore, and he missed the connection. The sofa back continued to defeat him.

Just put your arm around her, a voice in his head ordered. *She won't mind.*

Okay, he knew that was true. She wouldn't mind. But he wanted more than that. He wanted her to want him. Or at least be thinking about him the same way he was thinking about her. The fact that he didn't know exactly what he was thinking about her didn't matter.

He shifted a couple of times, but couldn't seem to get in a good position to casually hold her. He swore silently and leaned against the sofa. Enough, he told himself. This was crazy. If he and Kayla were attracted to each other, something would have happened a long time ago. Attraction and passion didn't suddenly explode in an already established relationship. Obviously, he had to get out more.

Kayla placed her elbows on her knees and hung her head. "Here it comes. Oh, I don't think I can watch."

The little girl on the screen stood on a narrow bunk in a long dormitory. She clutched a pillow to her midsection. Around her, children sat listening intently.

"We all want a family," Sally said earnestly. "And I know in my heart, someday we're going to find one. I pray for it every night. There's a mommy and daddy for each of us. Until they come to get us, we still have each other."

One of the little girls started to sniff. Kayla moaned. "It gets worse," she muttered.

"I'm enjoying it."

"Then you're a sick man."

He smiled.

"We are our own family. We love each other and take care of each other. That's what families do."

Kayla shrieked. "I can't stand this." She threw herself against Patrick and buried her face in his chest. "Turn it off, please. I beg you. I'll do anything."

He stared at her in amazement. Mission accomplished, he thought as he wrapped his arms around her. She snuggled close.

"If you won't turn it down," she said, "I'm going to hum loud enough so I can't hear it."

He didn't want to let go of her long enough to grab the remote, but he figured he would like the humming even less. He touched the volume control twice, and the sound quieted.

"Better," she murmured.

He agreed silently.

She had her arms around his waist, her head against his shoulder. With one hand he stroked her back, with the other he played with her silky hair. The curly strands slipped through his fingers, cool and soft. Tempting.

They were close enough that he could smell her scent and feel the heat of her body.

As they watched the rest of the show together, he felt a certain "rightness" in their being in each other's arms. He also wrestled with concern. He knew better than most the cost of loving and losing. He'd watched his father slowly die for twenty years after his wife died. Patrick didn't want to have to suffer that much for anyone. He wanted to belong, but not get hurt.

At least he was safe with Kayla. While he couldn't explain what was going on between them, he knew it wasn't love. They were just friends dealing with wayward hormones. In a few days, everything would return to normal. He would have bet on it.

Kayla laughed and reached for the remote control. She increased the volume, then pointed at the screen. "I remember her," she said as a woman in her late forties or early fifties chased three children out of the orphanage's kitchen. The woman raised her fist menacingly, but the children just grinned and held out the cookies they'd stolen.

"Her name is Mrs. Beecham, and she was always so sweet to my sisters and me. She made cookies every Friday on the set, remembered our birthdays." She sighed. "She used to talk to us about all the places she'd traveled and the men she'd met. Of course, with the hindsight of an adult, I've figured out that most of what she told us was probably made up, but that doesn't make it any less wonderful."

"I'm glad you had her in your life."

"Me, too. She used to say that love was like a tornado. It would sweep into our lives and carry us away."

"Interesting analogy, when you consider tornadoes tend to destroy everything in their path."

Kayla looked up at him and frowned. "That's not how she meant it."

"But it's true."

"Maybe, but I don't believe it." Her expression softened, and her eyes focused on something far in the future. "When I dance with my prince, I'm going to feel that tornado."

Patrick tried not to stiffen, but it was damned hard not to react. Here he'd been holding her in his arms, thinking romantic thoughts, and she'd been dreaming of some imaginary prince.

"I hope the two of you are very happy," he said, and released her. Before she could protest, he moved to the far end of the sofa.

Kayla stared at him, bewildered. "What's wrong?"

"Nothing."

"Then why are you acting weird?"

"I'm not. I just find it interesting that an independent woman such as yourself is dreaming about being rescued by Prince Charming."

"I don't want to be rescued," she said. "I want to be swept away. There's a difference."

"And only a prince can accomplish that?"

"It is a nice touch." Her voice sounded teasing.

He wasn't amused. "All those royals are probably stuck up and jaded with life."

"I don't care. It's not about the prince, it's what he represents." She leaned back against the sofa and sighed. "I'm going to Paris. I'm going to buy wonderful clothes and get my hair cut and speak French. I'm going to sit in sidewalk cafés and be sophisticated."

"You can't buy sophistication."

She waved him off. "Don't interrupt my fantasy. Men are going to find me irresistible. I'm going to write witty letters to all my friends and be perfectly happy."

Something dark and unexplained turned over in Patrick's chest. It wasn't that he objected to Kayla's dreams, or even her travel. What he didn't like was the fact that she planned to leave him behind without a second thought.

"With the prince—" she glanced at him "—or a prince-like person, I'm going to see the world. He'll take me riding and on his yacht. We'll drink champagne."

"I thought that's what we had been doing," he growled, nudging the nearly empty bottle with his foot.

"Patrick, if you're not going to participate, then at least don't make fun of me."

Confusion filled him. Confusion and annoyance. He couldn't compete against a prince, or any other perfect man she imagined. He was just the local vet, with dreams of his own, none of which could hold a candle to a castle or a yacht.

Without stopping to consider the consequences, he turned toward her. Rational thought fled. He reacted to what she'd said, to what he was feeling, and to what he really wanted.

He grabbed her shoulders and pulled her against him. Kayla didn't resist; she simply stared up at him, her eyes wide, her mouth parted.

"See if your prince makes you feel like this," he said.

Then he kissed her. Really kissed her.

Kayla was too stunned to react. Patrick hauled her closer, held her in his arms and settled his mouth against hers. She sensed his anger, which she didn't understand, his confusion, which she shared, and his passion, which tempted her as she'd never been tempted before.

Of their own accord, her hands rose to his shoulders and rested there. He was solid strength, the only stable part of a world that had started spinning.

His mouth clung to hers, touching, taunting. She felt the firm pressure and wanted more.

He read her mind. Even as she thought of him deepening the kiss, he did so. He parted his mouth and brushed her lips with his tongue. She parted for him, anticipation stirring her body into passionate restlessness.

He invaded slowly, as if he were a petitioner and she sacred ground. He paused to whisper her name, as though it were a prayer.

From the sleek softness of her inner lip, to her teeth and at last to her tongue. He moved slowly, discovering pleasure points dormant since her birth. He stroked these small sparks into roaring flame that threatened to consume her.

She slid her hands up his neck to his short hair. Individual strands tickled her palms. She learned the shape of his head, his ears, then cupped his jaw, caressing smooth skin with just the faintest hint of stubble.

His head tilted, allowing him to move deeper inside her. She met him, alternately blocking progress and leading the way. When she hesitated, he paused, as well, touching her gently, showing her how much better it would be if she allowed him to pleasure her.

He moved his hands against her. First they traced the

length of her back, then her hips. He placed his palm on her knee, warming her, then urged her to move toward him.

She resisted, not sure what he wanted.

He broke the kiss and stared at her. Desire darkened his irises to dark blue velvet. His mouth was damp, his skin flushed. She'd forgotten why he'd kissed her in the first place. She had the vague recollection of him trying to prove a point. If he was to ask her at this moment, she would swear that he had won and not care what or how. She only wanted him to kiss her again.

He brought one of her hands around to his mouth and pressed his tongue against her palm. Heat flared up her arms and settled in her breasts. Hot, bright need filled her with sensations she neither understood nor controlled, yet she wasn't afraid. Not of Patrick.

"Come closer," he whispered against her now damp skin.

She shifted toward him.

"Closer."

He put his hand on her hip and urged her to straddle him. She hesitated, unsure of herself, if not of him.

"Please."

The single word was more air than sound, yet it touched her soul. She did as he requested, sliding one thigh over his, settling herself on him, their most intimate places only inches apart.

Her hands once again rested on his shoulders. Because of her position, she sat slightly higher than he. She could see all of him—his face, the breadth of his shoulders, his powerful arms, the way her knees cradled his hips.

He threaded his fingers through her hair and drew

the long strands away from her face. "Cat eyes," he said. "So beautiful."

She ducked her head and flushed, not sure if the blush came from pleasure or from confusion. Questions filled her head. In the name of sanity, she needed to answer them. She needed to stop and think about what they were doing. But she didn't want to. She wanted this moment to go on forever.

He raised his head slightly. She met him more than halfway, lowering her mouth to his. This time, he parted, and she was allowed to enter the sacred place. She discovered the texture of his mouth, tasted him, felt the heat, the need that drove them both forward.

The uncharted course should have frightened her. Perhaps, if she'd allowed herself to think, it would have. But she refused to consider, or weigh what was happening. She only wanted to feel.

His hands moved slowly from her thighs to her hips to her waist. Fire coiled low, liquid flames stretching toward her breasts, making them swell and tighten. His fingers reached up and stroked the underside of her breasts.

She froze in place. Even her breath caught in her throat. Waves of pleasure filled her. They were like nothing she'd ever experienced before. A small whimper escaped when she tried to breathe.

Strong, capable hands slipped higher, taking her curves in their palms, cupping her gently, reverently. She broke the kiss, unable to concentrate on anything but his touch and the feelings he invoked. His fingers swept around, discovering her, moving closer to the taut centers, nearing but not reaching. Ache and fulfillment combined into the sweetest sensation.

When he moved his hands higher still, she nearly wept in frustration. Then she felt him unfastening the top button of her shirt. Too shy to look or help, she arched her head back and closed her eyes.

Whispers of cool air licked against her skin. The shirt parted easily, and he pulled it off her shoulders. Without thinking, she relaxed her arms and let the garment slip to the floor.

He placed his hands on her back and drew her closer. She went to him, her thighs sliding along his until they touched intimately. Her fingers laced behind his head. She knew what he would do next. Knew and eagerly anticipated. Every part of her tensed, until at last she felt his warm breath, moments before his mouth claimed the valley between her breasts.

Moist, hot, firm. There weren't enough words to describe the sensation of his mouth on her skin. He moved a little, licking the full curve, then moved again and settled over her left nipple.

Through the thin layer of her bra, he teased her. Teeth barely brushed against the tight peak. She sucked in her breath. Not able to control herself, she pressed her fingers into his scalp and urged him closer.

He obliged her silent request, opened his mouth and drew her inside.

Relief was instant. His mouth closed around her as his tongue sweetly tormented the sensitized peak. What she had felt before faded in the light of this new pleasure. Want and need melded until her very life depended on this exact moment. Sharp cries gathered in her throat until she couldn't control them. When one escaped, she stiffened slightly.

"Don't stop," he whispered against her, then transferred his attention to her other breast.

He moved back and forth, creating such fire inside her that she thought she must glow from the flames. Involuntarily her hips arched against him.

This time, he was the one to suck in his breath. His hands moved to her hips and encouraged her to repeat the action. She did, moving as he guided her. In her aroused state, it took her a minute to realize the significance of the hard ridge pressing between her thighs, brushing erotically against her jeans and creating friction in that most private place.

She pulled back and looked at him.

Patrick's face was alive with passion. She'd always thought him attractive, but now the tight lines of his jaw and around his mouth made him more than just someone she'd known. Need transformed him into a tempting stranger...someone dangerous.

Someone she wanted more than she wanted her next breath.

They stared at each other. As the passion faded, sanity returned. What were they doing? she asked herself. This wasn't right. They weren't lovers.

He touched her bottom lip and smiled faintly. "Do you want me to apologize?"

His voice was low and husky. She knew if she glanced down she would see the proof of his arousal straining against his jeans. A shiver rippled through her. Not one of fear or cold, but, instead, of anticipation. The innate understanding of how wonderful it would have been.

She shook her head. "Of course not. I'm just a little confused. What happened?"

"I don't know. I—" He dropped his hands to the sofa. "I guess we're lucky we never tried that before."

"I guess."

She slid back until her feet touched the floor, then she straightened. Although her bra covered her adequately, she felt self-conscious about being shirtless and quickly retrieved the garment.

Her insides were shaking. Not so much from passion anymore, but in reaction to what had happened… and almost happened.

Patrick stood up and approached her. She finished buttoning her blouse, then risked glancing at him. The fire was gone, and he'd returned to being the man she'd known for years.

"Hey." He touched her face. "Don't be scared, okay?"

"I'm not." She wasn't frightened, exactly. She wasn't sure what she felt. "But I'd better get home."

He walked her to the door. When she stepped onto the porch, he called her name. "Do you want to pretend this never happened?"

As if she had a choice. She had a bad feeling that she would remember this night—in sensual detail—for the rest of her life.

"I need you to be my friend, Patrick. I depend on you."

"I understand," he told her. "We'll both forget."

As she walked back to her apartment, she wondered if he was going to have to work as hard as she would to act normal.

She told herself it hadn't meant anything, that it *wouldn't* mean anything. They could both go on as they had before. Nothing had changed.

When she unlocked her door, she glanced over her

shoulder. Patrick stood watching, as he did every night when she walked home. He wanted to make sure she was safe.

She waved, then ducked inside.

Once she was alone, she sank down on the floor and tried to make sense of it all. She and Patrick were friends, and friends were different from lovers. Everyone knew that. Not that she had a whole lot of experience. She'd never had a lover.

A shiver rippled through her, this one leftover sensation from their time in each other's arms. The intimacy should have frightened her. For years she hadn't been able to imagine doing that with a stranger. She still couldn't. Yet with Patrick, everything had felt right. Maybe because she trusted him.

She didn't trust many people. Not since she'd watched her parents fight over everything when they were divorcing. Their raw anger had terrified her. Surely they had been in love once. What had gone wrong?

She didn't want that for herself. That was why the dream was so much safer than reality. But Patrick was real, and he didn't scare her.

She pressed her hands to her face and sighed. Was there an answer? Should she bother looking for one? Or should she just wait? When she got to Paris, life would be so much simpler.

Everything would be perfect—just as she'd always planned.

CHAPTER SIX

Mrs. Carter, the director of the rehabilitation facility, smiled. "We don't usually allow dogs on the premises, but in this case, we'll make an exception."

Rhonda sat on Kayla's lap. At the woman's words, her tail wagged, as if she were pleased at being allowed inside. Patrick knew dogs didn't understand what was being said, but sometimes he believed they had more powers of interpretation than they were given credit for.

Kayla stroked the dog's head. "I hope we can help, Mrs. Carter. I've taken the dogs to a retirement home for a couple of years, and they have really made a difference. Sometimes I think it's easier to relate to animals than to people, especially when the person involved is sick or injured. Dogs don't demand witty conversation and are grateful for a quick pat or cuddle."

"We have to do something." The director drew her eyebrows together. She was in her early thirties, well dressed, in a red suit. Dark eyes spoke of her concern and compassion. "Allison has been here nearly a week, and she hasn't said a word to anyone. Apparently it was the same at the hospital. It's not that she can't talk, she simply chooses not to. She's smart and verbal…at least she was until the accident. Her family is concerned, as is her doctor. At this point, we're considering psychiatric intervention."

Patrick leaned forward. He hadn't met the child, but already he felt his heart go out to her. "She was injured in a car accident?"

"She was on a bike," Mrs. Carter said. "A car hit her. There were almost no head injuries, so in that respect, she was lucky. We're hoping for a full recovery, but one can never be sure. She's in a body cast. She's only nine. This is difficult for her."

"Let's see what we can do," Kayla said. She picked up Rhonda, then rose to her feet.

"Would you like me to come with you?" Mrs. Carter asked.

Kayla shook her head. "Just tell us where the room is. I think we'll do better if we slip inside casually. It will look less like a setup. Not that she isn't going to figure out why we're here."

Mrs. Carter gave them the room number and directions. They said their goodbyes and promised to stop on their way out. Once they were in the hall, Kayla released the breath she'd been holding.

"Poor kid," she said quietly.

"Yeah. I can't imagine what it must be like."

Kayla glanced at him. "I can, and it's pretty tough." She hugged Rhonda. "You're going to work magic, aren't you?" The dog swiped at her nose with her pink tongue. Kayla giggled.

Patrick followed her down the cool, silent corridors. If Rhonda didn't work magic, then Kayla would. He remembered her talking about her own accident. He didn't know the details; Kayla didn't talk about them. Over the years, he'd put together enough of the story to know that she'd been badly injured and spent a year in recovery. For a while, the doctors had thought she wouldn't be able to walk, but she'd proved them wrong. Looking at her today, it was difficult to believe she'd ever been that seriously injured. The only lingering physical evidence was the faint network of scars on her thighs and torso.

They paused in front of the last door at the end of the hall. Windows at the end of the corridor showed a beautiful rose garden. He figured the rooms on either side would have the same view. So far, the rehab center had been impressive. Little Allison was in good hands.

"Do you want me to wait out here, or do you want me to come inside?" he asked.

Kayla touched his arm. "I think I might need the moral support."

"That's why I'm here."

They went inside together.

The room was large and bright, with white walls and colorful posters on the walls and ceiling. The latter was explained by the position of the occupant on the hospital bed in the center of the floor. A sheet covered her from her feet to her chest, but the thin layer of cotton didn't disguise the large cast over her body. The thick material covered her from her ankles to her neck and trapped her arms to just above the elbow.

Music drifted through the room, its source a speaker in the corner. There was a television mounted up high, the screen dark. On various tables and chairs scattered around were dolls, stuffed animals and books. Yet the child lay in solitary stillness.

Around her, on the floor, were a few more stuffed animals. From their awkward positions, he assumed they'd been placed on the bed and she'd thrown them off. A chair, tall enough to allow the visitor to be at equal level with the girl, sat next to the nightstand.

Kayla moved to the bed. "Hi, Allison. My name is Kayla. My friend Patrick and I thought you might like a visitor today." She set the small dog on the bed and smiled. "Her name is Rhonda. She's very friendly and very sweet. Do you like dogs?"

Silence.

Patrick stepped closer and looked at Allison. Shiny raven hair framed a pale face. Large blue eyes stared blankly at the ceiling. She had the innocent beauty of an angel, but the dark shadows under her lower lids and the tight set of her mouth told him that she'd spent more time in hell than in heaven.

It was all he could do not to hold the girl tight and promise to make it all right. He held back. No doubt her father had already tried that, and it hadn't helped. He could only hope Rhonda would succeed where the rest of them had failed.

"Rhonda's a special dog," Kayla said, stepping around to the far side of the bed. She sat in the chair and looked at the child. "She was left in our care so she could visit people and make them feel better. Dogs are wonderful friends. They love you no matter what. They want to be with you, even when you don't feel good. They don't even mind if you don't want to talk."

Rhonda sniffed at the sheets, then at the girl's hand. Her tail swept back and forth as she licked the slender, pale fingers.

Nothing. Not a flicker of response.

Kayla looked at him, and he shrugged. He felt helpless in the presence of this child's pain. What did he know about healing her?

"When Rhonda first came to us, she didn't have a name," Kayla said. "She was skinny and dirty, but when we fed her and cleaned her up, she turned out to be a very pretty dog, with a sweet, loving nature. It's amazing what you can find when you take the time to look on the inside. That's what's happened with you, isn't it? You've got a different outside. I'm sure you hate the cast, but when it's gone, there will be a whole new you on the inside."

This time, the silence wasn't as unexpected. Allison blinked every few seconds, but aside from that, there was no sign of life. The cast prevented him seeing the rise and fall of her chest.

Kayla glanced around the room. The sunlight caught her gold-blond hair and made it glow. She was in her usual attire of jeans and a T-shirt. No makeup, no jewelry save an inexpensive watch. Yet, to Patrick, she was as beautiful as she'd ever been.

She picked up a photograph on the nightstand. "This is your family. You guys look great together. Your mom's real pretty. You look a lot like her. I see you have a younger brother. I never had a brother. Just two sisters. It was fun. We shared clothes and played together."

Rhonda nudged at Allison's fingers, but they didn't move. The dog snorted in frustration, sank onto the mattress and tried to squeeze her head under the girl's hand. When that proved unsuccessful, she rested her muzzle on Allison's wrist and closed her eyes.

· "I don't see a dog in the picture. Do you have any pets at home?"

There wasn't an answer.

Kayla set the photo back on the nightstand. Patrick wondered if she would give up. She didn't. She stared at Allison for a long time, then reached over and brushed the girl's dark bangs off her forehead.

"I know," she said quietly. "Everyone is telling you how sorry they are and pretending they know exactly how you feel. They don't, though. They don't know what it's like to be trapped in a room day after day. They don't know how scared you are. They don't know that you lie awake at night, that you don't want to go to sleep, because when you do, you dream about the accident. They don't know that you're afraid you're going to spend the rest of your life in a cast, that sometimes you just want to scream so loud the world splits in two. They don't know how much you hate everyone who can walk and play and run and jump. They don't know that you hate your family most of all—your brother because he can do all the things you can't, and your parents because if they really loved you, they would be able to fix it."

Patrick sank into a chair by the door. He tore his gaze away from Kayla long enough to glance at Allison. So far, there was no reaction, but she seemed to be blinking a little faster.

"I know," Kayla said. "I know everything. You see, it happened to me, too. I was twelve. You were riding your bike when you were hit by a car. I was in a car when another car hit us. The man driving me was killed, and I almost died. I was in a hospital for weeks. They told me I wouldn't walk, that I would live in a wheelchair for the rest of my life."

She touched Allison's cheek with her fingers and smiled slightly. "I didn't believe them. I thought it was a dream. I kept trying to wake up, but I couldn't. My arms were in casts and I was in traction. I couldn't even pinch myself so I could wake up. I kept thinking if I could just pinch myself, everything would be okay."

While continuing to stroke the girl's cheek, she used her free hand to wipe her own face. Her tears made Patrick ache. But he didn't go to her. Instead, he remained in his seat, sensing that the telling of this story was as important for Kayla as it was for Allison.

"It's been over twelve years, and I still cry when I think about that time," she continued. "I was in hospitals and places like this for almost a whole year. My sisters, the ones I told you about, came to see me. They really cared and tried to make it better, but they only made it worse. You see, my sisters look just like me. We're identical triplets. So every time I looked at them, it was like looking at myself, only I couldn't do all the things I used to do. I felt as if I were looking in a mirror, the kind they have at carnivals. Instead of seeing myself, I saw an ugly joke. Someone else walking and playing. Someone who used to be me, but wasn't anymore."

Sometime while she was talking, the music had stopped. Patrick glanced over and saw that the playlist had ended. Kayla hadn't noticed. She sucked in a deep breath, as if the rest of the story would require even more emotional energy.

"I hated being in bed, and I hated being in pain," she said. Her voice was thick from tears. They fell freely now. One touched Allison's cheek. The child turned her head toward Kayla, who, with her head slightly bowed, didn't notice.

"After a while I started wishing I'd died in that accident," she whispered. "I prayed every night that God would let me die. Then one day I really did start to get better. It was slow at first, and it took a long time. There was a lot of work and a lot of frustration. But I made it. And then I was glad I hadn't died." She looked up and smiled at Allison. "I even got to be a regular girl again, and you're going to get that chance, too. I promise."

Tears trickled out of the corners of Allison's eyes. Kayla gently wiped them away. "It's good to cry," she said. "It helps wash away the sadness."

Patrick concentrated on staying in his chair. Every instinct screamed at him to go to Kayla and hold her tight, yet he knew there was nothing he could give her, no comfort he could offer. He'd heard her talk about her accident many times before. She often joked about it, made fun of her scars, or dismissed that year out of her life as unimportant. He realized now that there were scars he'd never known about—scars crisscrossing on the inside, scars that touched her heart.

She had a depth, a sense of self, he'd never fully understood. The circumstances of her past explained her interest and compassion with the elderly and the animals. She always looked out for those in need. She was a hell of a woman.

Rhonda stood up and stepped cautiously around Allison's shoulder encased in the cast. She bent over and began to lick away the child's tears. Allison sniffed, and then a smile tugged at her lips.

"She's very pretty," Allison said, speaking for the first time.

"I think so, too." Kayla stood up and walked around the bed. When she was by Rhonda, she moved the dog back so that Allison could pet her. "She has a soft coat. Would you like to touch her?"

Allison nodded and stroked Rhonda's head. The small dog's body shook with pleasure, and she gave a little yip of excitement. Allison laughed.

"Hi, Rhonda. You're a nice doggie, aren't you?"

Rhonda snuggled close in agreement.

"What do you feed her?" Allison asked.

As Kayla started to explain the intricacies of pet care, the door next to Patrick's chair opened. A nurse stepped into the room.

"I just came to check on—" The young woman paused in midsentence. She stared at the smiling child, then looked at Patrick. "What happened? Was it the dog that finally got through to her?"

"Rhonda helped, but mostly it was Kayla. She's been through a similar situation, and I think Allison is pleased to finally find someone who understands what's happening to her."

"I've got to tell Mrs. Carter," the nurse said. "I'll be right back." She closed the door, and Patrick heard her soft footsteps hurrying away.

A few minutes later, Mrs. Carter stepped into the room. "Amazing," she breathed.

Patrick rose to his feet. "I think so, too."

"Her parents are going to be thrilled. The doctor, too. Do you think Kayla will be willing to come back and bring the dog with her?"

Patrick stared at the woman he'd thought he knew so well. After seven years, he was just beginning to see the real Kayla Bedford.

"I know she'll come back," he said. "That's the kind of person she is."

Mrs. Carter excused herself and went to call Allison's parents. Patrick waited patiently while Kayla and Allison talked about Rhonda and what Allison missed most. He heard Kayla promise to sneak in some french fries the next time she visited.

The ache in his chest intensified. Every fiber of his being longed for her. Not just sexually, although he desperately needed her in his bed, but also in other ways. He wanted her in his life.

He'd spent the past four days trying to forget what had happened between them last Saturday. Nothing he did or thought had been able to erase those memories. They had embedded themselves in his person, much as the scars from her accident had left her physically changed.

For now, his scars didn't cause any pain, because she was still with him. But in time, he was going to have to let her go. No matter what he thought about her, no matter what he felt, he had no right to keep her beside him. She'd lived through too much, waited too long. She deserved to have every one of her dreams come true. Even if those dreams didn't include him.

Kayla squinted at the magazine, but that didn't help her understand the words. She laughed. "I keep feeling that if I stare at this long enough, it will make sense. But it's not working."

Sarah glanced up, looking over the half glasses resting on her nose. "I thought you were listening to French on your phone and doing the lessons in the workbook."

Kayla cleared her throat. "Yes, well, I've been trying, but with the dogs and all my additional responsibilities, I don't really have time."

"You need to make time, dear. This is important."

"I know."

She felt guilty, but that didn't give her any more hours in her day. The past four weeks had just flown by. Between her duties at the clinic, visiting Sarah and her friends and spending three afternoons a week with Allison, there wasn't a spare minute.

"If I'm not at work, I'm here, or at the rehab center. In the evenings I've been helping Patrick replace his wallpaper. I barely know what day it is."

"I didn't know that you were seeing Patrick." Sarah raised pale eyebrows.

"Oh, don't start on me, Sarah. There's absolutely nothing going on. I swear."

But as she spoke the words, she felt a faint heat climb up her cheeks.

There was no reason to blush, she told herself. She hadn't lied. There was *nothing* going on. Since that night…since he'd kissed her in a way she'd never been kissed before…he had done as he promised. He'd forgotten the incident. Not by a look or a word had he hinted they'd ever spent passionate moments in each other's arms.

Frankly, she preferred it that way. Better for both of them if they remained just friends.

But sometime over the past few weeks, those logical

words had ceased providing comfort. At times she wondered how he'd been able to forget so easily. Hadn't he felt the same incredible heat? The same need?

Unless she was willing to risk humiliation, she was never going to find out the answer to those questions. And she would rather be covered with honey and staked out naked on an anthill than ask him anything.

Eventually she would forget. At least that was what she told herself a hundred and fourteen times a day.

She tossed aside the French magazine and stood up. As she walked to the window, she tried to shake the restlessness that gripped her. She'd noticed that tingling jump-out-of-her-skin feeling more and more in the past week or so.

"We've put together a list of places you should go while you're in France," Sarah said. "I've put a little mark by Mr. Peter's suggestions. He's not as reliable as one would like. I have a feeling he might be sending you to a brothel."

Kayla laughed. "That would be interesting for everyone."

The vegetable garden was visible from Sarah's room. Young, tender plants sprouted in the rich soil. This year, she wouldn't be around to take home fresh green beans and carrots. In the fall, the pomegranates she loved so much would dry up on the tree. No one else ate them.

"What's wrong, dear?" Sarah asked. "You look out of sorts."

Kayla turned and smiled at her friend. "That's what I forgot when I was getting dressed this morning. My sorts."

Sarah didn't return the smile. She patted the side of the bed. "Tell me."

Kayla settled next to her and touched the older woman's hand. Sarah's skin was still soft, but it was tissue-thin. The network of veins was easily visible.

"I don't know what's wrong," Kayla said. "Sometimes I just want to run and run until—" She broke off and shrugged.

"Until what?"

"I'm not sure. Maybe if I had the answer to that, I'd feel better."

"Are you having second thoughts about your trip?"

"No," Kayla said quickly. "I want to go. I've wanted to go since I was little. I've been waiting for years."

Sarah pulled her hand free and touched Kayla's chin. "We grow, dreams change."

"Not mine."

Sarah nodded. "Then your problem is solved. When you leave, you're doing the right thing." The older woman rubbed Rip's ears. The black poodle, stretched across the bed and using her stomach for a pillow, groaned in contentment.

"I hope so." Kayla grimaced. "I worry about Allison. She's making great progress. In my head, I know she'll be fine, but in my heart, I want to be here to see it. Which is silly. She has a lot of friends and family. She's able to enjoy their visits more. She doesn't really need me."

"Maybe you need her."

Kayla wanted to dismiss Sarah's remark, but she knew better. "Maybe. I suppose watching her reminds me of myself. It's bringing back a lot of memories I thought had been long buried."

"You have many friends. Unfortunately, you're going to have to leave them behind when you fly to Paris. But our memories and our love will go with you."

Kayla leaned close and rested her head on Sarah's shoulder. The older woman wrapped her arm around her.

"I tell myself that's enough," Kayla said. "Then I worry that it isn't. I think my adventure would be a lot better if everyone I cared about came along with me."

"Sorry, but I've made plans for that day."

Sarah's tone was light and playful, but Kayla knew her friend would love to see Paris again. Kayla would have invited her in a heartbeat, but Sarah's infirmity prevented her traveling.

For a moment, she allowed herself the fantasy of having Patrick at her side as she explored Paris. But he had the new research facility to worry about, people to hire, changes to make. He didn't have time for anything else. Besides, having a man along would interfere with her plans to meet and get swept off her feet by a prince.

"I think I'm going to talk to Allison's mother and see if the family wants to adopt Rhonda," Kayla said.

"That's nice. I'm sure the child would adore to have Rhonda around."

"I agree. I'm going to make sure Patrick gets someone fun to bring the dogs here."

"He'll do a fine job, but your replacement will never be you, Kayla. We'll miss you."

"I wish—" Kayla broke off. What was there to wish for? She was getting everything she'd ever wanted. She should be the happiest person in the world.

* * *

Patrick stared at the university transcripts in front of him, then shifted his attention to the résumé on his desk. Melissa Taylor had recently graduated from the University of California at Davis. Her degree was with honors, and her work experience included hands-on practice in a clinic about the same size as his own. She had letters of recommendation from professors he remembered from his time spent at the same university. She was perfect for the job.

"I'm impressed," he said, stacking the papers into a neat pile and closing the folder. "I'm surprised you don't want to go to work for a larger practice, or at one in an affluent neighborhood."

Melissa smiled. She had auburn hair that tumbled down her back, a lithesome figure, and legs that seemed endless. If she didn't want to be a vet, she could probably make a great living as a cover model.

"I've had other offers," she said, her voice low and husky. "I suppose I could go into a different kind of practice, but this is what I prefer. I like dealing with family pets and regular people." She glanced away, as if suddenly shy. "I'm willing to admit that once I found out about your research project, I was intrigued. If you hire me, I hope you'll consider me for that, as well. I understand my primary duties would be to the clinic, but in my free time…" Her words trailed off.

"I appreciate the honesty," he told her. "It would be an advantage to have you help out."

He rose to his feet, and she followed suit. They shook hands.

"I'll be in touch," he told her. "I'll be making my decision in the next two weeks. Please let me know if you accept another position in the meantime."

She paused by the door and gave him a smile that could have sold gas heating to nuclear-power executives. "I probably shouldn't tell you this, Dr. Walcott, but I have no intention of accepting any other offers until I hear from you. You're my first choice." She smiled, then left.

He slumped back in his chair and waited. Unfortunately, his hormones did not come to life. In fact, no part of his body had been particularly moved by Melissa Taylor's charms. He wanted to think it was because he was more tired than usual. But he knew the truth was more devastating than that.

He could tell himself that Melissa wasn't funny enough, or experienced enough, or any number of other lies. The truth was, he would hire her and be grateful to have someone of her caliber to work at the clinic. Then, when she worked out perfectly—and he knew she would—he would do his best to ignore her only flaw.

After all, it wasn't her fault she wasn't Kayla.

CHAPTER SEVEN

KAYLA SHIFTED HER weight from foot to foot as she hovered by the front door of the clinic.

"You're going to wear out the tile," Cheryl, the petite, dark-haired receptionist said. "I'll tell you when your sister arrives."

Kayla shook her head and glanced at her watch for the fourteenth time in five minutes. "I'm too excited. She'll be here any minute. It's the middle of the day. She shouldn't have hit much traffic driving down."

Sure enough, before she could check her watch again, a familiar white Honda pulled into the parking lot. Kayla was out the door and down the walkway in a flash.

Elissa stepped out of her car and laughed. "I guess I don't have to ask if you're happy to see me."

"Of course not. And I happen to know you're just as thrilled to be here."

They embraced and grinned at each other. Elissa touched her sister's hair, then stepped back and looked her over. "You're just as beautiful as ever."

Kayla grinned at the familiar compliment. "As are you." Keeping her arm linked with Elissa's, she led her toward the clinic's front door. "I still find it amazing we've gotten away with telling each other that for years and no one has figured out how conceited we're being."

"It's not conceited," Elissa said. "It's—" She paused, her green eyes dancing. "It's a kindness to make others feel good about their physical appearance."

"Oh, right. But when most people compliment each other, they aren't talking to someone who looks exactly like them."

Kayla pulled open the glass door, and they stepped into the facility. She turned toward the counter. "Cheryl, this is my sister, Elissa."

The receptionist stared blankly. "Oh, my goodness."

"Didn't you warn her?" Elissa asked.

"Of course. Does it ever help?"

Cheryl walked around the counter and stopped in front of them. She glanced from one sister to the other. A large mirror hung on the far wall. Kayla could see what Cheryl saw—two women who looked exactly alike. Oh, the clothes were different. She wore her usual jeans and T-shirt, while Elissa dressed like a Laura Ashley model. Today she'd tucked a pale pink long-sleeved blouse, complete with a bit of ruffle around the collar, into a soft, flowing calf-length gray skirt. She wore gray flats and pearl earrings.

But the clothing and accessories were the only differences. They had the same gold-blond hair, the same green eyes, the same faces, hands, smiles, the same everything else.

Cheryl shook her head in amazement. "There's a third sister?"

"Yes," Elissa said. "Fallon. She's also identical."

"You girls must get a lot of attention when you're out together."

Kayla rolled her eyes. "Constantly. It was worse when we were younger. At least now we can choose not to dress alike."

"Oh, remember those velvet dresses every Christmas?"

"I bet you three were darling," Cheryl said.

"Maybe," Kayla told her, "but we were also really uncomfortable. Those big collars itch."

They continued chatting for a few more minutes, then Kayla took Elissa back to show her the rest of the clinic. She'd planned their route so they would end up in Patrick's office last.

"You didn't dress to meet dogs," Kayla said as she pushed open the door to the kennel.

"I didn't think it would matter what I wore," Elissa told her. "I assumed all your dogs were well-behaved."

"They should be." Kayla glanced at the pale, expensive-looking skirt. "I think I'll keep Trudi safely behind bars. She likes to jump on people."

They slowly walked down the center corridor. Kayla pointed out different boarders. Duchess was back for her monthly grooming. Kayla had already bathed and dried her, so she was fluffy and sweet-smelling.

"Duchess had a gentleman admirer a few weeks back," she said as she stuck her fingers through the gate. Duchess gave her a friendly lick. "Mr. Cookie, an eight-pound Yorkie, fell madly in love. Unfortunately, his owners objected, and the young lovers were torn apart, never to see each other again."

Elissa eyed the very large, very hairy Duchess. "An

eight-pound Yorkie? Maybe it was for the best. I don't think they could have overcome their rather obvious physical differences."

Kayla grinned. "Love can be spiritual, as well as physical."

"I'm not sure dogs see it that way."

"Maybe you're right." She motioned to the last cage. "This is our newest addition. Her name is Rhonda."

When Kayla opened the gate, Rhonda walked out. Elissa crouched down and patted the friendly dog. "This is the one you were telling me about, isn't she? The one helping you with that little girl?"

"Yes. Rhonda and I visit Allison three times a week. She's made great progress. The doctors are impressed with how quickly she's healing. The initial reports are good. There shouldn't be any permanent damage."

"She was lucky," Elissa said.

"I know. If that car had been going a little faster, or had hit her differently, she could have been paralyzed or killed."

"That's not what I meant." Elissa picked up Rhonda, then rose to her feet. She cuddled the dog in her arms. "Allison is lucky to have you to help her. You understand what she's going through. I wish you'd had someone like that when you were in the hospital."

Kayla shrugged, the praise leaving her feeling uncomfortable. "Anyone would have done the same thing."

"Most people would have wanted to, but you're one of a very few who could actually help. I'm trying to pay you a compliment. Accept it politely and say thank-you."

"Thank you. Let's get out of here."

Kayla led the way to her alcove. Elissa spotted the

calendar right away. She set Rhonda down and pointed to the crossed-out days.

"Doesn't this bother people?" she asked.

Kayla frowned. "Why would it?"

"You're leaving a week after your birthday, our birthday, which is right around the corner. You've made friends here. I'm sure they're going to miss you."

"Sure, but what does that have to do with the calendar?"

Elissa stared at her as if she'd grown a second head. "You're rubbing their nose in the fact that you can't wait to get away. Wouldn't you be offended if one of your friends did that to you?"

Kayla opened her mouth, then closed it. She didn't know what to say. Everyone had seemed happy for her, vicariously excited about her adventure. "I didn't mean it like that," she managed at last.

"I know. I'm sure they know, too. I'm being silly. Just forget it. What else is there to see around here?"

Kayla continued the tour. Rhonda trotted along beside them. Kayla pointed out examining rooms, the storage area, the small room where the employee on duty spent the night. But all the while she made conversation with her sister, a small part of her brain turned over Elissa's words. She remembered the strange look on Patrick's face when he'd seen her crossing off the day on the calendar before she went home. Did he think she was an insensitive clod?

They turned into the corridor. "That's the grand tour," Kayla said, forcing herself to concentrate on the moment. She could deal with the rest of it when she was alone. "There's only Patrick's office."

Elissa frowned. "I'm not sure this is such a good idea."

"It's perfect. You two belong together. You're going to have to trust me on this."

"The last time you said that to me was when I didn't want to jump my bike over the ravine behind the house. You said to trust you, and I ended up with a broken arm."

Kayla laughed and gave her a hug. "Hey, at least the attending physician was cute. That sort of made up for it, don't you think?"

"As I was the one stuck in a cast over Christmas, no, it doesn't make up for it. But I forgive you anyway."

"Thanks. Besides, Patrick is a lot less scary than that ravine. He's funny, intelligent, and very good-looking. You two went to the same college."

Elissa's smile faded. "I only lasted two years. I never graduated."

"That's not the point. You were there, weren't you?"

"I suppose." Elissa crossed to the window overlooking the parking lot.

"Do you have regrets?" Kayla asked.

"About leaving college?"

"About all of it."

"I haven't decided. I made the best decision I could under the circumstances. I was only twenty. That's awfully young to make those kinds of choices."

Kayla remembered that time. "I always admired you for what you did."

Elissa turned toward her and raised her eyebrows in surprise. "Why?"

"Because you followed your heart. I remember Mrs.

Beecham on the show talking about love being a tornado. That's what happened to you."

"Exactly. That *is* what happened to me. Look where I ended up. Love might be a tornado, but storms with that kind of power tend to destroy everything in their paths."

Kayla gave a start as she realized Patrick had said the same thing. "I don't care," she told both her sister and the memory. "I want to be swept away."

Elissa managed a shaky smile. "Then I'm sure you will be."

"What about you? It's not too late. When the trust money is released, you could go back to college."

"Maybe. I've thought about it. I have a lot of decisions I need to make."

Kayla didn't want to upset her sister, so she changed the subject. "I appreciate you helping me out with Patrick. One of the doctors he's hired is this evil woman. We have to protect him from her."

"Evil?"

Kayla sighed. "Well, maybe not evil, but I don't like her. She's beautiful, really tall, really smart. Oh, and she has red hair, which is, unfortunately, Patrick's favorite. I know she wants him." She shuddered. "I can't let that happen. You're my only hope."

Elissa laughed. "How can I refuse such an impassioned plea? Lead on, Kayla. Introduce me to this poor man in desperate need of rescuing."

They were still laughing when Kayla knocked on the door, then pushed it open.

Patrick stood up as they entered. He glanced from one sister to the other. "I know you warned me, but it's an amazing resemblance. However, I think I can tell you apart by your clothes, if nothing else." He came around the desk and held out his hand to Elissa. "I'm very pleased to meet you. Kayla has been singing your praises for weeks."

Elissa smiled. "So you only have the bad things left to discover."

"I doubt there are any bad things."

Elissa glanced at her. "Is he always this charming?"

Kayla nodded, even as she remembered all the times Patrick had taken great pleasure in pointing out *her* faults. They were, she noticed, still holding each other's hands. As if sensing her attention, they reluctantly released the contact.

"Please have a seat," Patrick said, pulling out a chair for Elissa. He left Kayla to find her own seat.

She picked up several charts resting on a chair and set them on the corner of his desk, then slumped down next to her sister.

"Kayla tells me you live in Los Angeles," Patrick said.

"That's right. Santa Monica."

"By the beach. It's pretty there."

"You know the area?"

"I've been there a few times. Actually, I've spent more time in Marina del Rey. I sailed out of there."

Elissa leaned forward in her chair. "Really? I didn't know you sailed."

"Nothing very big. Most twenty-five- or thirty-footers. Day trips, mostly. I've gone over to Catalina a couple of times."

Elissa shot her a glance. "You didn't tell me Patrick sails."

Kayla stared at her employer. "That's because I didn't know. You don't sail around here."

He barely spared her a smile. "I have. You must have been gone when I went out."

Or he hadn't bothered to invite her along. Maybe he used a day at sea to seduce his women. Her gaze narrowed. What other secrets did Patrick keep?

"How long are you going to be in town?" he asked. "Maybe you can make time for a sail."

"That would be lovely. Kayla and I haven't really discussed our plans for the weekend yet. Can I get back to you?"

"Sure."

The conversation continued to flow easily between them. Kayla folded her arms tightly across her chest and told herself she was really happy. Thrilled. She couldn't have been more excited. Elissa and Patrick chatted as if they'd known each other for years. They were perfect together.

It couldn't have worked out better.

So why did she want to throw up her hands and scream?

Take deep breaths, she told herself. Slow, calming breaths. She tried to force the tension from her body. Unfortunately, once it started to fade, she was able to feel something hot and painful in the pit of her stomach. It sat there heavily, like a ball of poison.

Patrick focused all his attention on Elissa. She might as well not have been in the room. Had he been like this when he interviewed Melissa Taylor? The thought stabbed her like a scalpel. How dare he—

She pressed her lips together. How dare *she?* She

had no rights where Patrick was concerned. They were friends. She'd often encouraged him to find someone and start a relationship. She'd introduced him to Elissa with the hopes the two of them would hit it off. Why was she suddenly having second thoughts? And why was Patrick so damned interested in Elissa?

She looked at her sister. Except for the different clothing, they were exactly alike. So it wasn't Elissa's looks. Was it her personality? Elissa was the middle of the triplets and acted like a middle child. She was calm and caring, settling fights between Fallon and Kayla. Maybe he was drawn to Elissa's gentle, restful spirit. Kayla knew she had many good qualities, but a restful spirit wasn't one of them.

In seven years, Patrick had never once looked at her the way he was looking at Elissa. It was all she could do not to grab her sister and hustle her from the room.

Before she could act on her impulse, the phone buzzed. Patrick excused himself and hit the speaker button.

Cheryl's voice came over the intercom.

"Is Kayla in with you? There's a package up front for her. It's from her travel agent."

"She's right here," Patrick said, at last sparing her a second's worth of attention. "She'll be right up." He hit the speaker button again to disconnect the call. "I'm sure it's brochures, or something equally wonderful. Don't worry. I can keep Elissa company."

"Yes, I know," she said before she could stop herself, then quickly left the room.

All the way to the front desk she told herself she was acting like a fool. This was what she wanted, and she would learn to be happy about it. Even if she had to fake it for the rest of her life.

As she stopped in front of the reception desk, Cheryl waved a box in the air. It was about as long and wide as a shoe box, but about a third as tall.

"Something exciting," Cheryl said.

"I hope so." Right now, she needed a distraction.

She grabbed a pair of scissors and slit the tape sealing the box. The top slipped off easily. Cheryl stared over her shoulder and gave a gasp of surprise. "Africa?"

"I'm not sure," Kayla told her. "I'm going to be in Paris for a while, then I'll come back to spend the holidays with my sisters. I thought I might try a photo safari in the spring."

Cheryl picked up one of the brochures. "It's beautiful."

Kayla nodded as she read over the letter from her travel agent. There were several documents attached. Visas were required for some countries, and there was a vaccination list. If Kayla was going to seriously consider the trip, she would need to start some of her series of shots now.

"Series of shots?" Kayla echoed out loud, then swallowed hard. She flipped to the next page, then the next, until she found the sheet she wanted.

She stared at the list of required shots and felt her stomach fall to her toes. She'd wanted a distraction, and she'd sure gotten one.

Series of shots? The last time she gave blood, she'd fainted. She sank into the nearest chair and lowered her head between her legs. Maybe Africa wasn't such a good idea.

* * *

After Kayla left, Elissa rose and closed the door. When she resumed her seat, she stared at Patrick.

He returned her gaze. At first the similarities between the women had been startling. Now he was starting to see that there were tiny differences in their features. While they both used their hands when they talked, Kayla had a body language that was unique. Her smile was broader, her gaze more intense. Irrationally, he thought she was prettier. Which told him he was in more trouble than he'd first realized.

Elissa leaned back in her chair and rested her hands on her lap. "That was a very impressive performance, Patrick. If I didn't know better, I would be flattered by the attention."

He swore under his breath. "Was it that obvious?"

"Yes." She smiled. "You said all the right words, but your heart wasn't in it. Were you trying to make Kayla jealous?"

He wasn't sure. When Kayla walked in and introduced her sister, something inside him had snapped. He'd been furious that she'd gone ahead with her plan to get him involved with another woman. Not only was he insulted by her assumption that he couldn't get a date on his own, he resented her not figuring out that she was the one he wanted to be with.

"It's a little more complicated than that," he said.

"Too bad, because the plan worked."

"You think so?" he asked, not wanting to sound too eager.

"I was afraid she was going to drag me out of here by my hair." Elissa leaned forward. "To give her credit,

I think she genuinely wanted us to like each other. But then something happened. I don't suppose you'd be willing to fill in the details."

"There aren't any. Kayla and I are good friends."

"If I could have hooked up a battery to the sparks flying between the two of you, I could have run an electric car for a month. If nothing's going on, why the act?"

She had him there.

"I want to help," Elissa said. "Kayla's my sister, and I love her. I want her to be happy. I've known there was something wrong for a while, but I didn't know what. Now that I've met you, it all makes sense."

"Then maybe you could explain it to me."

"Are you attracted to my sister?"

"I don't know." He held up a hand before Elissa could interrupt. "I mean that sincerely. If you'd asked me the same question six months ago, or even three months ago, I would have said no. I've known Kayla for years, and in all that time we've only ever been friends. Lately, though, something is different."

"Go on."

He fought a smile. "It's almost eerie talking to you, Elissa. You look so much like Kayla."

"Could you tell us apart?"

"Sure. Why?"

The corners of her mouth turned up. "No particular reason. I was curious. Some people can't. What's changed between you and my sister?"

"A while back, out of the blue, she announced that she and I would be a great couple. She listed all the reasons we belonged together. To tell you the truth, I was stunned. Then she laughed and said it was joke. That she was leaving and wasn't really the perfect woman for me—you were."

Elissa shook her head. "Sometimes Kayla can be stubborn. She gets an idea in her head and nothing can budge it. So that comment started you thinking?"

"In a way." He shifted in his chair. "Then there was this kiss."

Elissa raised her eyebrows.

"It's not what you think," he said, telling himself it wasn't a lie. He *had* been talking about that first kiss, the one at her place when he found out about the grant. The second kiss, the one that had set him on fire and left him sleepless with longing, was too private to share with anyone.

"Kayla and I have always kissed," he continued. "You know, as friends. Brother and sister, even. But it changed. I don't know why or how."

"Do you love her?"

He thought for a moment. "I care about her, but she's leaving in a few weeks. I don't want her to go, yet I'm not about to ask her to stay. She's been planning this trip for as long as I've known her, probably longer. She deserves a chance to make her dreams come true."

"I agree," Elissa said. "But is this her real dream, or something left over from when she was a child? Kayla has an unusual past. She learned how to put her life on hold."

"If you're talking about the accident, I know about it."

"I'm surprised she told you. She usually doesn't talk about it."

"I'd heard bits and pieces. She pretends that it wasn't anything. I didn't get the details until recently."

Elissa nodded. "Then you can understand why dreams are so important to her. For nearly a year, dreams were all she had. Lying in that hospital bed, she decided something wonderful was going to happen when she grew up. After the trust fund was established, she made the decision to see the world and marry a handsome prince."

If she was trying to make him feel better, she was doing a lousy job. Patrick pushed his chair back a couple of feet and rested his ankle on his opposite knee. "I can't compete with that."

"Oh, I'm not so sure. You've got the handsome part taken care of."

"Thanks. I'm not sure Kayla shares your opinion."

"Oh, but she does. She told me herself."

He refused to let himself hope. His feelings for Kayla were new and unexpected, and he had a bad feeling he'd already left himself open to heartbreak.

Elissa glanced over her shoulder, as if making sure the door was still closed. "I have a plan," she said quietly, leaning toward him. "It's a great way to test the waters without anyone getting hurt."

"I'm listening."

"I want you to invite me out to dinner tonight. Somewhere romantic, with dancing."

"Not that you wouldn't be a delightful companion, but how does this help me with Kayla?"

Elissa grinned. At that moment, she looked so much like her sister that he couldn't help grinning back.

"I won't be going," she said. "At the last minute, I'll

tell Kayla I can't go through with it." She waved her hand. "There are some things in my life that will make her believe me. I'll insist that she go in my place so you won't feel stood up. Your job is to pretend not to know. If I'm right, and I'm sure that I am, she's going to be very upset that you've asked me out. She'll jump at the chance to spend the evening with you. Then the fun starts. She'll be with you, but as me. That will give her something to think about."

The plan had merit. If Kayla was pretending to be her sister, she might slip up and say something she wouldn't normally. Maybe he could get an idea of her feelings for him. Even if he didn't learn a thing, at least he would get to spend the evening with her.

"Are you sure this is all right with you?" he asked. "After all, you're being abandoned on your first night here."

"I don't mind." She looked pensive for a moment. "Kayla is trying to do a nice thing. While I appreciate that, it wouldn't have worked out between you and I. Not that you're not everything she promised," she added quickly.

"Thanks."

"There are a few other things I have to take care of before I can start dating. Besides all that, I don't think Kayla has really thought this through. Her feelings for you seem a little confused to me. Maybe a date will clear up everything. I'd like you to give it a try."

"I'm willing," he said.

"I'm glad you agree. I know that traveling and fulfilling her dreams are important to Kayla. She deserves to do both. But I'm afraid she's spent so long living in her dreams, she's forgotten that the life she already has is pretty wonderful."

CHAPTER EIGHT

"HE REALLY ASKED you out for dinner?" Kayla asked, trying to keep the disbelief out of her voice.

Elissa stuck her head out of the bathroom and smiled. "I've told you fifteen times, yes, Patrick invited me out for dinner." Her gaze narrowed. "What's wrong, Kayla? Don't you want me to go?"

"Of course I want you to go," she answered quickly. "I'm thrilled. This is what I hoped would happen. It's terrific. Really."

She forced herself to hold perfectly still and look pleasant, when all she wanted to do was scream.

Apparently Elissa bought the act. She nodded and stepped back into the bathroom. "If you're sure."

"Oh, I am."

Kayla leaned against the door jamb and watched her sister put on makeup. Elissa wore her hair in a loose ponytail on the top of her head. Electric curlers sprouted from the rubber band like metallic flowers. She wore a towel wrapped around her, with the end tucked in by her left arm. The white terry cloth covered her from breasts to midthigh. She'd finished most of her makeup, and she reached for a tube of mascara to apply the final coat.

When she was done, she shooed Kayla out of the way. "You haven't seen this dress, and I want it to be a surprise. Go wait in the living room until I'm ready," she said.

Kayla stepped back and shuffled into the main room. "You'll look great," she mumbled under her breath. "Patrick will be blown away."

She slumped on the sofa and pulled one of the throw pillows close to her chest. "It's not fair. Patrick never asked me out to a romantic dinner by the water. He's never asked me out at all. Not that I wanted him to. We're not a couple. But still, he could have…"

Her voice trailed off. She wasn't sure what Patrick could have done, but there had to be something. Confusing feelings swirled inside her. Questions and thoughts mingled and separated.

Why was she jealous? She'd invited Elissa down specifically so her sister could meet Patrick. They obviously got along—Patrick had asked her out within minutes of meeting her, and Elissa was nearly dressed and ready, a good half hour before their date. Kayla's plan had worked. Everything was turning out exactly as it should.

So why did she feel so empty inside? Why was her heart aching and her body heavy with dread?

She wanted to believe it was because she sensed something wrong with the relationship, that she had a premonition that Elissa and Patrick shouldn't be together. Unfortunately, the reason wasn't that noble. She had an ugly suspicion that she was playing dog in the manger with Patrick. She didn't want him for herself, but she didn't want anyone else to have him, either.

But why? She'd never been like that before. It wasn't in her nature. She wasn't a mean-spirited person, and certainly not about her sister and her best friend. She cared about them both.

The bathroom door opened, interrupting her thoughts. Elissa stepped into the tiny hall, then forward into the living room.

The last rays of sunlight flowed through the window and caught the gold in Elissa's hair. The shimmering curls tumbled over her shoulders in casual, sexy disarray. Makeup highlighted large green eyes, brightening them to the color of summer grass. The short black dress ended several inches above her knees. Twin pairs of skinny straps secured the fitted bodice and waist, while the fuller skirt swayed with each step. Dark stockings and black pumps completed the outfit.

Kayla's breath caught in her throat. "You're beautiful," she said. This time there was no mistaking the bitter stab of jealousy, but she put her feelings aside. Tonight was for her sister. Elissa deserved some fun in her life. If that meant Patrick fell for her, then Kayla would learn to be happy with that.

Elissa twirled in a circle. The skirt fluttered with the movement. "You really think so?"

"I'm positive. Patrick isn't going to know what hit him."

Elissa's smile faltered. She bit her lower lip and sank into the love seat next to the sofa. "I can't," she whispered, and covered her face with her hands.

"You can't what?"

"I can't go through with this." She motioned to the dress, then touched her hair. "It's not right."

Kayla firmly squashed the first hint of elation. She was determined not to be selfish. "Why? Patrick asked you out, and you want to go. What's the problem?"

Elissa straightened. "Cole." She spoke the single word with two parts pain, one part resignation.

"You haven't spoken to him?" Kayla asked cautiously.

"Not since—" Her voice broke, and she waved her hand, as if that were enough to complete the thought.

It was. Kayla was at her side in an instant. She took Elissa's hand and squeezed it. "I'm sorry," she said. "It's been so long that I thought you were ready. I thought it would help you to meet someone else."

"I thought so, too, but it's not time. I just can't do this."

In an odd way, Kayla didn't feel relieved. She loved her sister and hated to see her unhappy. If Patrick could have helped Elissa recover from her past, then Kayla would have lived with the consequences.

Elissa drew in a deep breath. "I'll call Patrick and tell him I can't make it. I hope he doesn't get angry. I don't want to go into the reasons why I'm canceling our date."

"He won't be mad," Kayla said, as a flicker of expectation fluttered through her. If Patrick didn't go out with Elissa, he wouldn't have a chance to fall for her. She hated herself for thinking that, but she couldn't seem to make the thought disappear.

"I'm going to sound like a flake," Elissa said. "It's really too bad. He seems so nice, and I know he's a close friend of yours. But he dates a lot, right? It's not as if I'm the first woman he's asked out in months. This isn't going to upset him."

"Ah, right," Kayla said, and swallowed. Just as Elissa didn't want to discuss her past with Patrick, she knew Patrick wouldn't want her telling Elissa about his lack of a social life over the past couple of years. Elissa *was* the first woman he'd asked out in months. He very well might think he'd been blown off.

"What?" Elissa asked. "Why do you have that funny look on your face?"

"I don't. It's just—"

"He's going to be hurt."

"No, it's just—"

Elissa sprang to her feet. "I knew it. This is crazy. I should never have accepted. I wouldn't have, but you seemed so eager for us to go out. I didn't want to let you down."

Kayla felt as if she were having tea with the Mad Hatter. "This is *my* fault?"

"If not yours, then whose? Patrick is going to be crushed, I'm upset, all because we were trying to make you happy."

"But I— You—" She leaned back on the love seat and closed her eyes. "Fine. Everything is my fault. I'll call Patrick and explain that." She held up her hand to stop Elissa's interruption. "Don't worry, I won't say a thing about you and Cole. Patrick is polite. He won't ask questions."

She walked over to the phone hanging on the kitchen wall. When had everything gotten so out of control? Two months ago she and Patrick had been good friends and she hadn't cared about who he dated. Two weeks ago she'd been sure Elissa was the perfect woman for him. Ten minutes ago she'd been eating herself alive with jealousy because her sister was going out with Patrick. Now she was the bad guy for setting them up together. Maybe that African safari wasn't such a bad idea. At least there she wouldn't be able to mess up anyone's life, including her own.

She started dialing the familiar number. Before the call went through, Elissa grabbed the receiver and broke the connection. "Wait a minute. I have a plan," she said.

Fifteen minutes later, Kayla dropped the blush brush on the bathroom counter. "This is never going to work."

"Sure it is. Patrick doesn't know me at all."

"But he knows *me*."

"Exactly. So don't be yourself. Be me. We used to trade places all the time."

Kayla wrinkled her nose. "That was in junior high school. We haven't done it in years. Besides, I was never good at that game."

Elissa waved away her concerns. "He won't be expecting this at all. It's just dinner. The alternative is one of us calls him up and tells him I can't go. Frankly, I think he deserves better than that."

Kayla stared at her reflection in the mirror and had an eerie sensation of déjà vu. Her hair had been pulled to the top of her head in a ponytail. Electric curlers pressed against her scalp. Instead of a towel, she wore a short white robe, but otherwise, she could have been Elissa getting ready for her date.

Elissa handed her the mascara. She took it, but didn't put it on. As much as she wanted to go and spend a romantic evening with Patrick, there was one ugly truth she had to face. "He asked you out, not me."

"That's hardly important."

Kayla turned to face her. "It's very important. He's never asked me out. If he was interested in me that way, he would have."

"Are you sure about that? Have you ever given him a hint that *you* were interested in him in that way? Aren't you the one always talking about what good friends you are?"

"Yes."

"Then why would he ask you out? It's not as if you're secretly longing for him. Right?"

Longing for him. She liked the sound of that. It fit her feelings perfectly. Longing wasn't as big as love, but it seemed larger than friendship. She thought about him all the time, and didn't understand why. She longed to be with him, near him, maybe even held by him. She longed to repeat those amazing kisses.

"It's all very confusing," Kayla said, avoiding her sister's question. If Elissa noticed, she didn't let on.

"The bottom line is, he's your friend and you don't want to hurt him. Isn't that all that matters?"

"I guess."

Kayla finished applying her makeup, then pulled the curlers and rubber band out of her hair. By the time she'd slipped on the dress, applied a final layer of hair spray and hunted down her dressy black pumps, Patrick was due to arrive.

Tiny shudders rippled through her. She knew they were just a combination of nerves, excitement and a bit of dread. Would she be able to pull this off?

Elissa handed her a small black handbag. "He should be here any minute," she said. "I'll go wait in the bedroom. Our plan has a better chance of working if he doesn't see us together. After all, he knows you well enough that if we're next to each other, he might be able to tell us apart. And we don't want that."

"Okay."

Elissa kissed her cheek. "Have a great time. I won't wait up."

"We're not going to be out that late."

"You never know."

There was a knock on the front door.

"Don't forget you're supposed to be me," Elissa murmured, then waggled her fingers and disappeared into the bedroom.

Kayla walked to the front door, took a deep breath and pulled it open. Here goes nothing, she thought.

Until he saw her standing in front of him, Patrick wasn't sure Elissa would actually be able to pull off the switch. But the moment the door opened, he recognized the woman in front of him. The relief was instant, as was the anticipation.

"Hi," he said, as Kayla stared at him. "You look amazing."

"Ah, thanks. So do you. I've never seen you—" She stopped suddenly. "That is, you look great in a suit."

"Thanks."

He stepped toward her and glanced over her shoulder. "Where's Kayla?"

"What? Oh, she's in her bedroom. Um, lying down. She has a headache."

"I'm sorry to hear that. I should probably pop my head in and say hi."

Kayla grabbed his arm, then, just as quickly, let go. "I don't think she wants to be disturbed."

"All right. Be sure to tell her I hope she feels better."

"I'm sure she'll appreciate your concern."

He held out his arm. "Shall we go?"

Kayla stared blankly for a moment, then slipped her hand into the crook of his elbow. As they walked down the steps to the driveway, he felt the faint tremors in her fingers. Turning his head so she wouldn't see him smile, he sent a silent "Thank you" back to Elissa.

At first he'd had his doubts about her plan. Would it make a difference if he was out with Kayla pretending to be Elissa? But now he saw the possibilities. For the first time, they were on a date.

He'd had his car washed. It gleamed in the porch light. When he held open the passenger's door, she glanced at him before slipping in. Confusion darkened her eyes. He understood her apprehension. Nerves had a grip on him, too. But this was a time for them to get to know each other in a whole new way.

He waited until she'd secured her seat belt, then walked around the back of the car and got in beside her. Before starting the engine, he glanced at her.

He'd seen her in makeup before, and he was reasonably sure he'd seen her dressed up. Yet in some ways it was as if she were a stranger. A beautiful, mysterious stranger he'd just discovered.

"Is something wrong?" she asked, her voice low and husky.

"No. I was just thinking how beautiful you are." He touched her bare shoulder. "The dress isn't bad, either."

Color flared on her cheeks. Her gaze lowered as she murmured, "Thank you."

He hoped for that one moment she'd forgotten she

was supposed to be her sister. He wanted her to know the compliment was meant for her, and no one else.

Perhaps the reason they had never clicked as a couple was that they had never allowed themselves to see each other that way. Tonight was their chance. They could show that side of themselves. The night, he thought with a smile, had many possibilities.

The small, dimly lit waterfront restaurant was as romantic and seductive as satin sheets and chilled champagne. Their table sat in front of the window. Lights from the building and a nearby dock reflected on the inky ocean, providing just enough illumination for Kayla to see the pale foam of waves breaking against the pilings.

The place settings had been arranged close together, allowing them to talk intimately and stare out at the view. The last fingers of sunlight had disappeared as they were seated, and the darkness outside gave Kayla the impression that she and Patrick were alone.

It wasn't true. Bits of quiet conversation drifted to them from other tables. A four-piece band played in the far corner, and several couples moved together on the dance floor. The night, the place, the music and the man were all perfect. Except he thought he was with someone else.

The waiter returned with a bottle of white wine and a free-standing ice bucket. He presented the selection, holding the foil-wrapped top with one hand while resting the bottle against his opposite forearm.

Patrick glanced at the label. "That's the one," he said.

The waiter opened the bottle and poured a small amount into Patrick's glass. He sipped, then nodded.

After the wine had been poured, Patrick raised his drink.

"To a wonderful evening."

"My thoughts exactly," she said, and tasted the wine. "It's very nice."

"An old favorite," he said. "I like it on special occasions. But don't expect me to be an expert. I know a little about wine, but I'm more a beer or soda kind of guy."

Kayla remembered their celebration when he'd received his grant. They'd opened a bottle of champagne. "How do you feel about champagne?" she asked, trying to act innocent.

"I like it. In fact, I had some recently. When I—" He broke off and shook his head. "I don't want to talk about me. I want to hear about your life. You work in a hospital? What do you do there?"

Kayla gave him a brief description of Elissa's job, leaving out technical details because she didn't know them. It would be easier, she decided, if they talked about things she knew about.

"I toured the clinic today," she said. "I was impressed. You're doing good work there."

"Thank you. It's not just me. I have a great staff. Did Kayla take you back into the kennels?"

"Yes. I met several of your permanent residents."

Her forearm rested on the padded arm of the captain's chair. He shifted in his seat, moving closer. As his body angled toward hers, he stroked his fingers against the back of her fingers. The sensation was so unexpected, so electrifying, she lost her train of thought and couldn't pay attention to what Patrick was saying.

Not that she cared. No words could be as life-changing as the feel of his hand touching hers. He moved slowly, gently, teasing her. Nerves ignited. Untouched, undiscovered parts of her body began to make their presence known.

She stared into his blue eyes and knew that if she found a way to crawl inside Patrick's heart, he would hold her close and keep her safe forever. The thought should have terrified her. Perhaps, when she thought about it later, it would. Except this *was* Patrick, and she trusted him with her life.

"...so there stood Kayla, facing down this guy," he said, as if he'd been talking for several minutes.

She realized he probably had. With an effort, she wrenched her attention away from the delicious sensations he produced with his touch and tried to focus on his words.

"He was huge," Patrick continued. "Six-four, maybe six-five. A former linebacker with a pro football team. At least two hundred and fifty pounds of solid muscle. He'd bought a house in the area, had a successful business, and wanted to adopt a cat."

Kayla's mind cleared long enough for her to remember the incident. Working with a couple of local shelters, the clinic had sponsored an Adopt-a-Pet afternoon one Sunday last year. Kayla had put together the event by herself, and she'd been very picky about who took home the animals. She didn't remember anything extraordinary about that day, and wasn't sure why he was telling the story.

"It was late in the afternoon," he said. "We were down to a couple of dogs and one kitten." He grinned at the memory. "It was a tiny thing. All black, with big yellow eyes. A female, barely seven weeks. You know, when they still look like fur balls rather than small cats."

Kayla nodded.

"This one was a tiger at heart. She spit at everyone. Families with children had been afraid to take her home."

"She was too young to be with a household of children," Kayla said without thinking.

At Patrick's inquisitive look, she sank back in her chair. "I've, ah, been around small kittens. It's easy for them to get hurt."

"Oh. You're right."

She exhaled slowly and reminded herself she was Elissa. Elissa didn't work at the clinic. Pretending to be her sister was harder than she'd thought.

"So in walks this guy. I can't remember his name. Peter, I think."

His name had been Paul, but Kayla didn't dare correct him.

"He took one look at the kitten and fell in love. Of course, when he tried to pick her up, she spit and scratched until the poor man was bleeding."

Kayla smiled, remembering the crushed look on Paul's face. It was as if he'd been kicked by his own mother.

"What happened?" she asked, still not sure what intrigued Patrick about that afternoon.

"Kayla told Peter that the kitten had been handled all day and was scared. He had to show her he was safe. She made him lie on the floor on his back. Then she put tuna in his palm, his forearm, and a tiny dab of it on the front of his shirt." Patrick grinned. "No napkin, no plate, just tuna on the man's shirt."

Kayla felt herself flush. She hadn't thought about using a napkin until later, when Paul tried to rub away the smell.

"I was in the corner, trying not to laugh. This little tiny kitten, maybe three whole pounds of fur and not much else, came sneaking up to this big guy. She ate the tuna on his hand and arm, then climbed up to his chest. Now, kittens have needle-sharp claws. They really hurt. Peter flinched with each step, but he didn't budge. The kitten ate the tuna on his chest, stared into his face for a minute, then curled up and went to sleep."

Kayla smiled at the memory.

"Peter didn't want to get up and disturb her, so he stayed on the floor for about a half hour, until we were ready to leave."

"Did things work out with the kitten?" she asked, already knowing the answer.

"Absolutely. That cat runs his life. He brings her in every six months for a checkup. I keep telling him he only needs to come in once a year if she's not sick, but he won't listen." He shook his head. "Kayla is the only person in the world who would have dared to tell this rich, successful, famous guy to lay on the floor and then smear him with tuna, all because of a damn cat." Amusement crinkled the lines fanning out from the corners of his eyes. "She's one unique woman, and she's going to be impossible to replace."

Pleasure filled her. She wanted to thank him for the compliment and for thinking so highly of her. She held the words back, knowing that he wouldn't like her nearly as much if he knew she was here masquerading as her sister.

He squeezed her hand. "Sorry, Elissa. This night is so you and I can get to know each other, and here I am talking about your sister. You must think I'm a jerk."

"Not at all," she said quickly. "I like Kayla, too. Besides, she is the one person we have in common."

He stared at her. "You're right about that."

She wanted to ask what he meant, but the waiter appeared with their menus.

She glanced over the selections. Everything looked delicious, but she knew she was too nervous and excited to eat much. Patrick commented on several items, and they discussed the fresh fish of the day, then placed their orders.

"Aren't you hungry?" he asked when the waiter had moved off, leaving them in relative privacy.

"First dates make me nervous," she said, knowing she spoke the absolute truth. She and Patrick might have been friends for years, but this was their first official date. Except for the fact that she was lying about her identity, she thought it was going pretty well.

"Are you going to be leaving your job at the hospital?" he asked.

She stared at him. "No. Why do you ask?"

"I wondered if all three of the Bedford triplets would be taking off for parts unknown once the trust money was released."

Privately Kayla thought her two siblings were unadventurous and missing a great opportunity—but both had chosen not to come with her to Paris. Still, she couldn't say that.

"We all have plans," she said cautiously as she realized she wasn't sure what Elissa wanted to do with her money. Her sister had always been frightened of wealth. "But Kayla is definitely the traveler. In some ways, I envy her the trip she'll be taking in a few weeks." She took a sip of wine. "We plan to spend the holidays together in the Caribbean. That will be fun."

Patrick's mouth straightened. "You'll have to forgive me for not sharing your enthusiasm. Kayla's been a part of my life for a long time. I can't remember what the clinic was like without her, and I'm not looking forward to having to rediscover it. She's going to be impossible to replace. I'll miss her."

Kayla met his gaze. She read the sorrow in his eyes, the promise of pain he would suffer on her behalf. Her chest tightened. The knowledge that Patrick cared about her wasn't new; they'd always cared about each other. Maybe it was the depth of his feelings that surprised her…or the fact that he was telling a stranger things he'd never said to her face.

"I'm—" She cleared her throat. "She's really going to miss you, too."

"I doubt that. She'll be too busy chasing after European aristocracy. She wants to marry a prince."

"No, really. She is going to miss you. You mean a lot to her. She talks about you all the time. You're an important part of her life."

His mouth turned up in a faint smile. "You're being kind."

"I'm telling the truth. I swear." She made an X over her left breast. "Kayla thinks you're wonderful."

"I think she's great, too. I've always wondered one thing."

Her breath caught. What had he wondered? Why they'd never gotten together? She was starting to seriously ask that question herself. Being with Patrick felt so right. She could talk to him about nearly anything. It might have been difficult to admit her feelings to him as herself, but as Elissa it was amazingly easy to confess everything. That she liked him more than he knew. That she replayed his kisses over and over in her mind. She smiled. Okay, maybe it would be nearly impossible to work the comment about the kissing into a casual conversation, but she really wished there was a way to let him know.

"Kayla is so bright and funny. Nearly as good-looking as her sister."

He flashed her a grin designed to add to the compliment. Kayla wasn't sure if she was flattered or insulted.

"And?" she asked, hoping he would lay it all out on the table, confess everything. Then she could tell him the truth, and they would—

"Why hasn't some guy swept her off her feet? She never goes out. I keep hoping for someone special to come into her life, but it doesn't happen."

Kayla sagged back in her chair. Great. Patrick thought she was a lonely old maid in need of a social life. Not exactly the romantic declaration she'd anticipated.

Before she could formulate an answer, he touched her hand again.

"Elissa, you must think I'm the biggest jerk around. I keep talking about your sister, when you're the one I'm interested in. Can you forgive me?"

"Sure," Kayla mumbled, even though it wasn't true. Forgive him? For being interested in Elissa? Not likely. Didn't he get it? Didn't he sense the connection between them? Oh, yeah, of course he did; he thought the chemistry was between him and Elissa, not between him and her.

"Let's dance," he said, standing up and holding out his hand.

She let him lead her to the small floor in the far corner, all the while not sure what to make of her feelings. In a way, she should be happy that he couldn't stop talking about her. But it annoyed her that he kept apologizing for it. Nothing made sense.

Then he took her into his arms, and she didn't care about making sense or her sister or anything but being with him.

Her heels put her at exactly the right height to rest her chin on his shoulder. He pulled her close right away, and she didn't think to protest until it was too late. Frankly, she didn't care. This was Patrick, and if he thought she was acting brazen, what did it matter? He was with Elissa.

They touched from shoulder to thigh. One of his hands settled on the small of her back, the other held her fingers tucked in against his chest. She could feel the steady pounding of his heart—the strong and solid beat so much like the man himself.

They swayed together with a familiarity that belied the truth that this was their first dance. The music surrounded them like a sensual fog, leaving her dizzy and disoriented. Yet safe. Nothing bad would ever happen while she was in Patrick's arms.

The hard, muscled planes of his body provided the perfect counterpoint to her yielding curves.

"We do this well," he said lightly as the combo switched to another slow dance.

"I agree. I was going to tell you I'm not much of a dancer, but I guess that's not true with you."

His cheek rested against her forehead, and she felt him smile. "It must be my close contact with Kayla. You two are so much alike."

Kayla didn't want him to think about Elissa right now. "Have you danced much with Kayla?" she asked.

He chuckled. "No. We've never been romantically involved."

She had to struggle to keep her tone light, but she was determined to ask the question. "Why not?"

"She was never interested in me that way."

His statement hung in the air, floating on the music. A half-finished thought that begged for completion.

Were you ever interested in her...that way?

She didn't ask, and he didn't offer.

The right answer would fill her with elation and make her face her own questions. The wrong answer would leave her devastated. Rather than risk it, she contented herself with silence and the stirring pleasure of being in his arms.

By the time the dessert dishes had been cleared away, Kayla had given up worrying about the fact that all Patrick's attentiveness, all his gentle touches to her hand, arm and back, were actually meant for Elissa. Her sister wasn't here, she wasn't the one making Patrick laugh, so Kayla refused to worry about giving her the credit.

"You must have been very proud when you opened the clinic," she said.

Patrick nodded. "I'd wanted to be a vet since I was a kid. It was a dream come true. The first year was tough, but the community supported me in a big way."

"Now you're famous and you have a big staff."

He laughed. "I'm certainly not famous, but the staff is a decent size. They work hard, and I appreciate that. Especially you-know-who."

The not-so-subtle reference to her made her smile. The wine had relaxed her, as had the passion flaring in his eyes. She decided to up the stakes of the game.

"I have a confession," she said softly, leaning close.

He mirrored her posture, placing one hand on her back and tilting his head toward hers. "Which is?"

"You have to promise not to tell anyone. Especially Kayla."

For a moment, Patrick looked puzzled. Then his expression cleared. "You have my word. What's the confession?"

"Kayla had a huge crush on you when she first started working at the clinic."

Instead of laughing, Patrick turned serious. "She hid it well. I never had any idea. When did she get over it?"

Now it was Kayla's turn to be uncomfortable. It wasn't that she didn't want to speak the truth; instead, she wasn't sure what the truth *was*. When had she gotten over the crush? Or had she at all?

He settled the problem by taking her hand in his and squeezing gently. "You're trying to spare my feelings. She was over me in a week."

"You're not even close."

He shrugged. "Kayla and I take great pleasure in

tormenting each other. I have a confession of my own. She thinks I have a thing for redheads. I talk about it all the time."

Her heart pounded a little faster. "You don't favor them?"

"No. I like—" he reached up and touched one of her curls "—blondes." His hand dropped to her bare shoulder. "You're so lovely."

"Thank you."

She became lost in his steady gaze. She had no recollection of gathering her purse and leaving the restaurant, but suddenly they were standing on the dock overlooking the dark ocean. The restaurant was behind them. They could see other couples dining, but no one saw them. The side of the building and a wooden gate created an alcove of shadow that sheltered them in privacy.

The moment was so perfect, no words were necessary. And when he pulled her into his arms, she knew this dance had nothing to do with music, and everything to do with the rhythmic heat swelling between them.

His mouth came down on hers, a tender, welcome assault. Lips pressed to lips. She inhaled his scent, absorbed his taste, clung to him, to his broad shoulders. He wrapped his arms around her, pulling her close, so close she felt the edges of their beings start to meld together.

His fingers teased at her nape, seeking sensitive hollows under the protective layer of her curly hair. At his touch, electric shivers raced through her, making her rise up on her toes and kiss him more firmly.

His mouth parted, as did hers. They both waited a breath, then their tongues met, pressing tip-to-tip at the place where their lips clung.

As her body awakened to passion, her heart also embraced new and exciting sensations. They had no name. Some part of them, almost the echo of their presence, was familiar. As if a shadow of them had been present before.

She wasn't ready to identify them. It was enough to be with Patrick, to know those feelings existed in her world.

She slipped her arms around his waist and felt the strength of his back. Tracing the length of his spine, she moved her hands up to his shoulder blades, then slipped down to the waistband of his trousers. Her fingers itched to cup the tight, muscled shape of his rear. The itch went unsatisfied. Neither Kayla nor the pretend-Elissa had the courage to do that.

As if he'd read her mind, he broke the kiss and exhaled sharply. "You have no idea what you do to me," he said, his voice husky with passion.

"If it's what I'm experiencing, I have a good idea."

His gaze met hers. In the darkness, his irises looked like bottomless pools. She wondered how it would feel to disappear inside him.

"I knew tonight would be special," he said.

"Me, too. I've never felt like this before."

He hugged her tight. "Thank you for saying that." His mouth touched her cheek, her jaw, then moved lower, to her neck. She arched back her head, sinking into mindlessness as he forged a damp trail to her collarbone.

Intense pleasure made her toes curl. She needed this moment to last forever.

He licked the hollow of her throat. "I want you," he murmured. "Sweet Elissa, I want you."

CHAPTER NINE

NOW WHAT? Kayla asked herself as they drove through the dark streets. She focused her attention on the lit signs they passed, on the clear night sky, on her hands, clenched tightly in her lap. Anything to keep her from glancing at the man calmly sitting next to her.

Soft music drifted out from hidden speakers. Mood music—slow and romantic. Was that part of his plan? To relax her with the right combination of nighttime and sax solo?

Now what?

He wanted her. He'd kissed and held her and told her he wanted her. She'd felt the heat from his body, felt his passion, shared the moment.

But he thought he was with Elissa.

Her heart ached, with a dull, twisting kind of pain that made her want to get out of the car and start walking. Maybe if she went long enough and far enough, she could leave the misery behind. Maybe she would eventually forget.

How could he want her sister after just one evening, when he'd never once wanted her, Kayla? And he'd been with *her*. She pressed her lips tightly together to keep from swearing. It wasn't fair. She'd been his friend, she'd worked for him. How many nights had they sat up together, tending sick animals, or even each other? When he caught that bad flu three years ago, she'd been the one to make him soup and spoon-feed it to him. She'd been the one calling the doctor at three in the morning, then running out to get the prescription filled.

When a nasty bout of food poisoning laid her low for several days, Patrick had been there for her, too. He'd held her as she huddled in a ball and moaned in pain. He'd forced her to drink water so she wouldn't get dehydrated, and he'd cheered when she was able to keep down a piece of dry toast.

What about helping him with his grant and wallpapering his living room? What about the shared time on his porch, what about the sunsets and the laughter? Didn't they mean anything to him? How dare he think he wanted Elissa and not her!

That was the worst of it, she admitted to herself. Patrick's reaction was to her. She'd been the woman at the restaurant. His lips had touched *hers,* not Elissa's. She'd been the one to turn him on. But he didn't know that, and she didn't know how to tell him.

As they neared the house, she risked glancing at him. His expression gave little away. He looked relaxed, which wasn't fair at all.

What was she going to say? Should she confess all? If she didn't, she was going to have to explain to Elissa what had happened. After all, Patrick would expect to see Elissa again, and after tonight he would think they were more than friends.

She squeezed her eyes shut and whimpered softly.

What a mess. She didn't want to tell him the truth; it was too humiliating. However, there didn't seem to be another choice. Elissa hadn't been able to go on a friendly date with Patrick. There was no way she could deal with the relationship as it had evolved.

Unless Kayla kept pretending to be her sister.

A recipe for disaster, or a shortcut to happiness?

Before she could decide, the car slowed. She opened her eyes and saw that they'd pulled into Patrick's driveway. Instead of stopping by the detached garage and walking her up the stairs to her—make that Kayla's—apartment, he continued to the main house and parked the car near the front door.

After turning off the engine, he angled toward her. The porch light illuminated the left half of his face, highlighting strong planes and penetrating eyes.

"Despite what I said at the restaurant, I don't have plans to ravish you," he said lightly. "At least, not without your permission. With those ground rules established, would you like to come in?"

"Yes," Kayla said, without thinking. A small piece of sanity screamed out that it was a really bad idea. The rest of her didn't listen. It was tough to hear the voice of reason, when every cell of her body yearned to be in Patrick's arms again. Maybe a good ravishing would clear her mind.

He walked around the car and opened the door for her. As she stepped out, he took her hand and brought her fingers to his mouth. He touched the tips to his lips, dampening each sensitive pad with his tongue. The combination of the romantic and the erotic made her thighs tremble. She felt as if she'd just run five miles.

He pulled her close and kissed the top of her head. "I promise to act like a gentleman, no matter how tough that's going to be," he said, his voice thick. He slid his hands through her hair, cupped her scalp and raised her chin. "I want to kiss you. Is that all right?"

He hadn't closed the passenger's door, and the dome light allowed her to see his expression. Passion flared in his eyes. She could both feel and see the heat. The fire touched her skin, but instead of burning her, it caressed her, dancing against her in pirouettes of pleasure.

The problem of her identity disappeared in the need of the moment. Did it matter who she was, when she was the woman he wanted? If this was just a game, then she'd waited far too long to play. The rules weren't clear, nor was she completely familiar with the ultimate goal, but she was willing to risk losing, if that meant she would have the pleasure of watching Patrick win.

His question still hung between them. He waited patiently for her reply. Words formed in her throat, but a flood of emotion prevented her from speaking. Instead, she rose on tiptoe and pressed her mouth to his.

It was a chaste kiss. Closed lips clung, captivated by unleashed need. Kayla ached for more. She wanted his tongue in her mouth, his hands on her body, bare skin next to bare skin. And yet, this was right. Pure. As if it were important for their souls to join first.

First? Were they going to make love? Was that what she wanted? Patrick as her lover...her first lover?

He pulled back and stared at her. "You take my breath away."

"I know what that feels like," she said, and was pleased when her voice didn't shake. She was still wrestling with the idea of them becoming lovers. Was that what she wanted?

"Do you want me to take you home?" he asked.

Unexpectedly, tears sprang to her eyes. The gentle question made her want to throw herself at him. Even now, even with the desire raging between them, he was giving her a choice. That was the kind of man he was. Thoughtful, understanding, caring, considerate.

He would make love the same way he kissed—with quiet force and unbelievable passion. She'd never felt comfortable enough to give herself completely to the other men she'd dated. Maybe it had been a matter of not trusting them enough. She trusted Patrick.

She blinked away the tears. She wasn't ready to leave him, not tonight. "I'd like to come in," she said.

He closed the car door, then put his arm around her. They walked to the front door, which he unlocked, and then she led the way into his house.

The living room looked exactly as it had a hundred times before. Wallpaper was missing from two walls and partially peeled off a third.

"Redecorating, I see," she teased.

He shook his head. "It looks awful, I know. But it's not my fault. Your sister is supposed to be helping me. She's great with the animals, but not exactly committed when it comes to helping me around here."

"You look smart enough to take care of it yourself. After all, this is *your* house."

"Yeah, but the new wallpaper was her idea." He took off his suit jacket and tossed it over the sofa. "Do you really want to talk about decorating?" he asked, loosening his tie and moving close to her.

She tilted her head so she could meet his gaze. "Not really."

"Me either."

He placed his hands on her shoulders. Strong fingers kneaded her bare skin, and then he plucked at the skinny straps holding up her dress.

"These have been driving me crazy all evening," he said. "Just these little scraps of cloth. Weren't you worried they'd break?"

Her breathing increased. She placed her evening bag on the back of the sofa and wondered if he would think he was brazen if she stepped out of her shoes.

"They're sewn on well," she told him. "They don't break."

"But they do slide down."

The image his words painted filled her mind. In reality, the dress was snug enough that even if the straps were cut off, nothing would fall. Releasing the zipper in the back was another story. Would he want to do that, too?

Unable to speak, she nodded.

He bent and touched his mouth to her neck. Instinctively, she tilted her head to give him more room. He rewarded her with an openmouthed kiss against her already heated skin.

She couldn't think, she couldn't move, she could only stand there absorbing the wondrous sensation of erotic dampness, of his tongue licking her, tasting her. Her body grew heavy. An ache began in her chest and between her legs. She pressed her thighs tightly together, but that didn't help. She needed more; she needed him.

He slipped the straps off her shoulders, following his

fingers with his mouth. First on her left side, nibbling at the curve of her shoulder, moving his mouth lower, to the top of her chest, pausing to trace the line of her collarbone before repeating the actions on her right side.

Her hands fluttered in the air. As he dipped toward her breasts and touched the exposed, shadowed valley between, she swayed and caught herself by placing her hands on his waist.

"Touch me," he said, the words muffled against her skin.

Touch me. A man's plea for a woman's gentle embrace. Raw need exposing vulnerability. Did he fear her reaction—and the potential for rejection—or did he trust her?

Touch me.

"I want to touch you," she said, and slipped her hands up his chest.

Tense muscles quivered with her every move. The defined ridges and valleys of his stomach rippled as she passed over them. His body broadened, and she had to spread her fingers to caress all of him. When she reached his shoulders, she glanced up and found him watching her.

In her head, she knew Patrick was a man, with the wants and needs men experienced. But until that second, until their gazes locked and she felt the impact of his arousal, she hadn't thought of him as a sexual being. Hunger tightened his mouth, his nostrils flared with each breath, a muscle twitched in his right cheek.

His power overwhelmed her. For the first time, she felt small and fragile next to him—female to his male, her curves and softness designed to receive that which he gave.

He took one of her hands in his and brought it to his mouth. He kissed her palm, then gently bit the fleshy place below her thumb. Never breaking eye contact, he pressed her hand against the center of his chest. Slowly, but with a determination that left her no doubt about his final destination, he moved her hand lower. Past the smooth cotton of his shirt, past the cool metal of his belt buckle. Lower, until she felt the placket covering his zipper, lower, until she cradled the hard ridge.

While she was still a virgin, she wasn't completely inexperienced. Some of her dating relationships had lasted several months, and in that time, she'd felt comfortable enough to fool around. It wasn't as if she didn't know what an aroused man looked like. She'd seen and touched and even tasted, but she'd never gone all the way.

But touching Patrick was different. It was as if she'd never been with anyone before, yet she wasn't afraid. Perhaps it was because, for the first time, the situation felt right.

She traced the length of him, feeling him flex against her hand, even as his eyes half closed and the hand touching hers tensed.

He leaned forward and kissed her. Her lips parted, and he slipped inside. His tongue circled hers, setting up a rhythm that called her with an ancient and irresistible beat. She could imagine them together, locked in each other's arms, bodies slick and ready, joining, sharing, reaching, becoming one. The image was so clear, she had the oddest feeling they'd made love before, if not in this lifetime, then in another.

He nudged her hand away and pulled her up against

him. His hardness pressed into her belly. His hands touched her shoulders, her back, her hips, before dropping lower and cupping her rear. Her hips flexed, bringing her closer to him. She arched into the contact, released, then repeated the thrusting motion. He buried his face in the crook of her neck and groaned. She fought back a sigh of her own as that place between her legs grew damp, and need pumped through her like liquid fire.

He straightened, then took a single step toward the hallway, and the bedrooms beyond. A single step, and he paused.

"Do you want me to stop?" he asked, once again giving her complete control over what happened—or didn't happen—between them.

No, of course not. She wanted them to make love. She wanted to know what it was like to be in Patrick's arms, to feel safe and cared for. She wanted him to be the first man to touch her in that unique way that would bond them as one.

But a lie stood between them.

She didn't know what to say. He took her silence as affirmation. "I'll walk you home." Nothing in his body language or tone hinted that he was disappointed. His graciousness only made her feel worse.

"I don't want to go home," she said quickly, and turned away from him. "I just—" She shook her head. "It's not what you think."

The carpet was amazingly interesting, she thought as she stared at it, unblinking. The color, the weave. If she concentrated very hard, maybe she could pretend she didn't have to tell him the truth.

"It's exactly what I think, Kayla."

"No. I've been pretending."

"You don't want me?"

She spun toward him. "Of course I do. You're—" Her hands fluttered in front of her waist as she searched for words. How could she tell him how much this night had meant to her? Even though he thought she was Elissa, his physical response had been to *her*. She was the one he'd talked to and laughed with. He'd kissed *her* lips, touched *her* body, been held captive by *her* hand on that most male part of him.

"It's just..." Her voice trailed off. Her brain cleared slowly, as if waking from a vivid dream. Words filtered through. Words he had said. Words—a word—that just now made sense.

She straightened her arms and stared at him. "What did you say?"

One corner of his mouth turned up. "I said it's exactly what I think."

"After that."

"I asked if you had been pretending about wanting me."

Her body tensed as the truth sank in. "In between those two statements."

"I said your name. Kayla."

She nearly sank to the floor. As it was, she had to consciously tighten her leg muscles to keep standing. "You knew?"

"The moment you opened the door." He had the audacity to smile. "We've been friends a long time, kid. Did you really think you could fool me?"

"Me, fool you? If anyone's been fooled, it's me. You

let me go on pretending? You let me talk, say those things?" Her face burned as she recalled admitting her crush and who knew what else. "You could have told me."

The humor fled his face. "I could say the same thing."

"But I—" Her confusion disappeared, leaving behind embarrassment and shame. "Elissa couldn't go through with the date. I can't go into the reasons, because they're personal, but they have nothing to do with you. She was afraid you would think she was blowing you off. Neither of us wanted to hurt your feelings. She suggested we trade places. I'm not sure why I agreed. I suppose I thought it was a good idea at the time."

She turned away from him and walked to the sofa. "I'm sorry, Patrick. That was a lousy thing to do to a friend." She thought about the dancing together, the funny conversations, the way he'd kissed her as they stood on the dock. "I guess you got your own back, making me think you wanted her. I don't blame you."

She didn't. How could she? Switching places had been a stupid thing to do. She knew better. She reached for her purse. "I hope you can forgive me," she whispered, knowing tears were merely seconds away.

She'd had her chance, and she'd blown it.

"I knew it was you, Kayla."

"You told me." Fighting for control, she blinked several times.

"I knew it was you," he repeated. "From the beginning. You're the one I touched in the restaurant. You're the one I danced with. You're the one I kissed."

You're the one I want.

He didn't say the words, but she heard them. The purse fell from her suddenly slack fingers. It hit the ground, but she ignored it. "You wanted me?"

His pupils dilated. "Want. There's no past tense in that statement." He motioned to the front of his trousers. "It's hard for a guy to fake interest, or to hide it."

Hot color returned to her face, but this time it was because she was suddenly shy. She didn't dare drop her gaze from his face.

"You never said anything about this. Before, I mean," she added.

"Neither did you."

"But I wasn't sure. We've always been friends. I don't want to mess that up."

He shrugged. "Neither do I."

She cleared her throat. "This is an amazingly awkward moment. What happens now?"

"That's up to you. Do you want me to walk you home?"

That would be the safest course, she told herself. She and Patrick could put this moment behind them and pick up their old relationship where they'd left it. That made the most sense.

Except she'd already imagined them making love. Her body sensed what it would feel like with Patrick touching her, holding her, being inside her. She wanted him to be the one to teach her what really happened between a man and a woman. Because she trusted him, and because she loved him.

As a friend, of course. A good friend.

She looked at him, then at the front door, and finally at the dark hallway that led to his room. She'd been in there before, helping him put away laundry, or picking out a tie for him to wear when he spoke at a symposium. She'd sat on the king-size bed, even stretched out on it, giving him her fashion advice, along with a reminder that he not forget his ticket.

Safety or seduction?

She closed her eyes and tried to imagine what she would feel like forty years from now. Would she regret leaving or staying? She thought of Sarah and her boxes of memories. Precious, timeworn photos, bits of lace, a frayed teddy bear once loved by her children. Would she, Kayla, want to open her own memory box and know that she could have had this chance with Patrick, but instead had walked away?

The answer was simple.

She stepped out of her pumps and left them in the living room. Without saying a word, she moved past him, down the hall toward his bedroom. Before she got there, she felt his hand on her shoulder.

"Thank you," he whispered, and kissed her bare skin.

She turned to him and held out her arms. He slid close, pulling her toward him, covering her mouth with his.

Paradise found. She'd chosen wisely.

CHAPTER TEN

KAYLA STOOD BY his bed, a trembling, sensual creature, nearly otherworldly in her beauty. Patrick cupped her face. He traced her high cheekbones, the shape of her mouth, her jaw, before stroking her elegant neck.

She watched him steadily, her gaze never leaving his. Her green eyes had softened to the color of emerald mist.

They stood in semidarkness. A lamp in the corner cast a pale glow toward the ceiling. The bathroom light was on, the door partially closed. There was enough light to see by, but not enough to be obtrusive.

He smiled.

"What's that for?" she asked.

"I'm waiting to find out this is just a dream."

She tilted her head to one side. Blond curls drifted over her bare shoulders. "Do you dream about me often?"

They were about to make love; there was no reason for him not to tell the truth. "In the past few weeks, yes."

She returned his smile. "Since the, ah…"

"Kiss?"

"Yeah."

He nodded. "Since the kiss. Everything changed. I'm not sure why. It just got different."

"I agree." She ducked her head, as if she were feeling shy. "I meant what I said, Patrick. No matter what, I want us to always be friends."

Friends and lovers? He'd never experienced that before. Was it possible? "I want that, too. You mean a lot to me. I need you in my life."

She stepped toward him and rested her forehead against his chest. "I need you, too. I know everything is changing between us, but I need to know you'll always be the same."

"I promise. I'm not going anywhere."

He meant the words in an emotional sense, as in, he had no plans to stop caring about her, but as soon as he said them, they took on a different meaning. *I'm not going anywhere, but you are.*

A sharp pain took up residence in his chest. Apparently Kayla felt it, too, because she whimpered softly and wrapped her arms around his waist.

"Patrick."

She spoke his name as a plea. He wasn't sure what she wanted or needed, but the feel of her so close to him forced him to respond with a kiss.

She arched her head back and met him more than halfway. Yielding flesh, warm and sweet, opened to him. He tasted her, felt the tender inner smoothness of her lips, the slickness of her teeth, then began to stroke her tongue.

Once again passion threatened to spiral out of control. She clung to him, her fingers kneading into his back. He touched her everywhere. Hands on her hair,

her back, her hips, her rear. He rubbed the cool fabric
of her dress, his groin swelling painfully when he found
the zipper tab nestled against her spine.

He pulled it down slowly. The dress parted, gossamer
silk revealing the warm cream of her skin. His fingers
traced a line from her shoulders down her spine, pausing to discover the lacy band of her bra.

Never breaking their kiss, she lowered her hands to
her sides. The dress slipped down, pausing at her hips.
She wiggled slightly, and the garment was gone.

He rested his hands on her bare waist. His thumbs
pressed into her hipbones. Not able to stop himself, he
continued the voyage of discovery. Silk panties gave
way to smooth thighs. A couple of inches later, he felt
the band of her stockings.

He stepped back and straightened. He'd touched her
bareness, but the tactile exploration hadn't prepared him
for the visual impact of seeing her. A black strapless
bra supported generous breasts. Small panties teased
him by revealing more than they covered. But it was
the stockings that captured his attention.

"I've never seen that before," he admitted, running
a finger over the skin just above the band.

She ducked her head. "I don't wear dresses much so
I never got used to panty hose. I hate them. These are
a lot easier."

The heat inside him grew. He'd wanted her from the
moment she opened her apartment door and smiled at
him. He'd spent the evening hard. He knew what they
were about to do. He anticipated the passionate release
he would feel when their bodies joined. Yet, in some odd
way, being with her, wanting her, was nearly as satis-

fying. He didn't want to rush this moment. He wanted to talk and touch and tease, driving them both to the brink of madness, then pulling back. He didn't want their lovemaking to ever end.

She folded her hands over her chest, then dropped her arms to her sides. Her obvious nervousness reminded him that she was nearly naked, while he was fully dressed and staring at her.

Moron, he muttered silently to himself as he took her hand and led her to the bed.

As she settled onto the mattress, he sat next to her. He quickly removed his shoes and socks, then pulled his shirt free of his trousers and unbuttoned it. Then he smoothed her curly hair off her face.

"You okay with this?" he asked.

"Yes."

"Good." He smiled. "Let's deal with the logistical stuff first." He pointed at the nightstand. "I have protection with me, and I plan to use it."

She bit her lower lip, then nodded. "Thank you," she whispered.

"No problem." He bent close and licked her shoulder. "Anything you hate doing?"

"Uh, not really." A tremor rippled through her.

"Do you need me to spank you or call you a bad little girl?"

She pulled away and stared at him. Shock widened her eyes. Bright spots of color blossomed on her cheeks.

He chuckled. "I'll take that as a no."

"You spank women?" She sounded stunned.

"By hand or with a paddle?"

Her mouth dropped open.

He put his finger under her chin and pressed. "I'm kidding, Kayla. I've never spanked anyone. We're both a little nervous. I was trying to distract you."

She exhaled sharply. "You did a great job. I can't believe you asked that. In fact, I—"

He reached behind her and unfastened her bra. It fell to her lap. She stopped speaking with the suddenness of a television going out during a blackout. The next sound she made wasn't actually a word. It was more of a sigh as he pressed her onto the mattress and touched his mouth to her right breast.

She tasted of promise and sin. Sweet and intoxicating. He circled her taut nipple, discovering the pebbly texture, the heat, the smoothness of her curves.

He shifted his weight so that he was kneeling over her, then moved to her other breast. She arched into his caress. With his hands, he began to discover her—the strong yet delicate collarbone, the shape of her upper arms, the tiny mole on the left side of her chest. He counted her ribs, felt the faint lines of scars from her accident years ago, circled her belly button, rubbed her hipbones, then brushed across her panties.

Her body stirred restlessly. She grabbed and released the comforter beneath her. Her eyes closed, her mouth parted.

Over and over he lavished attention on her breasts. He licked the sensitive undersides, blew air across her nipples. He learned every millimeter of the valley between, gently nibbled at the place where the curves began.

When he couldn't stand it anymore, he stretched out beside her and kissed her mouth. Apparently he wasn't the only one aroused by what he was doing. She cupped his face and parted her lips. When he entered her, she suckled him. Fire flared inside. Had she touched his arousal at that second, he would have exploded without warning. Every muscle tensed; control slipped. He had to consciously force himself back from the edge.

He broke the kiss and stared into her eyes. "You're amazing."

"I'm okay," she said.

"Perfect."

She closed her eyes. "Never perfect."

He started to ask why, then remembered the scars. Did she really think they mattered?

"Perfect," he repeated forcefully, and placed his hand on her belly.

He outlined the pattern left by the barely visible marks. She flinched at his touch, so he gently kissed her. As he circled her mouth with his tongue, his fingers danced over the marks that shamed her. He concentrated on touching her with all the caring and passion he contained. He wanted his body to speak to hers, silently saying the right thing so she would believe.

One scar dipped below her panty line. He slipped the scrap of silk down her legs and tossed it on the floor. The white line disappeared into the dark curls at the apex of her thighs.

Returning his mouth to hers, he parted his lips and waited for her to enter. When she did, he sucked her tongue and felt sudden tension stiffening her. Intent on following the scar, he didn't realize how far he'd strayed until his fingers encountered unexpected heat and warmth.

He'd wanted to take longer, but the temptation was too great. He circled through the curls until he found the center of her being. Slowly, gently, taking his cues from her subtle reactions, he touched her there. Over and over. Her legs parted, her mouth pressed hard against his, her hands clung to him.

He listened to the increase in her breathing, felt the climbing temperature of her skin. Muscles tensed and contracted, time had no meaning. She drew nearer; he went faster, not pushing, but assisting.

Gasping for air, she broke the kiss. Her gaze met his.

"Perfect," he murmured.

"Yes, you are," she answered, then closed her eyes and arched her back.

He stopped moving his fingers. For a heartbeat, she hung suspended.

"Patrick!"

Her cry filled him with an intense pleasure he'd never known. He touched her lightly, quickly, circling her as her body shuddered in release.

He took her in his arms and held her as she recovered. When she slipped a leg between his and began kissing his chest, he knew he wouldn't be able to hold back much longer.

"I want you," she said, finding and licking his nipples.

Her hair brushed against his skin. The combination made control impossible.

He sat up and jerked off his shirt. His pants and briefs followed. When she reached for his arousal, he grabbed her wrist and kept her from touching him.

"You can't," he said, feeling like a sixteen-year-old. At her quizzical gaze, he added, "I'm really close."

She put her hand on his thigh and grinned. "How close?"

The pressure of her fingers on his leg made his hardness surge upward.

"My," she said, sounding impressed. "I see what you mean."

He grunted in response and pulled open the nightstand drawer. While he opened the package of protection, she moved behind him and pressed against his back.

"Thank you," she said. "For everything. For being wonderful and a great lover, and for making this exactly what I wanted it to be."

He slipped on the condom, then turned toward her. "Hey, it's not over yet."

"I know." She touched his face. "I just wanted you to know how I felt."

Some unidentified emotion tugged at his heart. He didn't dare analyze it. Not now. Usually, he was able to hold a piece of himself back when he made love. He didn't have to give it all. With Kayla, it was different. They connected in a way that terrified him, yet made him never want to be apart from her. What the hell did it mean?

She stretched out on the bed and tugged at his hand. "Don't look so serious. This is supposed to be fun."

He moved between her legs and dropped a kiss on her belly. "Yes, ma'am."

He stroked between her legs, savoring the heat and the moistness. She parted her thighs wider, closing her eyes as he touched her still-sensitive center. From there he moved down to the place that would accept him. Every part of him clenched in anticipation.

For a moment, the magnitude of what they were about to do stopped him. He believed that, no matter what, they would always be friends, but this one act would change everything forever. It was a risk. He had to take it or not, and had to make that decision without knowing the potential price.

"Hey." She glared at him. "Don't get weird on me, okay? There's no way I'm going to spank you or call you a bad little boy."

He grinned. "Just one little swat?"

"Patrick!"

"Okay, okay. I'll behave."

"Oh, don't do that, either."

They stared at each other. The humor faded, leaving only desire. He looked at her face, her breasts, her belly, the scars, then at the place that would accept and pleasure him.

"Now," she pleaded, and raised her hips slightly.

He entered her slowly. She was tight and wet, an unbelievable combination. He paused halfway and reached down to part her a little to make it easier. At his touch, she jumped.

He glanced at her. Her eyes were tightly closed, her face was fierce with concentration. Not passion, though. He noticed the tension in her arms and legs.

"Kayla?"

"Please, Patrick. Don't stop."

He moved in a little more. Slowly. As if waiting for some kind of resistance. As if—

He swore silently and started to withdraw. Her eyes flew open, and she grabbed his left arm to hold him in place. "No! I want you to do this."

"You're a virgin."

The statement hung between them. He waited for her to deny it, prayed she would. He wasn't all the way in, but he suspected he would have already felt the physical proof. There wasn't any, just a sixth sense inspired by her reaction to the intimate act.

She took a deep breath. "Make love to me. I want you. I want you inside. I want to feel you in me. I want to know what it's like."

"I've never been with a virgin before."

"Then we're even. I've never been with a man. At least not all the way."

A thousand questions filled his mind. Why him? Why now? Why was she still innocent? Why hadn't he guessed before?

There were no answers. There was nothing but the pleading in her eyes and the painful arousal between his thighs.

She braced her hands against the mattress and pushed her hips toward him. Slick tightness surrounded him, making him moan. She tilted her hips and made the decision for him.

He moved in and out slowly, cautiously, determined not to hurt her. The questions disappeared as pleasure took over. He had enough awareness left to slip one hand between them and touch her center. He couldn't return the gift she offered, but he could make sure she enjoyed the experience.

Her body quickened around his. He thrust faster,

feeling her muscles tense as he continued to stroke her. This time, though, he recognized it as coming from desire, not apprehension.

Gritting his teeth, calling on every trick, every ounce of strength, he held back until she called out his name and her body convulsed. He plunged inside and let her contractions take him on a journey so incredible, so unique, it was as if he'd never made love before, as well.

Kayla exhaled softly and rested her head on Patrick's shoulder. His steady heartbeat soothed her, adding to the lethargy creeping through her body.

She'd played around with other men before. While she hadn't gone all the way, she'd experienced physical release. But this was different. Every part of her felt complete, as if a missing piece of her had been found. Contentment swelled up inside her, making her want to lie in his bed, in his embrace, forever. The slight ache between her thighs only heightened her awareness that something wonderful had happened.

Making love had been better than anything she'd imagined.

Patrick stroked her head, running his fingers through her curls, tracing the curve of her ears, brushing the underside of her jaw. As their legs tangled together and his touch soothed her, she wanted to purr like a well-fed cat.

They had been such good friends that she supposed she should have worried that their becoming lovers would change everything between them. Perhaps it had, but not in a bad way. If anything, their connection was stronger. She looked inside, wondering about fear, but couldn't find any.

"Kayla?"

She hovered at the edge of sleep, but his voice called her back. "What?"

The hand on her hair stilled. "Why me?"

Why Patrick? The question was reasonable. Why, after years of holding back, of not trusting someone else with her innocence, why had she given it to him?

"I knew you'd make it right," she said. "In this day and age, it's sort of silly to sleep with just anyone, so I never did. Plus, I always worried about the scars. They've sort of faded, but they're still there. I always imagined having to answer a lot of questions, which I didn't look forward to. You already knew everything."

She paused and raised her head to look at him. Blue eyes met her gaze. She rubbed her fingers against his mouth. "I knew you'd make it special and right. I trusted you." She gave him a quick smile. "I hope that's okay."

He kissed her fingertips. "It's more than okay. I was pleased, if a little surprised. It never occurred to me you were a virgin, but once I realized it, I couldn't figure out why you hadn't saved yourself for a prince."

His voice teased, but there was something cautious in his expression. Something that warned her that her response would matter to him.

She wrinkled her nose. "Princes have virgins all the time."

"You know that for a fact?"

"I suspect it to be true. A prince wouldn't care, you would."

He wrapped his arms around her and held her close. She lowered her head back to his shoulder and absorbed the sensations of heat, strength and security. The moment stretched between them, a moment when her heart opened and waited. *She* waited, too. Waited for words to fill the silence.

She didn't know what those words would be, yet she found herself holding her breath in anticipation. She needed to hear them, to believe them. They would change her life forever.

He stroked her hair again. "Kayla, I—"

Her body tensed.

"I'm going to miss you when you're gone. I want you to promise you'll always remember this night."

The air left her body in a giant rush. Her heart squeezed painfully, and her eyes filled with tears.

Until he said he would miss her, she'd actually forgotten she was leaving.

But that wasn't what caused her hurt. Instead, it was what he hadn't said. Unspoken words could inflict lethal blows.

"Kayla?" He shook her gently. "Do you promise?"

"Yes," she murmured. "I'll never forget."

How could she? This night had changed her life.

She remembered hearing a song a few years ago. A certain man had come into a woman's life, but too late. She was already committed to someone else. He was, she told him in the song, the first time she'd thought about leaving.

Patrick was the first time Kayla had thought about staying. That was what she'd wanted to hear. Not that he would miss her, but that he didn't want to let her go. That he cared about her.

Her mind shied away from the *l* word. She wasn't

ready to talk about love, let alone think it. Neither of them was in love. Except as friends.

It wasn't love that had her thinking about staying, it was the way she felt in his arms. As if, for the first time in her life, she'd come home.

"You can't go to sleep," he said. "Not that I wouldn't love your company, but I suspect Elissa is waiting up to hear the outcome of your experiment."

Kayla sat up and glanced at the clock. It was after one in the morning. "You're right. I should have thought of that myself. She'll be worried."

He kissed her gently. "She's pretty smart. I think she has a fair idea of what happened."

It wasn't until they were dressed and walking her to her apartment that she found herself tongue-tied. What was she supposed to say? Thanks for the good time? I enjoyed the sex? Can we do it again, soon?

Nothing sounded right. She didn't know the rules for post-lovemaking etiquette. She didn't worry that she was never going to see Patrick again. After all, he was her boss, her landlord, her neighbor, and very much a part of her life. He wasn't going to disappear. But would they continue to be lovers? Was it *just* a onetime thing?

As they reached the stairs leading up to her apartment, she almost asked. But at the last minute, she bit back the question. It wasn't fair to ask, when she didn't have an answer herself. She didn't know what she wanted.

In a few weeks, she was leaving for Paris. Could she still do that if she was emotionally and physically involved with Patrick? Could she live with herself if she gave up her dream?

At the top of the stairs, he turned toward her and took her hands in his. He'd pulled on jeans and a T-shirt. Stubble darkened his jaw. He was tall and handsome, and she ached to be with him again.

"Thank you," he said, his gaze intense. "For everything. I—"

Instead of completing the sentence, he cupped her jaw, then kissed her. She parted to admit him, clinging to him, trying to put all her emotions, the joy, the confusion, the questions, into that one kiss.

When he pulled back, he nodded ruefully. "Me, too," he said, and she knew he understood.

The front door opened. Elissa leaned against the door jamb and yawned. "Hi, guys. I heard you coming up the stairs. I'm not interrupting, am I?"

"No." Patrick smiled at her.

Elissa raised her eyebrows. "Then everything worked out?"

"Absolutely."

"Good." She looked at Kayla. "Want a couple more minutes of privacy?"

Kayla shook her head. "Night, Patrick." She kissed him on the cheek and stepped inside.

He gave her a wave and started down the stairs. She watched him until he reached his house and disappeared from view. Only then did she realize tears were trickling down her cheeks.

Ten minutes later, she curled up in a corner of the sofa. She tucked her bathrobe around her feet and sipped at the herbal tea Elissa had made.

Her sister plopped onto the love seat and grinned.

"Okay, I want details. Start with the moment he picked you up. And talk slowly. I want time to imagine everything."

Kayla drew in a breath and let it out. "We… There was this restaurant by the ocean, and we danced. I thought he thought I was you and, oh, Elissa, I'm so confused."

She squeezed her eyes shut, determined not to keep crying.

Elissa was instantly at her side. "Honey, I'm sorry." She put her arm around her and pulled her close. "Hush, Kayla. You don't have to tell me anything."

Kayla wiped away her tears. "I want to. I don't mind talking about him. I, we, I'm not sure what happened or what it means. I don't want to feel differently than I do about him. I want it to be okay. I thought it was, but now that he's gone, I'm not so sure."

Her sister patted her shoulder. "The problem is that you're the only one who hasn't figured out how you feel about Patrick."

Kayla didn't like the sound of that. "What do you mean?"

Green eyes, exactly like her own, opened wide. "Kayla, you're in love with him. If not completely, then almost."

Love? No. Not that. "We're friends," she said firmly. "We have been for years. If you're talking about that kind of love, then okay, I agree with you. But romantic love—no way."

"Why is it so difficult to imagine?"

Kayla set her tea on the coffee table and pulled her knees to her chest. "It just is."

"Fine. If you're not in love with him, why are you so upset?"

"I'm not upset!"

Elissa stared at her with knowing eyes.

Kayla grimaced. "I'm a little upset. We made love, and we've never done that before." She didn't bother mentioning *she* hadn't done that before, either. "I don't want it to change everything, but I think in my heart I know it will."

"He loves you."

"No. He doesn't. He can't. Not now." She rubbed her temples. "I'm leaving, Elissa. After we turn twenty-five, I'm off to Paris. I've waited for this for years. I refuse to change my plans. I've earned this trip."

Elissa nodded. "No one's denying that. You're right, you have earned it, and you deserve it. But this isn't about going to Paris, even though that's what you want it to be about. It's about something bigger. All your life you've been waiting for something wonderful to happen. You live in the future and not in the present. I suppose the accident changed everything for you. No one else can understand what you went through that year you were recovering. It was painful to watch your suffering, but not nearly as horrible as it was for you to experience it."

"That doesn't matter now," Kayla said impatiently. "The accident was a long time ago. I've grown up."

"Certainly, but you haven't changed. Inside, you're still twelve years old and trapped in a cast. What on earth is waiting for you in Paris? What could be better than this? You've got a job that you love. People adore you. Kayla, I spend my day wrestling with numbers and a budget. You spend yours making people feel cared about. You change lives."

"You make it sound so dramatic. I haven't saved anyone. I'm not a doctor."

Elissa smiled sadly. "You save their souls. Isn't that more important?"

Kayla shrugged. Her sister made her sound like a hero, but it wasn't true. "Anyone can drive dogs around to visit seniors, or sick kids."

"Sure, anyone can, but who else bothers?" Elissa leaned forward. "You have two sisters who love and respect you, a wonderful man who's crazy about you. If you want to go to Paris, then go. But realize that dream has a price. You're leaving a lot behind, and there's no guarantee it's going to be waiting for you when you get back home."

"You guys will be here," Kayla said, trying not to imagine her life without Patrick. Even so, she could feel the bone-chilling coldness of an empty world.

"Stubborn brat, of course *we'll* be here, but that's not what we're talking about. Listen to me, Kayla. Life isn't a dress rehearsal. It's the real thing. If you don't learn to live in the present, if you don't stop ignoring what's right in front of you and constantly reaching for an impossible dream, you're going to wake up and realize you missed out on everything you could have had. And you'll have no one to blame but yourself."

Kayla didn't like what her sister was saying. "I know you think you're helping, but—"

She broke off when she saw tears in Elissa's eyes. Her sister turned away, but not fast enough. Now it was Kayla's turn to offer comfort.

She touched Elissa's arm. "Cole," she said softly.

Elissa nodded. "Thinking about you with Patrick brought it all back. You'd think after all this time I could let it go."

Kayla remembered her sister's brief marriage to Cole Stephenson. The hotshot young attorney had swept Elissa off her feet and taken her to New York. Elissa had been barely twenty, so in love she left her sisters and college willingly. Less than a year later, she'd returned. She never talked about her marriage, but Kayla and Fallon had seen the shadows in her eyes and the pain behind her smile.

"You're not over him?" Kayla asked.

Elissa shook her head. "I want to be. I should be. The fire burned so hot between us. Too hot. It burned itself out. Something like that isn't easy to let go." She wiped her face and managed a crooked grin. "Sorry. This isn't supposed to be about me. You're the one with the problem."

"I'm fine," Kayla said. "I just need to think this through. A lot of what you told me makes sense. I do need to live in the present and not the future. But does that mean giving up my dreams?"

"Not if you're sure your dreams are what you really want, and not some leftover fantasy from your childhood."

Was Paris a fantasy? Part of the fantasy of being swept away by a handsome prince? If love wasn't like a tornado, then what was it?

"I don't know what to do," she admitted, feeling helpless. "Which path is right for me?"

Elissa kissed her cheek. "Only you can answer that."

CHAPTER ELEVEN

PATRICK AND KAYLA stood at the edge of the construction site.

"I can't believe how quickly everything is moving," she said, pointing to the metal-reinforced framing growing out of the concrete foundation.

Patrick nodded. "The contractors know this is a grant-funded project, and I think they're scared the money might dry up. They want to get the work done fast, which works in my favor. We're going to be up and running by the end of the year."

She flashed him a smile. "You must be excited."

"There are a lot of details to work through."

He wondered if he sounded more enthusiastic than he felt. He hoped so. This research facility would be the fulfillment of an important dream. In time, he would appreciate how lucky he'd been to find grant funding. Over the next few years, he and his team of experts would make medical discoveries that would impact animals' lives. He'd been on the cutting edge of that kind of work in college, and he'd missed it.

So he'd done everything he'd planned.

But without Kayla, his world felt empty. She wasn't

gone yet—in fact, there were still a few weeks left until she left for Paris—but every day brought new proof of her upcoming departure. He didn't want to think about her leaving, but he couldn't seem to focus on anything else.

They stood next to each other, leaning against the clinic's van and watching the large equipment move heavy metal beams.

He glanced down at her and realized she'd been quiet for a couple of minutes. "You okay?" he asked.

"No."

The quick reply surprised him. He turned his back on the lot and stared at her. For the first time in several days, he really looked at her.

Shadows bruised the delicate skin under her green eyes. Her mouth was pulled straight, and the set of her jaw was faintly defeated. Although her golden hair was as shiny and curly as ever, instead of wearing it loose, or in one of her fancy braids, she had it pulled back in a simple ponytail. There wasn't any one thing that was so different, it was all of her.

"What's wrong?" he asked.

She shrugged. "Gee, Patrick, you're a smart man. You figure it out."

He didn't like playing games, and he certainly didn't like it with her. "Kayla, tell me what's going on."

She crossed her arms over her chest. Different expressions skittered across her face. He tried to gauge her mood. She wasn't angry—resigned, maybe? Disappointed?

At last she raised her gaze to his. Pain dilated her pupils. "It's been two weeks. Why haven't you asked how I was until now? You've been avoiding me, as if you wanted to pretend it never happened. How do you think that makes me feel?"

Her accusations caught him low in the belly. Guilt flared. Familiar guilt, because he'd known what he was doing, even as he stayed away from her, and it had made him feel like slime.

"I'm sorry," he told her. "You have every right to be angry and upset with me. I've acted badly."

She bit her lower lip. "Gee, I thought hearing you say that would make me feel better, but it doesn't."

The construction machinery fell silent. He glanced over and saw that a food truck had pulled up on the opposite side of the site. The men used the opportunity to take a break.

"Why?" she asked.

A single word; on the surface, a simple question. Yet he knew the real meaning behind the word, and what she was really asking.

Why did you make love to me? Why did you hold me that way, then avoid me? Why aren't you talking to me? Did I make a mistake by choosing you to be the one? Don't I mean anything to you? We're supposed to be friends, but this isn't how friends treat each other.

"I'm sorry," he said quietly, forcing himself to look at her. "I never meant to hurt you."

"What *did* you mean to do?"

"I wanted to make it okay between us." He figured he could risk a little honesty, but not too much. He had to keep control of himself, so he didn't blurt out that he'd withdrawn from her because the alternative was to fall in love. To want to hold on to her forever. That wasn't an option. She had her plans, and he cared about her enough to want her to get exactly what she wanted and deserved.

"Is this okay?" she asked, motioning to indicate the distance between them.

"No." He reached out to touch her shoulder, then withdrew his hand. He didn't dare touch her. It hurt too much. It reminded him of what he had had once and would never have again.

"You're sorry we made love." Her voice was flat.

"Never," he answered quickly. "I'm honored that I was your first."

She half turned away, staring out toward the city. "No, you're not. It's a responsibility that you didn't want, and now you don't know what to do about it."

He tried to speak, but she cut him off with a wave of her hand. "You don't have to *do* anything," she said. "That wasn't the point. There are no strings attached. We were friends before, and I thought we could still be friends after."

"We are." Yet, even as he spoke the words, he knew they sounded lame.

"Oh, yeah. Best friends." She hunched forward. "If I could take that night back, I would. I'm sorry we made love."

Her words sliced through him like a gleaming blade. He felt the physical cutting, but the pain took longer to kick in. When it did, it nearly drove him to his knees. He had to hold on to the side of the van to maintain his balance.

"Don't say that," he told her. "Don't regret it, please. That night was wonderful for me. I'll never be able to forget it. Or you. No matter what."

She threw herself at him. "Oh, Patrick, I didn't mean to say that. I don't regret anything we did. I loved being with you. It was magic. I just—" She sniffed. "I felt so confused, and I was afraid to talk to you."

"Don't be silly. You can talk to me about anything."

Her arms wrapped around his waist, and she pressed her face against his chest. He raised his hand to stroke her hair, then pulled away. He couldn't do it; he couldn't touch her. Not knowing she was leaving.

"We'll always be friends," he promised.

She nodded, then raised her head. Confusion made her mouth tremble. "You're not hugging me back."

He knew he didn't dare explain why. The truth would only make them both uncomfortable. So he settled on a cheap way out.

"That's because I have something to give you," he said, stepping back and opening the driver's side door. From under the seat, he pulled out a long, thick envelope. "This came for you today, before we left."

She debated whether or not to let him distract her, then finally reached for the envelope. "If this is another shot list, I'm not interested."

"I don't think that's it at all."

She tore open the back and pulled out a dark blue passport. Her breath caught. She flipped it open and stared at her picture, then fingered the blank pages.

In his mind's eye, he could see those pages filled with stamps from countries she'd visited. She was about to enter a world that held no place for him. She wanted to discover new adventures, he wanted to put down roots.

She turned it over in her hands. "It's so real."

"I guess you're on your way."

"Paris, here I come."

Her smile dazzled him. He forced himself to return it, when inside, his soul blackened and his heart turned to glass before shattering.

In that moment, with Kayla clutching her passport to her chest and chattering about all the things she would do, he finally got it.

He'd avoided her for nothing. He'd hoped to protect himself from the pain, but it was too late. It had probably been too late the first day he met her. It didn't matter that she would only ever think of him as a friend, it didn't matter that she was leaving and he might never see her again. It didn't matter that he'd tried to avoid this his whole life.

He loved her.

He'd thought he'd played it safe. He'd wanted a sure thing if he was going to risk love at all. Now he realized he didn't get to choose who or when. When love arrived, it did so without warning, without worrying about convenience or potential heartbreak.

He loved Kayla with all his heart, and now he had to let her go.

She flipped through the pages again. "It's happening. This feels strange. I know I've planned for it and everything, but I think in some part of my brain, I figured something would stop me."

"Don't tell me you're having second thoughts," he teased, pleased that he sounded completely normal. No matter what it cost, he would never let her know how he felt. He would never be responsible for the death of her dreams.

"Not exactly." She glanced at him, then away. "Things are a little different, that's all. Sometimes I wonder if the idea of going to Paris is going to be better than any actual trip."

It was, he realized, the perfect opening. He could tell her how he felt and ask her to stay. She might even agree. But then what? Would his world be enough for her? How long until she got restless? Until she felt the need to search out that tornado she talked about? His love for her had come upon him slowly. He didn't doubt its validity, or that it was forever, but would she believe that? He'd never once swept her away. It didn't matter that he believed tornadoes to be destructive. Kayla didn't want ordinary. She wanted the fairy tale and Prince Charming.

If her path led her back to him, then he would confess all. But he believed she needed to experience her dreams before she could make a decision about what mattered most. Her happiness was more important to him than his own.

Which probably made him a damn fool.

Loud motors started, drawing Kayla's attention to the construction. "You're going to be so busy with the research center, you're not even going to notice I'm gone."

"I'll notice."

She laughed. "Patrick, by the second week, you won't even remember my name."

He knew it was wrong of him, but he wished her statement was true. Unfortunately, he would remember. It would take more than three lifetimes to ever forget Kayla.

"There's this teacher…" Allison said, pausing to pat Rhonda on her head before turning her attention back to Kayla. "She came to see me and said there's these videos I can watch, so I can keep up with my studies." Her nose wrinkled. "I'm glad, 'coz I didn't want to get left behind in school."

"I know what you mean," Kayla said. "When I was recovering from my accident, my sisters visited me every day and helped me with my lessons. I didn't want to get left behind, either."

Talk about adding insult to injury, she thought, recalling those difficult months. As if surviving the accident and rehabilitation weren't bad enough, to be left a grade behind in school would make the situation intolerable. She remembered overhearing a conversation between an instructor and her mother. The instructor had been concerned about Kayla's "social" skills not keeping up, either. What the woman had never understood was that interacting with hospital employees, dealing with pain, physical therapy, adjusting to physical limitation, enduring the dark, endless nights alone, had forced her to grow up faster than any child should. She'd had no trouble socially adjusting with her peers. If anything, she'd passed them by.

Rhonda hopped over Allison's chest and landed on the other side of the bed. She tugged at a ribbon in the child's hair, pulling it loose, then racing to the end of the mattress. Once there, she dangled it and wagged her tail.

Allison laughed. "Silly dog. Bring that back to me."

Kayla had seen them play this game countless times before. As she watched the dog interact with the little girl, she had the oddest feeling that Rhonda really understood Allison's limitations. She played gently, darting away, but always quickly returning, as if she knew

Allison couldn't come after her. Even when Allison's parents and older brother visited, she would run and chase balls with them for a few minutes, then spend the rest of the time on Allison's bed.

"I saw your show on TV," Allison said. "I think I know which one was you."

Kayla leaned forward in her chair and held the girl's hand. "What was the show about?"

"The cook left, and there was no one to make dinner. Mrs. Beecham tried, but she doesn't know what little kids like to eat."

Kayla grinned. "We had so much fun filming that one. Remember the food fight everyone got into in the kitchen?"

Allison nodded.

"That was real. We spent hours on that one scene. By the end of it, everyone was covered in pudding and flour and green beans."

"Were you the one scooping the pudding out and throwing it at the boys?"

"Yup. And I was in the scene with Mrs. Beecham when we tried to make toast in the big oven and everything caught on fire."

Allison shook her head. "I didn't know that was you. 'Sally McGuire' is on every night, so I'm going to keep watching it."

"I hope you enjoy it. That was a long time ago." She stroked Allison's bangs off her forehead. While she and Rhonda were visiting, she made it a point to touch the child as much as possible. Kayla remembered feeling isolated when she was in a body cast. There hadn't been much of her skin showing, and everyone had seemed nervous about getting too close.

Rhonda returned the ribbon and flopped down next to Allison, resting her head on the girl's shoulder. Allison bent her neck so her cheek rested against Rhonda's soft fur.

"I'm gonna be moving soon," Allison whispered.

Kayla wasn't sure if she didn't want Rhonda to hear, or if the thought of going to another facility frightened the girl.

"I'd heard," she said. "You're doing really well, and the doctors want you to have more physical therapy. You're going to like the new place. It's closer to your family, there are going to be other children around, and—"

A single tear trickled out of the corner of Allison's eye. Kayla leaned close and brushed it away. Then she hugged the child as best she could, bending toward her and cradling her head.

"Honey, I know you're scared. Since the accident, everything new is frightening. You've been so brave and strong, but it feels like you're never going to get better." She rocked gently. "You feel like you're going to be broken forever, that you'll never have any friends, that you'll never run again, or even walk, and that you'll never be pretty."

Hot tears dampened Kayla's T-shirt. She ached for Allison. She knew the difficult road to recovery better than anyone.

"I j-just want to be like i-it was," Allison said, between sobs. "I d-don't want to go away. I w-won't see you anymore."

Kayla's eyes began to burn. She'd barely avoided crying that morning, when she was with Patrick. Apparently she wasn't going to be able to avoid tears much longer.

"I'm not going to forget you," she said fiercely. "I swear. I'll write you, and you can write me back."

"But I can't write," Allison moaned. "I can barely hold a pencil let alone type, and there's nowhere to put the p-paper." The additional problem unleashed more tears.

Kayla kissed her forehead. "You can dictate letters to me. Make your brother be the one who has to sit here and write everything down."

The crying slowed. "I don't think he'd want to do that."

"I think your parents might insist. Did your older brother used to tease you when you were younger?"

Allison nodded solemnly.

"Wouldn't this be a great way to pay him back?"

A smile tugged on the corner of the girl's mouth. "He broke a couple of my dolls, too."

"Well, then, you're going to be able to make him write a lot of letters."

"Maybe every day," Allison said, warming up to the possibility.

What Kayla didn't tell her was that Allison's brother was suffering from guilt. The uninjured siblings often felt left out and ignored. They wanted parental attention, but felt guilty for that, because they weren't the ones in the hospital. By spending time together, brother and sister would have the chance to get close to each other in a way that wouldn't have been possible without the accident. If things went well, that bond would last them a lifetime.

Kayla straightened. Rhonda moaned at Allison's distress and licked away the rest of her tears. The girl giggled.

"That tickles, Rhonda. But thank you for caring."

Kayla glanced at her watch. "Your mom's going to be here any minute, so I'm going to go out in the hall and wait for her. We've got a couple of things to talk about."

Allison wrinkled her nose. "You gonna tell her I cried?"

"Nope," Kayla said, then kissed her cheek. "That was just between you and me."

Kayla stepped into the hallway and saw that Allison's mother had already arrived. The tall, slender woman had passed her thick raven hair and blue eyes on to her daughter. In about four years, Allison was going to start breaking hearts.

Sheila Kay looked up from the magazine she was reading and smiled. "The nurse told me you were with Allison." She patted the vinyl sofa. "Have a seat and tell me what's going on."

Kayla settled next to her. "I heard she's being moved to another facility."

Sheila nodded, then named the place. "It comes highly recommended. There are children there, and we want her to have a chance to make friends. I worry about her being so isolated. Plus, it's closer to home, so her father can visit more often."

"I think it's a great idea." Kayla touched her arm. "Don't worry. No one judges you for wanting the best for your daughter."

"I know. It's just she's upset about the move. And she's not going to be able to see you anymore. That's going to be hard on her."

Just one more relationship she was leaving behind, Kayla thought grimly. "Even though I never discussed my travel plans with Allison, you and I have talked about them. I would have been leaving you in less than a month, anyway. I think it will be easier if she goes first. The new experiences will give her something to think about."

"I hadn't thought of it that way," Sheila said. "It makes sense. I keep thinking how hard this is for me, then I realize it must be so much worse for my little girl. I just want to hold her until she's better."

"She wants that, too. The time will go quickly. Then she'll be up and walking, and this will just be a bad dream." Kayla thought about the scars on her body, scars that Patrick had touched so tenderly. He'd made her feel perfect, as if those marks didn't matter. She sent up a quick prayer that Allison would find someone as wonderful. And that she would have the good sense to hang on to the guy.

"This is a lot to ask, but I was wondering..." Sheila's voice trailed off. Her gaze darted around the hallway before settling on Kayla's face. "About Rhonda. We'd like to adopt her for Allison. Is that possible?"

Kayla hugged the other woman. "Yes. I think it's a great idea."

"Really?" Sheila asked. "She doesn't belong to anyone?"

"No. Rhonda was abandoned. I've brought her here to be with Allison, and I'd planned to take her to visit the seniors, but I never got around to it. I think she already considers herself Allison's dog." Kayla straightened. "You want to take her home with you today?"

"That would be great. Oh my gosh! What do we feed her? Do we take her for walks? I haven't had a dog since I was Allison's age."

"It's easy," Kayla told her. "The most important thing is for Rhonda to be with people who really love her, and you guys have that one down. I'll give you written instructions for everything else."

Sheila sprang to her feet. "I have to tell Allison. She'll be so thrilled! Do you mind waiting for a couple of minutes?"

"Not at all."

Kayla watched the other woman enter Allison's room. She smiled to herself. At least part of her day had turned out exactly right.

Kayla opened the kennel door. Elizabeth stepped out and led the way to the grooming table.

"Good girl," Kayla said as the collie jumped into place.

Kayla collected brushes and combs, then turned on the radio. Soft country music filled the small room at the back of the clinic.

Elizabeth's long coat required frequent grooming, but Kayla didn't mind. She found the work relaxing, and after what she'd been through, she needed this. She knew giving Rhonda to Allison and her family had been the right decision. The dog deserved a great home, and Allison needed a friend. But Kayla had grown used to Rhonda's sweet face. She would miss her.

"Of course, I'm going to miss all of you when I'm gone," she muttered.

Elizabeth gave her an inquiring look, and Kayla stroked her silky ears. "Sorry, girl. Just moaning about nothing in particular. Ignore me."

There was a polite knock at the door. Kayla stuck out her tongue. There was only one person in the clinic who would bother knocking when she groomed a dog.

"Come in," she called, making a serious effort to keep the annoyance from her voice.

As expected, Melissa Taylor glided into the room. Despite the late hour—it was after six—the vet looked as if she'd just stepped out of her bathroom. Long auburn hair curled around her shoulders. Makeup accentuated large, well-shaped eyes. Kayla vaguely recalled showering that morning. She'd even used mascara. Nearly twelve hours later, her clothes were covered with hair, she smelled like dog, and any hint of beauty products had been erased by time, sweat and enthusiastic doggie kisses.

Either Melissa kept a stash of cosmetics and clothes in her car or she had a secret Kayla had yet to discover.

Melissa pointed to the collie. "Elizabeth, right? You take her to visit seniors?"

Kayla forced a smile. "Two correct answers."

Melissa smiled in return, exposing perfect teeth. Had she worn braces as a child? Kayla hoped so. The big ones, with rubber bands and a head brace. Of course, with her luck, Melissa had been born beautiful.

Melissa approached Elizabeth and let the dog sniff her hand. When she'd been accepted, she petted the collie.

Kayla didn't bother watching. Whatever personal reasons she might have for disliking Patrick's new vet, she couldn't fault the woman's treatment of the animals. She handled them well, knew how to calm them, and was a skilled surgeon. No wonder Patrick had hired her. The fact that her body was so incredible it looked airbrushed didn't have anything to do with it.

But it was still darned annoying.

"What can I do for you?" Kayla asked, when it became obvious that Melissa had something to discuss but was nervous about bringing it up. The tight knot in Kayla's stomach gave her a good idea about the subject matter. Oh, well. The day had been painful from the beginning.

"I have a question," Melissa said, not quite meeting her gaze. "Girl talk, really. But it's personal."

"Uh-huh."

"If that makes you uncomfortable, we don't have to discuss it."

Kayla leaned against the grooming table and folded her arms across her chest. Elizabeth sat down to wait patiently. "You want some information?" Kayla asked, even though she knew the answer. There was no point in playing stupid. Might as well get it over with. "I assume this is about Patrick."

"Well, yes." Melissa cleared her throat. "I know the two of you are friends."

"Good friends," Kayla put in before she could stop herself.

"Right. Good friends. And as his good friend, I thought you might know if he was involved right now. You know, dating someone important."

The only sign of Melissa's nervousness came from the way she tossed her hair over her shoulders. A subtle clue, but enough of one for Kayla to see that the other woman wasn't asking casually. Had she taken the job hoping to reach the point where she and Patrick would send out Christmas cards signed "Dr. and Dr. Walcott wish you all the joyousness of the season"?

Six months ago, the thought of someone being that interested in Patrick would have thrilled her. She'd only wanted his happiness. Now, while she still wanted his happiness, she wasn't sure the word *thrilled* described her feelings about him dating someone else.

Melissa wanted to know if Patrick was dating someone important.

Kayla remembered the night they'd made love, the warmth of his arms around her, the passion they'd shared. She thought about being near him, with him. Then she remembered back just a few hours, to that morning, when they'd been at the construction site. Despite everything they talked about, despite their once having been lovers, he hadn't even hugged her.

She looked at the beautiful redhead. "No," she told Melissa. "Patrick isn't dating anyone important at all."

CHAPTER TWELVE

"YOU DON'T HAVE to do this," Patrick said as Kayla smoothed the wallpaper into place. "I could hire someone."

She stepped back to admire her work. The paper was perfectly straight; the subtle pattern, cream with tiny flecks of blue and tan, gave texture and depth to the wall.

"No way. I started this project, I'll finish it. Besides, with everything going on, you won't have time to hire anyone. If I don't finish this, five years from now your living room will still be in a state of shambles."

She smiled as she spoke, trying to act as though everything was all right between them. As though they were just good friends getting together to work on a project. Obviously, she was doing a great job, because he patted her on the back and went to grab them both a soda.

She watched him go, trying not to notice the way his shoulders filled out his shirt and his butt filled out his jeans. She'd always thought he had a nice body, but since becoming intimately familiar with the length and breadth of him, she found it difficult to focus on anything else.

Time slipped through her fingers like shiny marbles, and there was nothing she could do to hold it back. Her twenty-fifth birthday was in three days, her trip to Paris a week after that. She'd thought...or hoped...that she and Patrick would be able to reconnect. Especially after their talk a few days ago at the construction site.

But they hadn't. He treated her as he always had. As if she were a combination of best friend and kid sister.

Maybe she was at fault. After all, hadn't she been the one to change the rules? If she hadn't gone on that date with him, if they hadn't made love, everything would be okay.

Patrick returned with the drinks and the wrapped sandwich she hadn't been able to finish earlier. She settled on the floor and unwrapped the plastic. He sat next to her and opened a bag of chocolate cookies.

"I like it," he said, glancing up at the wall they'd already finished. "The pattern is better than that floral junk the previous owner had used."

"That's what you get for buying a house from a little old lady with a thing for flowers," Kayla teased, remembering the pink sinks in the bathrooms and the dusty-rose flooring in the kitchen. Patrick had replaced both the first month he lived there.

He motioned to the remaining blank space. "We're not going to finish it tonight."

"Probably not, but it won't be much longer. Now that the old stuff is off and the walls are prepared, it will go fast."

As he talked about buying new furniture, which she knew he would get around to doing in the next millennium, bits of their past washed over her. Time they'd spent together, things they'd done. Since graduating from college, she'd spent more time with him than with anyone else. She knew her sisters better, but they lived in other parts of the state.

So many memories, so much caring and respect. Had it all been ruined by a single night of passion? She didn't want to think so. She couldn't regret being in his arms. For as long as she lived, she would carry with her the recollection of that night. No one else could have made her first time more special, more right. Having to do it all over again, she wouldn't want to do anything differently. Yet if the price of passion was their special friendship, would she have a choice?

Patrick picked up his soda and motioned to the wall. "I should have hired you to decorate the research facility."

"No thanks. I'm strictly an amateur. Besides, I don't think the scientists are going to notice wallpaper and paintings. They'll be too caught up in what they're doing."

Instead of smiling, he looked away. "I hope so."

She shifted toward him. "What does that mean?"

He shrugged. "Nothing, really. I guess I'm a little nervous about the whole thing."

"But this is what you've always wanted."

"I know." He stared at her. "In my head, I can see it all happening. I have these great plans for continuing research I started before. If we're lucky, we'll make progress and do some good."

"You will," she said, and placed her hand on his arm. "You're the best, Patrick. You have vision, and the guts to go after what you want."

"Turning vision into reality isn't guaranteed."

"I believe in you."

He covered her hand with his own. "Thanks. That means a lot. You don't give your support lightly."

"You'll always have my support. And anything else you need."

She made the comment lightly, but he didn't seem to catch the humor. To make matters worse, he pulled his arm toward his side, dropping her hand to the floor.

"I have something for you," he said, leaning to his left as he pulled something out of his right rear pocket.

She wasn't fooled by the casual action. Patrick had deliberately physically disconnected from her. A band tightened around her chest. What had happened to them? Was it over forever?

"Here." He handed her a piece of paper.

She opened it and found a list of names and cities. Next to each was a phone number. "I don't understand."

"These are a few people I know over in France." He pointed to the top two names. "Luc and Michael both live in Paris. I called them and told them you were a friend of mine and that you would be visiting. If you need anything, they'll be happy to help you. Luc especially. Watch out for him. He's a practiced heartbreaker. Not exactly in the same league as a prince, but the family owns a château somewhere in the South of France. Michael's married. I've never met his wife, but she's supposed to be nice."

Kayla frowned. "I'm still confused. How do you know these people?"

"I've met them at the various symposiums I've been to. I also have a couple of friends in England and Italy.

If you decide to go there, let me know, and I'll put you in touch with them."

Light brown hair fell over his forehead. His white T-shirt enhanced his tan and brought out his blue eyes. She'd stared at his face thousands of times. She could draw it from memory.

And yet she didn't know him.

Oh, she knew facts about his life, but she didn't really know *him*. Patrick traveled to different symposiums and lectures several times a year. He often talked about the people he'd met there. People from other countries. She knew he kept in touch with several of them through email and occasional phone calls.

Still, the list of names shocked her. Patrick, whose difficult childhood had made him want to put down roots, had seen worlds she'd only dreamed about. He'd visited places, talked with strangers, made friends and invited them into his life.

"Thanks," she said, setting her untouched sandwich on the floor, folding the paper and tucking it into her shirt pocket. "I'm sure I'll be fine, but it's nice to know there's someone I can contact if I need something."

"You'll have a great time," he said, and ate another cookie.

"It's going to be weird being away from everyone."

"You won't miss anybody. There's all of Paris to see, and besides, you'll be too busy with your princes."

"Yeah." Princes. That wasn't likely to happen. And she didn't care. Frankly, Luc's château or a prince's fortune weren't as appealing as she would have thought. She was perfectly comfortable right here in Patrick's living room.

"You're going to be busy, too," she said, knowing she was about to make the situation worse, but not able to help herself.

"With the research facility."

"And with your new employee."

He raised his eyebrows.

"Melissa is attracted to you," she said, her voice teasing. Maybe she should consider a career on the stage. She was able to sound completely normal, as if the situation didn't bother her in the least. Yet the pain inside was so bad, she half expected to faint.

Patrick shrugged off her declaration. "Not interested."

"But she's a redhead. Aren't they your favorite?"

He stared at her. "I told you they weren't. Or don't you remember?"

His serious expression made her want to cry. Of course she remembered. She remembered everything about that night. What they'd talked about, how they'd danced together, the kiss on the dock outside the restaurant.

"I—" She didn't know what to say.

Patrick finished his soda and set the empty can on the floor.

Silence filled the room. The air thickened with tension. Kayla wanted to run away, but she didn't have the strength to move. They both remembered. In the stillness, memories crowded around them.

She longed for him, to be in his arms again. Her body heated. Tonight, they could be together. Tonight, they could relive the perfection and make it right between them. Here, in this house, where they'd spent their best moments together.

She reached her hand toward him. "Patrick."

Either he didn't notice, or he didn't care. He stood up and placed his hands on his hips. "We should get back to work."

Somehow she stumbled to her feet and reached for the roll of wallpaper. Only when she attempted to focus on the subtle pattern and couldn't did she realize her eyes had filled with tears.

As she blinked them away, she tried to figure out what was wrong. So Patrick didn't remember the past the same way she did. It wasn't the end of the world. It wasn't as if she were in love with him.

Love. The word hovered in her mind. Elissa claimed she, Kayla, was already in love with Patrick. Kayla wasn't so sure. All she knew of romantic love was what she'd seen, read and been told. Mrs. Beecham had sworn love was a tornado that swept away everything in its path. Patrick said tornadoes destroyed. Who was right?

But if she didn't love him, why did she hurt so much?

"Do you want me to measure for the next piece?" he asked.

She looked at him, then at the wall. "No," she said. "I don't think I can do this anymore."

She wasn't talking about the wallpaper, but he didn't get that.

"I can finish it up myself," he told her. "No problem."

"You don't have to. I can help. Just not tonight." She walked to the door. "I—"

He followed her. "You look tired, Kayla. Get some sleep."

Even as she told herself she was making a mistake, she turned and hugged him. She pressed her body tightly against his, letting all her feelings flow through her into him. Surely he would understand and respond. He had to.

As her arms held him close and her hands stroked his back, she registered that he didn't return the embrace. Shock immobilized her. It wasn't until he gently put her away from him that she was able to move.

She dashed out the door and along the driveway. Tears streamed down her face. Even as she raced up the stairs to her apartment, she listened for a voice that didn't speak. Despite her fervent prayers, he never once called for her to come back.

Kayla finished pouring the champagne and glanced at her sister. Fallon held the phone to her ear and listened.

"Yes," she said. "Okay, that's great. I'll tell them. We really appreciate everything. Uh-huh. Oh, thanks. Yes, I'll pass along your best wishes." She hung up and grinned. "That's it. The money is released and has already been wired to our banks. It's done!"

"Finally," Kayla said, feeling her mood lighten for the first time in days. She passed out the fluted glasses.

Elissa took hers. "What else did Mr. Applegate want? He kept you for a long time."

Fallon sank back into the sofa and kicked off her loafers. "The usual. If we have any questions, he will be happy to help us personally. Oh, and birthday felicitations to all of us."

"*Felicitations?* There's a word you don't hear often enough." Kayla raised her glass. "Happy birthday."

Her sisters echoed her toast and they all tasted the champagne.

Fallon wrinkled her nose. "While it's nice..." she said, her voice trailing off.

Elissa grinned. "I was thinking the same thing."

"Me, too." Kayla took another sip. "For the first time in our lives, we splurged and spent two hundred dollars on a bottle of champagne. And we all like the twelve-dollar stuff better."

Laughter filled the room. Kayla stared at her sisters, then at the silly decorations on the walls and ceilings. Balloons floated everywhere. She'd hung crepe paper and banners. Party favors more suitable for a six-year-old's birthday littered the coffee table.

She felt as if she were seeing light for the first time in days. She'd been walking around in a fog of pain and confusion. Even though she hadn't come to terms with whatever was happening between Patrick and herself, even though her reaction and her feelings still confused her, she was done with the suffering. Her sisters were with her for a week, until she left for Paris. She was determined to enjoy their time together.

"Are we going to watch romantic movies and sob?" Fallon asked.

"Of course." Elissa glanced at Kayla. "Aren't we?"

"Sure. It's a tradition. I have tons of popcorn and soda. I've collected take-out menus from every restaurant within ten miles. Wednesday there's a great sale at our favorite department store."

"Heaven." Elissa sat on the floor by the sofa. Her long, flowing skirt covered her feet. With her ruffled blouse and her hair piled on top of her head, she looked like a nineteenth-century woman come to life. "Maybe I'll buy a few things."

"Jeans," Kayla said. "You don't own any."

"I do so. I have at least one pair." Elissa frowned. "Somewhere."

Fallon brushed her tailored trousers. "Why does it have to be jeans? Just regular long pants would be nice."

"Maybe *you* should buy something with ruffles," Kayla teased.

Fallon rolled her eyes. "I'll do that the day you wear a business suit."

Kayla stretched out on the love seat and propped her feet up on the armrest. "Remember those hideous matching dresses Mom put us in all through elementary school?"

"All frilly skirts and puffy sleeves." Fallon shuddered.

"In pink and peach and cream," Kayla added.

Elissa stared at them both. "They weren't so bad."

Kayla leaned down and grabbed some confetti from the floor, then tossed it at her sister. "Bite your tongue."

Elissa ignored her. "I'm glad we didn't go away to celebrate our birthday."

"Me, too," Fallon said. "What if the money hadn't been released? We would have been stuck with an expensive vacation and no way to pay for it."

"Practical as ever," Kayla told her. "But the money has come through, so there's no excuse for backing out of our Christmas plans."

"I'll be there." Fallon made an X over her heart. "The Caribbean over the holidays. Sounds heavenly."

"I want to go, too," Elissa said. She glanced at Kayla. "Are you still going to Africa in the spring?"

Kayla sipped her champagne. "I don't think so. My travel agent sent me the shot list."

"Did you faint?" Fallon asked.

"Almost. So I was thinking about something a little safer. Maybe a cruise."

"That's what I want to do." Fallon leaned forward and rested her elbows on her knees. "I've been thinking about the money. I'm going to give some of it to charity, and I'm going to put some of it away for the future. The rest is for me. I toyed with the idea of getting a new car, but I think I'd rather do a little traveling."

"You could come to Paris with me," Kayla said, thinking the trip would be better with one of her sisters along.

"I can't. Classes start in late August, and I'm committed to that until mid-December. Then I'll be off for a year. Maybe we can do something in the spring."

"That would be nice." Spring seemed so far away. Who knew what would have happened by then? Right now, even her trip to Paris felt surreal. She suspected that by the time she got back, everything would have changed. What would happen then? Would she pick up the pieces of her life? Was that even going to be an option? No doubt Melissa would succeed in her quest for Patrick's attention.

Don't think about it, she told herself. Not today. She would mourn Patrick later.

"I'm going to cut the cake," Fallon said. She put her champagne on the coffee table and walked to the kitchen. "What kind is it?"

"What do you think?" Kayla asked.

"Double chocolate with fudge filling and icing?" There was a hopeful note in her voice.

"What else?" Kayla glanced at Elissa. "You're being awfully quiet."

Elissa shrugged. "Just thinking."

"About the trust fund?"

Her sister hesitated, then nodded. "I know you two think I'm crazy, but I just can't help it. All that money scares me."

Fallon stuck her head around the kitchen wall. "What are you talking about? Speak up, I can't hear."

"Elissa's still scared of the money," Kayla called.

Fallon stepped into the living room and stared down at Elissa. "Get a financial planner, put it in another trust fund, buy yourself a dog, but please promise me you won't write a check and just give it all away. This is yours, Elissa, as much as it's mine or Kayla's. We earned this money working on that damn show, week after week." She tossed her head, sending blond curls tumbling down her back. "Make plans for the future."

Elissa grimaced. "I promise I won't write a check and give it away all at once."

"And that you won't give all of it away in pieces," Fallon said.

"Agreed. I'll keep some for a rainy day."

Kayla leaned over and patted Elissa's shoulder. "Don't be so afraid of it," she said. "It's just paper, or numbers on a bank statement."

Elissa nodded, but Kayla knew she was more interested in not upsetting the happy mood than in agreeing. Ever since they starred on "The Sally McGuire Show,"

Elissa had believed money was the root of the family's problems. In her mind, fighting over the girls' earnings had caused their parents' divorce. Their father had lived an extravagant life-style he couldn't afford. In the end, it had killed him, when he lost control of his expensive sports car and plunged into a canyon.

"I miss him, too," Kayla said softly.

Elissa gave her a grateful look. "I've been thinking about him a lot."

Fallon walked to the love seat and nudged Kayla's legs out of the way. "Me, too," she said, sinking onto the cushion. "It's tough now, and around the holidays."

For a second, nobody said anything. Then Elissa spoke. "She didn't call."

It was a statement, rather than a question. The "she" was their mother.

Kayla smiled ruefully. "It's pilot season, girls. What did you expect?"

"Pilot season," Fallon said, in the same tone Kayla would expect her to use to announce she had lice.

"I remember those days," Elissa said. "The waiting, the auditions."

Pilot season. "I don't want to remember," Kayla said. "It was awful."

Late spring and early summer meant the networks were casting their new fall television shows. Hopeful children came in from all over the country. The yearly pilgrimage had been more nightmarish for the triplets, because when it wasn't pilot season, their mother took them on movie and commercial auditions. Free afternoons were quickly filled with singing and dance lessons, not to mention the occasional acting class. If they'd been interested in entertainment as a career, they might have enjoyed the processes, but none of the sisters had done anything but endure.

"How old are the twins?" Fallon asked.

"Six," Kayla answered. "Plus Clarice is nearly eight, Andy is ten." Three half sisters and a half brother the triplets had never met.

"Mom sure didn't waste any time," Elissa said. "She was remarried and pregnant within a year of the divorce." She sighed. "I hope those kids enjoy the business more than we did."

Their mother had been furious when the girls refused to continue on television. She'd been determined to "make it" with a new set of children. Kayla hoped she was successful. It must be difficult to spend one's whole life chasing an impossible dream.

"Enough," Elissa said, and stood up. "We're here to celebrate, not dwell on the past. We're young, we're healthy and attractive, and now we're rich." She grinned. "Sort of."

"Comfortably well-off," Fallon said.

Kayla motioned to the kitchen. "I need chocolate cake or I'm going to die."

"Coming right up." As Elissa walked in that direction, there was a knock on the door. She unfastened the lock and pulled the door open. "Patrick. This is nice." She looked over her shoulder. "Patrick's here, and he has gifts. I think we should let him in."

Kayla scrambled to her feet, brushing at the front of her jeans and tugging on her T-shirt. She hadn't thought they would have company today, so she hadn't bothered with makeup or fixing her hair.

"By all means," Fallon said, also standing. "I've wanted to meet Kayla's friend for a long time."

Patrick grinned engagingly at the women. Kayla stared at him, hoping their eyes would meet, but he seemed to pass over her.

"I don't want to intrude," he said. "I have a few things for the birthday celebration, then I'll leave you ladies alone."

"Don't even think you're intruding," Elissa said, taking his arm and pulling him into the apartment. "We'd love the company. We're going to be together for a week, so there's plenty of time to catch up." She touched the roses he held in his arms. "Do you need some help with these?"

"Absolutely." He shifted them in his arms, then held out a dozen paper-wrapped peach roses. "Happy birthday."

Elissa clapped her hands together. "You shouldn't have, but I won't refuse them." She took the roses and inhaled their fragrance. "What a sweetie. Thank you." She rose on tiptoe and kissed his cheek.

Fallon was next. "We haven't been introduced," he said, handing her a dozen red roses. "I'm Patrick Walcott."

Fallon also kissed his cheek. "I like your style," she said, smiling. She glanced at Kayla and winked. "Okay, now I get it. You've kept him hidden away all these years because you knew we'd try to steal him from you."

Patrick grinned. "I'm yours for the taking."

Blond eyebrows arched. "That's not what I heard."

Kayla didn't want to think about how much Elissa had told Fallon. The sisters didn't have a lot of secrets between them. It wasn't that she minded them knowing, it was just that things were so unsettled between Patrick and herself right now. She didn't want either of them to be embarrassed.

Patrick stepped in front of her and held out the last dozen roses. They were exceptional, with creamy petals touched with peach at the top. Their scent enveloped her. Yet, for all their beauty, she couldn't stop looking at him.

He wore a suit and tie. She'd known he had a meeting with several of the scientists that morning. No doubt he had appointments at the clinic, too. She hadn't expected to see him, especially after how they'd parted last week. But she was glad he'd made the time to stop by.

"Thank you," she said quietly. "You're very thoughtful to remember all of us."

"You three are the only triplets I'm ever likely to know. Of course I want to help you celebrate such an important birthday." He turned to Elissa. "Did the money come through?"

She nodded.

He patted Kayla's shoulder. "So you're off to Paris. Good for you." He moved away before she could follow her sisters' lead and kiss him.

Patrick sat on the sofa. The roses were safely put away in vases and pitchers. Elissa brought him cake, Fallon showed him what they were drinking and offered champagne.

"I'd love a glass." He pointed to the bottle he'd brought with him. "I guess this is a pitiful offering."

Fallon glanced at their expensive champagne, then reached down and grabbed his. "To be honest, we like this stuff much better. I guess we don't really have millionaire tastes."

"Yet," he said.

Fallon leaned close. "None of us has a million dollars. Does that upset your plans to marry Kayla for her money?"

"Absolutely. I'm crushed."

They shared a smile.

Patrick had been prepared for the three women to look exactly alike, but the reality was more disconcerting than he'd imagined. Even without the difference in clothing, he would have been able to pick out Kayla. He was so familiar with her face and the way she moved that he could spot her without effort. Elissa and Fallon were more difficult. Had they been wearing the same clothes, he suspected, he would have easily confused them.

He leaned back against the sofa. Kayla sat on the love seat, as far away from him as possible. He didn't blame her.

Even after Fallon had poured his champagne and Elissa had passed out cake to everyone, Kayla didn't join in the conversation. She sat quietly observing, occasionally giving him questioning looks. His actions over the past couple of weeks had confused her, and she wanted to know what was going on.

He wanted to tell her the truth. He wanted her to know that he had to avoid her, for both their sakes. If they got emotionally involved now, it would make her leaving that much more difficult. Better to keep apart, to at least pretend to be friends.

But he couldn't speak the words. He knew in his

heart he would be too tempted to say it all. To tell her that it was too late for him. He already *was* emotionally involved. Without wanting to, he'd fallen in love with her.

What would happen if she knew the truth? Would she smile pityingly at him? Would she get uncomfortable and awkward? Would she try to respond in kind, only to have the lie lodge in her throat? Would she feel guilty?

He didn't want any of that. Better that she be angry for a while. When she was over it, and when his pain of loving but not having had subsided to a manageable ache, they could go on as before. Friends.

At least if they stayed friends, he would never lose her completely.

Fallon and Elissa kept him entertained with stories from their childhood. In many of them, Kayla was the star. She didn't seem to mind the teasing, laughing with her sisters, but she still didn't say much.

He found it difficult to pay attention to what was being said. He just wanted to sit there and stare at Kayla, memorizing everything about her, absorbing her so he wouldn't be so lonely when she was gone.

After about a half hour, he stood up. "I hate to eat and run, but I've got appointments at the clinic in about forty minutes."

Fallon and Elissa walked him to the door. "It's been wonderful," Elissa said. "We're here for the whole week. It's an extended slumber party. So come by again. We'd love to see you."

Fallon gave him a quick hug. "She's right. We're planning a session of truth or dare tomorrow, and I'm sure you don't want to miss that."

He could imagine a few dares he would like to make, but didn't think that was what Fallon had in mind.

He waited for a second, but Kayla didn't join them. No doubt she wanted to avoid another rebuff.

"Kayla, would you mind seeing me out?" he asked.

She looked startled, then rose to her feet. Elissa and Fallon stepped back to give her room, then retreated to the kitchen. He moved out onto the porch, and she followed him.

The late-afternoon sun was drifting toward the western horizon. When she joined him on the small wooden porch, he pulled the front door shut behind her and leaned against the railing.

There wasn't much room, so she was forced to stand close to him. He watched emotions chase across her face. Apprehension, determination and a few others he couldn't identify.

"I want the chance to say happy birthday in private," he told her.

"Great. Thanks." She reached for the door handle.

He wrapped his fingers around her wrist to stop her. "Don't go in yet. There's something else."

Her gaze lifted to his. The wariness there made him want to confess all and beg her forgiveness. But he couldn't do that. It wasn't fair to either of them. Or was he just taking the coward's way out?

He released her, reached into his jacket pocket and pulled out a gift. The box was nearly square, although not as tall as it was wide. A pale silver ribbon crisscrossed over foil paper.

"You already gave me roses," she said, not taking the present.

"This is special." Like you. But he didn't say it.

She took it and tugged off the wrapping. Inside was a gray jeweler's box. She lifted the cover and gasped. The wrapping paper and ribbon fell from her fingers, and she nearly dropped the box. As she caught it, she pulled out a bangle bracelet—an oval of gold with inset square-cut diamonds.

She turned the bracelet over in her hands, staring at it. "I can't accept this," she whispered. "It's too lovely."

"I want you to have it. Something to remember me by."

Before she could object, he took the bangle and opened the clasp. He slid the piece over her hand and settled it around her wrist. When the clasp closed, the bracelet fit perfectly.

Before he could stop himself, he cupped her cheek. "That's the deal, kid. As long as you wear this, you're not allowed to forget me."

"I could never do that. You're a part of me."

She raised her head. His gaze locked on her mouth. He could think of nothing but kissing her, tasting her, holding her close.

He set the box on the railing and reached for her. She came willingly, choking out a sob that tore at his heart. They hugged each other close, gripping tightly, as if they feared being torn apart.

"Kayla, I've missed you," he whispered into her hair.

"I've been right here."

"For now."

She started to step back to look at him, but he didn't release her. He didn't want her to see his face and know what he was thinking.

"What does that mean?" she asked.

Instead of answering, he pressed his mouth to hers.

Their lips touched gently, brushing against each other. Neither tried to deepen the kiss. Passion burned hot, yet this chaste contact was enough. He knew that if he did more, he would have to be with her. Not just for tonight, but for always.

"Patrick." The word whispered against his cheek.

He dropped his hands to his sides and turned to the stairs.

"Stay," she said. "You'd be welcome. My sisters are dying to get to know you."

"I have to get to work."

"Then come back after the clinic closes. We'll still be here."

He shook his head. She didn't know what she was asking. "I can't."

"Why?"

He climbed halfway down the flight, then glanced back at her. Her golden curls tumbled over her shoulders. Her old jeans and T-shirt outlined her body, and the vision tempted him. *She* tempted him. The sun dipped lower, catching a finger of light on one of the diamonds in her bracelet.

She clutched the railing. "Why can't you come back?"

He had no strength to lie. "Because it hurts too much."

CHAPTER THIRTEEN

SOMEONE WAS POUNDING on the front door. Patrick glanced at the clock and saw it was barely past seven in the morning. As he tossed the newspaper on the sofa, he stood up and headed for the door.

Kayla, he thought with one part anticipation, two parts dread. If she'd come looking for an explanation of what he'd told her yesterday, she wasn't going to get one. If she'd come to tempt him, he was weak enough not to resist.

But when he opened the door, the tall, golden-blond, green-eyed beauty on his porch wasn't Kayla.

"I know it's early," Elissa said, and shrugged. "Kayla mentioned you wouldn't be leaving for the clinic until eight-thirty. I was going to wait for another hour before I bothered you, but when I saw you come out and get the paper, I knew you were up."

"Come in," he said, stepping back and motioning her inside. What was she doing here? Something about the set of her shoulders and the determination in her gaze told him this wasn't just a social call.

"I've made coffee," he told her.

She shook her head. "I've had some, thanks."

As she sat on the sofa, he took in her neat braid and

the pale blue sundress that fell nearly to her ankles. He rubbed the stubble on his jawline and glanced down at his old shorts and torn T-shirt. "I wasn't expecting company."

"I know. Sorry."

He pushed the loose newspaper onto the floor and settled at the opposite end of the couch. "Why do I think I'd feel better if you actually looked sorry?"

She gave him a faint smile that faded quickly. "You want to know why I'm here."

"That's a start." Although he had a fair idea. He and Elissa only had one thing in common.

"It's about Kayla," she said.

"Okay. What about Kayla?"

Elissa angled toward him. She pressed her knees tightly together and rested her hands on her lap. "You're breaking her heart."

He'd expected a lot of accusations, but not that one. If anyone's heart was on the line in this situation, it was his. "You're exaggerating," he said. "Kayla may be a little confused by some of my actions—"

She cut in before he could finish. "Confused? You gave her a beautiful birthday present, yet instead of being happy she spent the rest of the day fighting off tears. When I asked her why, she didn't want to say. Finally she admitted you were ignoring her."

"I haven't been ignoring her. I came by yesterday."

"That's not what she meant, and you know it." Elissa's eyes darkened to the color of emeralds. Her shoulders straightened, as if she were preparing to fight to protect those she cared about. "Kayla was a virgin when you made love. I can't believe how you're treating her.

I thought you were a decent guy, but obviously I was wrong."

Her words caught him off guard, like an unexpected slap. The sting lingered as he wrestled with conflicting emotions. He knew he'd been distant with Kayla, but his intentions were honorable. At least that was what he told himself.

Elissa sighed. "By the look on your face, my comments aren't that far from the truth. And before you ask, the answer is no. Kayla didn't discuss the details of what happened that night. It was easy to figure out you two had been intimate. As for the other thing—" She waved her hand in the air.

Patrick assumed "the other thing" meant Kayla's virginity.

"I was guessing about her innocence," Elissa continued, confirming his thoughts. "The look on your face tells me I was right."

"Why did you think she was innocent?"

"Because she's always been a little wary of romantic relationships. She holds men at arm's length. Not in an obvious way. She's friendly and spends a lot of time with them, but doesn't really allow them to get close. At least not physically. I've never been able to figure out why. I think some of it has to do with her accident. She realizes, more than most, how quickly life can change. Maybe she wants to avoid being vulnerable. And then she'd got that silly idea about love being a tornado. She wants to be swept away."

He nodded. Elissa was right. "There's also the scars."

Delicate eyebrows drew together. "What?"

"The scars from the accident. She feels self-conscious about them."

"She still has scars?"

"On her stomach and chest. The tops of her thighs, too. They're faint, but there."

Elissa relaxed slightly, leaning against the back of the sofa. "I never knew. I saw them when we were still kids, but I assumed they'd faded away. Scars. Fallon and I should have thought about that. No wonder she felt self-conscious about going to the beach. She always wore a one-piece bathing suit and shorts. I figured she was shy."

She looked at him. "As triplets, you'd think we'd be better at guessing her secrets."

"The accident changed everything."

"I know. When Kayla was injured for a year, it's almost like the three of us disconnected a little. I regret that." Her mouth twisted. "So she hasn't shown the scars to us, but she let you see them."

And touch them and kiss them, he thought, remembering how lovely she'd been. Those faint white lines on her skin had simply made her unique. They were as much a part of her as her smile, or the way she spoke his name. He treasured her trust.

"Do you care about her?" Elissa asked.

Easy question, difficult choice of answers. He could take the cheater's way out and say of course he did—they were friends. He could make up some story about people having different needs at different times in their lives. Or he could tell her the truth.

He chose the latter. "I love her."

Elissa's eyes widened. "I didn't expect that."

"Neither did I. But now I do, and I can't make those feelings disappear."

"I don't understand," she said. "If you love her, why are you ignoring her? She said she tried to hug you a couple of times, but you didn't respond. I thought you'd decided being lovers had been a mistake. Obviously that's not the reason."

He shook his head. "There's no way I can regret what happened between us that night. I'll keep those memories forever. But I can't risk making the situation worse. Kayla has already decided what she wants, and it's not me. If I told her how I felt, she would be confused. Because I love her, I want to make it easy for her to walk away."

She leaned forward and touched his knee. "I can't decide if you're the most noble man I've ever met, or a fool. I want to say you're a fool. I want to make you tell her the truth, but in this situation, I think you're making the right choice."

He hadn't expected validation. Instead of making him feel justified, her words left him with the sensation of being trapped in an underground prison. There was no light, no relief, no chance of escape.

"Life is about timing," she said. "This is Kayla's time to live her dreams. Maybe, when she's met her prince, she'll realize there's someone just as wonderful waiting at home."

Or maybe she won't, he thought, swallowing hard. Either way, as long as Kayla was happy, he would survive.

She gave him a sad smile. "I fell in love once. To someone I'd known for a long time. When the three of us were still doing 'The Sally McGuire Show,' we 'adopted' an orphanage, visiting the children there, writing letters, sending gifts, that sort of thing. One boy, Cole, used to talk to me. He was five years older than me and, at eleven, I was thrilled a sixteen-year-old boy would even notice me. We started writing to each other and became friends."

She kept her gaze fixed on him, but he sensed she'd left the room and was instead caught up in the past. "We started dating when I was seventeen. For me, it was love at first sight. The second I saw him standing on the doorstep, smiling at me, I knew he was the one. But he was older and concerned, so he took it very slowly. We were married when I was twenty."

"It didn't work out?" he asked.

"No." She shook her head. "I accept most of the blame. I was away from home, I missed my sisters and my friends. I—"

She gave him a rueful smile. "Sorry. I'm sure you're not interested in the details. The point is, it wasn't our time. We both loved each other, but love turned out not to be enough."

"It's not time for Kayla and me, either," he said. And even if it was, he didn't know if she loved him. She cared. Obviously. But caring wasn't love. He suspected her feelings were a result of their physical intimacy and not because she'd discovered a new emotional depth to their relationship. In time, she would see that and let the memories of their night together fade until they blurred, like words from an old newspaper.

"I agree it doesn't appear to be your time, but neither of us can know for sure. A minute ago, I told you keeping your feelings from Kayla was right. Now I'm not so sure. If you let her go without telling her you love her, you're asking her to make a decision without all the facts. Telling her you love her isn't the same as asking her to stay."

She had a point. "I wouldn't want to pressure her."

"Are you concerned about pressure or getting rejected?"

"Both."

"At least you're honest."

"It's easy to tell you the truth. There's no risk."

She smiled at him. "There's a little one. I could tell Kayla everything we've talked about."

"You won't."

"Thanks for trusting me."

He touched her shoulder. "You have one very special sister. I doubt you're all that different from her."

"If you trust me to keep your secrets, can't you trust me enough to take my advice? At least think about telling her your feelings before she leaves."

He didn't want to think about Kayla leaving at all, let alone what he would say to her when the moment came.

"Please?" Elissa asked. "For Kayla's sake?"

For Kayla's sake, he would do anything. "I'll consider it," he promised.

"And I'll write you every day," Allison said, sniffing. Kayla tried to smile. "That's a big commitment. How about every week, instead?"

"Okay." The little girl wiped away her tears. "My mom said you're leaving, too. On vacation. Are you gonna send me postcards from Paris?"

"Of course. Lots of them."

Allison was leaving for her new rehabilitation facility later that afternoon. Kayla had wanted to stop by to say goodbye.

"Is it pretty there?" Allison asked.

"Very pretty. There are lots of old buildings and museums, little cafés and wonderful stores."

"Oh. I guess it's nice, but I'd rather stay here and play with the dogs. Won't you miss them?"

"Very much. But I'll be back."

"Then you're gonna start visiting kids again?"

That part of her future hadn't been decided. Kayla wasn't sure what would happen when she came back. She hadn't yet decided how long she would be gone. After Paris, there was the triplets' Christmas plans for the Caribbean. In the spring—she wasn't sure. As much as she might want her old job back, she doubted Patrick would offer it to her. Too much had changed; they would never go back to the way things had been just a few months ago.

"I'll never visit a kid as special as you are," Kayla said, and hugged Allison. Her eyes began to burn. She'd wanted to avoid crying, but that seemed unlikely. Leaving was a lot harder than she'd imagined.

"When I grow up, I'm going to be just like you," Allison said, her voice muffled.

"No, honey. You're going to be your own person, and that's the way it's supposed to be."

Allison nodded. "I want to be a doctor who takes care of kids like me."

"You'll be a great doctor."

A nurse stepped into the room. "I hate to interrupt, but we have to get her ready to travel."

"I understand." Kayla kissed Allison's cheek, then straightened. "I'll write."

"Me, too."

"Be good to Rhonda."

"I promise I'll love her forever." Allison's gaze was so intense, and she spoke so earnestly, Kayla had no trouble believing her.

"I know you will. Bye." She waved, then walked out of the room.

Once in the hallway, she leaned against the wall and squeezed her eyes shut. The action didn't help. Tears flowed down her cheeks faster than she could brush them away. She heard footsteps.

"Give me a second," she said, her voice thick with emotion.

"I'm in no rush."

She couldn't judge Patrick's feelings from his voice. Not that looking at him would help at all. Lately, he'd become a stranger.

She gulped back a sob and struggled for control. "Did you see Allison's mother?"

"Yes. Rhonda is doing fine and enjoying all the attention. They have an appointment to bring her into the clinic at the end of the month, just to make sure she's adjusting. But I don't think there's going to be a problem."

She sniffed and wiped her face again. "I'm sure you're right. A family is just what she needs."

The tears had stopped, and she risked opening her eyes. Patrick stood a couple of feet away, his attention focusing on the nurse's station at the far end of the corridor. She didn't know if he was being polite and giving her privacy, or if he just didn't care.

She studied his face, the shape of his head, his body. She'd been so sure she knew everything about him. What had changed?

"Stay."

"I can't."

"Why?"

"Because it hurts too much."

Their brief conversation played over and over in her head, as it had ever since her birthday, last Monday. Why had he said that to her? What hurt? Being with her? Being around her? Had she done something horrible? Had he grown to hate her that much?

He glanced at her. "Feeling better?"

She nodded.

"Then let's go," he said lightly.

He started down the corridor, but she didn't move. He retreated to her side. "What's wrong?"

She stared into his blue eyes and wondered what he was thinking. "Does any of this matter?" she asked.

"What are you talking about?"

"Me. Us. You're a stranger. I don't know how or why, but you've gone away."

Impatience pulled his mouth straight. "You're exaggerating. You're the one going away. I'm simply trying to make that easier for both of us."

"By ignoring me?"

He crossed his arms over his chest. "I'm not ignoring you, Kayla. I'm here, aren't I?"

She wanted to step toward him, to hug him close and be hugged in return. But despite the kiss they'd shared on her birthday, she remained wary. He'd rejected her before. She wasn't sure she could handle his coldness again.

"Here but not here," she said, and dropped her gaze to the floor. "This is hard for me, Patrick. It hurts." She wasn't sure if she was describing missing him, or leaving. It didn't matter—both were painful. "Don't you care anymore?"

"Of course I care." *I love you.*

She didn't actually hear the words, but for a moment they seemed to echo in the room. Something shifted in her heart. Something frightened and hibernating burst into life. It was as if she were seeing colors for the first time.

Paris, her dreams, a prince, her job, his research facility, their night together, the details and complications, the wonder, all tumbled together. They would work it out. Why not? He loved her. He—

He reached forward and ruffled her bangs. "We've been a part of each other's lives for years. You're the best friend I have, Kayla. I'm willing to admit I've been a little withdrawn, but that's because I'm going to miss you when you're gone. Maybe it's selfish, but it's easier for me if I pull back early." He gave her a crooked smile. "Besides, compared to European royalty, I'm going to look pretty tame, right? I figure three days after hitting Paris you'll be kicking yourself for not visiting sooner. You're going to forget all about me."

Pain enveloped her like a thick, wet blanket. His words came from a long way off, filtered almost, the sound muffled. But she heard every one of them. The meaning was clear. He didn't love her. Not romantically. It wasn't supposed to matter, but it did.

"You ready to head back to the clinic?" he asked.

She nodded, not sure she trusted her voice. If she spoke, she might give something away. She couldn't have said what that "something" was; she only knew she must keep it from Patrick.

Poor Kayla, always living in a fantasy world. Poor

Kayla, trapped in a hospital bed while other children could run and play. Poor Kayla, with no real career, no boyfriend, no plans for the future except to go to Paris and marry a prince.

Poor Kayla, who got crazy for a moment and thought her best friend might love her. She tried to laugh at the notion, but all that came out was a weak squeak. If he noticed, he didn't say anything.

Patrick didn't love her, and she didn't love him. Why would she? They'd had a great night together, nothing more. Passion had grown slowly between them. It hadn't been like a tornado, so it wasn't real.

Get over it, she told herself. Paris awaits.

The expensive stuff went down easy, Patrick thought as he held the bottle of Chivas Regal up to the light. He wasn't exactly drunk. As long as he didn't try to get up and walk, he would be fine.

He turned his head and looked at the photograph lying on the coffee table in his living room. The picture of his father had been taken twenty years ago. A thin, preoccupied man standing in front of an anemic Christmas tree. Tiny lights glowed in an assortment of colors, making the man's skin pasty by comparison.

"You weren't having a good time then, were you, Dad?" Patrick asked aloud. "You hated the holidays. Hell, you hated every day. And I hated *you* for that."

He brought the bottle to his lips and swallowed another mouthful. "It was like living with someone already dead. You walked through the room just like you were alive, but there were times I swore I could see right through you. I called you a lot of names back then. I thought you were a coward and a loser. I thought you were weak."

His eyes burned as he stared at the photograph. There were so few. The family had never taken many pictures. After Patrick's mother died, his father hadn't seen anything but the past.

"I hated that, too," he went on. "I knew that I wasn't enough. That without her, you had no reason to live. Sometimes I wanted to grab you and shake you, all the while screaming that I was still alive. That I mattered."

He leaned back in the chair and sighed. "I never got it. I never realized how much you loved Mom. I'm sorry about all those things I said and thought. I'm sorry I didn't try harder to get close to you."

His gaze focused on the picture. Maybe it was the alcohol, but he almost felt as if his father could hear him. "I understand now. Life doesn't give you a choice. You can't pick who you're going to love, or when that love is going to strike. And if it's not destined to be, there's not a damn thing you can do except walk through the days, as empty and transparent as a ghost."

He glanced down at his lap, half expecting to be able to see through his body to the pattern of the chair. His legs were solid.

For now, he thought, taking another swallow. But, like his father, he'd fallen in love with a woman who couldn't stay. And, like his father, he would spend the rest of his life walking from room to room, waiting for the pain to end.

CHAPTER FOURTEEN

"HOW MANY FOR DINNER?" the hostess asked.

Fallon glanced at Kayla. "Patrick's going to meet us here, right?"

"That's what he said," she answered, trying to sound cheerful. She didn't know anything about Patrick anymore, but she assumed he would at least be coming to her farewell dinner.

"Four," Fallon said. "And we'd like a table by the water."

The hostess nodded and made a note on her clipboard. "There's about a thirty-minute wait," she said, handing Fallon a small square pager. "This will buzz when your table's ready."

"Thanks." The three of them stepped back from the small desk.

"I need to visit the ladies' room," Elissa said. "You two want to wait or come with me?"

Fallon linked her arm through Kayla's. "We'll come with you."

Kayla had spent the past couple of days trying to act normal, but it was getting difficult. With both sisters staying in her small apartment, there wasn't much privacy, and there was even less time alone to think. She kept telling herself that if she could just sit quietly somewhere, she would be able to understand everything that was going on.

But before she could say that she would be happy to wait in the foyer, Fallon was already pulling her along toward the back of the restaurant.

The Empress Café sat on the water. To the left, the bridge to Coronado rose up like a beautiful piece of abstract art. As usual for July, no clouds marred the perfection of the deep blue sky. As the sun crept toward the horizon, the colors would change, but never lose their intensity.

"Just think," Elissa called over her shoulder. "Forty-eight hours from now you'll be in Paris."

"I can't wait," Kayla said automatically, then frowned as Elissa reached the back of the restaurant and turned left. "The bathrooms are to the right," she told her.

Elissa kept on walking.

"They've remodeled," Fallon said, and patted her arm.

"How do you know?"

"The hostess mentioned it."

"I didn't hear her say that."

Fallon arched her eyebrows. "Are you going to be cranky the whole evening? Because if you are, we're not going to pay for your dinner."

They paused in front of an unmarked door. "I didn't know you were considering it."

Fallon grinned. "Mind your manners and you just might be pleasantly surprised."

Elissa pulled open the door.

"This is *not* the bathroom," Kayla said loudly.

"You're so right."

Elissa stepped out of the way, and Fallon tugged Kayla into a darkened room. Kayla resisted, uneasy about the situation. Then her sister released her arm. Lights flashed on and a large group of people yelled, "Surprise!"

Kayla knew her mouth was hanging open, but she couldn't get herself together enough to close it. The large room at the back of the restaurant had been decorated for a going-away party. Balloons swayed from chair backs and table centerpieces. A badly drawn mural of Paris covered most of one wall. On a window facing an amazing view of the ocean, someone had written We'll Miss You, Kayla. Have A Good Time And Kick Some Royal Butt.

The round tables had been covered with red-and-white-checked tablecloths, French music flowed from speakers. But while the decorations were terrific, what really touched her was the group of people smiling at her.

In addition to her sisters were the staff from the clinic, including Jo, Cheryl and Melissa. Kayla ignored the twinge she felt knowing the beautiful vet would be around to comfort Patrick while she was gone. Assuming he was going to miss her.

Mr. Peters, Mrs. Grisham and other residents from Sunshine Village waved when she noticed them. Sarah sat in a wheelchair, a thick lap robe covering her frail legs. There were several families who had adopted pets from her, including Allison's parents, Duchess's owners, and Paul, the former football player. She wondered if his cat still ran his life.

Elissa and Fallon came up and hugged her.

"Okay, so dinner was just an excuse to get you here," Elissa said. "Are you surprised?"

"Very." Kayla couldn't stop looking at the crowd of people. "I can't believe you guys put this all together for me."

Sarah pushed a button on her electric wheelchair and moved forward. "We love you, child," she said, taking Kayla's hand. "We're going to miss you, but we all want you to have a wonderful adventure."

"Thank you." Kayla bent down and kissed her cheek.

"Hey, let's turn off this hokey French music and play some real tunes," Mr. Peters demanded.

"You're a cranky old man," Mrs. Grisham told him, slapping his hand. "We're setting a mood."

"But I saw a jukebox in the corner. We could jitterbug."

Mrs. Grisham raised dark eyebrows. "At your age?" She laughed. "You'd strain something."

Mr. Peters leaned close to her. "Then we could play doctor and patient."

Mrs. Grisham rolled her eyes, but Kayla noticed she didn't move away or scold him again. Romance at Sunshine Village?

The crowd surrounded her. As she greeted people, Fallon and Elissa explained how they'd planned the party.

"We started about two months ago," Elissa said. "I spoke to Cheryl at Patrick's clinic, and she agreed to take care of collecting RSVPs from the guests."

She continued talking about the logistics, but Kayla wasn't listening. As she shook hands with Allison's parents and nodded as they told her how well their daughter was doing, a part of her brain repeated a single phrase over and over. As if a needle had become stuck on an old record.

Where was Patrick?

She scanned the crowd, but he wasn't around.

When she could escape, she grabbed Elissa and pulled her into a corner. "Is Patrick supposed to be here?"

Elissa nodded. Her eyebrows drew together in a frown. "I don't understand why he's late. I confirmed a couple of things with him this morning, and everything was fine. Maybe there was a last-minute emergency at the clinic."

"I'm sure that's it," Kayla said, even though the knot in her stomach told her it was something else. There was a problem with Patrick. She could feel it.

She thought about phoning the clinic, then figured that if he *was* in the middle of surgery, she wouldn't want to disturb him. So she tried to ignore her concern and get into the spirit of the party.

While waiters circulated with trays of appetizers and drinks, Elissa led Kayla to a chair in the center of the room. Presents had been piled high.

Kayla stared at the proof of her friends' generosity and had to swallow. "You guys are going to make me cry."

"You'll spoil your makeup," Jo warned.

"True."

Fallon handed her a small rectangular box. "Open this first."

Kayla tore off the paper and laughed when she saw the disposable camera inside. "Is this for the party?" she asked.

Fallon nodded. "You can use it tonight, then take it in to a one-hour place tomorrow. That way you'll have photos to remember us while you're seducing your prince."

Kayla raised the camera and took a picture of the entire group. Everyone got into the spirit, suggesting shots, posing for her. Cheryl had a camera of her own and instructed the triplets to line up together.

"Amazing," Sarah said as the women stood next to each other. "They're nearly exactly alike."

"Yes, but I'm prettier," Fallon teased.

"You are not," Kayla and Elissa answered together.

When Cheryl had taken her photo, Kayla watched her sisters move around the room, talking to guests. They didn't know anyone here, yet they were friendly and gracious, and so completely different, Kayla didn't know how people could confuse them.

Fallon, always tailored, always correct, wore a royal blue sheath. The sleeveless dress ended precisely two inches above her knees. Elissa, the true romantic, dressed in pastel pink. A scoop-neck, capped-sleeved, gauzy two-piece outfit hugged her from shoulders to waist before flaring out in gentle pleats to fall nearly to her ankles. The dress swayed when she walked.

Kayla had picked out a simple silk T-shirt and a short straight skirt, both in purple. She hadn't bothered with stockings and wore flats instead of heels. Usually she didn't care about jewelry, but tonight she wore the bracelet Patrick had given her.

Her sisters continued to make sure their guests were comfortable. Kayla watched, realizing that it wasn't just clothing that told them apart. Even their hairstyles identified their personalities. Fallon had a French braid, Elissa piled her curls on top of her head, while Kayla wore her hair loose.

To her, the differences were much more than physical. And those differences were what made them unique.

"There are other presents," Sarah said, pointing to the pile on the floor. "Have a seat and get at it."

An hour later, Kayla was surrounded by crumpled sheets of wrapping paper and a stack of wonderful gifts. She had everything she would need for her travels. From a voltage changer for her blow dryer and curling iron, to a phrase book, to a pillow for sleeping on the plane. There were maps of Paris and France, clever travel kits with sewing supplies and medical goodies, a current French newspaper, and a beautiful hand-crocheted shawl from Sarah.

The largest gift, a set of luggage, had been opened, although the giver hadn't arrived. For the hundredth time, Kayla scanned the room and wondered what was keeping Patrick.

After dinner, Mr. Peters got his wish. The French music faded, and he picked the first tune from the juke-box. Instead of Glenn Miller, most of the songs were from the fifties and sixties. After pushing the tables aside, most of the guests pulled off their shoes and danced in the center of the room.

"You guys are too young to remember the sixties," Cheryl said, demonstrating the mashed potato.

"So are you," Kayla countered.

"Yeah, but I'm the youngest of six, and I watched my brothers and sisters very closely."

They laughed and danced, arms swinging in the air, hips swaying, feet shifting. A whisper of warmth brushed the back of her neck, and Kayla spun around.

He wasn't close enough to have touched her. From the way he glanced around the room, he hadn't even spotted her yet. But he was here, now, and that was enough.

Kayla started walking toward him. She knew the exact moment he spotted her. His solemn face relaxed into a smile.

"Hi," she said, when she was a few feet away.

"Hi, yourself."

For a second, she wondered if he was going to reject her tonight. She hesitated, rather than offering him a hug. He eased her mind when he held open his arms.

As she stepped into his embrace, he held her tightly against him. She returned his touch, wrapping her arms around his waist and pressing her head against his shoulder. She could feel the steady pounding of his heart.

"Sorry I'm late," he murmured. "Something came up at the clinic."

"Everything okay?"

"Sure."

There was something about his tone of voice. Something that made her want to question him. What was he holding back?

Before she could ask, the record ended and another dropped into place. The room filled with the scratchy sound of a needle on vinyl, and then the opening notes of "Smoke Gets in Your Eyes" flowed over them.

Without saying anything, they began to dance. Their bodies moved together in perfect communication. His heat and scent surrounded her, filling her with contentment. She'd always been at her best when she was with him.

As they circled the room, she glanced at the people around them. A few couples had joined them, including Allison's parents and Mrs. Grisham and Mr. Peters. Melissa caught her gaze, then turned away. Kayla didn't have it in her to feel triumph or pity. Tonight there was no room for petty emotion.

In the security of Patrick's arms, she studied the individuals who brought joy to her world. Sarah, Fallon and Elissa. Elissa waved, then snapped a picture of Kayla and Patrick dancing. She was pleased she would have that moment to take with her.

She thought of all she would be leaving behind this time tomorrow. Her plane took off Sunday evening and arrived in Paris in the early afternoon on Monday.

She thought of the sights she would see, the people she would meet. After waiting nearly thirteen years, her dream had arrived.

But instead of feeling light with joy, questions weighed on her. Was she doing the right thing? Was she being selfish? Would she have a life to come back to, or would everyone have moved on and forgotten her?

She knew that by "everyone" she really meant Patrick. The record ended, but he continued to hold her. Another slow song drifted through the room, and they swayed to the sound. Her eyes drifted closed. She tried to imagine herself in Paris, sipping coffee at a café, watching the world walk by.

But instead of the famous French capital, she saw a pair of ruby slippers and a young girl clicking her heels three times.

"There's no place like home."

She held Patrick tighter. Home. Was that where she belonged? Was she making a huge mistake?

They turned in a slow circle, and her gaze fell on the pile of presents everyone had bought her. Her tickets waited at her apartment, she had reservations at a hotel, appointments to meet with Sarah's friend's granddaughter and the people Patrick knew. Everything was in place.

There was no turning back.

Light from the full moon spilled into her bedroom. Kayla tossed back the sheets and sat up. A quick glance at the clock told her it was nearly one. She and her sisters had come home from the party two hours ago and gone right to bed, but she hadn't been able to sleep.

She quietly walked to the window and stared up at the sky. The moon sat high, nearly directly overhead. Its brightness concealed most of the stars, except for those close to the horizon.

The apartment was silent. Elissa slept on a cot in the corner of Kayla's bedroom. In the living room, Fallon rested on the sleeper sofa.

Kayla thought about returning to bed, but she was too restless. In less than twenty-four hours, she would be gone. Her life would change forever. How could anyone sleep?

She grabbed a pair of shorts and a T-shirt she'd left on her dresser that afternoon, then slipped into the bathroom. Five minutes later, her face washed, her hair brushed, she made her way into the living room, then out the front door.

Once settled on the steps, she drew in a deep breath. The night air was cool. She hugged herself, knowing she would be freezing in about twenty minutes, but determined to enjoy the solitude until then.

Memories of the party made her smile. She had good friends, people who really cared about her. She wasn't sure what she'd done to deserve that much support, but she was grateful for it.

She thought about Patrick. Something had been bothering him. He'd left right after they served cake. She'd hoped for another dance, but before she could ask, he was gone.

Patrick. Her gaze settled on his house at the end of the driveway below.

She wished… She shook her head. What did she wish? That they could go back to the way things had been between them? Did she really want that? Or had she secretly been hoping for something more?

"Of course I care."

Those words. They'd stunned her, left her breathless, anticipating something she couldn't even name. He'd created a moment of magic, then made it disappear.

"We're friends."

Friends. While she loved the friends in her life, she hated the word. It confused her—*he* confused her.

A flicker of light caught her attention. She stared more intently and realized a light had been on when she first came out. Because the drapes were pulled, she hadn't noticed. Until Patrick moved in front of it and momentarily blocked the glow.

He was awake.

She was halfway across the driveway before she realized what she was doing. At his front door, she raised her hand to knock, then paused. What was she going to say?

"I'll think of something," she muttered under her breath. "How humiliating can it be? After all, I'm leaving the country tomorrow."

With that, she rapped on the door.

He opened the door and stared down at her in surprise. She returned the stare. He wore nothing but loose shorts that hung low on his hips. His hair stood up in spikes, as if he'd been asleep.

"Did I wake you?" she asked.

"No. I tried to lie down, but I couldn't sleep."

"Me, either." She motioned toward the stairs leading up to her apartment. "I was sitting outside when I noticed you had a light on. I thought you might like some company."

Instead of answering, he pushed the door open.

"Want something to drink?" he asked when she'd settled on one edge of the sofa.

"No, thanks."

There was a tumbler filled with ice and clear liquid on the coffee table. He sat in front of it and leaned back against the cushions.

There was less than two feet between them, yet she

felt as if they were separated by the world. Tension knotted in her stomach, as it had at the party.

"Something's wrong," she said.

He glanced at her and smiled. "I'm gonna miss you, kid. Who else would know what I was thinking?"

"No one. So tell me what's going on."

He shook his head, leaned forward and grabbed his drink. "Just some odds and ends. Nothing for you to worry about the night before you leave."

His voice sounded funny. Was he drunk? Kayla didn't think she'd ever seen Patrick drink more than a couple of beers. She leaned toward him and took the glass. She sniffed, but couldn't smell anything. When she took a sip, she tasted ice water. Obviously whatever was bothering him wasn't that serious.

"What did you think?" he asked as he retrieved the glass. "That I was drowning my sorrows?"

"It crossed my mind."

He set the glass on the table and angled toward her. "Only as a last resort."

His hands lay loose in his lap. She had the strongest urge to reach forward and take one in hers. To touch him. Be near him. Is that why she'd come over?

To distract herself, she said, "Thanks for the luggage."

"You already thanked me."

"I know, but—" She shrugged. "I'd told you which ones I'd thought about buying, and you remembered. That makes the gift more special."

"You're welcome." He leaned his head against the sofa back. "You're going to enjoy Paris. I hope you remember to come back."

To you? she wanted to ask, but didn't.

"I'll be around," she said.

There was only a single lamp on in the room, and that was in the corner by the front door. They sat in semi-darkness. As Patrick shifted, shadows concealed, then exposed, parts of his face and body. She could make out the clean line of his jaw, his shoulders, his left arm. The thick, defined muscles of his chest were visible, as was his stomach. Or maybe she couldn't see them at all. Maybe she remembered them so well, she didn't need light to know what they looked like.

The heat began so slowly, she didn't notice it at first. It slipped down her legs and arms, then up through her torso. Her breasts swelled and ached. That magical place between her legs throbbed in time with her increasing heartbeat.

Did he feel it, too? The need? The tension?

Her gaze sought his. She couldn't read anything in his eyes. Did he want her, or did he simply tolerate her presence?

Touch me!

The voice screamed loudly in her head, yet her lips didn't move. The room was still. She waited, commanding him to move toward her, to take her in his arms as he had at the party. She was leaving tomorrow; she wanted tonight with him. She wanted the memory to carry with her for the rest of her life.

But he did nothing. He simply returned her gaze, waiting. For what? Permission? For her to leave?

When she couldn't stand it, she slid forward on the sofa. She moved deliberately, so that there could be no doubt of her intentions. So that he could stop her at any moment. She didn't want to think about being rejected, but if he turned her away, she would survive.

Her hands cupped his face. Stubble teased the sensitive pads of her fingers. She leaned toward him and pressed her lips to his.

He accepted the caress, but didn't return it. She closed her eyes and put her heart and soul into the kiss, letting her feelings pour over him. He stirred restlessly, yet neither moved away nor deepened the kiss.

She straightened. "What's going on?" she asked, confusion and frustration adding a sharpness to her tone. "Do you want me to leave or do you want me to beg?"

His eyes darkened to the color of the night sky. He raised his hands to her shoulders, then dropped them back to his lap. "I want you not to have regrets."

Was that all? She smiled. "I could never regret being with you, Patrick. I want this. I want you."

Without warning, he pulled her to him, turned her so that she lay on her back, and then he stretched out half on top of her. His arousal pressed into her hip. His hands were everywhere, touching her arms, her thighs, her breasts.

"Thank God," he said, his voice low and thick with passion. "Thank God."

CHAPTER FIFTEEN

HE KISSED HER with the intensity that left her breathless. His lips covered hers, his tongue plunged inside. She raised her arms to wrap them around his neck and draw him closer. She needed more; she needed to be one with him.

As he traced the sensitive places in her mouth, he drew her into a sitting position. From there, they rose to their feet. Still the kiss continued. He pressed against her. Bare legs brushed. Her hands lowered to his shoulders, then his back. He wasn't wearing a shirt, and she ached to feel his skin against hers.

She reached down and fumbled with the hem of her T-shirt. He backed away a little to give her room. Finally, as she tugged up the fabric, they broke the kiss.

They were both breathing heavily. Passion dilated his eyes. "I want you," he said hoarsely. "Now."

As she tossed down her shirt, he pulled her toward the bedroom. She kicked off her sandals, stumbling slightly when a strap caught around her heel.

He bent down and freed her. On his way up, he nibbled on her thigh, then licked her belly. Her muscles contracted at the contact. She had to clutch his shoulders to keep from falling to her knees.

When he'd straightened, they continued toward the bedroom. Patrick unfastened her bra, then tugged at her shorts. She pulled on his, so by the time they'd turned on a lamp and tumbled onto the sheets, they were both naked.

"I don't remember it being like this." She sighed as he kissed her neck, then down her chest. He took her already hard nipple in his mouth and sucked.

"I know," he said, before reaching for her other breast. "I want to take it slow, but—"

"No." She cupped his face and forced him to look at her. "Don't hold back anything."

Their gazes locked. The fire in his eyes heated her blood and made her feminine place dampen with need. She released him and moved her hands to his rear. Once there, she squeezed the tight, round flesh. He arched against her. His arousal bumped her belly, the tender sacs between his legs brushed against her center. Pleasure shot through her.

She parted her thighs, tilting her hips toward him. He repeated the action. The friction teased at her, not enough to take her closer to release, yet more than enough to make her willing to do anything he asked.

When he slipped away, she whimpered in protest.

"Don't worry," he promised. "I know something better to do."

With that, he knelt between her knees. He covered her breasts with his hands, then bent low and kissed her belly button. His fingers circled her nipples, brushing them gently, connecting those sensitive points with the one his mouth approached.

She felt warm breath at the top of her thigh. She knew what he was about to do. She'd read about it, heard friends talk about it, but no one had ever touched her there...not that way.

An intimate kiss. Elissa had once whispered it could be the most perfect pleasure. Kayla couldn't imagine anything more wonderful than what they'd done before, yet she was willing to be proved wrong.

He brought her hands to her center and urged her to part for him. With the protective folds pulled back, she was exposed to him. Her eyes shut tight, and she shuddered in embarrassment. Why would he want to look at her *there?*

"You're so beautiful," he whispered, stroking a single finger along her sensitive flesh. He didn't touch that tiny point of pleasure, instead discovering the rest of her.

As he circled the entrance, she pushed toward him, remembering the pleasure he'd brought her there. He dipped inside, deeper, hinting at what they would do later.

Then, when she'd nearly forgotten about being exposed and how he was going to touch her, he placed his tongue against her.

The moist, gentle contact impacted against her nerve endings. Small explosions went off in different parts of her body. There was no reason for breath or thought, no reason to exist, except for the sole purpose of experiencing the sensations he created.

He licked her slowly, as if exploring a perfect treasure. Her entire being concentrated on that one place and the power he wielded.

When he stroked faster, her body trembled. Involuntary quivers of muscles, an uncontrolled gasp. Her head moved from side to side. She might have said something. Maybe his name, maybe a plea that he not stop.

She wasn't sure of anything except the promise of a release so incredible that the anticipation alone was enough to speed her closer.

With one hand, he continued to move inside her. Long fingers pressed up, as if caressing her center of pleasure from both sides. With his other hand, he reached up and cupped her breast. He squeezed her taut nipple, matching the rhythm of his tongue.

She pressed her heels into the mattress, parting her legs wider, straining toward him. She didn't know how long he'd touched her there. Seconds…maybe days. She spiraled higher and higher.

"No!" she gasped. "Not yet. It feels too good."

But she had no control. Even as she absorbed intense pleasure, even as she became one with the heat and the flames, her body betrayed her. Muscles tensed, though she tried to relax them. She fought against the climax. She wanted to go on like this forever.

As if he had read her mind, Patrick stopped. Her body froze. Release was so close, she could feel the first whisper of ecstasy.

Before she could cry out in protest, he began again. Lighter, yet faster, touching everywhere he had before, his tongue creating magic. Completion hovered stubbornly out of reach, taunting her. She surged toward it. Closer. Closer. Closer still.

Then it was upon her. She and the pleasure were one. Every part of her vibrated with wondrous surrender.

As she relaxed, Patrick slipped next to her and pulled up the covers. He shifted so her head rested on his shoulder and her legs tangled with his. She rested one hand on his belly.

An aftershock rippled through her and she smiled. "How'd you do that?" she asked softly.

"I was inspired by my subject."

"Hmm. That was the most amazing experience of my life."

He stroked her hair. "For me, too."

She closed her eyes. Almost of its own accord, her hand slipped lower, through the curls, until she felt the length of him. He was hard and ready, and he jumped against her fingers when she touched him.

Now it was his turn to suck in his breath.

"All this for me?" she teased.

"Everything's for you."

He sounded so intense, she opened her eyes. Passion pulled his mouth straight and tightened the line of his jaw. Lethargy vanished in an instant. She wanted him again.

"Where is it?" she asked, speaking of the protection.

"I happen to have one ready."

She took the condom from him and pushed away the sheet. When he was exposed to her gaze, she caught her breath. The need and strength inherent in his maleness made her feel powerful. He was aroused because they were together. Because of what he'd done to her and what she was about to do to him.

She knelt between his thighs and took him in her hand. After stroking up and down several times, she bent low and licked the sensitive tip.

Her free hand rested on his thigh. She felt his muscles tense with her action. He groaned low in his throat. She licked again, then drew him into her mouth. She suckled him, moving her fingers at a matching rhythm, feeling the passion grow.

"Look at me," he said.

She glanced up and saw that he'd raised himself into a half-sitting position. Her hair tumbled onto his thigh and belly, her mouth embraced his maleness. It was a moment of connection so strong, she knew that whatever happened between them, they would both remember what had once been. It was, she told herself, enough.

He touched her wrist and indicated she should stop. She opened the protection, then slid it over him. Before he could shift her onto her back, she cleared her throat.

"Would you mind if I tried being, um, on top?"

He grinned, then stretched out on the bed. "Be my guest."

She straddled his hips. As she reached down to guide him inside, he did the same. Their fingers brushed. Again they looked at each other. He glanced down, and she followed his gaze. The tip of him pressed into her, their hands overlapped on his arousal. It was all there, the intimate joining of two people. She hadn't known it could be this wonderful.

She sank down on him, feeling him fill all of her. Recently satisfied need flared to life. He grasped her hips and set the pace for their joining. She tossed her head back, letting her hair flutter against her back. She liked being on top, being in control. Her thighs tightened around his hips, drawing him in deeper until he touched her soul.

When his hands clasped hers, she leaned forward, letting him lower her until she rested against his chest. He released her, then reached between them, opening her so that the most sensitive part of her rubbed him with each thrust.

Instant pleasure caught her off guard. She gasped his name, then kissed him.

As their tongues stroked together, she felt him collect himself for his release. Her own body began tensing, heading toward the promise.

"I can't hold back," he growled, obviously struggling for control.

"Don't. Just feel it," she urged, moving faster.

"Not yet." He pushed her upright, then groaned. "That's worse."

She saw him staring at her breasts. They bounced in time with their joining. She cupped them to hold them still.

"Better?" she asked.

"Not exactly."

Then his eyes closed. He surged toward her. As she prepared herself to absorb his pleasure, he reached between them and touched a fingertip to her core. Without warning, she soared into her climax, barely able to register that he followed her. She leaned forward and clutched at his shoulders, rocking and thrusting to drain everything from them both.

Later, when they were back under the sheets, nestled together, Kayla sighed. Their lovemaking had been more than she'd imagined it would be. Better than last time. Would it continue to get better as they learned about each other's secret desires? A voice inside whispered that it would.

A sense of rightness filled her. This was where she belonged. In Patrick's bed, in his arms. In his life.

He'd positioned them so they lay like spoons, his front nestled against her back.

"Kayla?" he murmured, sounding nearly asleep.

"Yes?"

"Stay with me."

Stay. It was what she'd always wanted. Why hadn't she seen that before?

"Yes, Patrick. I'll be right here." She placed her hand on top of his and squeezed.

He pressed a kiss to her bare shoulder. "Thanks. After making love with you, I don't want to sleep alone. There'll be plenty of time for that when you're gone."

His regular breathing told her he'd fallen asleep. She pressed her lips tightly together and let her tears fall silently onto the pillow.

She'd been prepared to stay for a lifetime, but he only cared about a night. When she first came over, she'd told herself any humiliation or rejection wouldn't be that awful. After all, in less than twenty-four hours she was leaving for Paris.

The pain in her chest deepened. She knew now what it meant, why she'd been so confused lately, what was wrong with her life.

Somewhere between the laughter and teasing, over sodas or sandwiches, after patients or while making love, she'd fallen in love with him.

There was no need to go searching for her handsome prince. He'd been living next door the whole time.

As the tears continued to flow, she wrestled with the fact that he hadn't once indicated he'd had a change of feelings. In his mind, they were just good friends.

The hurt in her chest deepened. She knew it was a problem to be on an airplane when you had a cold or certain illnesses, but how dangerous was it to fly with a broken heart?

Patrick sat in bed and watched Kayla sleep. She stirred occasionally, pushing the sheets as she turned, exposing her naked body to view. Each time she settled, he pulled the covers back into place. He'd long since memorized every part of her.

Physical contentment fought with emotional anguish. He loved her more than he'd ever loved anyone or anything in his life. He hadn't known such depth of emotion was possible. In the past couple of months, she'd become a part of his being, as if her presence had been grafted onto his soul. When she left him, he would mourn her absence with the same passion that he would mourn the death of hope. Like his father before him, he would move silently through his world, enduring, emotionally limping, as though a part of him had been ripped away.

He rose from the bed and pulled on his shorts, then made his way to the living room. Instead of turning on a light, he pulled open the drapes. It was nearly dawn. The start of a new day…the day Kayla would leave.

In a twisted sort of way, he should be grateful. He'd just endured the worst day of his life, and he'd survived. Kayla's departure allowed him to forget what else had happened. Compared to the devastation of losing her, the loss of funding for his research facility would barely warrant a footnote in the story of his life.

The sun rose, slipping above the horizon in slow motion, as if in no hurry to start the day. A *thunk* on his porch informed him the paper had been delivered. Patrick resisted moving for a couple of minutes, then pushed to his feet and went to retrieve it. There was no way he wanted Kayla reading the front page. That would ruin everything.

He opened the front door and saw someone crossing

toward him. In the half-light, he might have mistaken her for Kayla. The same body shape, the same hair, the same temper blazing in the same green eyes.

Elissa tugged her robe tighter around herself and glared at him. "What do you think you're doing?" she demanded, then thrust her copy of the newspaper at him. "Have you read this?"

He reached behind him and closed the front door. He didn't want Kayla to wake up and hear their voices. Then she would know what had happened. He would do anything to avoid that.

"Have a seat," he said, settling on the porch's single step.

Elissa continued to glare at him.

"I'll explain everything."

"You'd better." She sank next to him, every fiber of her being vibrating with anger. "She spent the night with you, didn't she?"

He nodded.

Her gaze narrowed. "And you didn't tell her a thing."

It wasn't a question, so he didn't bother answering.

He folded both newspapers together and stared at the still-dark western sky. "I received a phone call yesterday, from the foundation I've been dealing with. A highly placed officer has embezzled millions. He's already left the country, and they're not sure they can recover their money."

"I read that much in the paper. It's why you were late to the party yesterday, isn't it?"

"Oh, yeah." He'd been on the phone, trying to figure out how the news affected him. The answer had been succinct.

"What does the embezzlement mean to you?"

He continued to stare at the horizon, but instead of treetops and sky, he saw the research building as it should have been. He saw the equipment he'd ordered, the scientists working. What could have been a chance to make a difference had turned to dust.

"They're real sorry, but there's no money to give me."

She caught her breath. "Oh, Patrick, I'm sorry."

She placed her hand on his arm. A comforting touch, so like her sister's that it should have eased his pain. It didn't. Elissa was a wonderful person, but she was a poor substitute for the real thing.

"They're going to try and get me alternative funding. It'll take a while, and there's no guarantee it will come through. They might recover some of what was stolen. If it's enough, they'll help me out." He shrugged. "It's been a gamble from the beginning. I knew there were a thousand things that could go wrong."

"But you never expected to lose the money once you had it."

"No, I never expected that."

Life had broadsided him in a couple of different ways. First with Kayla, and now with this. At least he still had the clinic. He would bury himself in work and try to forget.

"Why didn't you tell her?"

"That's easy. Her plane leaves tonight, and I want her on it. If she knew about this, she would want to fix it. That's what Kayla does, she heals the world. I'm not going to stand in the way of what she wants, and I'm not going to be one of her damn strays. So I'm not going to say anything, and neither are you."

For the first time since sitting down, he looked at

Elissa, pinning her with his gaze. "I want your word on that," he said.

"Why? What's so wrong with her wanting to fix it? She cares about you."

Cares. It was a start, he supposed. Better than hating him, or having no feelings at all. But he'd wanted everything. Both with the research facility and with her. Better to walk away than to get it half-right.

"I don't want her pity and I don't want her money. You know that's what she'd offer me."

Elissa nodded. "She'd write you a check without blinking." She drew in a deep breath. "Do you know what you're giving up?"

He knew she was talking about more than the research facility. "I'm intimately familiar with the pain I'm going to face." He'd watched his father live through it for twenty years. Walcott men were cursed that way. He knew because history was about to repeat itself.

He turned his attention back to the horizon. "Your word, Elissa."

"All right. I won't say anything to her before she gets on the plane."

"And you won't call and tell her the truth."

"Agreed. But if she calls me and already knows something, I'm going to fill in the details."

"Fine."

He wasn't worried about that. Once Kayla was in Paris, there was no way she was going to find out anything. She would be too busy living her dream.

Happily ever after. That was all he'd ever wanted for her.

CHAPTER SIXTEEN

KAYLA SAT IN front of the French café. Her small round table and single chair were near the sidewalk, allowing her a perfect view of the quaint street and passersby. Despite the fact that it was late July, the temperature was pleasant, rather than hot, the sky was clear, and the sun shone down brightly.

She fingered the brochure she'd picked up that morning on her second visit to the Louvre. Earlier that week, she'd viewed the old masters; today she'd concentrated on the sculptures. The artwork amazed her. Some of the statues were so perfect, they looked as if they'd come from a mold, instead of being hand-carved.

She sipped her coffee, then reached for the postcards she'd bought yesterday. After staring at them for a second, she let them fall back on the table. Who would have thought that after ten days in Paris, she would have nothing to say to her friends?

A family walked by the café. Three children, all chatting happily, their parents smiling at each other. Their French was too quick for her to decipher, but she didn't need to understand the conversation to know they were happy and excited about their day together. Seeing them made Kayla feel her solitary existence even more.

"Bonjour, mademoiselle."

Kayla glanced up and saw a flower vendor standing in front of her. He held up a small bouquet and raised his eyebrows questioningly.

She shook her head. *"Non."*

The vendor moved on.

She watched him pause at the next table. A couple sat there. They were young, probably still in their teens, and very much in love. They stared at each other as if the rest of the world had long since ceased to exist. The young man bought the bouquet and placed it in his girl-friend's hands. She kissed him.

Kayla turned away from them and forced herself to look at the shops across the street. Dresses and shoes were displayed provocatively behind sparkling-clean windows. Paris was a shopper's paradise, she thought to herself, then glanced down at her tailored pantsuit. An impulsive spending spree in an exclusive boutique had provided her with several sophisticated outfits, match-ing shoes and handbags. The afternoon had cost about as much as she'd made in the previous three months, but she refused to worry about that. She had her trust fund. Her goal had always been to enjoy life.

"Postcards," she said softly. "Someone has to write them, and you seem to be the only person volunteering."

She reached into her handbag for a pen. Her fingers closed over a thick envelope instead. The pictures from her going-away party. She'd already looked at them a hundred times, but she couldn't help pulling them out again.

Mr. Peters and Mrs. Grisham dancing together. Jo from the clinic, talking with Sarah, probably making plans. Jo had taken over the visits to Sunshine Village. The sisters laughing together. She touched the smooth paper, remembering the good time she'd had that night. So many people had come to see her off. So many people cared about her. There were no photos of the dogs, but she often thought about them, too.

"I miss you guys," she whispered, wishing her sisters were with her right now. Paris wasn't much fun for someone on her own.

She glanced around at the city and tried to convince herself it was as wonderful as she'd always imagined. But it wasn't. She didn't speak the language well, she didn't know anyone. At the end of the day, there was no one to ask what she'd done, no one to talk to, no one to hold.

Maybe it was her own fault. She had the list of Patrick's friends and Sarah's friend's granddaughter, but she'd avoided making definite plans with any of them. What was her problem? What was she waiting for?

She set the photos on the table, then found her pen and started to write. First to her sisters, then maybe Sarah.

But instead of "Dear Elissa" or "Dear Fallon," what appeared on the card was "Patrick."

Patrick—Here I am in Paris. It's beautiful and the people are much nicer than everyone told me. I've been to the Louvre twice. As I write this, I'm sitting in a little café watching the world go by.

And I miss you more than I thought I could ever miss anyone.

The last sentence went unwritten. Partly because she didn't think he would care all that much, partly because tears filled her eyes and it was difficult to see.

She slammed the pen onto the table. Her fingers hit the pile of pictures and the top one slid to one side, exposing the photo underneath. She didn't need to blink away the tears to be able to make out the subject. She'd memorized that particular shot on the plane.

She and Patrick held each other close as they danced. The background blurred, leaving only the couple in focus. They looked right together, their bodies blending with the familiarity of lovers. She closed her eyes and remembered what it had felt like to be with him. To love him, not just physically, but with her heart and her soul.

"This is crazy," she muttered, and thrust the photos back in their envelope. "Get a grip, kid, or you're never going to make it."

She scrawled an inane sentence about the weather, signed her name, then addressed the postcard and set it to one side. Next, she wrote her sisters, Sarah and Allison, and sent a group postcard to Sunshine Village and the clinic. She had just pulled out several stamps when someone placed a bouquet of flowers on the table.

She glanced up and stared into the face of the most handsome man she'd ever seen. He was tall, with dark hair pulled back in a ponytail and black eyes. A white cotton shirt emphasized the breadth of his shoulders and chest before disappearing into the waistband of his jeans. He should have looked like a dangerous pirate, but the boyish smile he gave her chased away any fears.

"Vous permettez?" he asked, motioning to the flowers.

Kayla's French was improving, but she had a long way to go. She thought he was asking permission to give her flowers.

"Merci, non. Je ne suis pas—" She searched her brain for the verb "to want" and found nothing. "Thank you, but I don't want the flowers."

Great, as if speaking English would help.

He frowned, but then the smile returned. "American, *non?*"

"Yes, ah, *oui.*"

He pulled a chair over from an empty table, then sat next to her. *"Bon.* I speak English," he said, his voice thick with a French accent, then laughed. *"Un peu."* He held his right thumb and forefinger about an inch apart.

She grinned. *"Je parle français un peu.* Okay, I admit I speak French less than a little, but I'm trying."

"Bon." He shook his head. "Good. I'm Jean." He held out his hand.

She shook hands with him, then pulled her fingers free. "I'm Kayla."

"Enchanté." He repeated her name several times. "Pretty, yes?"

Despite the fact that he was talking about her name, his intense gaze made her wonder if he was referring to something else. "Thank you," she murmured.

"How long have you been in Paris?"

"Ten days."

"Your *mari,* ah, your husband is with you, *non?*"

She shook her head. "I'm not married."

Jean looked at her single cup of coffee, then took her hand in his again, and squeezed her fingers. "You are alone in Paris? *Je suis désolé.* It is not permitted. We could have dinner tonight. The, ah, restaurant is public, *non?* You would be comfortable *avec moi,* ah, with me. We talk, we laugh, I explain Paris."

She didn't know if he thought he was picking up a rich American on her own or if he was genuinely a nice man. Maybe even a prince in disguise. It didn't matter. He wasn't the one she wanted.

She looked at the flowers, then at Jean, and pulled her hand from his. "I can't," she said.

"Tomorrow?"

She shook her head. The tears returned, and when one slipped down her cheek, he frowned. "Kayla? What is wrong?"

"Nothing." She collected her postcards and photographs and shoved them into her purse. After throwing a few bills on the table, she stood up and started for the exit.

"Kayla?"

Jean sounded confused, but he didn't come after her. Thank goodness. She was crying so hard, she couldn't see where she was going.

She kept wiping her face and walking. After ten or fifteen minutes, she gained enough control to look around and try to figure out where she was. Her hotel was only a couple of blocks away.

When she sank onto her bed, she buried her face in her hands and sobbed. This wasn't what she wanted. She missed everyone back home. She missed her life. Traveling was fine, but not without someone to share it with. Not without someone to love.

"Oh, Patrick." Her voice cracked.

She reached for the phone. It didn't matter if he didn't love her in return. She just had to hear his voice and tell him what he meant to her. In time, they could be friends again. She would rather have him as a friend than not have him at all.

She spoke haltingly with the hotel operator and asked to be connected to an international phone line. It was late afternoon in Paris. The clinic would just be opening. After several misdirections and sudden hang-ups, trying her patience to the point where she wanted to scream, she heard a ring, followed by a familiar voice saying, "Walcott Animal Clinic. May I help you?"

"Cheryl?"

Silence.

"Cheryl? Can you hear me?"

"Kayla? Is that you?"

"Yes. I'm in Paris."

Cheryl laughed. "Girl, what on earth are you doing phoning here? If I was in Paris, I would be looking for a handsome Frenchman to show me why those people have a reputation for being such great lovers."

"I could give you a name," she muttered, then cleared her throat. "Is Patrick there yet?"

"Patrick?" Cheryl said the name as if she'd never heard it before.

"Your boss. Is he in?"

"No. He's not here."

"Is he still at the house?" She could probably catch him there. She had to talk to him. She had to tell him how she felt.

"I thought you knew," Cheryl said.

Kayla's chest tightened. "What are you talking about? Knew what?"

"He's in Washington, D.C., trying to get his grant money restored."

"What?" Kayla stared at the phone. What was she talking about? Grant money restored? But that was all taken care of.

Then different memories filtered into her consciousness. Patrick being late to her going-away party, and his preoccupation that night. Elissa's odd behavior before Kayla left on the plane. As if her sister were hiding something.

"Never mind," Kayla said. "I know who to call. Do you know where he's staying?"

"Yes, but he's coming home in a couple of days. If you wait, you can phone him here."

"Thanks. I'll talk to you soon, Cheryl."

Kayla hung up and quickly reconnected with the operator. The call went through faster this time. In less than two minutes, she was speaking with her sister.

"How's Paris?" Elissa asked. "Are you having a wonderful time?"

"No, but that's not important. I called the clinic and found out that Patrick's in Washington because he's having trouble with his grant. What do you know about that?"

Elissa sighed. "I wanted him to tell you before you left, but he wouldn't hear of it. I'm sorry, Kayla. He made me promise not to say anything. Of course, I didn't promise not to fill you in if you asked."

She went on to explain about the embezzlement and the delay in funding.

"So he's in Washington to see what he can do?" Kayla asked, stunned by the information.

"Right. He's working with the original foundation. They're also helping him with emergency funding through other sources."

While Elissa told her what was going on, Kayla paced beside the bed, walking as far as the phone cord would let her before turning around and heading for the nightstand. Now disbelief made her sink to the floor.

"Why didn't he want me to know?" she asked.

"He knew you'd want to help."

"Oh, and that's a bad thing?" He hadn't trusted her. Why?

"He thought you'd delay your trip and try to give him money," Elissa said softly. "He didn't want to ruin your plans."

"You mean he didn't want me hanging around." She knew she sounded bitter, but she couldn't help herself. She'd thought—

Her throat tightened. "I love him, Elissa. I would have done anything for him."

"Did you ever tell him that?"

"No. I'd sort of hoped he would give me a hint as to how he felt. Everything has changed between us. It happened so fast that I wasn't sure what was going on. That last night, I hoped he would ask me to stay."

"Did you offer?"

"I thought about it."

"So you expected him to take all the risks?"

Kayla didn't like the sound of that. "Not really."

"Gee, that's what it sounds like to me. Maybe you can explain it."

Kayla picked at the bedspread. "I... I..."

"You were afraid."

"Yeah."

"I know that feeling. Fear is powerful. It was easier to avoid the risk, and so very simple to go away. But what did you leave behind?"

That was an easy question. "The man I love."

"And?"

"I have to tell him how I feel. But I can't. He's in Washington. He's coming home in a couple of days. Should I call him, or just come back?"

"That's your decision."

Kayla squeezed her eyes shut. She thought about Patrick, about what he meant to her, about the years they'd been together. "He's the best man I've ever known. How could I have been such a fool?"

"We all make mistakes," Elissa said, and it was obvious she wasn't just talking about Kayla's situation.

"Thank you for telling me what happened with him. And for listening. I'm going to get a flight back tomorrow. I should be in San Diego sometime the day after."

"Call and let me know what happens."

"I will."

They chatted for a couple more minutes, then hung up. Kayla got up and found her French phrase book. For the third time, she braved the hotel operator, requesting a connection with the airlines.

Patrick waited until the plane had emptied before grabbing his carry-on bag and heading for the gangway. Once in the terminal, he walked slowly toward the baggage claim and the car park beyond.

It had been a grueling five days. He'd spoken to dozens of people, met with committees, told his story over and over, until he was hoarse.

His hard work had paid off. The funding had been restored. He'd called his contractor from the Washington airport; work should start back up in the morning.

So why wasn't he excited? This was his dream come true, after all. Everything was going according to plan.

He passed a bank of phones and wished he had someone to call. His employees would be happy when he told them, but that wasn't the same as having one special person to share the moment. When he got home, he would be alone. There was no one to hold, no one to love. Maybe he should get a dog. There were plenty of strays in the clinic kennels. He could pick one out this afternoon.

But a dog would be a poor substitute for who and what he really wanted.

Without meaning to, he pictured Kayla. Her golden-blond curls, her smile, her laughter, the way she always weaseled out of doing the dishes. The scent of her skin, the feel of her body next to his, the way she gave herself completely, unselfconsciously, the way she held him as if she never wanted to let go.

The picture shifted unexpectedly, and he saw his father. Old before his years, walking through life like a spirit biding time until he could be with the woman he loved.

"Dammit, she's not dead," Patrick said out loud. Several people turned to stare at him, but he ignored them.

The realization slammed home like a gunshot. Kayla *wasn't* dead. His father hadn't had a choice. There was no way to be with his love, but Patrick was suffering simply because he'd chosen to be noble. Or maybe he'd just chosen to be stupid. After all, he'd never told Kayla how he felt. Maybe she wanted to know that he loved her. Maybe she had feelings for him, too, but was afraid to be the first one to confess them.

He understood all about being afraid, and he was sick of it. He was sick of suffering and being noble, and maybe even of being a fool. By God, he was going to tell her the truth. If she rejected him, then at least he would know. He might spend the rest of his life missing her, but he wouldn't have the added agony of wondering, "What if?"

"I don't care if she travels," he muttered. "As long as she comes home to me."

He scanned the signs overhead and saw the one pointing to the international terminal. Walking quickly, he headed that way.

"Patrick?"

He turned toward the familiar sound, scanning faces, wondering if his mind was playing tricks on him.

"Patrick, I'm right here."

He looked at a woman separating herself from the crowd. She wore a blue suit with matching high heels. Golden curls had been trimmed to shoulder length and tamed into a sophisticated style. She wore makeup and jewelry. His heart recognized her first, and then he saw the gold and diamond bangle on her wrist and was sure.

"Kayla?"

She laughed and flew toward him. "Yes. I just got in a couple of hours ago. I called the office and Cheryl gave me your flight number. When you didn't get off the plane, I didn't know what to do."

"I got off, but I was last."

She stopped in front of him. "I should have waited longer."

They stared at each other. His heart thundered in his chest. The awful pain that had seeped down into his bones began to fade. He opened his arms, and she slammed into him.

"Why are you back?" he asked, holding her tightly against him. Her scent, her heat, the feel of her, comforted him, thrilled him. Even if it was just for today, it was perfect.

"I had to come back." She buried her face against his chest. "I missed everyone. No, that's not true. I missed you, Patrick." She looked up at him. "Why didn't you tell me about the funding?"

There were a thousand things he could have said. Half truths, almost truths. He was done with that. "Because I love you. Because I wanted you to have your dream."

"Oh, Patrick." She rose up on tiptoe and brushed his mouth with hers. "I love you, too."

It was as if the band around his chest had been unlocked. It fell away, freeing him to breathe, to feel, to love.

"I was such a fool," she said.

"No, I was."

She shook her head. "It was me. I spent so much time putting my life on hold to wait for a magical future, I never bothered to notice I already had a wonderful present. I don't need Paris, or any of that. I have lots of

people who care about me. I have a job I love, and—"
She paused. "Do you really love me?"

"More than anything."

"Friendship, love, or something more?"

The doubt in her eyes pained him. "I love you the
way a man loves a woman, Kayla. Romantically and
passionately. I want you in my life. I want us to be part
of each other."

Her smiled nearly blinded him. "I want that, too. I
don't deserve you, but I want to be with you always."

He desperately wanted to believe her. "What about
your prince?"

She frowned. "I saw a couple of pictures of the
princes of Europe. They're not as good-looking as I'd
thought. I think the prince thing is really overrated."

They both smiled. He touched her hair. "You look
different."

"Dumb, you mean."

"I like it. Very sophisticated."

"Don't get used to it. As soon as we get home, I'm
washing off this makeup and I'm going to start growing my hair back. I'm not the glamour type. I'm just
the girl next door."

"The girl of my dreams."

She hugged him tight. "Always."

Later, when they'd made love and were holding each
other, he asked, "Would you like to go to Paris for our
honeymoon?"

She raised herself onto one elbow and smiled at him.
"Is that a proposal?"

She was so beautiful. He touched her face and her

neck. "I know our love isn't the tornado you've been waiting for, but it's strong enough to last both our life-times. I come from a long line of men who love with their whole hearts." He tucked her hair behind her ears. "Yes, it's a proposal. Kayla, will you marry me?"

Her eyes filled with tears. She wiped them away and groaned. "Do you know how many times I've cried since I left here? It's horrible. I missed you so much. Yes, I'll marry you. I'll love you forever. I'll make you proud."

His heart filled with contentment. "I already am."

She bent over and kissed him. Their lips parted. She swept inside his mouth, igniting fires that had so recently been quenched. He put his hands on her waist, then drew her on top of him. She wiggled when she felt his arousal, teasing him with the promise of their joining.

"You're wrong about something," she said, breaking the kiss and touching her index finger to his lower lip.

"What's that?"

"You said our love isn't like a tornado, but it is. Every time I'm with you, every time I think about you, every time you hold me, I get swept away."

* * * * *

PLAYING BY
THE GREEK'S RULES

Sarah Morgan

To the wonderful Joanne Grant,
for her enthusiasm and encouragement
and for always keeping the door open.

CHAPTER ONE

LILY PULLED HER hat down to shade her eyes from the burn of the hot Greek sun and took a large gulp from her water bottle. 'Never again.' She sat down on the parched, sunbaked earth and watched as her friend carefully brushed away dirt and soil from a small, carefully marked section of the trench. 'If I ever, *ever* mention the word "love" to you, I want you to bury me somewhere in this archaeological site and never dig me up again.'

'There is an underground burial chamber. I could dump you in there if you like.'

'Great idea. Stick a sign in the ground. *"Here lies Lily, who wasted years of her life studying the origin, evolution and behaviour of humans and still couldn't understand men".*' She gazed across the ruins of the ancient city of Aptera to the sea beyond. They were high on a plateau. Behind them, the jagged beauty of the White Mountains shimmered in the heat and in front lay the sparkling blue of the Sea of Crete. The beauty of it usually lifted her mood, but not today.

Brittany sat up and wiped her brow with her forearm. 'Stop beating yourself up. The guy is a lying, cheating rat bastard.' Reaching for her backpack, she glanced across the site to the group of men who were deep in conversation. 'Fortunately for all of us he's flying back to London tomorrow to his wife. And all I can say to that is, God help the woman.'

Lily covered her face with her hands. 'Don't say the word "wife". I am a terrible person.'

'Hey!' Brittany's voice was sharp. 'He told you he was single. He *lied*. The responsibility is all his. After tomorrow you won't have to see him again and I won't have to struggle not to kill him.'

'What if she finds out and ends their marriage?'

'Then she might have the chance of a decent life with someone who respects her. Forget him, Lily.'

How could she forget when she couldn't stop going over and over it in her head?

Had there been signs she'd missed?

Had she asked the wrong questions?

Was she so desperate to find someone special that she'd ignored obvious signs?

'I was planning our future. We were going to spend August touring the Greek Islands. That was before he pulled out a family photo from his wallet instead of his credit card. Three little kids wrapped around their dad like bindweed. He should have been taking them on holiday, not me! I can't bear it. How could I have made such an appalling error of judgement? That is a line I *never* cross. Family is sacrosanct to me. If you asked me to pick between family and money, I'd pick family every time.' It crossed her mind that right now she had neither. No money. No family. 'I don't know which is worse—the fact that he clearly didn't know me *at all*, or the fact that when I checked him against my list he was perfect.'

'You have a list?'

Lily felt herself grow pink. 'It's my attempt to be objective. I have a really strong desire for permanent roots. Family.' She thought about the emotional wasteland of her past and felt a sense of failure. Was the future going to look the same way? 'When you want something badly it can distort your decision-making process, so I've put in some layers of protection for myself. I know the basic qualities I need in a man to be happy. I never date anyone who doesn't score highly on my three points.'

Brittany looked intrigued. 'Big wallet, big shoulders and big—'

'No! And you are appalling.' Despite her misery, Lily laughed. 'First, he has to be affectionate. I'm not interested in a man who can't show his feelings. Second, he has to be honest, but short of getting him to take a lie detector test I don't know how to check that one. I thought Professor Ashurst was honest. I'm never calling him David again, by the way.' She allowed herself one glance at the visiting archaeologist who had dazzled her during their short, ill-fated relationship. 'You're right. He's a rat pig.'

'I didn't call him a rat pig. I called him a rat b—'

'I know what you called him. I never use that word.'

'You should. It's surprisingly therapeutic. But we shouldn't be wasting this much time talking about him. Professor Asshat is history, like this stuff we're digging up.'

'I can't believe you called him that.'

'You should be calling him far worse. What's the third thing on your list?'

'I want a man with strong family values. He has to want a family. But not several different families at the same time. Now I know why he gave off all those signals about being a family man. Because he already *was* a family man.' Lily descended into gloom. 'My checklist is seriously flawed.'

'Not necessarily. You need a more reliable test for honesty and you should maybe add "single" to your list, that's all. You need to chill. Stop looking for a relationship and have some fun. Keep it casual.'

'You're talking about sex? That doesn't work for me.' Lily took another sip of water. 'I have to be in love with a guy to sleep with him. The two are welded together for me. How about you?'

'No. Sex is sex. Love is love. One is fun and the other is to be avoided at all costs.'

'I don't think like that. There is something wrong with me.'

'There's nothing wrong with you. It's not a crime to want a relationship. It just means you get your heart broken more than the average person.' Brittany pushed her hat back from her face. 'I can't believe how hot it is. It's not even ten o'clock and already I'm boiling like a lobster.'

'And you know all about lobsters, coming from Maine. It's summer and this is Crete. What did you expect?'

'Right now I'd give anything for a few hours back home. I'm not used to summers that fry your skin from your body. I keep wanting to remove another layer of clothing.'

'You've spent summers at digs all over the Mediterranean.'

'And I moaned at each and every one.' Brittany stretched out her legs and Lily felt a flash of envy.

'You look like Lara Croft in those shorts. You have amazing legs.'

'Too much time hiking in inhospitable lands searching for ancient relics. I want your gorgeous blonde hair.' Brittany's hair, the colour of polished oak, was gathered up from her neck in a ponytail. Despite the hat, her neck was already showing signs of the sun. 'Listen, don't waste another thought or tear on that man. Come out with us tonight. We're going to the official opening of the new wing at the archaeological museum and afterwards we're going to try out that new bar on the waterfront. My spies tell me that Professor Asshat won't be there, so it's going to be a great evening.'

'I can't. The agency rang this morning and offered me an emergency cleaning job.'

'Lily, you have a masters in archaeology. You shouldn't be taking these random jobs.'

'My research grant doesn't pay off my college loans and I want to be debt free. And anyway, I love cleaning. It relaxes me.'

'You love cleaning? You're like a creature from another planet.'

'There's nothing more rewarding than turning someone's messy house into a shiny home, but I do wish the job wasn't tonight. The opening would have been fun. A great excuse to wash the mud off my knees and dress up, not to mention seeing all those artefacts in one place.

Never mind. I'll focus on the money. They're paying me an emergency rate for tonight.'

'Cleaning is an emergency?'

Lily thought about the state of some of the houses she cleaned. 'Sometimes, but in this case it's more that the owner decided to arrive without notice. He spends most of his time in the US.' She dug in her bag for more sunscreen. 'Can you imagine being so rich you can't quite decide which of your many properties you are going to sleep in?'

'What's his name?'

'No idea. The company is very secretive. We have to arrive at a certain time and then his security team will let us in. Four hours later I add a gratifyingly large sum of money to my bank account and that's the end of it.'

'Four hours? It's going to take five of you four hours to clean one house?' Brittany paused with the water halfway to her mouth. 'What is this place? A Minoan palace?'

'A villa. It's big. She said I'd be given a floor plan when I arrive, which I have to return when I leave and I'm not allowed to make copies.'

'A *floor plan*?' Brittany choked on her water. 'Now I'm intrigued. Can I come with you?'

'Sure—' Lily threw her a look '—because scrubbing out someone's shower is so much more exciting than having cocktails on the terrace of the archaeological museum while the sun sets over the Aegean.'

'It's the Sea of Crete.'

'Technically it's still the Aegean, and either way I'm missing a great party to scrub a floor. I feel like Cinderella. So what about you? Are you going to meet someone tonight and do something about your dormant love life?'

'I don't have a love life, I have a sex life, which is not at all dormant fortunately.'

Lily felt a twinge of envy. 'Maybe you're right. I need to lighten up and use men for sex instead of treating every relationship as if it's going to end in confetti. You were an only child, weren't you? Did you ever wish you had brothers or sisters?'

'No, but I grew up on a small island. The whole place felt like a massive extended family. Everyone knew everything, from the age you first walked, to whether you had all A's on your report card.'

'Sounds blissful.' Lily heard the wistful note in her own voice. 'Because I was such a sickly kid and hard work to look after, no one took me for long. My eczema was terrible when I was little and I was always covered in creams and bandages and other yucky stuff. I wasn't exactly your poster baby. No one wanted a kid who got sick. I was about as welcome as a stray puppy with fleas.'

'Crap, Lily, you're making me tear up and I'm not even a sentimental person.'

'Forget it. Tell me about your family instead.' She loved hearing about other people's families, about the complications, the love, the experiences woven into a shared history. To her, family seemed like a multicoloured sweater, with all the different coloured strands of wool knitted into something whole and wonderful that gave warmth and protection from the cold winds of life.

She picked absently at a thread hanging from the

hem of her shorts. It felt symbolic of her life. She was a single fibre, loose, bound to nothing.

Brittany took another mouthful of water and adjusted the angle of her hat. 'We're a normal American family, I guess. Whatever that is. My parents were divorced when I was ten. My mom hated living on an island. Eventually she remarried and moved to Florida. My dad was an engineer and he spent all his time working on oil rigs around the world. I lived with my grandmother on Puffin Island.'

'Even the name is adorable.' Lily tried to imagine growing up on a place called Puffin Island. 'Were you close to your grandmother?'

'Very. She died a few years ago, but she left me her cottage on the beach so I'd always have a home. I take several calls a week from people wanting to buy the place but I'm never going to sell.' Brittany poked her trowel into the ground. 'My grandmother called it Castaway Cottage. When I was little I asked her if a castaway ever lived there and she said it was for people lost in life, not at sea. She believed it had healing properties.'

Lily didn't laugh. 'I might need to spend a month there. I need to heal.'

'You'd be welcome. A friend of mine is staying at the moment. We use it as a refuge. It's the best place on earth and I always feel close to my grandmother when I'm there. You can use it any time, Lil.'

'Maybe I will. I still need to decide what I'm going to do in August.'

'You know what you need? Rebound sex. Sex for the fun of it, without all the emotional crap that goes with relationships.'

'I've never had rebound sex. I'd fall in love.'

'So pick someone you couldn't possibly fall in love with in a million years. Someone with exceptional bedroom skills, but nothing else to commend him. Then you can't possibly be at risk.' She broke off as Spyros, one of the Greek archaeologists from the local university, strolled across to them. 'Go away, Spy, this is girl talk.'

'Why do you think I'm joining you? It's got to be more interesting than the conversation I just left.' He handed Lily a can of chilled Diet Coke. 'He's a waste of space, *theé mou*.' His voice was gentle and she coloured, touched by his kindness.

'I know, I know.' She lifted the weight of her hair from her neck, wishing she'd worn it up. 'I'll get over it.'

Spy dropped to his haunches next to her. 'Want me to help you get over him? I heard something about rebound sex. I'm here for you.'

'No thanks. You're a terrible flirt. I don't trust you.'

'Hey, this is about sex. You don't need to trust me.' He winked at her. 'What you need is a real man. A Greek man who knows how to make you feel like a woman.'

'Yeah, yeah, I know the joke. You're going to hand me your laundry and tell me to wash it. This is why you're not going to be my rebound guy. I am not washing your socks.' But Lily was laughing as she snapped the top of the can. Maybe she didn't have a family, but she had good friends. 'You're forgetting that when I'm not cleaning the villas of the rich or hanging out here contributing nothing to my college fund, I work for the ultimate in Greek manhood.'

'Ah yes.' Spyros smiled. 'Nik Zervakis. Head of the mighty ZervaCo. Man of men. Every woman's fantasy.'

'Not mine. He doesn't tick a single box on my list.'

Spy raised his eyebrows and Brittany shook her head. 'You don't want to know. Go on, Lily, dish the dirt on Zervakis. I want to know everything from his bank balance to how he got that incredible six pack I saw in those sneaky photos of him taken in that actress's swimming pool.'

'I don't know much about him, except that he's super brilliant and expects everyone around him to be super brilliant, too, which makes him pretty intimidating. Fortunately he spends most of his time in San Francisco or New York so he isn't around much. I've been doing this internship for two months and in that time two personal assistants have left. It's a good job he has a big human resources department because I can tell you he gets through *a lot* of human resources in the average working week. And don't even start me on the girlfriends. I need a spreadsheet to keep it straight in my head.'

'What happened to the personal assistants?'

'Both of them resigned because of the pressure. The workload is inhuman and he isn't easy to work for. He has this way of looking at you that makes you wish you could teleport. But he *is* very attractive. He isn't my type so I didn't pay much attention, but the women talk about him all the time.'

'I still don't understand why you're working there.'

'I'm trying different things. My research grant ends this month and I don't know if I want to carry on doing this. I'm exploring other options. Museum work doesn't pay much and anyway, I don't want to live in a big city.

I could never teach—' She shrugged, depressed by the options. 'I don't know what to do.'

'You're an expert in ceramics and you've made some beautiful pots.'

'That's a hobby.'

'You're creative and artistic. You should do something with that.'

'It isn't practical to think I can make a living that way and dreaming doesn't pay the bills.' She finished her drink. 'Sometimes I wish I'd read law, not archaeology, except that I don't think I'm cut out for office work. I'm not good with technology. I broke the photocopier last week and the coffee machine hates me, but apparently having ZervaCo on your résumé makes prospective employers sit up. It shows you have staying power. If you can work there and not be intimidated, you're obviously robust. And before you tell me that an educated woman shouldn't allow herself to be intimidated by a guy, try meeting him.'

Spyros rose to his feet. 'Plenty of people would be intimidated by Nik Zervakis. There are some who say his name along with the gods.'

Brittany pushed her water bottle back into her backpack. 'Those would be the people whose salary he pays, or the women he sleeps with.'

Lily took off her hat and fanned herself. 'His security team is briefed to keep them away from him. We are not allowed to put any calls through to him unless the name is on an approved list and that list changes pretty much every week. I have terrible trouble keeping up.'

'So his protection squad is there to protect him from women?' Brittany looked fascinated. 'Unreal.'

'I admire him. They say his emotions have never played a part in anything he does, business or pleasure. He is the opposite of everything I am. No one has ever dumped him or made him feel less of a person and he always knows what to say in any situation.' She glanced once across the heat-baked ruins of the archaeological site towards the man who had lied so glibly. Thinking of all the things she could have said and hadn't plunged her into another fit of gloom. 'I'm going to try and be more like Nik Zervakis.'

Brittany laughed. 'You're kidding, right?'

'No, I'm not kidding. He is like an ice machine. I want to be like that. How about you? Have either of you ever been in love?'

'No!' Spy looked alarmed, but Brittany didn't answer. Instead she stared sightlessly across the plateau to the ocean.

'Brittany?' Lily prompted her. 'Have you been in love?'

'Not sure.' Her friend's voice was husky. 'Maybe.'

'Wow. Ball-breaking Brittany, in love?' Spy raised his eyebrows. 'Did you literally fire an arrow through his heart?' He spread his hands as Lily glared at him. 'What? She's a Bronze Age weapons expert and a terrifyingly good archer. It's a logical suggestion.'

Lily ignored him. 'What makes you think you might have been in love? What were the clues?'

'I married him.'

Spyros doubled up with soundless laughter and Lily stared.

'You—? Okay. Well that's a fairly big clue right there.'

'It was a mistake.' Brittany tugged the trowel out of the ground. 'When I make mistakes I make sure they're *big*. I guess you could call it a whirlwind romance.'

'That sounds more like a hurricane than a whirlwind. How long did it last?'

Brittany stood up and brushed dust off her legs. 'Ten days. Spy, if you don't wipe that smile off your face I'm going to kick you into this trench and cover your corpse with a thick layer of dirt and shards of pottery.'

'You mean ten *years*,' Lily said and Brittany shook her head.

'No. I mean days. We made it through the honeymoon without killing each other.'

Lily felt her mouth drop open and closed it again quickly. 'What happened?'

'I let my emotions get in the way of making sane decisions.' Brittany gave a faint smile. 'I haven't fallen in love since.'

'Because you learned how not to do it. You didn't go and make the same mistake again and again. Give me some tips.'

'I can't. Avoiding emotional entanglement came naturally after I met Zach.'

'Sexy name.'

'Sexy guy.' She shaded her eyes from the sun. 'Sexy rat bastard guy.'

'Another one,' Lily said gloomily. 'But you were young and everyone is allowed to make mistakes when they're young. Not only do I not have that excuse, but I'm a habitual offender. I should be locked up until I'm safe to be rehabilitated. I need to be taken back to the store and reprogrammed.'

'You do not need to be reprogrammed.' Brittany stuffed her trowel into the front of her backpack. 'You're warm, friendly and lovable. That's what guys like about you.'

'That and the fact it takes one glance to know you'd look great naked,' Spy said affably.

Lily turned her back on him. 'Warm, friendly and lovable are great qualities for a puppy, but not so great for a woman. They say a person can change, don't they? Well, I'm going to change.' She scrambled to her feet. 'I am not falling in love again. I'm going to take your advice and have rebound sex.'

'Good plan.' Spy glanced at his watch. 'You get your clothes off, I'll get us a room.'

'Not funny.' Lily glared at him. 'I am going to pick someone I don't know, don't feel anything for and couldn't fall in love with in a million years.'

Brittany looked doubtful. 'Now I'm second-guessing myself. Coming from you it sounds like a recipe for disaster.'

'It's going to be perfect. All I have to do is find a man who doesn't tick a single box on my list and have sex with him. It can't possibly go wrong. I'm going to call it Operation Ice Maiden.'

Nik Zervakis stood with his back to the office, staring at the glittering blue of the sea while his assistant updated him. 'Did he call?'

'Yes, exactly as you predicted. How do you always know these things? I would have lost my nerve days ago with those sums of money involved. You don't even break out in a sweat.'

Nik could have told him the deal wasn't about money, it was about power. 'Did you call the lawyers?'

'They're meeting with the team from Lexos first thing tomorrow. So it's done. Congratulations, boss. The US media have turned the phones red-hot asking for interviews.'

'It's not over until the deal is signed. When that happens I'll put out a statement, but no interviews.' Nik felt some of the tension leave his shoulders. 'Did you make a reservation at The Athena?'

'Yes, but you have the official opening of the new museum wing first.'

Nik swore softly and swung round. 'I'd forgotten. Do you have a briefing document on that?'

His PA paled. 'No, boss. All I know is that the wing has been specially designed to display Minoan antiquities in one place. You were invited to the final meeting of the project team but you were in San Francisco.'

'Am I supposed to give a speech?'

'They're hoping you will agree to say a few words.'

'I can manage a few words, but they'll be unrelated to Minoan antiquities.' Nik loosened his tie. 'Run me through the schedule.'

'Vassilis will have the car here at six-fifteen, which should allow you time to go back to the villa and change. You're picking up Christina on the way and your table is booked for nine p.m.'

'Why not pick her up after I've changed?'

'That would have taken time you don't have.'

Nik couldn't argue with that. The demands of his schedule had seen off three assistants in the last six months. 'There was something else?'

The man shifted uncomfortably. 'Your father called. Several times. He said you weren't picking up your phone and asked me to relay a message.'

Nik flicked open the button at the neck of his shirt. 'Which was?'

'He wants to remind you that his wedding is next weekend. He thinks you've forgotten.'

Nik stilled. *He hadn't forgotten.* 'Anything else?'

'He is looking forward to having you at the celebrations. He wanted me to remind you that of all the riches in this world, family is the most valuable.'

Nik, whose sentiments on that topic were a matter of public record, made no comment.

He wondered why anyone would see a fourth wedding as a cause for celebration. To him, it shrieked of someone who hadn't learned his lesson the first three times. 'I will call him from the car.'

'There was one more thing—' The man backed towards the door like someone who knew he was going to need to make a rapid exit. 'He said to make sure you knew that if you don't come, you'll break his heart.'

It was a statement typical of his father. Emotional. Unguarded.

Reflecting that it was that very degree of sentimentality that had made his father the victim of three costly divorces, Niklaus strolled to his desk. 'Consider the message delivered.'

As the door closed he turned back to the window, staring over the midday sparkle of the sea.

Exasperation mingled with frustration and beneath that surface response lay darker, murkier emotions he had no wish to examine. He wasn't given to introspection and he believed that the past was only useful when it informed the future, so finding himself staring down into a swirling mass of long-ignored memories was an unwelcome experience.

Despite the air conditioning, sweat beaded on his forehead and he strode across his office and pulled a bottle of iced water from the fridge.

Why should it bother him that his father was marrying again?

He was no longer an idealistic nine-year-old, shattered by a mother's betrayal and driven by a deep longing for order and security.

He'd learned to make his own security. Emotionally he was an impenetrable fortress. He would never allow a relationship to explode the world from under his feet. He didn't believe in love and he saw marriage as expensive and pointless.

Unfortunately his father, an otherwise intelligent man, didn't share his views. He'd managed to build a successful business from nothing but the fruits of the land around him, but for some reason he had failed to apply that same intellect to his love life.

Nik reflected that if he approached business the way his father approached relationships, he would be broke.

As far as he could see his father performed no risk analysis, gave no consideration to the financial implications of each of his romantic whims and approached each relationship with the romantic optimism entirely inappropriate for a man on his fourth marriage.

Nik's attempts to encourage at least some degree of circumspection had been dismissed as cynical.

To make the situation all the more galling, the last

time they'd met for dinner his father had actually lectured him on his lifestyle as if Nik's lack of divorces suggested a deep character flaw.

Nik closed his eyes briefly and wondered how everything in his business life could run so smoothly while his family was as messy as a dropped pan of spaghetti. The truth was he'd rather endure the twelve labours of Hercules than attend another of his father's weddings.

This time he hadn't met his father's intended bride and he didn't want to. He failed to see what he would bring to the proceedings other than grim disapproval and he didn't want to spoil the day.

Weddings depressed him. All the champagne bubbles in the world couldn't conceal the fact that two people were paying a fortune for the privilege of making a very public mistake.

Lily dumped her bag in the marble hallway and tried to stop her jaw from dropping.

Palatial didn't begin to describe it. Situated on the headland overlooking the sparkling blue of the sea, Villa Harmonia epitomised calm, high-end luxury.

Wondering where the rest of the team were, she wandered out onto the terrace.

Tiny paths wound down through the tumbling gardens to a private cove with a jetty where a platform gave direct swimming access to the sea.

'I've died and gone to heaven.' Disturbed from her trance by the insistent buzz of her phone, she dug it out of her pocket. Her simple uniform was uncomfortably tight, courtesy of all the delicious thyme honey and Greek yoghurt she'd consumed since arriving in

Crete. Her phone call turned out to be the owner of the cleaning company, who told her that the rest of the team had been involved in an accident and wouldn't make it.

'Oh no, are they hurt?' On hearing that no one was in hospital but that the car was totalled, Lily realised she was going to be on her own with this job. 'So if it normally takes four of us four hours, how is one person going to manage?'

'Concentrate on the living areas and the master suite. Pay particular attention to the bathroom.'

Resigned to doing the best she could by herself, Lily set to work. Choosing Mozart from her soundtrack, she pushed in her earbuds and sang her way through *The Magic Flute* while she brushed and mopped the spacious living area.

Whoever lived here clearly didn't have children, she thought as she plumped cushions on deep white sofas and polished glass tables. Everything was sophisticated and understated.

Realising that dreaming would get her fired, Lily hummed her way up the curving staircase to the master bedroom and stopped dead.

The tiny, airless apartment she shared with Brittany had a single bed so narrow she'd twice fallen out of it in her sleep. *This* bed, by contrast, was large enough to sleep a family of six comfortably. It was positioned to take advantage of the incredible view across the bay and Lily stood, drooling with envy, imagining how it must feel to sleep in a bed this size. How many times could you roll over before finding yourself on the floor? If it were hers, she'd spread out like a starfish.

Glancing quickly over her shoulder to check there

was no sign of the security team, she unclipped her phone from her pocket and took a photo of the bed and the view.

One day, she texted Brittany, I'm going to have sex in a bed like this.

Brittany texted back, I don't care about the bed, just give me the man who owns it.

With a last wistful look at the room, Lily tucked her phone carefully into her bag and strolled into the bathroom. A large tub was positioned next to a wall of glass, offering the owner an uninterrupted view of the ocean. The only way to clean something so large was to climb inside it, so she did that, extra careful not to slip.

When it was gleaming, she turned her attention to the large walk-in shower. There was a sophisticated control panel on the wall and she looked at it doubtfully. Remembering her disastrous experience with the photocopier and the coffee machine, she was reluctant to touch anything, but what choice was there?

Lifting her hand, she pressed a button cautiously and gasped as a powerful jet of freezing water hit her from the opposite wall.

Breathless, she slammed her hand on another button to try and stop the flow but that turned on a different jet and she was blasted with water until her hair and clothes were plastered to her body and she couldn't see. She thumped the wall blindly and was alternately scalded and frozen until finally she managed to turn off the jets. Panting, her hair and clothes plastered to her body, she sank to the floor while she tried to get her breath back, shivering and dripping like a puppy caught in the rain.

'I hate, hate, *hate* technology.' She pushed her hair back from her face, took it in her hands and twisted it into a rope, squeezing to remove as much of the water as she could. Then she stood up, but her uniform was dripping and stuck to her skin. If she walked back through the villa like this, she'd drip water everywhere and she didn't have time to clean the place again.

Peeling off her uniform, she was standing in her underwear wringing out the water when she heard a sound from the bedroom.

Assuming it must be one of the security team, she gave a whimper of horror. 'Hello? If there's anyone out there, don't come in for a moment because I'm just—' She stilled as a woman appeared in the doorway.

She was perfectly groomed, her slender body sheathed in a silk dress the colour of coral, her mouth a sheen of blended lipstick and lip-gloss.

Lily had never felt more outclassed in her life.

'Nik?' The woman spoke over her shoulder, her tone icy. 'Your sex drive is, of course, a thing of legend but for the record it's always a good idea to remove the last girlfriend before installing a new one.'

'What are you talking about?' The male voice came from the bedroom, deep, bored and instantly recognisable.

Still shivering from the impact of the cold water, Lily closed her eyes and wondered if any of the buttons on the control panel operated an ejector seat.

Now she knew who owned the villa.

Moments later he appeared in the doorway and Lily peered through soaked lashes and had her second ever look at Nik Zervakis. Confronted by more good looks and sex appeal than she'd ever seen concentrated in one man before, her tummy tumbled and she felt as if she were plunging downhill on a roller coaster.

He stood, legs braced apart, his handsome face blank of expression as if finding a semi-naked woman in his shower wasn't an event worthy of an emotional response. 'Well?'

That was all he was going to say?

Braced for an explosion of volcanic proportions, Lily gulped. 'I can explain—'

'I wish you would.' The woman's voice turned from ice to acid and her expensively shod foot tapped rhythmically on the floor. 'This should be worth hearing.'

'I'm the cleaner—'

'Of course you are. Because "cleaners" always end up naked in the client's shower.' Vibrating with anger, she turned the beam of her angry glare onto the man next to her. 'Nik?'

'Yes?'

Her mouth tightened into a thin, dangerous line. 'Who is she?'

'You heard her. She's the cleaner.'

'*Obviously* she's lying.' The woman bristled. 'No doubt she's been here all day, sleeping off the night before.'

His only response to that was a faint narrowing of those spectacular dark eyes.

Recalling someone warning her on her first day with his company that Nik Zervakis was at his most dangerous when he was quiet, Lily felt her anxiety levels rocket but apparently her concerns weren't shared by his date for the evening, who continued to berate him.

'Do you know the worst thing about this? Not that you have a wandering eye, but that your eye wanders to someone as fat as her.'

'*Excuse* me? I'm not fat.' Lily tried vainly to cover herself with the soaking uniform. 'I'll have you know that my BMI is within normal range.'

But the woman wasn't listening. 'Was she the reason you were late picking me up? I *warned* you, Nik, no games, and yet you do this to me. Well, you gambled and you lost because I don't do second chances, especially this early in a relationship and if you can't be bothered to give an explanation then I can't be bothered to ask for one.' Without giving him the chance to respond, his date stalked out of the room and Lily flinched in time with each furious tap of those skyscraper heels.

She stood in awkward silence, her feelings bruised and her spirits drenched in cold water and guilt. 'She's very upset.'

'Yes.'

'Er—is she coming back?'

'I sincerely hope not.'

Lily wanted to say that he was well rid of her, but decided that protecting her job was more important than honesty. 'I'm *really* sorry—'

'Don't be. It wasn't your fault.'

Knowing that wasn't quite true, she squirmed. 'If I hadn't had an accident, I would have had my clothes on when she walked into the room.'

'An accident? I've never considered my shower to be a place of danger but apparently I was wrong about that.' He eyed the volume of water on the floor and her drenched clothing. 'What happened?'

'Your shower is like the flight deck of a jumbo jet, that's what happened!' Freezing and soaked, Lily couldn't stop her teeth chattering. 'There are no instructions.'

'I don't need instructions.' His gaze slid over her with slow, disturbing thoroughness. 'I'm familiar with the workings of my own shower.'

'Well I'm not! I had no idea which buttons to press.'

'So you thought you'd press all of them? If you ever find yourself on the flight deck of a Boeing 747 I suggest you sit on your hands.'

'It's not f-f-funny. I'm soaking wet and I didn't know you were going to come home early.'

'I apologise.' Irony gleamed in those dark eyes. 'I'm not in the habit of notifying people of my movements in advance. Have you finished cleaning or do you want me to show you which buttons to press?'

Lily summoned as much dignity as she could in the circumstances. 'Your shower is clean. Extra clean, because I wiped myself around it personally.' Anxious to make her exit as fast as possible, she kept her eyes fixed on the door and away from that tall, powerful frame. 'Are you sure she isn't coming back?'

'No.'

Lily paused, torn between relief and guilt. 'I've ruined another relationship.'

'Another?' Dark eyebrows lifted. 'It's a common occurrence?'

'You have no idea. Look—if it would help I could call my employer and ask her to vouch for me.' Her voice tailed off as she realised that would mean confessing she'd been caught half naked in the shower.

He gave a faint smile. 'Unless you have a very liberal-minded employer, you might want to rethink that idea.'

'There must be some way I can fix this. I've ruined your date, although for the record I don't think she's a very kind person so she might not be good for you in the long term and with a body that bony she won't be very cuddly for your children.' She caught his eye. 'Are you laughing at me?'

'No, but the ability to cuddle children isn't high on my list of necessary female attributes.' He flung his jacket carelessly over the back of a sofa that was bigger than her bed at home.

She stared in fascination, wondering if he cared at all that his date had walked out. 'As a matter of interest, why didn't you defend yourself?'

'Why would I defend myself?'

'You could have explained yourself and then she would have forgiven you.'

'I never explain myself. And anyway—' he shrugged '—you had already given her an explanation.'

'I don't think she saw me as a credible witness. It might have sounded better coming from you.'

He stood, legs spread, his powerful shoulders blocking the doorway. 'I assume you told her the truth? You're the cleaner?'

'Of course I told her the truth.'

'Then there was nothing I could have added to your story.'

In his position she would have died of humiliation, but he seemed supremely indifferent to the fact he'd been publicly dumped. 'You don't seem upset.'

'Why would I be upset?'

'Because most people are upset when a relationship ends.'

He smiled. 'I'm not one of those.'

Lily felt a flash of envy. 'You're not even a teeny tiny bit sad?'

'I'm not familiar with that unit of measurement but no, I'm not even a "teeny tiny" bit sad. To be sad I'd have to care and I don't care.'

To be sad I'd have to care and I don't care.

Brilliant, Lily thought. *Why* couldn't she have said that to Professor Ashurst when he'd given her that fake sympathy about having hurt her? She needed to memorise it for next time. 'Excuse me a moment.' Leaving a dripping trail behind her, she shot past him, scrabbled in her bag and pulled out a notebook.

'What are you doing?'

'I'm writing down what you said. Whenever I'm dumped I never know the right thing to say, but next time it happens I'm going to say *exactly* those words in exactly that tone instead of producing enough tears to power a water feature at Versailles.' She scribbled, dripping water onto her notebook and smearing the ink.

'Being "dumped" is something that happens to you often?'

'Often enough. I fall in love, I get my heart broken, it's a cycle I'm working on breaking.' She wished she hadn't said anything. Although she was fairly open with people, she drew the line at making public announcements about not being easy to love.

That was her secret.

'How many times have you fallen in love?'

'So far?' She shook the pen with frustration as the ink stalled on the damp page, 'Three times.'

'*Cristo*, that's unbelievable.'

'Thanks for not making me feel better. I bet you've never been unlucky in love, have you?'

'I've never been in love at all.'

Lily digested that. 'You've never met the right person.'

'I don't believe in love.'

'You—' She rocked back on her heels, her attention caught. 'So what do you believe in?'

'Money, influence and power.' He shrugged. 'Tangible, measurable goals.'

'You can measure power and influence? Don't tell me—you stamp your foot and it registers on the Richter scale.'

He loosened his tie. 'You'd be surprised.'

'I'm already surprised. Gosh, you are *so* cool. You are my new role model.' Finally she managed to coax ink from the pen. 'It is never too late to change. From now on I'm all about tangible, measurable goals, too. As a matter of interest, what is your goal in relationships?'

'Orgasm.' He gave a slow smile and she felt herself turn scarlet.

'Right. Well, that serves me right for asking a stupid question. That's definitely a measurable goal. You're obviously able to be cold and ruthlessly detached when it comes to relationships. I'm aiming for that. I've dripped all over your floor. Be careful not to slip.'

He was leaning against the wall, watching her with amusement. 'This is what you look like when you're being cold and ruthlessly detached?'

'I haven't actually started yet, but the moment my

radar warns me I might be in danger of falling for the wrong type, *bam*—' she punched the air with her fist '—I'm going to turn on my freezing side. From now on I have armour around my heart. Kevlar.' She gave him a friendly smile. 'You think I'm crazy, right? All this is natural to you. But it isn't to me. This is the first stage of my personality transplant. I'd love to do the whole thing under anaesthetic and wake up all new and perfect, but that isn't possible so I'm trying to embrace the process.'

A vibrating noise caught her attention and she glanced across the room towards his jacket. When he didn't move, she looked at him expectantly. 'That's your phone.'

He was still watching her, his gaze disturbingly intent. 'Yes.'

'You're not going to answer it?' She scrambled to her feet, still clutching the towel. 'It might be her, asking for your forgiveness.'

'I'm sure it is, which is why I don't intend to answer it.'

Lily absorbed that with admiration. 'This is a perfect example of why I need to be like you and not like me. If that had been my phone, I would have answered it and when whoever was on the end apologised for treating me badly, I would have told him it was fine. I would have forgiven them.'

'You're right,' he said. 'You do need help. What's your name?'

She shifted, her wet feet sticking to the floor. 'Lily. Like the flower.'

'You look familiar. Have we met before?'

SARAH MORGAN   295

Lily felt the colour pour into her cheeks. 'I've been working as an intern at your company two days a week for the past couple of months. I'm second assistant to your personal assistant.' *I'm the one who broke the photocopier and the coffee machine.*

Dark eyebrows rose. 'We've met?'

'No. I've only seen you once in person. I don't count the time I was hiding in the bathroom.'

'You hid in the bathroom?'

'You were on a firing spree. I didn't want to be noticed.'

'So you work for me two days a week, and on the other three days you're working as a cleaner?'

'No, I only do that job in the evenings. The other three days I'm doing fieldwork up at Aptera for the summer. But that's almost finished. I've reached a crossroads in my life and I've no idea which direction to take.'

'Fieldwork?' That sparked his interest. 'You're an archaeologist?'

'Yes, I'm part of a project funded by the university but that part doesn't pay off my massive college loans so I have other jobs.'

'How much do you know about Minoan antiquities?'

Lily blinked. 'Probably more than is healthy for a woman of twenty-four.'

'Good. Get back into the bathroom and dry yourself off while I find you a dress. Tonight I have to open the new wing of the museum. You're coming with me.'

'Me? Don't you have a date?'

'I had a date,' he said smoothly. 'As you're partially responsible for the fact she's no longer here, you're coming in her place.'

'But—' She licked her lips. 'I'm supposed to be cleaning your villa.'

His gaze slid from her face to the wash of water covering the bathroom floor. 'I'd say you've done a pretty thorough job. By the time we get home, the flood will have spread down the stairs and across the living areas, so it will clean itself.'

Lily gave a gurgle of laughter. She wondered if any of his employees realised he had a sense of humour. 'You're not going to fire me?'

'You should have more confidence in yourself. If you have knowledge of Minoan artefacts then I still have a use for you and I never fire people who are useful.' He reached for the towel and tugged it off, leaving her clad only in her soaking wet underwear.

'What are you doing?' She gave a squeak of embarrassment and snatched at the towel but he held it out of reach.

'Stop wriggling. I can't be the first man to see you half naked.'

'Usually I'm in a relationship when a man sees me naked. And being stared at is very unnerving, especially when you've been called fat by someone who looks like a toast rack—' Lily broke off as he turned and strolled away from her. She didn't know whether to be relieved or affronted. 'If you want to know my size you could ask me!'

He reached for his phone and dialled. While he waited for the person on the other end to answer, he scanned her body and gave her a slow, knowing smile. 'I don't need to ask, *theé mou*,' he said softly. 'I already know your size.'

CHAPTER TWO

NIK LOUNGED IN his seat while the car negotiated heavy evening traffic. Beside him Lily was wriggling like a fish dropped onto the deck of a boat.

'Mr Zervakis? This dress is far more revealing than anything I would normally wear. And I've had a horrible thought.' Her voice was breathy and distracting and Nik turned his head to look at her, trying to remind himself that girls with sweet smiles who were self-confessed members of Loveaholics Anonymous were definitely off his list.

'Call me Nik.'

'I can't call you Nik. It would feel wrong while I'm working in your company. You pay my salary.'

'I pay you? I thought you said you were an intern.'

'I am. You pay your interns far more than most companies, but that's a different conversation. I'm still having that horrible thought by the way.'

Nik dragged his eyes from her mouth and tried to wipe his brain of X-rated thoughts. 'What horrible thought is that?'

'The one where your girlfriend finds out you took me as your date tonight.'

'She will find out.'

'And that doesn't bother you?'

'Why would it?'

'Isn't it obvious? Because she didn't believe I was the cleaner. She thought you and I—well...' she turned scarlet '...if she finds out we were together tonight then it will look as if she was right and we were lying, even though if people used their brains they could work out that if she's your type then I couldn't possibly be.'

Nik tried to decipher that tumbled speech. 'You're concerned she will think we're having sex? Why is that a horrible thought? You find me unattractive?'

'That's a ridiculous question.' Lily's eyes flew to his and then away again. 'Sorry, but that's like asking a woman if she likes chocolate.'

'There are women who don't like chocolate.'

'They're lying. They might not eat it, but that doesn't mean they don't like it.'

'So I'm chocolate?' Nik tried to remember the last time he'd been this entertained by anyone.

'If you're asking if I think you're very tempting and definitely bad for me, the answer is yes. But apart from the fact we're totally unsuited, I wouldn't be able to relax enough to have sex with you.'

Nik, who had never had trouble helping a woman relax, rose to the challenge. 'I'm happy to—'

'No.' She gave him a stern look. 'I know you're competitive, but forget it. I saw that photo of you in the swimming pool. No way could I ever be naked in front of a man with a body like yours. I'd have to suck everything in and make sure you only saw my good side. The stress would kill any passion.'

'I've already seen you in your underwear.'

'Don't remind me.'

Nik caught his driver's amused gaze in the mirror and gave him a steady stare. Vassilis had been with him for over a decade and had a tendency to voice his opinions on Nik's love life. It was obvious he thoroughly approved of Lily.

'It's true that if you turn up as my guest tonight there will be people who assume we are having sex.' Nik returned his attention to the conversation. 'I can't claim to be intimately acquainted with the guest list, but I'm assuming a few of the people there will be your colleagues. Does that bother you?'

'No. It will send a message that I'm not brokenhearted, which is good for my pride. In fact the timing is perfect. Just this morning I embarked on a new project. Operation Ice Maiden. You're probably wondering what that is.'

Nik opened his mouth to comment but she carried on without pausing.

'I am going to have sex with no emotion. That's right.' She nodded at him. 'You heard me correctly. Rebound sex. I am going to climb into bed with some guy and I'm not going to feel a thing.'

Hearing a sound from the front of the car, Nik pressed a button and closed the screen between him and Vassilis, giving them privacy.

'Do you have anyone in mind for—er—Operation Ice Maiden?'

'Not yet, but if they happen to think it's you that's fine. You'd look good on my romantic résumé.'

Nik leaned his head back against the seat and started to laugh. 'You, Lily, are priceless.'

'That doesn't sound like a compliment.' She adjusted the neckline of her dress and her breasts almost escaped in the process. 'You're basically saying I'm not worth anything.'

Dragging his gaze from her body, Nik decided this was the most entertaining evening he'd had in a long time.

'There are photographers.' As they pulled up outside the museum Lily slunk lower in her seat and Nik closed his hand around her wrist and hauled her upright again.

'You look stunning. If you don't want them all surmising that we climbed out of bed to come here then you need to stop looking guilty.'

'I saw several TV cameras.'

'The opening of a new wing of the museum is news.'

'The neckline of this dress might also be news.' She tugged at it. 'My breasts are too big for this plunging style. Can I borrow your jacket?'

'Your breasts deserve a dress like that and no, you may not borrow my jacket.' His voice was a deep, masculine purr and she felt the sizzle of sexual attraction right through her body.

'Are you flirting with me?' He was completely different from the safe, friendly men who formed part of her social circle. There was a brutal strength to him, a confidence and assurance that suggested he'd never met a man he hadn't been able to beat in a fight, whether in the bar or the boardroom.

Her question appeared to amuse him. 'You're my date. Flirting is mandatory.'

'It unsettles me and I'm already unsettled at the thought of tonight.'

'Because you're with me?'

No way was she confessing how being with him really made her feel. 'No, because the opening of this new museum wing is a really momentous occasion.'

'You and I have a very different idea of what constitutes a momentous occasion, Lily.' There was laughter in his eyes. 'Never before has my ego been so effectively crushed.'

'Your ego is armour plated, like your feelings.'

'It's true that my feelings of self-worth are not dependent on the opinion of others.'

'Because you think you're right and everyone else is wrong. I wish I were more like you. What if the reporters ask who I am? What do I say? I'm a fake.'

'You're the archaeologist. I'm the fake. And you say whatever you want to say. Or say nothing. Your decision. You're the one in charge of your mouth.'

'You have no idea how much I wish that was true.'

'Tell me why you're excited about tonight.'

'You mean apart from the fact I get to dress up? The new wing houses the biggest collection of Minoan antiquities anywhere in Greece. It has a high percentage of provenanced material, which means archaeologists will be able to restudy material from old excavations. It's exciting. And I love the dress by the way, even though I'll never have any reason to wear it again.'

'Chipped pots excite you?'

She winced. 'Don't say that on camera. The collection will play an active role in research and in university teaching as well as offering a unique insight for the general public.'

As the car pulled up outside the museum one of Nik's security team opened the door and Lily emerged to what felt like a million camera flashes.

'Unreal,' she muttered. 'Now I know why celebrities wear sunglasses.'

'Mr Zervakis—' Photographers and reporters gathered as close as they could. 'Do you have a statement about the new wing?'

Nik paused and spoke directly to the camera, relaxed and at ease as he repeated Lily's words without a single error.

She stared at him. 'You must have an incredible short-term memory.'

A reporter stepped forward. 'Who's your guest tonight, Nik?'

Nik turned towards her and she realised he was leaving it up to her to decide whether to give them a name or not.

'I'm a friend,' she muttered and Nik smiled, took her hand and led her up the steps to the welcome committee at the top.

The first person she spotted was David Ashurst and she stopped in dismay. In answer to Nik's questioning look, she shook her head quickly, misery and panic creating a sick cocktail inside her. 'I'm fine. I saw someone I didn't expect to see, that's all. I didn't think he'd have the nerve to show up.'

'That's him?' His gaze travelled from her face to the man looking awkward at the top of the steps. 'He is the reason you're hoping for a personality transplant?'

'His name is Professor Ashurst. He has a *wife*,' she

muttered in an undertone. 'Can you believe that? I actually cried over that loser. Do I have time to get my notebook out of my bag? I can't remember what I wrote down.'

'I'll tell you what to say.' He leaned closer and whispered something in her ear that made her gasp.

'I can't say that.'

'No? Then how's this for an alternative?' Sliding his arm round her waist, he pressed his hand to the base of her spine and flattened her against him. She looked up at him, hypnotised by those spectacular dark eyes and the raw sexuality in his gaze. Before she could ask what he was doing he lowered his head and kissed her.

Pleasure screamed through her, sensation scorching her skin and stoking a pool of heat low in her belly. She'd been kissed before, but never like this. Nik used his mouth with slow, sensual expertise and she felt a rush of exquisite excitement burn through her body. Her nerve endings tingled, her tummy flipped like a gymnast in a competition, and Lily was possessed by a deep, dark craving that was entirely new to her. Oblivious to their audience, she pushed against his hard, powerful frame and felt his arms tighten around her in a gesture that was unmistakably possessive. It was a taste rather than a feast, but it left her starving for more so that when he slowly lifted his head she swayed towards him dizzily, trying to balance herself.

'Wh-why did you do that?'

He dragged his thumb slowly across her lower lip and released her. 'Because you didn't know what to say and sometimes actions speak louder than words.'

'You're an amazing kisser.' Lily blinked as a flashbulb went off in her face. 'Now there's *no* chance your girlfriend will believe I'm the cleaner.'

'No chance.' His gaze lingered on her mouth. 'And she isn't my girlfriend.'

Her head spun and her legs felt shaky. She was aware of the women staring at her enviously and David gaping at her, shell-shocked.

As she floated up the last few steps to the top she smiled at him, feeling strong for the first time in days. 'Hi, Professor Ass—Ashurst.' She told herself it was the heat that was making her dizzy and disorientated, not the kiss. 'Have a safe flight home tomorrow. I'm sure your family has missed you.'

There was no opportunity for him to respond because the curator of the museum stepped forward to welcome them, shaking Nik's hand and virtually prostrating himself in gratitude.

'Mr Zervakis—your generosity—this wing is the most exciting moment of my career—' the normally articulate man was stammering. 'I know your schedule is demanding but we'd be honoured if you'd meet the team and then take a quick tour.'

Lily kept a discreet distance but Nik took her hand and clamped her next to his side, a gesture that earned her a quizzical look from Brittany, who was looking sleek and pretty in a short blue dress that showed off her long legs. She was standing next to Spy, whose eyes were glued to Lily's cleavage, confirming all her worst fears about the suitability of the dress.

The whole situation felt surreal.

One moment she'd been half naked and shivering on the bathroom floor, the next she'd been whisked into an elegant bedroom by a team of four people who had proceeded to style her hair, do her make-up and generally make her fit to be seen on the arm of Nik Zervakis.

Three dresses had magically appeared and Nik had strolled into the room in mid phone call, gestured to one of them and then left without even pausing in his conversation.

It had been on the tip of Lily's tongue to select a different dress on principle. Then she'd reasoned that not only had he provided the dress, thus allowing her to turn up at the museum opening in the first place, but that he'd picked the dress she would have chosen herself.

All the same, she felt self-conscious as her friends and colleagues working on the project at Aptera stood together while she was treated like a VIP.

As the curator led them towards the first display Lily forgot to be self-conscious and examined the pot.

'This is early Minoan.'

Nik stared at it with a neutral expression. 'You know that because it's more cracked than the others?'

'No. Because their ceramics were characterised by linear patterns. Look—' She took his arm and drew him closer to the glass. 'Spirals, crosses, triangles, curved lines—' She talked to him about each one and he listened carefully before strolling further along the glass display cabinet.

'This one has a bird.'

'Naturalistic designs were characteristic of the Middle Minoan period. The sequencing of ceramic styles has helped archaeologists define the three phases of Minoan culture.'

He stared down in her eyes. 'Fascinating.'

Her heart bumped hard against her chest and as the curator moved away to answer questions from the press she stepped closer to him. 'You're not really fascinated, are you?'

'I am.' His eyes dropped to her mouth with blatant interest. 'But I think it might be because you're the one saying it. I love the way you get excited about things that put other people to sleep, and your mouth looks cute when you say "Minoan". It makes you pout.'

She tried not to laugh. 'You're impossible. To you it's an old pot, but it can have tremendous significance. Ceramics help archaeologists establish settlement and trading patterns. We can reconstruct human activity based on the distribution of pottery. It gives us an idea of population size and social complexity. Why are you donating so much money to the museum if it isn't an interest of yours?'

'Because I'm interested in preserving Greek culture. I donate the money. It's up to them to decide how to use it. I don't micromanage and gifts don't come with strings.'

'Why didn't you insist that it was called "The Zervakis Wing" or something? Most benefactors want their name in the title.'

'It's about preserving history, not about advertising my name.' His eyes gleamed. 'And ZervaCo is a modern, forward-thinking company at the cutting edge of technology development. I don't want the name associated with a museum.'

'You're joking.'

'Yes, I'm joking.' His smile faded as Spy and Brittany joined them.

'They're good friends of mine,' Lily said quickly, 'so you can switch off the full-wattage intimidation.'

'If you're sure.' He introduced himself to both of them and chatted easily with Spy while Brittany pulled Lily to one side.

'I don't even know where to start with my questions.'

'Probably just as well because I wouldn't know where to start with my answers.'

'I'm guessing he's the owner of Villa You-Have-to-be-Kidding-Me.'

'He is.'

'I'm not going to ask,' Brittany muttered and then grinned. 'Oh hell, yes I am. I'm asking. What happened? He found you in the cellar fighting off the ugly sisters and decided to bring you to the ball?'

'Close. He found me on the floor of his bathroom where I'd been attacked and left for dead by his power shower. After I broke up his relationship, he needed a replacement and I was the only person around.'

Brittany started to laugh. 'You were left for dead by his power shower?'

'You said you wouldn't ask.'

'These things only ever happen to you, Lily.'

'I am aware of that. I am really not good with technology.'

'Maybe not, but you know how to pick your rebound guy. He is spectacular. And you look stunning.' Brittany's curious gaze slid over her from head to foot. 'It's a step up from dusty shorts and hiking boots.'

Lily frowned. 'He isn't my rebound guy.'

'Why not? He is smoking hot. And there's something about him.' Her friend narrowed her eyes as she scanned

Nik's broad shoulders and powerful frame. 'A suggestion of the uncivilised under the civilised, if you know
what I mean.' Brittany put her hand on her arm and her
voice was suddenly serious. 'Be careful.'

'Why would I need to be careful? I'm never setting
foot in his shower again, if that's what you mean.'

'It isn't what I mean. That man is not tame.'

'He's surprisingly amusing company.'

'That makes him even more dangerous. He's a tiger,
not a pussycat and he hasn't taken his eyes off you for
five seconds. I don't want to see you hurt again.'

'I have never been in less danger of being hurt. He
isn't my type.'

Brittany looked at her. 'Nik Zervakis is the man
equivalent of Blood Type O. He is everyone's type.'

'Not mine.'

'He kissed you,' Brittany said dryly, 'so I'm guessing he might have a different opinion on that.'

'He kissed me because I didn't know what to say to
David. I was in an awkward position and he helped me
out. He did that for me.'

'Lily, a guy like him does things for himself. Don't
make a mistake about that. He does what he wants,
with whoever he wants to do it, at a time that suits him.'

'I know. Don't worry about me.' Smiling at Brittany,
she moved back to Nik. 'Looks like the party is breaking up. Thanks for a fun evening. I'll post you the dress
back and any time you need your shower cleaned let
me know. I owe you.'

He stared down at her for a long moment, ignoring
everyone around them. 'Have dinner with me. I have a
reservation at The Athena at nine.'

She'd heard of The Athena. Who hadn't? It was one of the most celebrated restaurants in the whole of Greece. Eating there was a once-in-a-lifetime experience for most people and a never-in-this-lifetime experience for her.

Those incredible dark eyes held hers and Brittany's voice flitted into her head.

He's a tiger, not a pussycat.

From the way he was looking at her mouth, she wondered if he intended her to be the guest or the meal.

'That's a joke, right?' She gave a half-smile and looked away briefly, awkward, out of her depth. When she looked back at him she was still the only one smiling.

'I never joke about food.'

Something curled low in her stomach. 'Nik…' she spoke softly '…this has been amazing. Really out of this world and something to tell my kids one day, but you're a gazillionaire and I'm a—a—'

'Sexy woman who looks great in that dress.'

There was something about him that made her feel as if she were floating two feet above the ground.

'I was going to say I'm a dusty archaeologist who can't even figure out how to use your power shower.'

'I'll teach you. Have dinner with me, Lily.' His soft command made her wonder if anyone had ever said no to him.

Thrown by the look in his eyes and the almost unbearable sexual tension, she was tempted. Then she remembered her rule about never dating anyone who didn't fit her basic criteria. 'I can't. But I'll never forget this evening. Thank you.' Because she was afraid she'd change her mind, she turned and walked quickly towards the exit.

What a crazy day it had been.

Part of her was longing to look back, to see if he was watching her.

Of course he wouldn't be watching her. Look at how quickly he'd replaced Christina. Within two minutes of her refusal, Nik Zervakis would be inviting someone else to dinner.

David stood in the doorway, blocking her exit. 'What are you doing with him?'

'None of your business.'

His jaw tightened. 'Did you kiss him to make me jealous or to help you get over me?'

'I kissed him because he's a hot guy, and I was over you the moment I found out you were married.' Realising it was true, Lily felt a rush of relief but that relief was tempered by the knowledge that her system for evaluating prospective life partners was seriously flawed.

'I know you love me.'

'You're wrong. And if you really knew me, you'd know I'm incapable of loving a man who is married to another woman.' Her voice and hands were shaking. 'You have a wife. A family.'

'I'll work something out.'

'Did you really just say that to me?' Lily stared at him, appalled. 'A family is *not* disposable. You don't come and go as it suits you, nor do you "work something out". You stick by them through thick and thin.' Disgusted and disillusioned, she tried to step past him but he caught her arm.

'You don't understand. Things are tough right now.'

'I don't care.' She dug her fingers into clammy palms. Knowing that her response was deeply personal, she looked away. 'A real man doesn't walk away when things get tough.'

'You're forgetting how good it was between us.'

'And you're forgetting the promises you made.' She dragged her arm out of his grip. 'Go back to your wife.'

He glanced over her shoulder towards Nik. 'I never thought you were the sort to be turned on by money, but obviously I was wrong. I hope you know what you're doing because all that man will ever give you is one night. A man like him is only interested in sex.'

'What did you say?' Lily stared at him and then turned her head to look at Nik. The sick feeling in her stomach eased and her spirits lifted. 'You're right. Thank you so much.'

'For making you realise he's wrong for you?'

'For making me realise he's perfect. Now stop looking down the front of my dress and go home to your wife and kids.' With that, she stalked past him and spotted the reporter who had asked her identity on the way in. 'Lily,' she said clearly. 'Lily Rose. That's my name. And yes, Rose is my second name.'

Then she turned and stalked back into the museum, straight up to Nik, who was deep in conversation with two important-looking men in suits.

All talk ceased as Lily walked up to him, her heels making the same rhythmic tapping sound that Christina's had earlier in the evening. She decided heels were her new favourite thing for illustrating mood. 'What time is that restaurant reservation?'

He didn't miss a beat. 'Nine o'clock.'

'Then we should leave, because we don't want to be late.' She stood on tiptoe and planted a kiss firmly on his mouth. 'And just so that you know, whatever you're planning on doing with the dress, I'm keeping the shoes.'

CHAPTER THREE

THE ATHENA WAS situated on the edge of town, on a hill overlooking Souda Bay with the White Mountains dominating the horizon behind them.

Still on a high after her confrontation with David, Lily sailed into the restaurant feeling like royalty. 'You have no idea how good it felt to tell David to go home to his wife. I felt like punching the air. You see what a few hours in your company has done for me? I'm already transformed. Your icy control and lack of emotional engagement is contagious.'

Nik guided her to his favourite table, tucked away behind a discreet screen of vines. 'You certainly showed the guy what he was missing.'

Lily frowned. 'I didn't want to show him what he was missing. I wanted him to learn a lesson and never lie or cheat again. I wanted him to think of his poor wife. Marriage should be for ever. No cheating. Mess around as much as you like before if that's what you want, but once you've made that commitment, that's it. Don't you agree?'

'Definitely. Which is why I've never made that commitment,' he said dryly. 'I'm still at the "messing around" stage and I expect to stay firmly trapped in that stage for the rest of my life.'

'You don't want a family? We're very different. It's brilliant.' She smiled at him and his eyes narrowed.

'Why is that brilliant?'

'Because you're completely and utterly wrong for me. We don't want the same things.'

'I'm relieved to hear it.' He leaned back in his chair. 'I hardly dare ask what you want.'

She hesitated. 'Someone like you will think I'm a ridiculous romantic.'

'Tell me.'

She dragged her gaze from his and looked over the tumbling bougainvillea to the sea beyond. *Was she a ridiculous romantic?*

Was she setting herself unachievable goals?

Seduced by the warmth of his gaze and the beauty of the spectacular sunset, she told the truth. 'I want the whole fairy tale.'

'Which fairy tale? The one where the stepmother poisons the apple or the one where the prince has to deal with a heroine with narcolepsy?'

She laughed. 'The happy-ending part. I want to fall in love, settle down and have lots of babies.' Enjoying herself, she looked him in the eye. 'Am I freaking you out yet?'

'That depends. Are you expecting to do any of that with me?'

'No! Of course not.'

'Then you're not freaking me out.'

'I start every relationship in the genuine belief it might go somewhere.'

'I presume you mean somewhere other than bed?'

'I do. I have never been interested in sex for the sake of sex.'

Nik looked amused. 'That's the only sort of sex I'm interested in.'

She sat back in her chair and looked at him. 'I've never had sex with a man I wasn't in love with. I fall in love, then I have sex. I think sex cements my emotional connection to someone.' She sneaked another look at him. 'You don't have that problem, do you?'

'I'm not looking for an emotional connection, if that's what you're asking.'

'I want to be more like you. I decided this morning I'm going to have cold, emotionless rebound sex. I'm switching everything off. It's going to be wham, bam, thank you, man.'

The corners of his mouth flickered. 'Do you have anyone in mind for this project?'

She sensed this wasn't the moment to confess he was right at the top of her list. 'I'm going to pick a guy I couldn't possibly fall in love with. Then I'll be safe. It will be like—' she struggled to find the right description '—emotional contraception. I'll be taking precautions. Wearing a giant condom over my feelings. Protecting myself. I bet you do that all the time.'

'If you're asking if I've ever pulled a giant condom over my feelings, the answer is no.'

'You're laughing at me, but if you'd been hurt as many times as I have you wouldn't be laughing. So if emotions don't play a part in your relationships, what exactly is sex to you?'

'Recreation.' He took a menu from the waiter and

she felt a rush of mortification. As soon as he walked away, she gave a groan.

'How long had he been standing there?'

'Long enough to know you're planning on having cold, unemotional rebound sex and that you're thinking of wearing a giant condom over your feelings. I think that was the point he decided it was time to take our order.'

She covered her face with her hands. 'We need to leave. I'm sure the food here is delicious, but we need to eat somewhere different or I need to take my plate under the table.'

'You're doing it again. Letting emotions govern your actions.'

'But he *heard* me. Aren't you embarrassed?'

'Why would I be embarrassed?'

'Aren't you worried about what he might think of you?'

'Why would I care what he thinks? I don't know him. His role is to serve our food and make sure we enjoy ourselves sufficiently to want to come back. His opinion on anything else is irrelevant. Carry on with what you were saying. It was fascinating. Dining with you is like learning about an alien species. You were telling me you're going to pick a guy you can't fall in love with and use him for sex.'

'And you were telling me sex is recreation—like football?'

'No, because football is a group activity. I'm possessive, so for me it's strictly one on one.'

Her heart gave a little flip. 'That sounds like a type of commitment.'

'I'm one hundred per cent committed for the time a woman is in my bed. She is the sole focus of my attention.'

Her stomach uncurled with a slow, dangerous heat. 'But that might only be for a night?'

He simply smiled and she leaned back with a shocked laugh.

'You are so *bad*. And honest. I love that.'

'As long as you don't love *me*, we don't have a problem.'

'I could never love you. You are so wrong for me.'

'I think we should drink to that.' He raised a hand and moments later champagne appeared on the table.

'I can't believe you live like this. A driver, bottles of champagne—' She lifted the glass, watching the bubbles. 'Your villa is bigger than quite a few Greek islands and there is only one of you.'

'I like space and light and property is always a good investment.' He handed the menu back to the waiter. 'Is there any food you don't eat?'

'I eat everything.' She paused while he spoke to the waiter in Greek. 'Are you seriously ordering for me?'

'The menu is in Greek and you were talking about sex so I was aiming to keep the interaction as brief as possible in order to prevent you from feeling the need to dine under the table.'

'In that case I'll forgive you.' She waited until the waiter had walked away with their order. 'So if property is an investment that means you'd *sell* your home?'

'I have four homes.'

Her jaw dropped. 'Four? Why does one person need four homes? One for every season or something?'

'I have offices in New York, San Francisco and London and I don't like staying in hotels.'

'So you buy a house. That is the rich man's way of solving a problem. Which one do you think of as home?' Seeing the puzzled look on his face, she elaborated. 'Where do your family live? Do you have family? Are your parents alive?'

'They are.'

'Happily married?'

'Miserably divorced. In my father's case three times so far, but he's always in competition with himself so I'm expecting a fourth as soon as the wedding is out of the way.'

'And your mother?' She saw a faint shift in his expression.

'My mother is American. She lives in Boston with her third husband who is a divorce lawyer.'

'So do you think of yourself as Greek American or American Greek?'

He gave a careless lift of his broad shoulders. 'Whichever serves my purpose at the time.'

'Wow. So you have this big, crazy family.' Lily felt a flash of envy. 'That must be wonderful.'

'Why?'

'You don't think it's wonderful? I guess we never appreciate something when we have it.' She said it lightly but felt his dark gaze fix on her across the table.

'Are you going to cry?'

'No, of course not.'

'Good. Because tears are the one form of emotional expression I don't tolerate.'

She stole an olive from the bowl on the table. 'What if someone is upset?'

'Then they need to walk away from me until they've sorted themselves out, or be prepared for me to walk away. I never allow myself to be manipulated and ninety-nine per cent of tears are manipulation.'

'What about the one per cent which are an expression of genuine emotion?'

'I've never encountered that rare beast, so I'm willing to play the odds.'

'If that's your experience, you must have met some awful women in your time. I don't believe you'd be that unsympathetic.'

'Believe it.' He leaned back as the waiter delivered a selection of dishes. 'These are Cretan specialities. Try them.' He spooned beans in a rich tomato sauce onto her plate and added local goat's cheese.

She nibbled the beans and moaned with pleasure. 'These are delicious. I still can't believe you ordered for me. Do you want to feed me, too? Because I could lie back and let you drop grapes into my mouth if that would be fun. Or you could cover my naked body with whipped cream. Is that the sort of stuff you do in bed?'

There was a dangerous glitter in his eyes. 'You don't want to know the sort of "stuff" I do in bed, Lily. You're far too innocent.'

She remembered what Brittany had said about him not being tame. 'I'm not innocent. I have big eyes and that gives people a false impression of me.'

'You remind me of a kitten that's been abandoned by the side of the road.'

'You've got me totally wrong. I'd say I'm more of a

panther.' She clawed the air and growled. 'A little bit predatory. A little bit dangerous.'

He gave her a long steady look and she blushed and lowered her hand.

'All right, maybe not a *panther* exactly but not a kitten either.' She thought about what lay in her past. 'I'll have you know I'm pretty tough. Tell me more about your family. So you have a father and a few stepmothers. How about siblings?'

'I have one half-sister who is two.'

Lily softened. 'I love that age. They're so busy and into everything. Is she adorable?'

'I've no idea. I've never met her.'

'You've—' She stared at him, shocked. 'You mean it's been a while since you've seen her.'

'No. I mean I've never seen her.' He lifted his champagne. 'Her mother extracted all the money she could from my father and then left. She lives in Athens and visits when she wants something.'

'Oh, my God, that's *terrible*.' Lily's eyes filled. 'Your poor, poor father.'

He put his glass down slowly. 'Are you crying for my father?'

'No.' Her throat was thickened. 'Maybe. Yes, a little bit.'

'A man you've never met and know nothing about.'

'Maybe I'm the one per cent who cares.' She sniffed and he shook his head in exasperation.

'This is your tough, ruthless streak? How can you be sad for someone you don't know?'

'Because I sympathise with his situation. He doesn't see his little girl and that must be so hard. Family is the most important thing in the world and it is often the least appreciated thing.'

'If you let a single tear fall onto your cheek,' he said softly, 'I'm walking out of here.'

'I don't believe you. You wouldn't be that heartless. I think it's all a big act you put on to stop women slobbering all over you.'

'Do you want to test it?' His tone was cool. 'Because I suggest you wait until the end of the meal. The lamb *kleftiko* is the best anywhere in Greece and they make a house special with honey and pistachio nuts that you wouldn't want to miss.'

'But if you're the one walking out, then I can stay here and eat your portion.' She helped herself to another spoonful of food from the dish closest to her. 'I don't know why you're so freaked out by tears. It's not as if I was expecting you to hug me. I've taught myself to self-soothe.'

'Self-soothe?' Some of the tension left him. 'You hug yourself?'

'It's important to be independent.' She'd been self-sufficient from an early age, but the ability to do everything for herself hadn't removed the deep longing to share her life with someone. 'Why did your dad and his last wife divorce?'

'Because they married,' he said smoothly, 'and divorce is an inevitable consequence of marriage.'

She wondered why he had such a grim view of marriage. 'Not all marriages.'

'All but those infected with extreme inertia.'

'So you're saying that even people who stay married would divorce if they could be bothered to make the effort.'

'I think there are any number of reasons for a couple to stay together, but love isn't one of them. In my father's case, wife number three married him for his money and the novelty wore off.'

'Does "wife number three" have a name?'

'Callie.' His hard tone told her everything she needed to know about his relationship with his last stepmother.

'You don't like her?'

'Are you enjoying your meal?'

She blinked, thrown by the change of subject. 'It's delicious, but—'

'Good. If you're hoping to sample dessert, you need to talk about something other than my family.'

'You control everything, even the conversation.' She wondered why he didn't want to talk about his family. 'Is this where you bring all the women you date?'

'It depends on the woman.'

'How about that woman you were with earlier— Christina? She definitely wouldn't have eaten any of this. She had carb-phobia written all over her.'

Those powerful shoulders relaxed slightly. 'She would have ordered green salad, grilled fish and eaten half of it.'

'So why didn't you order green salad and grilled fish for me?'

'Because you look like someone who enjoys food.'

Lily gave him a look. 'I'm starting to understand why women cry around you. You basically called me fat. For your information, most women would storm out if you said that to them.'

'So why didn't you storm out?'

'Because eating here is a once-in-a-lifetime experience and I don't want to miss it. And I don't think you meant it that way and I like to give people the benefit of the doubt. Tell me what happens next on a date. You bring a woman to a place like this and then you take her back to your villa for sex in that massive bed?'

'I never talk about my relationships.'

'You don't talk about your family and you don't talk about your relationships.' Lily helped herself to rich, plump slices of tomato salad. 'What do you want to talk about?'

'You. Tell me about your work.'

'I work in your company. You know more about what goes on than I do, but one thing I will say is that with all these technology skills at your disposal you need to invent an app that syncs all the details of the women who call you. You have a busy sex life and it's easy to get it mixed up, especially as they're all pretty much the same type.' She put her fork down. 'Is that the secret to staying emotionally detached? You date women who are clones, no individual characteristics to tell them apart.'

'I do not date clones, and I don't want to talk about my work, I want to talk about your work. Your archaeological work.' His eyes gleamed. 'And try to include the word "Minoan" at least eight times in each sentence.'

She ignored that. 'I'm a ceramics expert. I did a masters in archaeology and since then I've been working on an internationally funded project replicating Minoan cooking fabrics. Among other things we've been looking at the technological shift Minoan potters made when they replaced hand-building methods with the wheel.

We can trace patterns of production, but also the context of ceramic consumption. The word *ceramic* comes from the Greek, *keramikos,* but you probably already know that.'

He reached for his wine glass. 'I can't believe you were cleaning my shower.'

'Cleaning your shower pays well and I have college debts.'

'If you didn't have college debts, what would you be doing?'

She hesitated, unwilling to share her dream with a stranger, especially one who couldn't possibly understand having to make choices driven by debt. 'I have no idea. I can't afford to think like that. I have to be practical.'

'Why Crete?'

'Crete had all the resources necessary to produce pottery. Clay, temper, water and fuel. Microscopic ceramic fabric analysis indicate those resources have been used for at least eight thousand years. The most practical way of understanding ancient technology is to replicate it and use it and that's what we've been doing.'

'So you've been trying to cook like a Minoan?'

'Yes. We're using tools and materials that would have been available during the Cretan Bronze Age.'

'That's what you're digging for?'

'Brittany and the team have different objectives, but while they're digging I'm able to access clay. I spend some of my time on site and some of my time at the museum with a small team, but that's all coming to an end now. Tell me what you do.'

'You work in my company. You should know what I do.'

'I don't know *specifically* what you do. I know you're a technology wizard. I guess that's why you have a shower that looks like something from NASA. I bet you're good with computers. Technology isn't really my thing, but you probably already know that.'

'If technology isn't your thing, why are you working in my company?'

'I'm not dealing with the technology side. I'm dealing with people. I did a short spell in Human Resources— you keep them busy by the way—and now I'm working with your personal assistants. I still haven't decided what I want to do with my life so I'm trying different things. It's only two days a week and I wanted to see how I enjoyed corporate life.'

'And how are you enjoying "corporate life"?'

'It's different.' She dodged the question and he gave her a long, speculative look.

'Tell me why you became involved with that guy who looked old enough to be your father.'

Her stomach lurched. *Because she was an idiot.* 'I never talk about my relationships.'

'On short acquaintance I'd say the problem is stopping you talking, not getting you talking. Tell me.' Something about that compelling dark gaze made it impossible not to confide.

'I think I was attracted to his status and gravitas. I was flattered when he paid me attention. A psychologist would probably say it has something to do with not having a father around when I was growing up. Anyway, he pursued me pretty heavily and it got serious fast. And then I found out he was married.' She lowered her voice and pulled a face. 'I hate myself for that, but most of all I hate him for lying to me.' Knowing his views on marriage, she wondered if he'd think she was ridiculously principled but his eyes were hard.

'You cried over this guy?'

'I think perhaps I was crying because history repeated itself. My relationships always follow the same pattern. I meet someone I'm attracted to, he's caring, attentive and a really good listener—I fall in love, have sex with him, start planning a future and then suddenly that's it. We break up.'

'And this experience hasn't put you off love?'

Perhaps it should have done.

No one had ever stayed in her life.

From an early age she'd wondered what it was about her that made it so easy for people to walk away.

The dishes were cleared away and a sticky, indulgent dessert placed in the centre of the table.

She tried to pull herself together. 'If you have one bad meal you don't stop eating, do you? And by the way this is the best meal I've ever had in my whole life.' She stuck her spoon in the pastry and honey oozed over the plate. She decided this was the perfect time to check a few facts before finally committing herself. 'Tell me what happens in your relationships. We'll talk hypothetically as you don't like revealing specifics. Let's say you meet a woman and you find her attractive. What happens next?'

'I take her on a date.'

'What sort of date?' Lily licked the spoon. 'Dinner? Theatre? Movie? Walk on the beach?'

'Any of those.'

'Let's say it's dinner. What would you talk about?'

'Anything.'

'Anything as long as it isn't to do with your family or relationships.'

He smiled. 'Exactly.'

'So you talk, you drink expensive wine, you admire the romantic view—then what? You take her home or you take her to bed?'

'Yes.' He paused as their waiter delivered a bottle of clear liquid and two glasses and Lily shook her head.

'Is that raki? Brittany loves it, but it gives me a headache.'

'We call it *tsikoudia*. It is a grape liqueur—an important part of Cretan hospitality.'

'I know. It's been around since Minoan times. Archaeologists have found the petrified remains of grapes and grape pips inside *pithoi*, the old clay storage jars, so it's assumed they knew plenty about distillation. Doesn't change the fact it gives me a headache.'

'Then you didn't drink it with enough water.' He handed her a small glass. 'The locals think it promotes a long and healthy life.'

Lily took a sip and felt her throat catch fire as she swallowed. 'So now finish telling me about your typical date. You don't fall in love, because you don't believe in love. So when you take a woman to bed, there are no feelings involved at all?'

'There are plenty of feelings involved.' The look he gave her made her heart pump faster.

'I mean emotions. You have emotionless sex. You don't say *I love you*. You don't feel anything here—'

Lily put her hand on her heart. 'No feelings. So it's all about physical satisfaction. This is basically a naked workout, yes? It's like a bench press for two.'

'Sex may not be emotional, but it's intimate,' he said softly. 'It requires the ultimate degree of trust.'

'You can do that and still not be emotionally involved?'

'When I'm with a woman I care about her enjoyment, her pleasure, her happiness and her comfort. I don't love her.'

'You don't love women?'

'I do love women.' The corners of his mouth flickered. 'I just don't want to love one specific woman.'

Lily stared at him in fascination.

There was no way, *no way*, she would ever fall in love with a man like Nik. She didn't even need to check her list to know he didn't tick a single one of the boxes.

He was perfect.

'There's something I want to say to you and I hope you're not going to be shocked.' She put her glass down and took a deep breath. 'I want to have rebound sex. No emotions involved. Sex without falling in love. Not something I've ever done before, so this is all new to me.'

He watched her from under lowered lids, his expression unreadable. There was a dangerous stillness about him. 'And you're telling me this because—?'

'Because you seem to be the expert.' Her heart started to pound. 'I want you to take me to bed.'

CHAPTER FOUR

NIK SCANNED HER in silence. The irony was that his original plan had been to do exactly that. Take her to bed. She was fun, sexy and original but the longer he spent in her company the more he realised how different her life goals were from his own. By her own admittance, Lily wasn't the sort to emotionally disengage in a relationship. In the interests of self-protection, logic took precedence over his libido.

'It's time I took you home.'

Far from squashing her, the news appeared to cheer her. 'That's what I was hoping you'd say. I promise you won't regret it. What I lack in experience I make up for in enthusiasm.'

She was as bright as she was pretty and he knew her 'misunderstanding' was deliberate.

'*Theé mou*, you should *not* be saying things like that to a man. It could be taken the wrong way.'

She sliced into a tomato. 'You're taking it the way I intended you to take it.'

Nik glanced at the bottle of champagne and tried to work out how much she'd had. 'I'm not taking you to my home, I'm taking you to *your* home.'

'You don't want to do that. My bed is smaller than a cat basket and you're big. I have a feeling we're going to get very hot and sweaty, and I don't have air conditioning.'

Nik's libido was fighting against the restraining bonds of logic. 'I will give you a lift home and then I'm leaving.'

'Leaving?' Disappointment mingled with uncertainty. 'You don't find me attractive?'

'You're sexy as hell,' he drawled, 'but you're not my type.'

'That doesn't make any sense. You don't like sexy?'

'I like sexy. I don't like women who want to fall in love, settle down and have lots of babies.'

'I thought we'd already established I didn't want to do any of that with you. You don't score a single point on my checklist, which is *exactly* why I want to do this. I know I'd be safe. And so would you!'

He decided he didn't even want to know about her checklist. 'How much champagne have you had?'

'I'm not drunk, if that's what you're suggesting. Ask me anything. Make me walk in a straight line. I'll touch my nose with my eyes closed, or I'll touch *your* nose with my eyes closed if you prefer. Or other parts of you—' She gave a wicked grin and leaned forward. 'One night. That's all it would be. You will not regret it.'

Nik deployed the full force of his will power and kept his eyes away from the softness of her breasts. 'You're right. I won't, because it's not going to happen.'

'I do yoga. I'm very bendy.'

Nik gave a soft curse. 'Stop talking.'

'I can put my legs behind my head.'

'*Cristo*, you should *definitely* stop talking.' His libido was urging logic to surrender.

'What's the problem? One night of fun. Tomorrow we both go our own ways and if I see you in the office I'll pretend I don't know you. Call your lawyer. I'll sign a contract promising not to fall in love with you. A pre-non-nuptial agreement. All I want is for you to take me home, strip me naked, throw me onto that enormous bed of yours and have sex with me in every conceivable position. After that I will walk out of your door and you'll never see me again. Deal?'

He tried to respond but it seemed her confusing mix of innocence and sexuality had short-circuited his brain. 'Lily—' he spoke through his teeth '—trust me, you do *not* want me to take you home, strip you naked and throw you onto my bed.'

'Why not? It's just sex.'

'You've spent several hours telling me you don't do "just sex".'

'But I'm going to this time. I want to be able to separate sex from love. The next time a man comes my way who might be the one, I won't let sex confuse things. I'll be like Kevlar. Nothing is getting through me. Nothing.'

'You are marshmallow, not Kevlar.'

'That was the old me. The new me is Kevlar. I don't understand why you won't do this, unless—' She studied him for a long moment and then leaned forward, a curious look in her eyes. 'Are you *scared*?'

'I'm sober,' he said softly, 'and when I play, I like it to be with an opponent who is similarly matched.'

'I'm tougher than I look.' A dimple appeared in the

corner of her mouth. 'Drink another glass of champagne and then call Vassilis.'

'How do you know my driver's name?'

'I listen. And he has a kind face. There really is no need to be nervous. If rumour is correct, you're a cold, emotionless vacuum and that means you're in no danger from someone like little me.'

He had a feeling 'little me' was the most dangerous thing he'd encountered in a long while. 'If I'm a "cold, emotionless vacuum", why would you want to climb into my bed?'

'Because you are *insanely* sexy and all the things that make you so wrong for me would make you perfect for rebound sex.'

He looked into those blue eyes and tried to ignore the surge of sexual hunger that had gripped him from the moment he'd laid eyes on that pale silky hair tumbling damp round her gleaming wet body.

Never before had doing the right thing felt so wrong.

Nik cursed under his breath and rose to his feet. 'We're leaving.'

'Good decision.' She slid her hand into his, rose on tiptoe and whispered in his ear. 'I'll be gentle with you.'

With her wide smile and laughing eyes, it was like being on a date with a beam of sunshine. He felt heat spread through his body, his arousal so brutal he was tempted to haul her behind the nearest lockable door, rip off that dress and acquaint himself with every part of her luscious, naked body.

Vassilis was waiting outside with the car and Nik bundled her inside and sat as far from her as possible.

All his life, he'd avoided women like her. Women who

believed in romance and 'the one'. For him, the myth of love had been smashed in childhood along with Santa and the Tooth Fairy. He had no use for it in his life.

'Where do you live?' He growled the words but she simply smiled.

'You don't need to know, because we're going back to your place. Your bed is almost big enough to be seen from outer space.'

Nik ran his hand over his jaw. 'Lily—'

Her phone signalled a text and she dug around in her bag. 'I need to answer this. It will be Brittany, checking I'm all right. She and Spy are probably worried because they saw me go off with you.'

'Maybe you should pay attention to your friends.'

'Hold that thought—'

Having rebound sex. She mouthed the words as she typed. Speak to you tomorrow.

Nik was tempted to seize the phone and text her friends to come and pick her up. 'Brittany was the girl in the blue dress?'

'She's the female version of you, but without the money. She doesn't engage emotionally. I found out today that she was married for ten days when she was eighteen. Can you believe that? Ten days. I don't know the details, but apparently it cured her of ever wanting a repeat performance.' She pressed send and slid the phone back into her bag. 'I grew up in foster homes so I don't have any family. I think that's probably why my friends are so important to me. I never really had a sense of belonging anywhere. That's a very lonely feeling as a child.'

He felt something stir inside him, as if she'd poked a

stick into a muddy, stagnant pool that had lain dormant and undiscovered for decades. Deeply uncomfortable, he shifted in his seat. 'Why are you telling me this?'

'I thought as we're going to have sex, you might want to know something about me.'

'I don't.'

'That's not very polite.'

'I'm not striving for "polite". This is who I am. It's not too late for my driver to drop you home. Give him the address.'

She leaned forward and pressed the button so that the screen closed between him and the driver. 'Sorry, Vassilis, but I don't want to corrupt you.' She slid across the seat, closed her eyes and lifted her face to his. 'Kiss me. Whatever it is you do, do it now.'

Nik had always considered himself to be a disciplined man but he was rapidly rethinking that assessment. With her, there was no discipline. He looked down at those long, thick eyelashes and the pink curve of her mouth and tried to remember when he'd last been tempted to have sex in the back of his car.

'No.' He managed to inject the word with forceful conviction but instead of retreating, she advanced.

'In that case I'll kiss you. I don't mind taking the initiative.' Her slim fingers slid to the inside of his thigh. He was so aroused he couldn't even remember why he was fighting this, and instead of pushing her away he gripped her hand hard and turned his head towards her.

His gaze swept her flushed cheeks and the lush curve of her mouth. With a rough curse he lowered his head, driving her lips apart with his tongue and taking that mouth in a kiss that was as rough as it was sexually explicit. His intention was to scare her off, so there was no holding back, no diluting of his passion. He kissed her hard, expecting to feel her pull back but instead she pressed closer. She tasted of sugar and sweet temptation, her mouth soft and eager against his as she all but wriggled onto his lap.

The heavy weight of her breasts brushed against his arm and he gave a groan and slid his hand into her hair, anchoring her head for the hard demands of his kiss. She licked into his mouth, snuggling closer like a kitten, those full soft curves pressing against him. It was a kiss without boundaries, an explosion of raw desire that built until the rear of the car shimmered with stifling heat and sexual awareness.

He slid his hand under her dress, over the smooth skin of her thigh to the soft shadows between her legs. It was her thickened moan of pleasure that woke him up.

Cristo, they were in the car, in moving traffic.

Releasing her as if she were a hot coal, he pushed her away. 'I thought you were supposed to be smart.'

Her breathing was shallow and rapid. 'I'm very, very smart. And you're an amazing kisser. Are you as good at everything else?'

His pulse was throbbing and he was so painfully aroused he didn't dare move. 'If you really want to come home with me then you're not as smart as you look.'

'What makes you think that?'

'Because a woman like you should steer clear of men like me. I don't have a love life, I have a sex life. I'll use you. If you're in my bed it will be all about pleasure and nothing else. I don't care about your feelings. I'm not kind. I'm not gentle. I need you to know that.'

There was a long, loaded silence and then her gaze slid to his mouth. 'Okay, I get it. No fluffy kittens in this relationship. Message received and understood. Can this car go any faster because I don't think I've ever been this turned on in my life before.'

She wasn't the only one. His self-control was stretched to breaking point. Why was he fighting it? She was an adult. She wasn't drunk and she knew what she was doing. Logic didn't just surrender to libido, it was obliterated. All the same, something made him open one more exit door. 'Be very sure, Lily.'

'I'm sure. I've never been so sure of anything in my life. Unless you want to be arrested for performing an indecent act in a public place you'd better tell Vassilis to break a few speed limits.'

Lily walked into the villa she'd cleaned earlier, feeling ridiculously nervous. In the romantic setting of the restaurant this had seemed like a good idea. Now she wasn't quite so sure. 'So why did you hire a contract cleaning company?'

'I didn't.' He threw his jacket over the back of a chair with careless disregard for its future appearance. 'I have staff who look after this place. Presumably they arranged it. I didn't give them much notice of my return. I don't care how they do their job as long as it gets done.'

She paced across the living room and stared across the floodlit shimmer of the infinity pool. 'It's pretty at night.' It was romantic, but she knew this had nothing to do with romance. Her other relationships had been with men she knew and cared about. This scenario was new to her. 'Do you have something to drink?'

'You're thirsty?'

Nervous. 'A little.'

He gave her a long look, strolled out of the room and returned moments later carrying a glass of water.

'I want you sober,' he said softly. 'In fact I insist on it.'

Realising they were actually going to do this, she suddenly found she was shaking so much the water sloshed out of the glass and onto the floor. 'Oops. I'm messing up the floor I cleaned earlier.'

He was standing close to her and her gaze drifted to the bronzed skin at the base of his throat and the blue-shadowed jaw. Everything about him was unapologetically masculine. He wasn't just dangerously attractive, he was lethal and suddenly she wondered what on earth she was doing. Maybe she should have taken up Spy's offer of rebound sex, except that Spy didn't induce one tenth of this crazy response in her. A thrilling sense of anticipation mingled with wicked excitement and she knew she'd regret it for ever if she walked away. She knew she took relationships too seriously. If she was going to try a different approach then there was surely no better man to do it with than Nik.

'Scared?' His voice was deep, dark velvet and she gave a smile.

'A little. But only because I don't normally do this and you're not my usual type. It's like passing your driving test and then getting behind the wheel of a Ferrari. I'm worried I'll crash you into a lamppost.' She put the glass down carefully on the glass table and ran her damp hands over her thighs. 'Okay, let's do this. Ignore the fact I'm shaking, go right ahead and do your bad, bad thing, whatever that is.'

He said nothing. Just looked at her, that dark gaze uncomfortably penetrating.

She waited, heart pounding, virtually squirming on the spot. 'I'm not good with delayed gratification. I'm more of an instant person. I like to—'

'Hush.' Finally he spoke and then he reached out and drew her against him, the look in his eyes driving words and thoughts from her head. She felt the warmth of his hand against the base of her spine, the slow, sensitive stroke of his fingers low on her back and then he lifted his hands and cupped her face, forcing her to look at him. 'Lily Rose—'

She swallowed. 'Nik—'

'Don't be nervous.' He murmured the words against her lips. 'There's no reason to be nervous.'

'I'm not nervous,' she lied. 'But I'm not really sure what happens next.'

'I'll decide what happens next.'

Her heart bumped uncomfortably against her ribs. 'So—what do you want me to do?'

His mouth hovered close to hers and his fingers grazed her jaw. 'I want you to stop talking.'

'I'm going to stop talking right now this second.' Her stomach felt as if a thousand butterflies were trying to escape. She hadn't expected him to be so gentle, but those exploring fingers were slow, almost languorous as they stroked her face and slid over her neck and into her hair.

She stood, disorientated by intoxicating pleasure as he trailed his mouth along her jaw, tormenting her with dark, dangerous kisses. Heat uncurled low in her pelvis and spread through her body, sapping the strength from her knees, and she slid her hands over those sleek, powerful shoulders, feeling the hard swell of muscle beneath her palms. His mouth moved lower and she tilted her head back as he kissed her neck and then the base of her throat. She felt the slow slide of his tongue against supersensitive skin, the warmth of his breath and then his hand slid back into her hair and he brought his mouth back to hers. He kissed her with an erotic expertise that made her head spin and her legs grow heavy. With each slow stroke of his tongue, he sent her senses spinning out of control. It was like being drugged. She tried to find her balance, her centre, but just when she felt close to grasping a few threads of control, he used his mouth to drive every coherent thought from her head. Shaky, she lifted her hand to his face, felt the roughness of his jaw against her palm and the lean, spare perfection of his bone structure.

She slid her fingers into his hair and felt his hand slide down her spine and draw her firmly against him.

She felt him, brutally hard through the silky fabric of her dress, and she gave a moan, low in her throat as he trapped her there with the strength of his arms, the power in those muscles reminding her that this wasn't a safe flirtation, or a game.

His kisses grew rougher, more intimate, more demanding and she tugged at his shirt, her fingers swift and sure on the buttons, her movements more frantic with each bit of male muscle she exposed.

His chest was powerful, his abs lean and hard and she felt a moment of breathless unease because she'd never had sex with a man built like him.

He was self-assured and experienced and as she pushed the shirt from his shoulders she tried to take a step backwards.

'I'd like to keep my clothes on, if that's all right with you.'

'It's not all right.' But there was a smile in his voice as he slid his hand from her hips to her waist, pulling her back against him. His fingers brushed against the underside of her breast and she moaned.

'You look as if you spend every spare second of your life working out.'

'I don't.'

'You get this way through lots of athletic sex?'

His mouth hovered close to hers. 'You promised to stop talking.'

'That was before I saw you half naked. I'm intimidated. That photo didn't lie. Now I know what you look like under your clothes I think I might be having body-image problems.'

He smiled, and she felt his hands at the back of her dress and the slow slither of silk as her dress slid to the floor.

Standing in front of him in nothing but her underwear and high heels, she felt ridiculously exposed. It didn't matter that he'd already seen her that way. This was different.

He eased back from her, his eyes slumberous and dangerously dark. 'Let's go upstairs.'

Her knees were shaking so much she wasn't sure she could walk but the next moment he scooped her into his arms and she gave a gasp of shock and dug her hands in his shoulder.

'Don't you dare drop me. I bruise easily.' She had a close-up view of his face and stared hungrily at the hard masculine lines, the blue-black shadow of his jaw and the slim, sensual line of his mouth. 'If I'd known you were planning on carrying me I would have said no to dessert.'

'Dessert was the best part.' They reached the top of the stairs and he carried her into his bedroom and lowered her to the floor next to the bed.

She didn't see him move, and yet a light came on next to the bed sending a soft beam over the silk covers. Glancing around her, Lily realised that if she lay on that bed her body would be illuminated by the wash of light.

'Can we switch the lights off?'

His eyes hooded, he lowered his hands to his belt. 'No.' As he removed the last of his clothes she let her eyes skid downwards and felt heat pour into her cheeks.

It was only a brief glance, but it was enough to imprint the image of his body in her brain.

'Do you model underwear in your spare time? Because seriously—' Her cheeks flooded with colour. 'Okay so I think this whole thing would be easier in the dark—then I won't be so intimidated by your supersonic abs.'

'Hush.' He smoothed her hair back from her face. 'Do you trust me?' His voice was rough and she felt a flutter of nerves low in her belly.

'I—yes. I think so. Why? Am I being stupid?'

'No. Close your eyes.'

She hesitated and then closed them. She heard the sound of a drawer opening and then felt something soft and silky being tied round her eyes.

'What are you doing?' She lifted her hand but he

closed his fingers round her wrist and drew her hands
back to her sides.

'Relax.' His voice was a soft purr. 'I'm taking away
one of your senses. The one that's making you nervous.
There's no need to panic. You still have four remaining.
I want you to use those.'

'I can't see.'

'Exactly. You wanted to do this in the dark. Now
you're in the dark.'

'I meant that you should put the lights out! It was
so you couldn't see me, not so that I couldn't see you.'

'Shh.' His lips nibbled at hers, his tongue stroking
over her mouth in a slow, sensual seduction.

She was quivering, her senses straining with delicious anticipation as she tried to work out where he was
and where he'd touch her next.

She felt his lips on her shoulder and felt his fingers
slide the thin straps of her bra over her arms. Wetness
pooled between her thighs and she pressed them together, so aroused she could hardly breathe.

He took his time, explored her neck, her shoulder,
the underside of her breast until she wasn't sure her legs
would hold her and he must have known that because
he tipped her back onto the bed, supporting her as she
lost her balance.

She could see nothing through the silk mask but she
felt the weight of him on top of her, the roughness of
his thigh against hers and the slide of silk against her
heated flesh as he stripped her naked.

She was quivering, her senses sharpened by her lack
of vision. She felt the warmth of his mouth close over
the tip of her breast, the skilled flick of his tongue send-

ing arrows of pleasure shooting through her over-sensitised body.

She gave a moan and clutched at his shoulders. 'Do we need a safe word or something?' She felt him pause.

'Why would you need a safe word?'

'I thought—'

'I'm not going to do anything that makes you uncomfortable.'

'What do I say if I want you to stop?'

His mouth brushed lightly across her jaw. 'You say "stop".'

'That's it?'

'That's it.' There was a smile in his voice. 'If I do one single thing that makes you uncomfortable, tell me.'

'Is embarrassed the same as uncomfortable?'

He gave a soft laugh and she felt the stroke of his palm on her thigh and then he parted her legs and his mouth drifted from her belly to her inner thigh.

He paused, his breath warm against that secret place. 'Relax, *erota mou.*'

She lifted her hands to remove the blindfold but he caught her wrists in one hand and held them pinned, while he used the other to part her and expose her secrets.

Unbearably aroused, melting with a confusing mix of desire and mortification, she tried to close her legs but he licked at her intimately, opening her with his tongue, exploring her vulnerable flesh with erotic skill and purpose until all she wanted was for him to finish what he'd started.

'Nik—' She writhed, sobbed, struggled against him and he released her hands and anchored her hips, holding her trapped as he explored her with his tongue.

She'd forgotten all about removing the blindfold.

The only thing in her head was easing the maddening ache that was fast becoming unbearable.

She dug her fingers in the sheets, moaning as he slid his fingers deep inside her, manipulating her body and her senses until she tipped into excitement overload. She felt herself start to throb round those seeking fingers, but instead of giving her what she wanted he gently withdrew his hand and eased away from her.

'Please! Oh, please—' she sobbed in protest, wondering what he was doing.

Was he leaving her?

Was he stopping?

With a whimper of protest, she writhed and reached for him and then she heard a faint sound and understood the reason for the brief interlude.

Condom, she thought, and then the ability to think coherently vanished because he covered her with the hard heat of his body. She felt the blunt thrust of his erection at her moist entrance and tensed in anticipation, but instead of entering her he cupped her face in his hand and gently slid off the blindfold.

'Look at me.' His soft command penetrated her brain and she opened her eyes and stared at him dizzily just as he slid his hand under her bottom and entered her in a series of slow, deliciously skilful thrusts. He was incredibly gentle, taking his time, murmuring soft words in Greek and then English as he moved deep into the heart of her. Then he paused, kissed her mouth gently, holding her gaze with his.

'Are you all right? Do you want to use the safe word?' His voice was gently teasing but the glitter in his eyes and the tension in his jaw told her he was no-where near as relaxed as he pretended to be.

In the grip of such intolerable excitement she was in-capable of responding, Lily simply shook her head and then moaned as he withdrew slightly and surged into her again, every movement of his body escalating the wickedly agonising pleasure.

She slid her hands over the silken width of his shoul-ders, down his back, her fingers clamping over the thrust-ing power of his body as he rocked against her. His hand was splayed on her bottom, his gaze locked on hers as he drove into her with ruthlessly controlled strength and a raw, primitive rhythm. She wrapped her legs around him as he brought pleasure raining down on both of them. She cried out his name and he took her mouth, kissing her deeply, intimately, as the first ripple of orgasm took hold of her body. They didn't stop kissing, mouths locked, eyes locked as her body contracted around his and dragged him over the edge of control. She'd never experienced anything like it, the whole experience a shattering rev-elation about her capacity for sensuality.

It was several minutes before she was capable of speaking and longer than that before she could persuade her body to move.

As she tried to roll away from him, his arms locked around her. 'Where do you think you're going?'

'I'm sticking to the rules. I thought this was a one-night thing.'

'It is.' He hauled her back against him. 'And the night isn't over yet.'

CHAPTER FIVE

Nik spent ten minutes under a cold shower, trying to wake himself up after a night that had consisted of the worst sleep of his life and the best sex. He couldn't remember the last time he hadn't wanted to leave the bed in the morning.

A ton of work waited for him in the office, but for the first time ever he was contemplating working from home so that he could spend a few more hours with Lily. After her initial shyness she'd proved to be adventurous and insatiable, qualities that had kept both of them awake until the rising sun had sent the first flickers of light across the darkened bedroom.

Eventually she'd fallen into an exhausted sleep, her body tangled around his as dawn had bathed the bedroom in a golden glow.

It had proved impossible to extract himself without waking her so Nik, whose least favourite bedroom activity was hugging, had remained there, his senses bathed in the soft floral scent of her skin and hair, trapped by those long limbs wrapped trustingly around him.

And he had no one to blame but himself.

She'd offered to leave and he'd stopped her.

He frowned, surprised by his own actions. He had no need for displays of affection or any of the other meaningless rituals that seemed to inhabit other people's relationships. To him, sex was a physical need, no different from hunger and thirst. Once satisfied he moved on. He had no desire for anything deeper. He didn't believe anything deeper existed.

When he was younger, women had tried to persuade him differently. There had been a substantial number who had believed they had what it took to penetrate whatever steely coating made his heart so inaccessible. When they'd had no more success than their predecessors they'd withdrawn, bruised and broken, but not before they'd delivered their own personal diagnosis on his sorry condition.

He'd heard it all. That he didn't have a heart, that he was selfish, single minded, driven, too focused on his work. He accepted those accusations without argument, but knew that none explained his perpetually single status. Quite simply, he didn't believe in love. He'd learned at an early age that love could be withdrawn as easily as it was given, that promises could be made and broken in the same breath, that a wedding ring was no more than a piece of jewellery, and wedding vows no more binding than one plant twisted loosely around another.

He had no need for the friendship and affection that punctuated other people's lives.

He'd taught himself to live without it, so to find himself wrapped in the tight embrace of a woman who smiled even when she was asleep was as alien to him as it was unsettling.

For a while, he'd slept, too, and then woken to find her locked against him. Telling himself that she was the one holding him and not the other way round, he'd managed to extract himself without waking her and escaped to the bathroom where he contemplated his options.

He needed to find a tactful way of ejecting her.

He showered, shaved and returned to the bedroom. Expecting to find her still asleep, he was thrown to find her dressed. She'd stolen one of his white shirts and it fell to mid-thigh, the sleeves flapping over her small hands as she talked on the phone.

'Of course he'll be there.' Her voice was as soothing as warm honey. 'I'm sure it's a simple misunderstanding…well, no I agree with you, but he's very busy…'

She lay on her stomach on the bed, her hair hanging in a blonde curtain over one shoulder, the sheets tangled around her bare thighs.

Nik took one look at her and decided that there was no reason to rush her out of the villa.

They'd have breakfast on the terrace. Maybe enjoy a swim.

Then he'd find a position they hadn't yet tried before sending her home in his car.

Absorbed in her conversation, she hadn't noticed him and he strolled round in front of her and slowly released the towel from his waist.

He saw her eyes go wide. Then she gave him a smile that hovered somewhere between cheeky and innocent and he found himself resenting the person on the end of the phone who was taking up so much of her time.

He dressed, aware that she was watching him the

whole time, her conversation reduced to soothing, sympathetic noises.

It was the sort of exchange he'd never had in his life. The sort that involved listening while someone poured out their woes. When Nik had a problem he solved it or accepted it and moved on. He'd never understood the female urge to dissect and confide.

'I know,' she murmured. 'There's nothing more upsetting than a rift in the family, but you need to talk. Clear the air. Be open about your feelings.'

She was so warm and sympathetic it was obvious to Nik that the conversation was going to be a long one. Someone had rung in the belief that talking to Lily would make them feel better and he couldn't see a way that this exchange would ever end as she poured a verbal Band-Aid over whatever wound she was being asked to heal. Who would want to hang up when they were getting the phone equivalent of a massive hug?

Outraged on her behalf, Nik sliced his finger across his throat to indicate that she should cut the connection.

When she didn't, he was contemplating snatching the phone and telling whoever it was to get a grip, sort out their own problems and stop encroaching on Lily's good nature when she gestured to the phone with her free hand.

'It's for you,' she mouthed. 'Your father.'

His *father*?

The person she'd been soothing and placating for the past twenty minutes was his *father*?

Nik froze. Only now did he notice that the phone in her hand was his. 'You answered my phone?'

'I wouldn't have done normally, but I saw it was your

dad and I knew you'd want to talk to him. I didn't want you to miss his call because you were in the shower.' Clearly believing she'd done him an enormous favour, she wished his father a cheery, caring goodbye and held out the phone to him. The front of his shirt gapped, revealing those tempting dips and curves he'd explored in minute detail the night before. The scrape of his jaw had left faint red marks over her creamy skin and the fact that he instantly wanted to drop the phone in the nearest body of water and take her straight back to bed simply added to his irritation.

'That's my shirt.'

'You have so many, I didn't think you'd miss one.'

Reflecting on the fact she was as chirpy in the morning as she was the rest of the day, Nik dragged his gaze from her smiling mouth, took the phone from her and switched to Greek. 'You didn't need to call again. I got your last four messages.'

'Then why didn't you call me back?'

'I've been busy.'

'Too busy to talk to your own father? I have rung you every day this week, Niklaus. Every single day.'

Aware that Lily was listening Nik paced to the window, turned his back on her and stared out over the sea. 'Is the wedding still on?'

'Of course it is on! Why wouldn't it be? I love Diandra and she loves me. You would love her, too, if you took the time to meet her and what better time than the day in which we exchange our vows?' There was a silence. 'Nik, come home. It has been too long.'

Nik knew exactly how long it had been to the day.

'I've been busy.'

'Too busy to visit your own family? This is the place of your birth and you never come home. You have a villa here that you converted and you don't even visit. I know you didn't like Callie and it's true that for a long time I was very angry with you for not making more of an effort when she showed you so much love, but that is behind us now.'

Reflecting on exactly what form that 'love' had taken, Nik tightened his hand on the phone and wondered if he'd been wrong not to tell his father the unpalatable truth about his third wife. He'd made the decision that since she'd ended the relationship anyway there was nothing to be gained from revealing the truth, but now he found himself in the rare position of questioning his own judgement.

'Will Callie be at the wedding?'

'No.' His father was quiet. 'I wanted her to bring little Chloe, but she hasn't responded to my calls. I don't mind admitting it's a very upsetting situation all round for everyone.'

Not everyone, Nik thought. He was sure Callie wasn't remotely upset. Why would she be? She'd extracted enough money from his father to ensure she could live comfortably without ever lifting a finger again. 'You would really want her at your wedding?'

'Callie, no. But Chloe? Yes, of course. If I had my way she would be living here with me. I still haven't given up hope that might happen one day. Chloe is my child, Nik. My daughter. I want her to grow up knowing her father. I don't want her thinking I abandoned her or chose not to have her in my life.'

Nik kept his eyes forward and the past firmly suppressed. 'These things happen. They're part of life and relationships.'

His father sighed. 'I'm sorry you believe that. Family is the most important thing in the world. I want that for you.'

'I set my own life goals, and that isn't on the list,' Nik drawled softly. Contemplating the complexity of human relationships, he was doubly glad he'd successfully avoided them himself. Like every other area of his life, he had his feelings firmly under control. 'Would Diandra really want Chloe to be living with you?'

'Of course! She'd be delighted. She wants it as much as I do. And she'd really like to meet you, too. She's keen for us to be a proper family.'

A proper family.

A long-buried memory emerged from deep inside his brain, squeezing itself through the many layers of self-protection he'd used to suppress it.

It had been so long the images were no longer clear, a fact for which he was grimly grateful. Even now, several decades later, he could still remember how it had felt to have those images replaying in his head night after night.

A man, a woman and a young boy, living an idyllic existence under blue skies and the dazzle of the sun. Growing up, he'd learned a thousand lessons about living. How to cook with leaves from the vine, how to distil the grape skins and seeds to form the potent *tsikoudia* they drank with friends. He'd lived his cocooned existence until one day his world had crumbled and he'd learned the most important lesson of all.

That a family was the least stable structure invented by man.

It could be destroyed in a moment.

'Come home, Niklaus,' his father said quietly. 'It has been too long. I want us to put the past behind us. Callie is no longer here.'

Nik didn't tell him that the reason he avoided the island had nothing to do with Callie.

Whenever he returned there it stirred up the same memory of his mother leaving in the middle of the night while he watched in confusion from the elegant curve of the stairs.

Where are you going, Mama? Are you taking us with you? Can we come, too?

'Niklaus?' His father was still talking. 'Will you come?'

Nik dragged his hand over the back of his neck. 'Yes, if that's what you want.'

'How can you doubt it?' There was joy in his father's voice. 'The wedding is Tuesday but many of our friends are arriving at the weekend so that we can celebrate in style. Come on Saturday then you can join in the pre-wedding celebrations.'

'Saturday?' His father expected him to stay for four days? 'I'll have to see if I can clear my diary.'

'Of course you can. What's the point of being in charge of the company if you can't decide your own schedule? Now tell me about Lily. I like her very much. How long have the two of you been together?'

Ten memorable hours. 'How do you know her name?'

'We've been talking, Niklaus! Which is more than

you and I ever do. She sounds nice. Why don't you bring
her to the wedding?'

'We don't have that sort of relationship.' He felt a
flicker of irritation. Was that why she'd spent so much
time on the phone talking to his father? Had she decided
that sympathy might earn her an invite to the biggest
wedding of the year in Greece?

Exchanging a final few words with his father, he
hung up. 'Don't ever,' he said with silky emphasis as
he turned to face her, 'answer my phone again.' But he
was talking to an empty room because Lily was no-
where to be seen.

Taken aback, Nik glanced towards the bathroom and
then noticed the note scrawled on a piece of paper by
his pillow.

Thanks for the best rebound sex ever. Lily.

The best rebound sex?

She'd left?

Nik picked up the note and scrunched it in his palm.
He'd been so absorbed in the conversation with his father
he hadn't heard her leaving.

The dress from the night before lay neatly folded on
the chair but there was no sign of the shoes or his shirt.
He had no need to formulate a plan to eject her from
his life because she'd removed herself.

She'd gone.

And she hadn't even bothered saying goodbye.

'No need to ask if you had a good night, it's written
all over your face.' Brittany slid her feet into her hik-

ing boots and reached for her bag. 'Nice shirt. Is that silk?' She reached out and touched the fabric and gave a murmur of appreciation. 'The man has style, I'll give him that.'

'Thanks for your text. It was sweet of you to check on me. How was your evening?'

'Nowhere near as exciting as yours apparently. While you were playing Cinderella in the wolf's lair, I was cataloguing pottery shards and bone fragments. My life is so exciting I can hardly bear it.'

'You love it. And I think you're mixing your fairy tales.' Aware that her hair was a wild mass of curls after the relentless exploration of Nik's hands, Lily scooped it into a ponytail. She told herself that eventually she'd stop thinking about him. 'Did you find anything else after I left yesterday?'

'Fragments of plaster, conical cups—' Brittany frowned. 'We found a bronze leg that probably belongs to that figurine that was discovered last week. Are you listening to me?'

Lily was deep in an action replay of the moment Nik had removed the mask from her eyes. 'That's exciting! I'm going to join you later.'

'We're removing part of the stone mound and exploring the North Eastern wall.' Brittany eyed her. 'You might want to rethink white silk. So am I going to hear the details?'

'About what?'

'Oh, please—'

'It was fun. All right, incredible.' Lily felt her cheeks burn and Brittany gave a faint smile.

'That good? Now I'm jealous. I haven't had incredible sex since—well, let's just say it's been a while. So are you seeing him again?'

'Of course not. The definition of rebound sex is that it's just one night. No commitment.' She parroted the rules and tried not to wish it could have lasted a little more than one night. The truth was even in that one night Nik had made her feel special. 'Do we have food in our fridge? I'm starving.'

'He helped you expend all those calories and then didn't feed you before you left? That's not very gentlemanly.'

'He didn't see me leave. He had to take a call.' And judging from the reluctance he'd shown when she'd handed him the phone, if it had been left to him he wouldn't have answered it.

Why not?

Why wouldn't a man want to talk to his father?

It had been immediately obvious that whatever issues Nik might have in expressing his emotions openly weren't shared by his father, who had been almost embarrassingly eager to share his pain.

She'd squirmed with discomfort as Kostas Zervakis had told her how long it was since his son had come home. Even on such a short acquaintance she knew that family was one of the subjects Nik didn't touch. She'd felt awkward listening, as if she were eavesdropping on a private conversation, but at the same time his father had seemed so upset she hadn't had the heart to cut him off.

The conversation had left her feeling ever so slightly sick, an emotion she knew was ridiculous given that she hadn't ever met Kostas and barely knew his son. Why should it bother her that there were clearly problems in their relationship?

Her natural instinct had been to intervene but she'd recognised instantly the danger in that. Nik wasn't a man who appreciated the interference of others in anything, least of all his personal life.

The black look he'd given her had been as much responsible for her rapid exit as her own lack of familiarity with the morning-after etiquette following rebound sex.

She'd taken advantage of his temporary absorption in the phone call to make a hasty escape, but not before she'd heard enough to make her wish for a happy ending. Whatever damage lay in their past, she wanted them to fix their problems.

She always wanted people to fix their problems.

Lily blinked rapidly, realising that Brittany was talking. 'Sorry?'

'So he doesn't know you left?'

'He knows by now.'

'He won't be pleased that you didn't say goodbye.'

'He'll be delighted. He doesn't want emotional engagement. No awkward conversations. He will be relieved to be spared a potentially awkward conversation. We move in different circles so I probably won't ever see him again.' And that shouldn't bother her, should it? Although a one-night stand was new to her, she was the expert at transitory relationships. Her entire life had been a series of transitory relationships. No one had ever stuck in her life. She felt like an abandoned railway station where trains passed through but never stopped.

Brittany glanced out of the window at the street

below and raised her eyebrows. 'I think you're going to see him again a whole lot sooner than you think.'

'What makes you say that?'

'Because he's just pulled up outside our apartment.'

Lily's heart felt as if it were trying to escape from her chest. 'Are you sure?'

'Well there's a Ferrari parked outside that costs more than I'm going to earn in a lifetime, so, unless there is someone else living in this building that has attracted his attention, he clearly has things he wants to say to you.'

'Oh *no*.' Lily shrank against the door of the bedroom. 'Can you see his face? Does he look angry?'

'What reason would he have to be angry?' Brittany glanced out of the window again and then back at Lily. 'Is this about the shirt? He can afford to lose one shirt, surely?'

'I don't think he's here because of the shirt,' Lily said weakly. 'I think he's here because of something I did this morning. I'm going to hide on the balcony and you're going to tell him you haven't seen me.'

Brittany looked at her curiously. 'What did you do?'

Lily flinched as she heard a loud hammering on the door. 'Remember—you haven't seen me.' She fled into the bedroom they shared and closed the door.

What was he doing here?

She'd seen the flash of anger in his eyes when he'd realised it was *his* phone she'd answered, but surely he wouldn't care enough to follow her home?

She heard his voice in the doorway and heard Brittany say, 'Sure, come right on in, Nik—is it all right if I call you Nik?—she's in the bedroom, hiding.' The door opened a moment later and Brittany stood there, arms folded, her eyes alive with laughter.

Lily impaled her with a look of helpless fury. 'You're a traitor.'

'I'm a friend and I am doing you a favour,' Brittany murmured. 'The man is seriously *hot*.' Having delivered that assessment, she stepped to one side with a bright smile. 'Go ahead. The space is a little tight, but I guess you folks don't mind that.'

'No! Brittany, don't—er—hi…' Lily gave a weak smile as Nik strolled into the room. His powerful frame virtually filled the cramped space and she wished she'd picked a different room as a refuge. Being in a bedroom reminded her too much of the night before. 'If you're mad about the shirt, then give me two minutes to change. I shouldn't have taken it, but I didn't want to do the walk of shame through the middle of Chania wearing an evening dress that doesn't belong to me.'

'I don't care about the shirt.' His hair was glossy dark, his eyes dark in a face so handsome it would have made a Greek god weep with envy. 'Do you seriously think I'm here because of the shirt?'

'No. I assume you're mad because I answered your phone, but I saw that it was your father and thought you wouldn't want to miss his call. If I had a dad I'd be ringing him every day.'

His face revealed not a flicker of emotion. 'We don't have that sort of relationship.'

'Well I know that *now,* but I didn't know when I answered the phone and once he started talking he was so upset I didn't want to hang up. He needed to talk to someone and I was in the right place at the right time.'

'You think so?' His voice was silky soft. 'Because I would have said you were in the wrong place at the wrong time.'

'Depends how you look at it. Did you manage to clear the air?' She risked a glance at the hard lines of his face and winced. 'I'm guessing the answer to that is no. If I made it worse by handing you the phone, I'm sorry.'

He raised an eyebrow. 'Are you?'

She opened her mouth and closed it again. 'No, not really. Family is the most important thing in the world. I don't understand how anyone could not want to try and heal a rift. But I could see you were very angry that I'd answered the call and of course your relationship with your father is none of my business.' But she wanted to make it her business so badly she virtually had to sit on her hands to stop herself from interfering.

'For someone who realises it's none of her business, you seem to be showing an extraordinary depth of interest.'

'I feel strongly about protecting the family unit. It's my hot button.'

His searing glance reminded her he was intimately familiar with all her hot buttons. 'Why did you walk out this morning?'

The blatant reminder of the night before brought the colour rushing to her cheeks.

'I thought the first rule of rebound sex was that you rebound right out of the door the next morning. I have no experience of morning-after conversation and frankly the thought of facing you over breakfast after all the things we did last night didn't totally thrill me. And can you honestly tell me you weren't standing in that shower working out how you were going to eject me?' The expression on his face told her she was right and she nodded. 'Exactly. I thought I'd spare us both a major awkward moment and leave. I grabbed a shirt and was halfway out of the door when your father rang.'

'It didn't occur to you to ignore the phone?'

'I thought it might be important. And it was! He was *so* upset. He told me he'd already left a ton of messages.' Concern overwhelmed her efforts not to become involved. 'Why haven't you been home for the past few years?'

'A night in my bed doesn't qualify you to ask those questions.' The look in his eyes made her confidence falter.

'I get the message. Nothing personal. Now back off. Last night you were charming and fun and flirty. This morning you're scary and intimidating.'

He inhaled deeply. 'I apologise,' he breathed. 'It was not my intention to come across as scary or intimidating, but you should *not* have answered the phone.'

'What's done is done. And I was glad to be a listening ear for someone in pain.'

'My father is not in pain.'

'Yes, he is. He misses you. This rift between you is causing him agony. He wants you to go to his wedding. It's breaking his heart that you won't go.'

'Lily—'

'You're going to tell me it's none of my business and you're right, it isn't, but I don't have a family at all. I don't even have the broken pieces of a family, and you have no idea how much I wish I did. So you'll have to forgive me if I have a tendency to try and glue back together everyone else's chipped fragments. It's the archaeologist in me.'

'Lily—'

'Just because you don't believe in love, doesn't mean you have to inflict that view on others and judge them for their decisions. Your father is happy and you're spoiling it. He loves you and he wants you there. Whatever you are feeling, you should bury it and go and celebrate. You should raise a glass and dance at his wedding. You should show him you love him no matter what, and if this marriage goes wrong then you'll be there to support him.' She stopped, breathless, and waited to be frozen by the icy wind of his disapproval but he surprised her yet again by nodding.

'I agree.'

'You do?'

'Yes. I've been trying to tell you that but you wouldn't stop talking.' He spoke through clenched teeth. 'I am convinced that I should go to the wedding, which is why I'm here.'

'What does the wedding have to do with me?'

'I want you to come with me.'

Lily gaped at him. 'Me? Why?'

He ran his hand over the back of his neck. 'I am willing to be present if that is truly what my father wants, but I don't have enough faith in my acting skills to believe I will be able to convince anyone that I'm pleased to be there. No matter how much he tells me Diandra is "the one", I cannot see how this match will have a happy ending. You, however, seem to see happy endings where none exist. I'm hoping that by taking you, people will be blinded in the dazzling beam of your sunny optimism and won't notice the dark thundercloud hovering close by threatening to rain on the proceedings.'

The analogy made her smile. 'You're the dark thundercloud in that scenario?'

His eyes gleamed. 'You need to ask?'

'You really believe this marriage is doomed? How can you say that when you haven't even met Diandra?'

'When it comes to women, my father has poor judgement. He follows his heart and his heart has no sense of direction. Frankly I can't believe he has chosen to get married again after three failed attempts. I think it's insane.'

'I think it's lovely.'

'Which is why you're coming as my guest.' He reached out and lifted a small blue plate from her shelf, tipping off the earrings that were stored there. 'This is stylish. Where did you buy it?'

'I didn't buy it, I made it. And I haven't agreed to come with you yet.'

'You *made* this?'

'It's a hobby of mine. There is a kiln at work and sometimes I use it. The father of one of the curators at the museum is a potter and he's helped me. It's interesting comparing old and new techniques.'

He turned it in his hands, examining it closely. 'You could sell this.'

'I don't want to sell it. I use it to store my earrings.'

'Have you ever considered having an exhibition?'

'Er—no.' She gave an astonished laugh. 'I've made about eight pieces I didn't throw away. They're all exhibited around the apartment. We use one as a soap dish.'

'You've never wanted to do this for a living?'

'What I want to do and what I can afford to do aren't the same thing. It isn't financially viable.' She didn't even allow her mind to go there. 'And where would our soap live? Let's talk about the wedding. A wedding is a big deal. It's intimate and special, an occasion to be shared with friends and loved ones. You don't even know me.' The moment the words left her mouth she realised how ridiculous that statement was given the night they'd spent. 'I mean obviously there are *some* things about me you know very well, but other things like my favourite flower and my favourite colour, you don't know.'

Still holding her plate, he studied her with an unsettling intensity. 'I know all I need to know, which is that you like weddings almost as much as I hate them. Did you study art?'

'Minoan art. This is a sideline. And if I go with you, people will speculate. How would you explain our relationship to your father? Would you want us to pretend to be in a relationship? Are we supposed to have known one another for ages or something?'

'No.' His frown suggested that option hadn't occurred to him. 'There is no need to tell anything other than the truth, which is that I'm inviting you to the wedding as a friend.'

'Friend with benefits?'

He put the plate back down on the shelf and replaced the earrings carefully. 'That part is strictly between us.'

'And if your father asks how we met?'

'Tell him the truth. He'd be amused, I assure you.'

'So you don't want to pretend we're madly in love or anything? I don't have to pose as your girlfriend?'

'No. You'd be going as yourself, Lily.' A muscle flickered in his lean jaw. 'God knows, the wedding will be stressful enough without us playing roles that feel unnatural.'

It was his obvious distaste for lies and games that made up her mind. After David, a man whose instinct was to tell the truth was appealing. 'When would we leave?'

'Next Saturday. The wedding is on Tuesday but there will be four days of celebrations.' It was obvious from his expression he'd rather be dragged naked through an active volcano than join in those celebrations and a horrible thought crept into her mind.

'You're not going because you're planning to break off the wedding, are you?'

'No.' His gaze didn't shift from hers. 'But I won't tell you it didn't cross my mind.'

'I'm glad you rose above your natural impulse to wreck someone else's happiness. And if you really think it would help to have me there, then I'll come, if only to make sure you don't have second thoughts and decide to sabotage your father's big day.' Lily sank down onto the edge of her bed, thinking. 'I'll need to ask for time off.'

'Is that a problem? I could make a few calls.'

'No way!' Imagining how the curator at the museum would respond to personal intervention from Nik Zervakis, Lily recoiled in alarm. 'I'm quite capable of handling it myself. I don't need to bring in the heavy artillery, I'll simply ask the question. I'm owed holiday and my post ends in a couple of weeks anyway. Where exactly are we going? Where is "home" for you?'

'My father owns an island off the north coast of

Crete. You will like it. The western part of the island has Minoan remains and there is a Venetian castle on one of the hilltops. It is separated from Crete by a lagoon and the beaches are some of the best anywhere in Greece. When you're not reminding me to smile, I'm sure you'll enjoy exploring.'

'And he *owns* this island? So tourists can't visit.'

'That's right. It belongs to my family.'

Lily looked at him doubtfully. 'How many guests will there be?'

'Does it matter?'

'I wondered, that's all.' She wanted to ask where they'd be sleeping but decided that if his father could afford a private island then presumably there wasn't a shortage of beds. 'I need to go shopping.'

'Given that you are doing me a favour, I insist you allow me to take care of that side of things.'

'No. Apart from last night, which wasn't real, I buy my own clothes. But thanks.'

'Last night didn't feel real?' He gave her a long, penetrating look and she felt heat rush into her cheeks as she remembered all the very real things he'd done to her and she'd done to him.

'I mean it wasn't really my life. More like a dreamy moment you know is never going to happen again.' Realising it was long past time she kept her mouth shut, she gave a weak smile. 'I'll buy or borrow clothes, don't worry. I'm good at putting together a wardrobe. Colours are my thing. The secret is to accessorise. I won't embarrass you even if we're surrounded by people dressed head to toe in Prada.'

'That possibility didn't enter my head. My concern was purely about the pressure on your budget.'

'I'm creative. It's not a problem.' She remembered she was wearing his shirt. 'I'll return this, obviously.'

A smile flickered at the corners of his mouth. 'It looks better on you than it does on me. Keep it.'

His gaze collided with hers and suddenly it was hard to breathe. Sexual tension simmered in the air and she was acutely aware of the oppressive heat in the small room that had no air conditioning. Blistering, blinding awareness clouded her vision until the only thing in her world was him. She wanted so badly to touch him. She wanted to lean into that muscled power, rip off those clothes and beg him to do all the things he'd done to her the night before. Shaken, she assumed she was alone in feeling that way and then saw something flare in his eyes and knew she wasn't. He was sexually aroused and thinking all the things she was thinking.

'Nik—'

'Saturday.' His tone was thickened, his eyes a dark, dangerous black. 'I will pick you up at eight a.m.'

She watched him leave, wondering what the rules of engagement were when one night wasn't enough.

CHAPTER SIX

Nik put his foot down and pushed the Ferrari to its limits on the empty road that led to the north-western tip of Crete.

He spent the majority of his time at the ZervaCo offices in San Francisco. When he returned to Crete it was to his villa on the beach near Chania, not to the island that had been his home growing up.

For reasons he tried not to think about, he'd avoided the place for the past few years and the closer he got to their destination, the blacker his mood.

Lily, by contrast, was visibly excited. She'd been waiting on the street when he'd arrived, her bag by her feet and she'd proceeded to question him non-stop. 'So will this be like *My Big Fat Greek Wedding*? I loved that movie. Will there be dancing? Brittany and I have been learning the *kalamatianós* at the *taverna* near our apartment so I should be able to join in as long as no one minds losing their toes.' She hummed a Greek tune to herself and he sent her an exasperated look.

'Are you ever *not* cheerful?'

The humming stopped and she glanced at him. 'You want me to be miserable? Did I misunderstand the brief, because I thought I was supposed to be the sunshine to your thundercloud. I didn't realise I had to be a thundercloud, too.'

Despite his mood, he found himself smiling. 'Are you capable of being a thundercloud?'

'I'm human. I have my low moments, same as anyone.'

'Tell me your last low moment.'

'No, because then I might cry and you'd dump me by the side of the road and leave me to be pecked to death by buzzards.' She gave him a cheery smile. 'This is the point where you reassure me that you wouldn't leave me by the side of the road, and that there are no buzzards in Crete.'

'There are buzzards. Crete has a varied habitat. We have vultures, Golden Eagle, kestrel—' he slowed down as he approached a narrow section of the road '—but I have no intention of leaving you by the side of the road.'

'I'd like to think that decision is driven by your inherent good nature and kindness towards your fellow man, but I'm pretty sure it's because you don't want to have to go to this wedding alone.'

'You're right. My actions are almost always driven by self-interest.'

'I don't understand you at all. I love weddings.'

'Even when you don't know the people involved?'

'I support the principle. I think it's lovely that your father is getting married again.'

Nik struggled to subdue a rush of emotion. 'It is not lovely that he is getting married again. It's ill advised.'

'That's your opinion. But it isn't what *you* think that matters, is it? It's what *he* thinks.' She spoke with gentle emphasis. 'And he thinks it's a good idea. For the record, I think it says a lot about a person that he is prepared to get married again.'

'It does.' As they hit a straight section of road, he pushed the car to its limits and the engine gave a throaty roar. 'It says he's a man with an inability to learn from his mistakes.'

'I don't see it that way.' Her hair whipped around her face and she anchored it with her hand and lifted her face to the sun. 'I think it shows optimism and I love that.'

Hearing the breathy, happy note in her voice he shook his head. 'Lily, how have you survived in this world without being eaten alive by unscrupulous people determined to take advantage of you?'

'I've been hurt on many occasions.'

'That doesn't surprise me.'

'It's part of life. I'm not going to let it shatter my belief in human nature. I'm an optimist. And what would it mean to give up? That would be like saying that love isn't out there, that it doesn't exist, and how depressing would *that* be?'

Nik, who lived his life firmly of the conviction that love didn't exist, didn't find it remotely depressing. To him, it was simply fact. 'Clearly you are the perfect wedding guest. You could set up a business, weddingguests.com. Optimists-R-us. You could be the guaranteed smile at every wedding.'

'Your cynicism is deeply depressing.'

'Your optimism is deeply concerning.'

'I prefer to think of it as inspiring. I don't want to be one of those people who think that a challenging past has to mean a challenging future.'

'You had a challenging past?' He remembered that she'd mentioned being brought up in foster care and hoped she wasn't about to give him the whole story.

She didn't. Instead she shrugged and kept her eyes straight ahead. 'It was a bit like a bad version of *Goldilocks and the Three Bears*. I was never "just right" for anyone, but that was my bad luck. I didn't meet the right family. Doesn't mean I don't believe there are loads of great families out there.'

'Doesn't what happened to you cause you to question the validity of any of these emotions you feel? The fact that the last guy lied to you *and* his wife doesn't put you off relationships?'

'It was one guy. I know enough about statistics to know you can't draw a reliable conclusion from a sample of one.' She frowned. 'If I'm honest, I'm working from a bigger sample than that because he's the third relationship I've had, but I still don't think you can make a judgement on the opposite sex based on the behaviour of a few.'

Nik, who had done exactly that, stayed silent and of course she noticed because she was nothing if not observant.

'Put it this way—if I'm bitten by a shark am I going to avoid swimming in the sea? I could, but then I'd be depriving myself of one of my favourite activities so instead I choose to carry on swimming and be a little more alert. Life isn't always about taking the safe option. Risk has to be balanced against the joy of living. I call it being receptive.'

'I call it being ridiculously naïve.'

She looked affronted. 'You're cross and irritable because you're not looking forward to this, but there is no reason to take it out on me. I'm here as a volunteer, remember?'

'You're right. I apologise.'

'Accepted. But for your father's sake you need to work on your body language. If you think you're a thundercloud you're deluding yourself because right now you're more of a tropical cyclone. You have to stop being judgemental and embrace what's happening.'

Nik took the sharp right-hand turn that led down to the beach and the private ferry. 'I am finding it hard to embrace something I know to be a mistake. It's like watching someone driving their car full speed towards a brick wall and not trying to do something to stop it.'

'You don't know it's a mistake,' she said calmly. 'And even if it is, he's an adult and should be allowed to make his own decisions. Now smile.'

He pulled in, killed the engine and turned to look at her.

Those unusual violet eyes reminded him of the spring flowers that grew high in the mountains. 'I will not be so hypocritical as to pretend I am pleased, but I promise not to spoil the moment.'

'If you don't smile then you *will* spoil the moment! Poor Diandra might take one look at your face and decide she doesn't want to marry into your family and then your father would be heartbroken. I can't believe I'm saying this, but be hypocritical if that's what it takes to make you smile.'

'Poor Diandra will not be poor for long so I think it unlikely she'll let anything stand in the way of her wedding, even my intimidating presence.'

Her eyes widened. 'Is that what this is about? You think she's after his money?'

'I have no idea but I'd be a fool not to consider it.' Nik saw no reason to be anything but honest. 'He is mega wealthy. She was his cook.'

'What does her occupation have to do with it? Love is about people, not professions. And I find it very offensive that you'd even think that. You can't judge a person based on their income. I know plenty of wealthy people who are slimeballs. In fact if we're going with stereotypes here, I'd say that generally speaking in order to amass great wealth you have to be prepared to be pretty ruthless. There are plenty of wealthy people who aren't that nice.'

Nik, who had never aspired to be 'nice', was careful not to let his expression change. 'Are you calling me a slimeball?'

'I'm simply pointing out that income isn't an indicator of a person's worth.'

'You mean because you don't know the level of expenditure?'

'No! Why is everything about money with you? I'm talking about *emotional* worth. Your father told me about Diandra. He was ill with flu last winter after Callie left. He was so ill at one point he couldn't drag himself from the bed. I sympathised because it happened to me once and I hope I never get flu again. Anyway, Diandra cared for him the whole time. She was the one who called the doctor. She made all his meals. That was kind, don't you think?'

'Or opportunistic.'

'If you carry on thinking like that you are going to

die lonely. He met her when she cooked him her special moussaka to try and tempt him to eat. I *love* that he doesn't care what she does.'

'He should care. She stands to gain an enormous amount financially from this wedding.'

'That's horrible.'

'It is truly horrible. Finally we find something we agree on.'

'I wasn't agreeing with you! It's your attitude that's horrible, not this wedding. You're not only a judgemental cynic, you're also a raging snob.'

Nik breathed deeply. 'I am not a raging snob, but I am realistic.'

'No, what you are is damaged. Not everything has a price, Nik, and there are things in life that are far more important than money. Your father is trying to make a family and I think that's admirable.' She fumbled with the seat belt. 'Get me out of this car before I'm contaminated by you. Your thundercloud is about to rain all over my sunny patch of life.'

Your father is trying to make a family.

Nik thought about everything that had gone before.

He'd buried the pain and hurt deep and it was something he had never talked about with anyone, especially not his father, who had his own pain to deal with. What would happen when this relationship collapsed?

'If my father entered relationships with some degree of caution and objective contemplation then I would be less concerned, but he makes the same mistake you make. He confuses physical intimacy with love.' He saw the colour streak across her cheeks.

'I'm not confused. Have I spun fairy tales about the

night we spent together? Have I fallen in love with you? No. I know exactly what it was and what we did. You're in a little compartment in my brain labelled "Once in a Lifetime Experiences" along with skydiving and a helicopter flight over the New York skyline. It was amazing by the way.'

'The helicopter flight was amazing?'

'No, I haven't done that yet. I was talking about the night with you, although there were moments that felt as nerve-racking as skydiving.' Her mouth tilted into a self-conscious smile. 'Of course it's also a little embarrassing looking at you in daylight after all those things we did in the dark, but I'm trying not to think about it. Now stop being annoying. In fact, stop talking for a while. That way I'm less likely to kill you before we arrive.'

Nik refrained from pointing out she'd been the only one in the dark. He'd had perfect vision and he'd used it to his own shameless advantage. There wasn't a single corner of her body he hadn't explored and the memory of every delicious curve was welded in his brain.

He tried to work out what it was about her that was so appealing. Innocence wasn't a quality he generally admired in a person so he had to assume the power of the attraction stemmed from the sheer novelty of being with someone who had managed to retain such an untarnished view of the world.

'Are you embarrassed about the night we spent together?'

'I would be if I thought about it, so I'm not thinking about it. I'm living in the moment.' Having offered that simple solution to the problem, she reached into the back of the car for her hat. 'You could take the same approach to the wedding. You're not here to fix it or protect anyone. You're here as a guest and your only responsibility is to smile and look happy. Is this it? Are we here? Because I don't see an island. Maybe your father might have changed the venue when he saw the black cloud of your presence approaching over the horizon.'

Nik dragged his gaze from her mouth to the jetty. 'This is it. From here, we go by boat.'

Lily stood in the prow of the boat feeling the cool brush of the wind on her face and tasting the salty air. The boat skimmed and bounced over the sparkling ocean towards the large island in the distance, sending a light spray over her face and tangling her hair.

Nik stood behind the wheel, legs braced, eyes hidden behind a pair of dark glasses. Despite the unsmiling set of his mouth, he looked more approachable and less the hard-headed businessman.

'This is so much fun. I think I might love it more than your Ferrari.'

He gave a smile that turned him from insanely good-looking to devastating, and she felt the intensity of the attraction like a physical punch.

It was true he didn't seem to display any of the family values that were so important to her, but that didn't do anything to diminish the sexual attraction.

As far as she could tell, he couldn't be more perfect for a short-term relationship.

For the whole trip in the car she'd been aware of him. As he'd shifted gear his hand had brushed against her bare thigh and she'd discovered that being with him was an exciting, exhilarating experience that was like nothing she'd experienced before.

There had been a brief moment when they'd pulled into the car park that she'd thought he might be about to kiss her. He'd looked at her mouth the way a panther looked at its prey before it devoured it, but just when she'd been about to close her eyes and take a fast ride to bliss, he'd sprung from the car, leaving her to wonder if she'd imagined it.

She'd followed him to the jetty, watching in fascination as the group of people gathered there sprang to attention. If she needed any more evidence of the power he wielded, she had only to observe the way people responded to him. He behaved with an authority that was instinctive, his air of command unmistakable even in this apparently casual setting.

It was a good job he didn't possess any of the qualities she was looking for, she thought, otherwise she'd be in trouble.

Her gaze lingered on his bronzed throat, visible at the open neck of his shirt. He handled the boat with the same confident assurance he displayed in everything and she was sure that no electrical device had ever dared to misbehave under his expert touch.

Trying not to think about just how expert his touch had been, she anchored her hair and shouted above the wind. 'The beaches are beautiful. People aren't allowed to bathe here?'

'You can bathe here. You're my guest.' As they approached the island, he slowed the speed of the boat and skilfully steered against the dock.

Two men instantly jumped forward to help and Nik sprang from the boat and held out his hand to her.

'I need to get my bag.'

'They will bring our luggage up to the villa later.'

'I have a gift for your father and it's only one bag,' she muttered. 'I can carry a single bag.'

'You bought a gift?'

'Of course. It's a wedding. I couldn't come without a small gift.' She stepped out of the bobbing boat and allowed herself to hold his hand for a few seconds longer than was necessary for balance. She felt warmth and strength flow through her fingers and had to battle the temptation to press herself against him. 'So how many bedrooms does your father have? Are you sure there is room for me to stay?'

The question seemed to amuse him. 'There will be room, *theé mou*, don't worry. As well as the main villa, there are several other properties scattered around the island. We will be staying in one of those.'

As they walked up a sandy path she breathed in the wonderful scents of sea juniper and wild thyme. 'One of the things I love most about Crete is the thyme honey. Brittany and I eat it for breakfast.'

'My father keeps bees so he will be very happy to hear you say that.'

The path forked at the top and he turned right and took the path that led down to another beach. There, nestling in the small horseshoe bay of golden sand with the water almost lapping at the whitewashed walls, was a beautiful contemporary villa.

Lily stopped. '*That's* your father's house?' The position was idyllic, the villa stunning, but it looked more like a honeymoon hideaway than somewhere to accommodate a large number of high-profile international guests.

'No. This is Camomile Villa. The main house is fifteen minutes' walk in the other direction, towards the small Venetian fort. I thought we'd unpack and breathe for an hour or so before we face the guests.'

Witnessing his tension, she felt a rush of compassion. 'Nik—' She put her hand on his cheek and turned his face to hers. 'This is a wedding, not the sacking of Troy. You do not need to find your strength or breathe. Your role is to smile and enjoy yourself.'

His gaze locked on hers and she wished she hadn't touched him. His blue-shadowed jaw was rough beneath her fingers and suddenly she was remembering that night in minute detail.

Seriously unsettled, she started to pull her hand away but he caught her wrist in his fingers and held it there.

'You are a very unusual woman.' His voice was husky and she gave a faint smile, ignoring the wild flutter of nerves low in her stomach.

'I am not even going to ask what you mean by that. I'm simply going to take it as a compliment.'

'Of course you are.' There was a strange gleam in his eyes. 'You see positive in everything, don't you?'

'Not always.' She could have told him that she saw very little positive in being alone in the world, having no family, but given his obvious state of tension she decided to keep that confidence to herself. 'So how do you know we're staying in Camomile Villa? Cute name, by the way. Maybe your father has given it to one of the other guests. Shouldn't you go and check?'

'Camomile belongs to me.'

Lily digested that. 'So actually you own five properties, not four.'

'I don't count this place.'

'Really? Because if I owned this I'd be spending
every spare minute here.' She walked up the path, past
silvery green olive trees, nets lying on the ground ready
for harvesting later in the year. A small lizard lay bask-
ing in the hot sun and she smiled as it sensed company
and darted for safety into the dry, dusty earth.

The path leading down to the villa cut through a garden of tumbling colour. Bougainvillaea in bright pinks
and purples blended and merged against the dazzling
white of the walls and the perfect blue of the sky.

Nik opened the door and Lily followed him inside.

White beamed ceilings and natural stone floors gave
the interior a cool, uncluttered feel and the elegant white
interior was lifted by splashes of Mediterranean blue.

'If you don't want this place, I might live here.' Lily
looked at the shaded terrace with its beautiful infinity
pool. 'Why does anyone need a pool when the sea is
five steps from the front door?'

'Some people don't like swimming in the sea.'

'I'm not one of those people. I adore the sea. Nik,
this place is—' she felt a lump in her throat '—it's really special.'

He opened the doors to the terrace and gave her a
wary look. 'Are you going to cry?'

'It's perfect.' She blinked. 'And I'm fine. Happy. And
excited. I love Crete, but I never get the chance to enjoy
it like a tourist. I'm always working.' And never in her
life had she experienced this level of luxury.

She and Brittany were always moaning about the mosquitoes and lack of air conditioning in their tiny apartment. At night they slept with the windows open to make the most of the breeze from the sea, but in the summer months it was almost unbearable indoors.

'You are the most unusual woman I've ever met. You enjoy small things.'

'This is not a small thing. And you're the unusual one.' She picked up her bag. 'You take this life for granted.'

'That is not true. I know how fortunate I am.'

'I don't think you do, but I'm going to be pointing it out to you every minute for the next few days so hopefully by the time we leave you will.' She glanced around her and then looked at him expectantly. 'My bedroom?'

For a wild, unnerving moment she hoped he was going to tell her there was just one bedroom, but he gestured to a door that led from the large spacious living area.

'The guest suite is through there. Make yourself comfortable.'

Guest suite.

So he didn't intend them to share a room. For Nik, it really had been one night.

Telling herself it was probably for the best, she followed his directions and walked through an open door into a bright, airy bedroom. The bed was draped in layers of cream and white, deep piles of cushions and pillows inviting the occupant to lounge and relax. The walls were hung with bold, contemporary art, slashes of deep blue on large canvases that added a stylish touch to the room. In one corner stood a tall, elegant vase in graduated blues, the colour shifting under the dazzling sunlight.

Lily recognised it instantly. 'That's one of Skylar's pots.'

He looked at her curiously. 'You know the artist?'

'Skylar Tempest. She and Brittany were roommates at college. They're best friends, as close as sisters. I would know her work anywhere. Her style, her use of colour and composition is unique, but I know that pot specifically because I talked to her about it. Brittany introduced us because Skylar wanted to talk to me about ceramics. She's incorporated a few Minoan designs into some of her work, modernised, of course.' She knelt down and slid her hand over the smooth surface of the glass. 'This is from her *Mediterranean Sky* collection. She had a small exhibition in New York, not only glass and pots but jewellery and a couple of paintings. She's insanely talented.'

'You were at that exhibition?'

'Sadly no. I don't move in those circles. Nor do I pretend to claim any credit for any of her incredible creations, but I did talk to her about shapes and style. Of course the Minoans used terracotta clay. It was Sky's idea to reproduce the shape in glass. Look at this—' She trailed her finger lightly over the surface. 'The Minoans usually decorated their pots with dark on light motifs, often of sea creatures, and she's taken her inspiration from that. It's genius. I can't believe you own it. Where did you find it?'

'I was at the exhibition.'

'In New York? How did you even know about her?'

'I saw her work in a small artisan jewellers in Green-

wich Village and I bought one of her necklaces for—'
He broke off and Lily looked at him expectantly.

'For? For one of your women? We're not in a relationship, Nik. You don't have to censor your conversation. And even if we were in a relationship you still
wouldn't need to censor it.'

'In my experience, most women do not appreciate
hearing about their predecessors.'

'Yes, well the more I hear about the women you've
known in your life, the more I'm not surprised. Now
tell me about how you discovered Skylar.'

'I asked to see more of her work and was told she was
having an exhibition. I managed to get myself invited.'

Lily rocked back on her heels. 'She never mentioned
that she met you.'

'We never met. I didn't introduce myself. I went on
the first night and she was surrounded by well-wish-
ers, so I simply bought a few pieces and left. That was
two years ago.'

'So she doesn't know she sold pieces to Nik Zervakis?'

'A member of my team handled the actual transac-
tion.'

Lily scrambled to her feet. 'Because you don't touch
real money? She would be so excited if she knew her
work was here in your villa. Can I tell her?'

He looked amused. 'If you think it would interest
her, then yes.'

'Interest her? Of course it would interest her.' Lily
pulled her phone out of her bag and took a photo. 'I
must admit that pot looks perfect there. It needs a large
room with lots of light. Did you know she has another
exhibition coming up?' She slipped her phone back into

her bag. 'December in London. An upmarket gallery in Knightsbridge is showing her work. She's really excited. Her new collection is called *Ocean Blue*. It's still sea themed. Brittany showed me some photos.'

'Will you be going?'

'To an exhibition in Knightsbridge? Sure. I thought I'd fly in on my private jet, spend a night in the Royal Suite at The Savoy and then get my driver to take me to the exhibition.' She laughed and then saw something flicker in his eyes. 'Er—that's exactly what you're going to be doing, isn't it?'

'My plans aren't confirmed.'

'But you do have a private jet.'

'ZervaCo owns a Gulfstream and a couple of Lear jets.' He said it as if it was normal and she shook her head, trying not to be intimidated.

For her, wealth was people and family, not money, but still—

'Seriously, Nik. What am I doing here? To you a Gulfstream is a mode of transport, to me it's a warm Atlantic current. I used to own a rusty mountain bike until the wheel fell off. I'm the one who works in a dusty museum, digs in the dirt in the summer and cleans other people's houses to give myself enough money to live. And living doesn't include jetting across Europe to a friend's exhibition. I have no idea where I'll even be in December. I'm job hunting.'

'Wherever you are, I'll fly you there. And for your information, I wouldn't be staying in the Royal Suite.'

'Because you already own an apartment that most royals would kill for.' His lack of response told her she was right and she rolled her eyes. 'Nik, we had an illuminating conversation earlier during which you confessed that you think your new stepmother is only interested in your father's money. Money is obviously a very big deal to you, so I'm hardly likely to take you up on your offer of a ride in your private jet, am I?'

'That is different. I'm grateful that you agreed to come here with me,' he said softly, 'and taking you to Skylar's exhibition would be my way of saying thank you.'

'I don't need a thank you. And to be honest I'm here because of the conversation I had with your father. My decision didn't have anything to do with you. We had one night, that's all. I mean, the sex was great, but I had no trouble walking out of your door that morning. There were no feelings involved.' She shook her head to add emphasis. 'Kevlar, that's me.'

He gave her a long, steady look. 'I have never met anyone who less resembles that substance.'

'Up until a week ago I would have agreed with you, but now I'm a changed person. Seriously, I'm enjoying being with you. You're smoking hot and surprisingly entertaining despite your warped view of relationships, but I am no more in love with you than I am with your supersonic shower. And you don't owe me anything for bringing me here—in fact I owe you.' She glanced across the room to the terrace outside. 'This is the nearest I've come to a vacation in a long time. It's not exactly a hardship being here. I am going to lie in the sun like that lizard out there.'

'You haven't met my family yet.' He paused, his gaze fixed on hers. 'Think about it. If you change your mind about coming to Skylar's London exhibition, let me know. The invitation stands. I won't withdraw it.'

It was a different world.

What would it be like, she wondered, not to have to think about your budget? Not to have to make choices between forfeiting one thing to buy another?

This close she could see the flecks of gold in those dark eyes, the blue-black shadow of his jaw and the almost unbelievably perfect lines of his bone structure. If a scale had been invented to measure sex appeal, she was pretty sure he would have shattered it. She couldn't look at his mouth without remembering all the ways he'd used it on her body and remembering made her want it again. She wanted to reach out and slide her fingers into that silky dark hair and press her mouth to his. And this time she wanted to do it without the blindfold.

Aware that her mind was straying into forbidden territory she took a step back, reminding herself that money came a poor second to family and this man seemed to be virtually estranged from his father.

'I won't change my mind.'

Dragging her gaze from his, she dropped her bag on the floor and unzipped it. 'I need to hang up my dresses or they'll be creased. I don't want to make a bad impression.'

'There are staff over in the main villa who will help you unpack. I can call them.'

'Are you kidding?' Amused by yet more evidence of the differences between their respective lifestyles, she pulled out her clothes. 'This will take me five minutes at most. And I'd be embarrassed to ask anyone else to hang up a tee shirt that cost the same amount as a cup of coffee. So what happens next?'

'We are joining my father and Diandra for lunch.'

'Sounds good to me.'

The expression on his face told her he didn't share her sentiments. 'I need to make some calls. Make yourself at home. The fridge is stocked, there are books in the living room. Feel free to use the pool. If there is anything you need, let me know. I'll be using the office on the other side of the living room.'

What else could she possibly need?

Lily glanced round the villa, which was by far the most luxurious and exclusive place she'd ever stayed.

She had a feeling the only thing she was going to need was a reality check.

He hadn't been back here since that summer five years before. It had been an attempt to put the past behind him, but ironically it had succeeded only in making things worse.

The memory of his last visit sat in his head like a muddy stain.

Nik strolled out onto the terrace, hoping the view would relieve his tension, but being here took him right back to his childhood and that was a place he made a point of avoiding.

With a soft curse, he walked back into the room he'd had converted into an office and switched on his laptop.

For the next hour he took an endless stream of calls and then finally, when he couldn't postpone the moment any longer, he took a quick shower and changed for lunch.

Another day, another wedding.

Mouth grim, he pocketed his phone and strolled through the villa to find Lily.

She was sitting in the shade on the terrace, a glass of iced lemonade by her hand and a book in her lap, staring out across the bright turquoise blue of the bay.

She hadn't noticed him and he stood for a moment, watching her. The tension left him to be replaced by tension of a different source. That one night he'd spent with her hadn't been anywhere near long enough.

He wanted to rip off that pretty blue sundress and take her straight back to bed but he knew that, no matter what she said, she wasn't the sort of woman to be able to keep her emotions out of the bedroom so he gave her a cool smile as he strolled onto the terrace.

'Are you ready?'

'Yes.' She slid her feet into a pair of silver ballet flats and put her book on the table. 'Is there anything I should know? Who will be there?'

'My father and Diandra. They wanted this lunch to be family only.'

'In other words your father doesn't want your first meeting for a long while to be in public.' She reached for her glass and finished her drink. 'Don't worry about me while we're here. I'm sure I can find a few friendly faces to talk to while you're mingling.'

He looked down at the curve of her cheeks and the dimple in the corner of her mouth and decided she was the one with the friendly face. If he had to pick a single word to describe her, it would be approachable. She was warm, friendly and he was sure there would be no shortage of guests eager to talk to her. The thought should have reduced his stress because it gave him one less responsibility, but it didn't.

Despite her claims to being made of Kevlar, he wasn't convinced she'd managed to manufacture even a thin layer of protection for herself.

He offered to drive her to avoid the heat but she chose to walk and on the way up to the main house she grilled him about his background. Did his father still work? What exactly was his business? Did he have any other family apart from Nik?

His suspicion that she was more comfortable with this gathering than him was confirmed as soon as he walked onto the terrace.

He saw the table by the pool laid for four and felt Lily sneak her hand into his.

'He wants you to get to know Diandra. He's trying to build bridges,' she said softly, her fingers squeezing his. 'Don't glare.'

Before he could respond, his father walked out onto the terrace.

'Niklaus—' His voice shook and Nik saw the shimmer of tears in his father's eyes.

Lily extracted her hand from his. 'Hug him.' She made it sound simple and Nik wondered whether bringing someone as idealistic as Lily to a reunion as complicated as this one had been entirely sensible, but she and his father obviously thought alike because he walked towards them, arms outstretched.

'It's been too long since you were home. Far too long, but the past is behind us. All is forgiven. I have such news to tell you, Niklaus.'

Forgiven?

His feet nailed to the floor by the past and the weight of the secrets his father didn't know, Nik didn't move and then he felt Lily's small hand in his back pushing, harder this time, and he then stepped forward and was embraced by his father so tightly it knocked the air from his lungs.

He felt a heaviness in his chest that had nothing to do with the intensity of his father's grip. Emotions rushed towards him and he was beginning to wish he'd never agreed to this reunion when Lily stepped forward, breaking the tension of the moment with her warmest, brightest smile and an extended hand that gave his father no choice but to release Nik.

'I'm Lily Rose. We spoke on the phone. You have a very beautiful home, Mr Zervakis. It's kind of you to invite me to share your special day.' Blushing charmingly, she then attempted to speak a few words of Greek, a gesture that both distracted his father and guaranteed a lifetime of devotion.

Nik watched as his dazzled father melted like butter left in the hot sun.

He kissed her hand and switched to heavily accented English. 'You are welcome in my home, Lily. I'm so happy you are able to join us for what is turning out to be the most special week of my life. This is Diandra.'

For the first time Nik noticed the woman hovering in the background.

He'd assumed she was one of his father's staff, but now she stepped forward and quietly introduced herself.

Nik noticed that she didn't quite meet his eye, instead she focused all her attention on Lily as if she were the lifebelt floating on the surface of a deep pool of water.

Diandra clearly had sophisticated radar for detecting sympathy in people, Nik thought, wondering what 'news' his father had for them.

Experience led him to assume it was unlikely to be good.

'I've brought you a small gift. I made it myself.' Lily delved into her bag and handed over a prettily wrapped parcel.

It was a ceramic plate, similar to the one he'd admired in her apartment, decorated with the same pattern of swirling blues and greens.

Nik could see she had real talent and so, apparently, did his father.

'You made this? But this isn't your business?'

'No. I'm an archaeologist. But I did my dissertation on Minoan ceramics so it's an interest of mine.'

'You must tell me all about it. And all about yourself. Lily Rose is a beautiful name.' His father led her towards the table that had been laid next to the pool. Silver gleamed in the sunlight and bowls of olives gleamed glossy dark in beautiful blue bowls. Kostas put Lily's plate in the centre of the table. 'Your mother liked flowers?'

'I don't know. I didn't know my mother.' She shot Nik an apologetic look. 'That's too much information for a first meeting. Let's talk about something else.'

But Kostas Zervakis wasn't so easily deflected. 'You didn't know your mother? She passed away when you were young, *koukla mou*?'

Appalled by that demonstration of insensitivity, Nik shot him an exasperated look and was about to steer the conversation away from such a deeply personal topic when Lily answered.

'I don't know what happened to her. She left me in a basket in Kew Gardens in London when I was a few hours old.'

Whatever he'd expected to hear, it hadn't been that and Nik, who made a point of never asking about a woman's past, found himself wanting to know more. 'A basket?' Her eyes lifted to his and for a moment the presence of other people was forgotten.

'Yes. I was found by one of the staff and taken to hospital. They called me Lily Rose because I was found among the flowers. They never traced my mother. They assumed she was a teenager who panicked.' She spoke in a matter-of-fact tone but Nik knew she wasn't matter-of-fact about the way she felt.

This was why she had shown so much wistful interest in the detail of his family. At the time he hadn't been able to understand why it would make an interesting topic of conversation, but now he understood that, to her, it was not a frustration or a complication. It was an aspiration.

This was why she dreamed of happy endings, both for herself and other people.

He felt something stir inside him, an emotion that was entirely new to him.

He'd believed himself immune to even the most elaborately constructed sob story, but Lily's revelation had somehow managed to slide under those steely layers of protection he'd constructed for himself. For some reason, her simply stated story touched him deeply.

Unsettled, he dragged his eyes from her soft mouth and promised himself that no matter how much he wanted her, he wasn't going to touch her again. It wouldn't be fair, when their expectations of life were so different. He had no concerns about his own ability to keep a relationship superficial. He did, however, have deep concerns about her ability to do the same and he didn't want to hurt her.

His father, predictably, was visibly moved by the revelation about her childhood.

'No family?' His voice was roughened by emotion. 'So who raised you, *koukla mou*?'

'I was brought up in a series of foster homes.' She poked absently at her food. 'And now I think we should talk about something else because this is *definitely* too much detail for a first meeting, especially when we're here to celebrate a wedding.' Superficially she was as cheerful as ever but Nik knew she was upset.

He was about to make another attempt to change the topic when his father reached out and took Lily's hand.

'One day you will have a family of your own. A big family.'

Nik ground his teeth. 'I don't think Lily wants to talk about that right now.'

'I don't mind.' Lily sent him a quick smile and then turned back to his father. 'I hope so. I think family makes you feel anchored and I've never had that.'

'Anchors keep a boat secured in one place,' Nik said softly, 'which can be limiting.'

Her gaze met his and he knew she was deciding if his observation was random or a warning.

He wasn't sure himself. All he knew was that he didn't want her thinking this was anything other then temporary. He could see she'd had a tough life. He didn't want to be the one to shatter that optimism and remove the smile from her face.

His father gave a disapproving frown. 'Ignore him. When it comes to relationships my son behaves like a child in a sweetshop. He gorges his appetites without learning the benefits of selectivity. He enjoys success in everything he touches except, sadly, his private life.'

'I'm very selective.' Nik reached for his wine. 'And given that my private life is exactly the way I want it to be, I consider it an unqualified success.'

He banked down the frustration, wondering how his father, thrice divorced, could consider himself an example to follow.

His father looked at him steadily. 'All the money in the world will not bring a man the same feeling of contentment as a wife and children, don't you agree, Lily?'

'As someone with massive college loans, I wouldn't dismiss the importance of money,' Lily said honestly, 'but I agree that family is the most important thing.'

Feeling as if he'd woken up on the set of a Hollywood rom-com in which he'd been cast in the role of 'bad guy', Nik refrained from asking his father which of his wives had ever given him anything other than stomach ulcers and astronomical bills. Surely even he couldn't reframe his romantic past as anything other than a disaster.

'One day you will have a family, Lily.' Kostas Zervakis surveyed her with misty eyes and Nik observed this emotional interchange with something between disbelief and despair.

His father had known Lily for less than five minutes and already he was ready to leave her everything in his will. It was no wonder he'd made himself a target for every woman with a sob story.

Callie had spotted that vulnerability and dug her claws deep. No doubt Diandra was working on the same soft spot.

A dark, deeply buried memory stirred in the depths of his brain. His father, sitting alone in the bedroom among the wreckage of his wife's hasty packing, the image of wretched despair as she drove away without looking back.

Never, before or since, had Nik felt as powerless as he had that day. Even though he'd been a young child, he'd known he was witnessing pain beyond words.

The second time it had happened, he'd been a teenager and he remembered wondering why his father would have risked putting himself through such emotional agony a second time.

And then there had been Callie...

He'd known from the first moment that the relationship was doomed and had blamed himself later for not trying to save his father from that particular mistake.

And now here he was again, trapped in the unenviable position of having to make a choice between watching his father walk into another relationship disaster, or potentially damaging their relationship by trying to intervene.

Lily was right that his father was a grown man, able to make his own decisions. So why did he still have this urge to push his father out of the path of the oncoming train?

Emotions boiling inside him, he glanced across the table to his future stepmother, wondering if it was a coincidence that she'd picked the chair as far from his as possible.

She was either shy or she was harbouring a guilty conscience.

He'd promised he wouldn't interfere, but he was fast rethinking that decision.

He sat in silence, observing rather than participating, while staff discreetly served food and topped up glasses.

His father engaged Lily in conversation, encouraging her to talk about her life and her love of archaeology and Greece.

Forced to sit through a detailed chronology of Lily's life history, Nik learned that she'd had three boyfriends, worked numerous low-paid jobs to pay for college tuition, was allergic to cats, suffered from severe eczema as a child and had never lived in the same place for more than twelve months.

The more he discovered about her life, the more he realised how hard it had been. She'd made a joke about Cinderella, but Lily made Cinderella look like a slacker.

Learning far more than he'd ever wanted to know, he turned to his father. 'What is the "news" you have for me?'

'You will find out soon enough. First, I am enjoying having the company of my son. It's been too long. I have resorted to the Internet to find news of what is happening with you. You have been spending a great deal of time in San Francisco.'

Happy to talk about anything that shifted the focus from Lily, Nik relaxed slightly and talked broadly about some of the technology developments his company was spearheading and touched lightly on the deal he was about to close, but the diversion proved to be brief.

Kostas spooned olives onto Lily's plate. 'You must persuade Nik to take you to the far side of the island to see the Minoan remains. You will need to go early in the day, before it is too hot. At this time of year everything is very dry. If you love flowers, then you will love Crete in the spring. In April and May the island is covered in poppies, daisies, camomile, iris.' He beamed at her. 'You must come back here then and visit.'

'I'd like that.' Lily tucked into her food. 'These olives are delicious.'

'They come from our own olive groves and the lemonade in your fridge came from lemons grown on our own trees. Diandra made it. She is a genius in the kitchen. You wait until you taste her lamb.' Kostas leaned across and took Diandra's hand. 'I took one mouthful and fell in love.'

Losing his appetite, Nik gave her a direct look. 'Tell me about yourself, Diandra. Where were you brought up?' He caught Lily's urgent glance and ignored it, instead listening to Diandra's stammered response.

From that he learned that she was one of six children and had never been married.

'She never met the right person, and that is lucky for me,' his father said indulgently.

Nik opened his mouth to speak, but Lily got there first.

'You're so lucky having been born in Greece,' she said quickly. 'I've travelled extensively in the islands but living here must be wonderful. I've spent three summers on Crete and one on Corfu. Where else do you think I should visit?'

Giving her a grateful look, Diandra made several suggestions, but Nik refused to be deflected from his path.

'Who did you work for before my father?'

'Ignore him,' Lily said lightly. 'He makes every conversation feel like a job interview. The first time I met him I wanted to hand over my résumé. This lamb is *delicious* by the way. You're so clever. It's even better than the lamb Nik and I ate last week and that was a top restaurant.' She went on to describe what they'd eaten in minute detail and Diandra offered a few observations of her own about the best way to cook lamb.

Deprived of the opportunity to question his future stepmother further, Nik was wondering once again what 'news' his father was preparing to announce, when he heard the sound of a child crying inside the house.

Diandra shot to her feet and exchanged a brief look with his father before scurrying from the table.

Nik narrowed his eyes. 'Who,' he said slowly, 'is that?'

'That's the news I was telling you about.' His father turned his head and watched as Diandra returned to the table carrying a toddler whose tangled blonde curls and sleepy expression announced that she'd recently awoken from a nap. 'Callie has given me full custody of Chloe as a wedding present. Niklaus, meet your half-sister.'

CHAPTER SEVEN

LILY SAT ON the sunlounger in the shade, listening to the rhythmic splash from the infinity pool. Nik had been swimming for the past half an hour, with no break in the relentless laps back and forth across the pool.

Whatever had possessed her to agree to come for this wedding?

It had been like falling straight into the middle of a bad soap opera.

Diandra had been so intimidated by Nik she'd barely opened her mouth and he, it seemed, had taken that as a sign that she had nothing worth saying. Lunch had been a tense affair and the moment his father had produced his little half-sister Nik had gone from being coolly civil to remote and intimidating. Lily had worked so hard to compensate for his frozen silence she'd virtually performed cartwheels on the terrace.

And she couldn't comprehend his reaction.

He was too old to care about sharing the affections of his father, and too independently wealthy to care about the impact on his inheritance. The toddler was adorable, a cherub with golden curls and a ready smile, and his father and Diandra had been so obviously thrilled by the new addition to the family Lily couldn't understand the problem.

On the walk back from lunch she'd tentatively broached the subject but Nik had cut her off and made straight for his office where he'd proceeded to work without interruption.

Trying to cure her headache, Lily had drunk plenty of water and then read her book in the shade but she'd been unable to concentrate on the words.

She knew it was none of her business, but still she couldn't keep her mouth shut and when Nik finally vaulted from the pool in an athletic movement that displayed every muscle in his powerful frame, she slid off her sunlounger and blocked his path.

'You were horrible to Diandra at lunch and if you want to heal the rift with your father, that isn't the way. She is *not* a gold-digger.'

His face was an uncompromising mask. 'And you know this on less than a few minutes' acquaintance?'

'I'm a good judge of character.'

'This from a woman who didn't know a man was married?'

She felt herself flush. 'I was wrong about him, but I'm not wrong about Diandra, and you have to stop giving her the evil eye.'

Droplets of water clung to his bronzed shoulders. 'I was not giving her the evil eye.'

'Nik, you virtually grilled her at the table. I was waiting for you to throw her on the barbecue along with the lamb. You were terrifying.'

'*Theé mou,* that is *not* true. She behaved like a woman with a guilty conscience.'

'She behaved like a woman who was terrified of you! How can you be so *blind*?' And then she realised in a flash of comprehension that she was the one who was blind. He wasn't being small-minded, or prejudiced. That wasn't what was happening. She saw now that he was afraid for his father. His actions all stemmed from a desire to protect him. In his own way he was displaying the exact loyalty she valued so highly. Like a gazelle approaching a sleeping lion, she tiptoed carefully. 'I think your perspective may be a little skewed because of what happened with your father's other relationships. Do you want to talk about it?'

'Unlike you, I don't have the desire to verbalise every thought that enters my head.'

Lily stiffened. 'That was a little harsh given that I'm trying to help, but I'm going to forgive you because I can see you're very upset. And I think I know why.'

'Don't forgive me. If you're angry, say so.'

'You told me not to verbalise every thought that enters my head.'

Nik wiped his face with the towel and sent her a look that would have frozen molten lava. 'I don't need help.'

Lily tried a different approach. 'I can see that this situation has the potential for all sorts of complications, not least that Diandra has been given another woman's child to raise as her own just a few days before the wedding, but she seemed thrilled. Your father is clearly delighted. They're happy, Nik.'

'For how long?' His mouth tightened. 'How long until it all falls apart and his heart is broken again? What if this time he doesn't heal?' His words confirmed her suspicions and she felt a rush of compassion.

'This isn't about Diandra, it's about you. You love your father deeply and you're trying to protect him.' It was ironic, she thought, that Nik Zervakis, who was supposedly so cold and aloof, turned out to have stronger family values than David Ashurst, who on the surface had seemed like perfect partner material. It was something that her checklist would never have shown up. 'I love that you care so much about him, but has it occurred to you that you might be trying to save him from the best thing that has ever happened in his life?'

'Why will this time be different from the others?'

'Because he loves her and she loves him. Of course having a toddler thrown into the mix will make for a challenging start to the relationship, but—' She frowned as she examined that fact in greater depth. 'Why did Callie choose to do this now? A child is a person, not a wedding present. You think she was hoping to derail your father's relationship with Diandra?'

'The thought had occurred to me but no, that isn't what she is trying to do.' He hesitated. 'Callie is marrying again and she doesn't want the child.'

He delivered that news in a flat monotone devoid of emotion, but this time Lily was too caught up in her own emotions to think about his.

Callie didn't want the child?

She felt as if she'd been punched in the gut. All the air had been sucked from her lungs and suddenly she couldn't breathe.

'Right.' Her voice was croaky. 'So she gives her up as if she's a dress that's gone out of fashion? I'm not surprised you didn't like her. She doesn't sound like a very likeable person.' Horrified by the intensity of her response and aware he was watching her closely, she moved past him. 'If you're sure you don't want to talk then I think I'm going to have a rest before dinner. The heat makes me sleepy.'

He frowned. 'Lily—'

'Dinner is at eight? I'll be ready by then.' She steered her shaky legs towards her bedroom and closed the door behind her.

What was the matter with her?

This wasn't her family.

It wasn't her life.

Why did she have to take everything so *personally*?

Why was she worrying about how little Chloe would feel when she was old enough to ask about her mother when it wasn't really any of her business? Why did she care about all the potential threats she could see to his family unit?

The door behind her opened and she stiffened but kept her back to him. 'I'm about to lie down.'

'I upset you,' he said quietly, 'and that was not my intention. You were generous enough to come here with me, the least I can do is respond to your questions in a civil tone. I apologise.'

'I'm not upset because you didn't want to talk. I understand you don't find it helpful.'

'Then what's wrong?' When she didn't reply he cursed softly. 'Talk to me, Lily.'

'No. I'm having lots of feelings of my own and you hate talking about feelings. And no doubt you'll find some way to interpret what I'm feeling in a bad way, because that seems to be your special gift. You twist everything beautiful into something dark and ugly. You really should leave now. I need to self-soothe.'

She expected to hear the pounding of feet and the sound of a door closing behind him, but instead felt the warm strength of his hands curve over her shoulders.

'I do not twist things.'

'Yes, you do. But that's your problem. I can't deal with it right now.'

'I don't want you to self-soothe.' The words sounded as if they were dragged from him. 'I want you to tell me what's wrong. My father asked you a lot of personal questions over lunch.'

'I don't mind that.'

'Then what? Is this about Chloe?'

She took a juddering breath. 'It's a little upsetting when adults don't consider how a child might feel. It's lovely that she has a loving father, but one day that little girl is going to wonder why her mother gave her away. She's going to ask herself whether she cried too much or did something wrong. Not that I expect you to understand.'

There was a long pulsing silence and his grip on her arms tightened. 'I do understand.' His voice was low. 'I was nine when my mother left and I asked myself all those questions and more.'

She stood still, absorbing both the enormity and the implications of that revelation. 'I didn't know.'

'I don't talk about it.'

But he'd talked about it now, with her. Warmth spread through her. 'Did seeing Chloe stir it all up for you?'

'This whole place stirs it up,' he said wearily. 'Let's hope Chloe doesn't ask herself those same questions when she's older.'

'I was a baby and I still ask myself those questions.'

And she had questions for him, so many questions, but she knew they wouldn't be welcome.

'I appreciate you listening to me, but I know you don't really want to talk about this so you should probably leave now.'

'Seeing as I am indirectly responsible for the fact you're upset by bringing you here in the first place, I have no intention of leaving.'

'You should.' Her voice was thickened. 'It's the situation, not you. You've never even met your half-sister so you can't be expected to love her and your father is obviously pleased, but a toddler is a lot of work and he's about to be married. What if he decides he doesn't want Chloe either?'

'He won't decide that.' His hands firm, he turned her to face him. 'He has wanted her from the first day, but Callie did everything she could to keep the child from him. I have no idea what my father will say when Chloe is old enough to ask, but he is a sensitive man—much more sensitive than I am as you have discovered—and he will say the right thing, I'm sure.' His hands stroked her bare arms and she gave a little shiver.

She could see the droplets of water clinging to dark hair that shadowed his bare chest.

Unable to help herself, she lifted her hand to his chest and then caught herself and pulled back.

'Sorry—' She took a step backwards but he muttered something under his breath in Greek and hauled her back against him. Her brain blurred as she was flattened against the heat and power of his body, his arm holding her trapped. He used his other hand to tilt her face to his and she drowned in the heated burn of his

eyes in the few seconds before he bent his head and
kissed her. And then there was nothing but the hunger
of his mouth and the erotic slide of his tongue and it felt
every bit as good as it had the first time. So good that
she forgot everything except the pounding of her pulse
and the desperate squirming heat low in her pelvis.

Pressed against his hard, powerful chest she forgot
about feeling miserable and unsettled.

She forgot all the reasons this wasn't a good idea.

She forgot everything except the breathtaking excitement he generated with his mouth and hands. His kiss
was unmistakably sexual, his tongue tangling with hers,
his gaze locked on hers as he silently challenged her.

'Yes, yes.' With a soft murmur of acquiescence, she
wrapped her arms round his neck, feeling the damp
ends of his hair brush her wrists.

The droplets of water on his chest dampened her
thin sundress until it felt as if there were nothing between them.

She felt him pull her hard against him, felt his hand
slide down her back and cup her bottom so that she was
pressed against the heavy thrust of his erection.

'I promised myself I wasn't going to do this but I
want you.' He spoke in a thickened tone, and she gave
a sob of relief.

'I want you, too. You have no idea how much. Right
through lunch I wanted to rip your clothes off and remove that severe look from your face.'

He lifted his mouth from hers, his breathing uneven, the smouldering glitter of his eyes telling her everything she needed to know about his feelings. 'Do I
look severe now?'

'No. You look incredible. This has been the longest week of my life.' She backed towards the bed, pulling him with her. If he changed his mind she was sure she'd explode. 'Don't have second thoughts. I know this is about sex and nothing else. I don't love you, but I'd love a repeat of all those things you did to me the other night.'

With sure hands, he dispensed with her sundress. 'All of them?'

'Yes.' She wanted him so badly it was almost indecent and when he lowered his head and trailed his mouth along her neck she almost sobbed aloud. 'Please. Right now. I want your whole repertoire. Don't hold anything back.'

'You're shy, it's still daylight,' he growled, 'and I don't have a blindfold.'

'I'm not shy. Shy has left the party. I don't care, I don't care.' Her hands moved over his chest and lower to his damp swimming shorts. She struggled to remove them over the thrusting force of his erection but finally her frantic fumbling proved successful and she covered him with the flat of her hand.

He groaned low in his throat and tipped her onto the bed, covering her body with his, telling her how much he wanted her, how hard she made him, until the excitement climbed to a point where she was a seething, writhing mass of desire. She tore at his shirt with desperate hands and he swore under his breath and wrenched it over his head, his fingers tangling with hers.

'Easy, slow down, there's no rush.'

'Yes, there is.' She rolled him onto his back and pressed her mouth to the hard planes of his chest and lower until she heard him groan. She tried to straddle him but he flipped her onto her back and caught her shifting hips in his hands, anchoring her there.

Despite the simmering tension, there was laughter in his eyes. 'It would be a criminal waste to rush this, *theé mou*.'

'No, it wouldn't.' She slid her hands over the silken muscles of his back. 'It might kill me if you don't.'

It was hard to know which of them was most aroused. She saw it in the glitter of his eyes and heard it in his uneven breathing. Felt it in the slight shake of his fingers as he unhooked her bra and peeled it away from her, releasing her breasts, taking his time. Everything he did was slow, unhurried, designed to torture her and she wondered how he could exercise so much control, such brutal discipline, because if it had been up to her the whole thing would have been over by now. He kept her still with his weight, with soft words, with skilled kisses and the sensual slide of his hand that dictated both position and pace.

She felt the cool air from the ceiling fan brush the heated surface of her skin and then moaned aloud as he drew her into the dark heat of his mouth. Sensation was sweet and wild and she arched into him, only to find herself anchored firmly by the rough strength of his thigh. He worked his way down her body with slow exploratory kisses and she shivered as she felt the brush of his lips and the flick of his tongue. Lower, more intimate, his mouth wandered to the shadows between her thighs and she felt the slippery heat of his tongue opening her, tasting her until she could feel the pleasure thundering down on her. She was feverish, desperate, everything in her body centred on this one moment.

'Nik—I need—'

'I know what you need.' A brief pause and then he eased over her and into her, each driving thrust taking him deeper until she didn't know where she ended and he began and then he paused, his hand in her hair and his mouth against hers, eyes half closed as he studied her face. She was dimly aware that he was saying something, soft intimate words that blurred in her head and melted over her skin. She felt the delicious weight of him, the masculine invasion, the solidity of muscle, the scrape of his jaw against hers as he kissed her, murmured her name and told her all the things he wanted to do to her. And she moaned because she wanted him to do them, right now. He was controlling her but she didn't care because he knew things about her she didn't know herself. How to touch her, where to touch her. All she wanted was more of this breath-stealing pleasure and then he started to move, slowly at first, and then building the rhythm with sure, skilled thrusts until she was aware of nothing but him, of hard muscle and slick skin, of the frenzy of sensation until it exploded and she clung to him, sobbing his name as her body tightened on his, her muscles rippling around the thrusting length of him drawing out his own response.

She heard him groan her name, felt him slide his hand into her hair and take her mouth again so that they kissed their way through the whole thing, sharing every throb, ripple and flutter in the most intimate way possible.

The force of it left her shaken and stunned and she lay, breathless, trying to bring herself slowly back to earth. And then he shifted his weight and gathered her close, murmuring something in Greek as he stroked her hair back from her face and kissed her mouth gently.

They lay for a moment and then he scooped her up and carried her into the shower where, under the soft patter of steamy water, he proceeded to expand her sexual education with infinite skill until her body no longer felt like her own and her legs felt like rubber.

'Nik?' She lay damp and sated on the tangled sheets, deliciously sleepy and barely able to keep her eyes open. 'Is that why you don't like coming back here? Because it reminds you of your childhood?'

He stared down at her with those fathomless black eyes, his expression inscrutable. 'Get some sleep.' His voice was even. 'I'll wake you in time to change for dinner.'

'Where are you going?'

'I have work to do.'

In other words she'd strayed into forbidden territory. Somewhere in the back of her mind there was another question she wanted to ask him, but her brain was already drifting into blissful unconsciousness and she slid into a luxurious sleep.

Nik returned to the terrace and made calls in the shade, one eye on the open doors of Lily's bedroom.

So much for his resolve not to touch her again.

And what had possessed him to tell her about his mother? It was something he rarely thought about himself, let alone spoke of to other people.

It was being back here that had stirred up memories long buried.

He ignored the part of him that said it was the prospect of another wedding that stirred up the memories, not the place.

To distract himself he worked until the blaze of the sun dimmed and he heard movement from the bedroom.

He ended the call he'd made and a few minutes later she wandered onto the terrace, sleepy eyed and deliciously disorientated. 'Have you been out here the whole time?'

'Yes.'

'You're not tired?'

'No.'

'Because you're stressed out about your father.' She sat down next to him and poured herself a glass of water. 'For what it's worth, I like Diandra.'

He studied the soft curve of her mouth and the kindness in her eyes. 'Is there anyone you don't like?'

'Yes!' She sipped her water. 'I have a deep aversion to Professor Ashurst, and if we're drawing up a list then I should confess I didn't totally fall in love with your girlfriend from the other night, but that might be because she called me fat. And I definitely didn't like you a few hours ago, but you redeemed yourself in the bedroom so I'm willing to overlook the offensive things you said on the journey.' A dimple appeared in the corner of her mouth and Nik felt the instant, powerful response of his body and wondered how he was going to make it through an evening of small talk with people that didn't interest him.

She, on the other hand, interested him extremely.

'We should get ready for the party. The guests will be arriving soon and my father wants us up there early to greet them.'

'Us? You, surely, not me.'

'He wants you, too. He likes you very much.'

'I like him, too, but I don't think I should be greeting

his guests. I'm not family. We're not even together.' Her gaze slid to his and away again and he knew she was thinking about what they'd shared earlier.

He was, too. In fact he'd thought of little else but sex with Lily since she'd drenched herself in his shower a week earlier.

Sex had always been important to him, but since meeting her it had become an obsession.

'It would mean a lot to him if you were there.'

'Well, if you're sure that's what he wants. This all feels a bit surreal.'

'Which part feels surreal?'

'All of it. The whole rich-lifestyle thing. Living with you could turn a girl's head. You can snap your fingers and have anything you want.'

Relieved by the lightening of the atmosphere, he smiled. 'I will snap my fingers for you any time you like. Tell me what you want.'

She smiled. 'You can get me anything?'

'Anything.'

'So if I had a craving for lobster mousse, you'd find me one?'

'I would.' He reached for his phone and she covered his hand with hers, laughing.

'I wasn't serious! I don't want lobster mousse.' Her fingers were light on his hand. There was nothing suggestive about her touch. Nothing that warranted his extreme physical reaction.

'Then what?' His voice was husky. 'If you don't want lobster mousse, what can I get you?'

Her eyes met his and colour streaked across her cheeks. 'Nothing. I have everything I need.' She removed her hand quickly and said something, but her words were drowned out by the clacking of a helicopter.

Nik rose reluctantly to his feet. 'We need to move. The guests are arriving.'

'By helicopter?' Her eyes were round, as if it was only now dawning on her that this wasn't an ordinary wedding party. 'Is this party going to be glamorous?'

'Very. Lunch was an informal family affair, but tonight is for my father to show off his new wife.'

'How many guests?'

'A very select party. No more than two hundred, but they're arriving from all over Europe and the US.'

'Two *hundred*? That's a select party?' Her smile faltered. 'I'm a gatecrasher.'

'You are not a gatecrasher. You're my guest.'

She pushed her hair back from her face. 'I'm starting to panic that what I brought with me isn't dressy enough.'

'You look lovely in everything you wear, but I do have something if you'd like to take a look at it.'

'Something you bought for someone else?'

'No. For you.'

'I told you I didn't want anything.'

'I didn't listen.'

'So you bought me something anyway. In case I embarrassed you?'

'No. In case you had a panic that what you'd brought wasn't dressy enough.'

'I should probably be angry that you're calling me predictable, but as we don't have time to be angry I'm going to overlook it. Can I see?' She stood up at the same time he did and her body brushed against his.

'Lily…' He breathed her name, steadied her with his hands and she gave a low moan.

'No.' Her eyes were clouded. 'Seriously, Nik, if we do it again I'll fall asleep and never wake up. The Prince is supposed to wake Sleeping Beauty, not put her to sleep with endless sex.'

He lifted his hand to her flushed cheek and gently stroked her hair back from her face. It took all his will power not to power her back against the wall. 'We could skip the party. Better still, we could grab a couple of bottles of champagne and have our own party here by the pool.'

'No way! Not only would that upset your father and Diandra, but I wouldn't get to ogle all those famous people. Brittany will grill me later so I need to have details. Am I allowed to take photographs?'

'Of course.' With a huge effort of will he let his hand drop. 'You'd better try the dress.'

The dress was exquisite. A long sheath of shimmering turquoise silk with delicate beads hand-sewn around the neckline. It fitted her perfectly.

She picked up her phone, took a quick selfie and sent it to Brittany with a text saying *Rebound sex is my new favourite thing.*

People were wrong when they thought rebound sex didn't involve any emotion, she mused. Yes, the sex was spectacular, but even though she wasn't in love that didn't mean two people couldn't care about each other. She cared about making this wedding as easy as possible for Nik, and he'd cared enough not to leave her alone when she was upset.

Somewhere deep inside a small part of her wondered if perhaps that wasn't how she was supposed to be feeling, but she dismissed it, picked up her purse and walked through to the living room.

'I could be a little freaked out by how well you're able to guess my size.'

He turned, sleek and handsome in a dinner suit.

Despite the undisputable elegance and sophistication, formal dress did nothing to disguise the lethal power of the man beneath.

Testosterone in a tux, she thought as he reached into his pocket and handed her something.

'What's this?' She took the slim, elegant box and opened it cautiously. There, nestled in deep blue velvet, was a necklace of silver and sapphire she immediately recognised. 'It's one of Skylar's. I admired the picture.'

'And now you can admire the real thing. I thought it would look better on your neck than in a catalogue.' He took it from her and fastened it round her neck while she pressed her fingers to her throat self-consciously.

'When did you buy this?'

'I had it flown in after you admired her pot.'

'You had it *flown in*? From New York? There wasn't time.'

'This piece was in a gallery in London.'

'Unbelievable. So extravagant.'

'Then why are you smiling?'

'Because I like pretty things and Skylar makes the prettiest things.' Smiling, she pulled her phone out of her purse again. 'I need to capture the moment so when I'm sitting in my pyjamas in a cramped apartment in rainy London I can relive this moment. It's a loan, obviously, because I could never accept a gift this generous.'

She took a couple of photos and then made him pose with her. 'I promise not to sell these to the newspapers. Can I send it to Sky? I can say *Look what I'm wearing*.'

A smile touched the corners of his mouth. 'It's your photo. You can do anything you like with it.'

'Skylar will be over the moon. I'm going to make sure everyone sees this necklace tonight. Now, tell me how you're feeling.' She'd asked herself over and over again if his earlier confession was something she should mention or not. But how could she ignore it when it was clearly the source of his stress?

His expression shifted from amused to guarded. 'How I'm feeling?'

'This is a party to celebrate your father's impending wedding, which you didn't want to attend. Is it hard to be here thinking about your mother and watching your father marry again? It must make marriage seem like a disposable object.'

'I appreciate your concern, but I'm fine.'

'Nik, I know you're not fine, but if you'd rather not talk about it—'

'I'd rather not talk about it.'

She kept her thoughts on that to herself. 'Then let's go.' She slipped her hand into his. 'I guess everyone will be trying to work out whether you're pleased or not, so for Diandra's sake make sure you smile.'

'Thank you for your counsel.'

'Ouch, that was quite a put-down. I presume that was your way of telling me to stop talking.'

'If I want to stop you talking, I have more effective methods than a verbal put-down.'

She caught his eye. 'If you feel like testing out one of those methods, go right ahead.'

'Don't tempt me.'

She was shocked by how badly she wanted to tempt him. She considered dragging him back inside, but a car was waiting outside the villa for them. 'I didn't realise there were cars on the island. How do they get across here?'

'There is a ferry, but my father usually takes a helicopter to the mainland if he is travelling.'

'We could have walked tonight.'

'There is no way you'd be able to walk that far in those shoes, let alone dance.'

'Who says I'll be dancing?'

His gaze slid to hers. 'I do.'

'You seem very sure of that.'

'I am, because you'll be dancing with me.'

She felt a shiver of excitement, excitement that grew as they drew up outside the imposing main entrance. The villa was situated on the far side of the island, out of sight of the mainland. 'This is a mansion, not a villa. Normal people don't live like this.'

'You think I'm not a normal person?'

'I *know* you're not.' She took his arm as they walked past a large fountain to the floodlit entrance of the villa. 'Normal people don't own five homes and a private jet.'

'The jet is owned by the company.'

'And you own the company.' It was hard not to feel overwhelmed as she walked through the door into the palatial entrance of his father's home. Towering ceilings gave a feeling of space and light and through open doors she caught a glimpse of rooms tastefully fur-

nished with antiques and fine art. 'Tell me again what
your father does?'

Nik smiled. 'He ran a very successful company,
which he sold for a large sum of money.'

'But not to you.'

'Our interests are different.'

There was no opportunity for him to elaborate because Diandra was hovering and Lily noticed the nervous look she gave Nik.

To break the ice, she enthused over the other woman's dress and hair and then asked after Chloe.

'She's sleeping. My niece is watching her while we
greet everyone, then I'm going to check on her. It's been a
very unsettling time.' Diandra kept her voice low. 'I wanted
to postpone the wedding but Kostas won't hear of it.'

'You're right, I won't.' Kostas took Diandra's hand.
'Nothing is going to stop me marrying you. You worry
too much. She will soon settle and in the meantime we
have an army of staff to attend to her happiness.'

'She doesn't need an army,' Diandra murmured. 'She
needs the security of a few people she knows and trusts.'

'We'll discuss this later.' Kostas drew her closer.
'Our guests are arriving. Lily, you look beautiful. You
will stand with us and greet everyone.'

'Oh, but I—'

'I insist.'

Lily quickly discovered that Nik's father was as
skilled at getting his own way as his son.

Unable to extract herself, she stood and greeted the
guests, feeling as if she were on a movie set as a wave
of shimmering, glittering guests flowed past her.

'This isn't my life,' she whispered to Nik but he simply smiled and exchanged a few words with each guest, somehow managing to make everyone feel as if they'd had his full attention.

She discovered that even among this group of influential people everyone wanted a piece of him, especially the women.

It gave her a brief but illuminating insight into his life and she saw how it must be for him, surrounded by people whose motives in wanting to know him were as mixed up and murky as the bottom of the ocean.

She was beginning to understand both his reserve and his cynicism.

The evening was like something out of a dream, except that none of her dreams had ever featured an evening as glittering and extravagant as this.

What would it be like, she wondered, if this really *were* her life?

She pushed that thought aside quickly, preferring not to linger in fantasyland. Wanting a family was one thing, this was something else altogether.

Candles flickered, silverware gleamed and the air was filled with the heady scent of expensive perfume and fresh flowers. The food, a celebration of all things Greek, was served on the terrace so that the guests could enjoy the magnificent sight of the sun setting over the Aegean.

By the time Nik finally swung her onto the dance floor Lily was dizzy with it.

'I talked to a few people while you were in conversation with those men in suits. I didn't mention the fact I'm a penniless archaeologist.'

'Are you enjoying yourself?'

'What do you think?'

'I think you look stunning in that dress.' He eased her closer. 'I also think you are better at mindless small talk than I am.'

'Are you calling me mindless?' She rested her hand lightly on his chest. 'Did you know that the very good-looking man over there with the lovely wife owns up-market hotels all over the world? He's Sicilian.'

He glanced over her shoulder. 'Cristiano Ferrara? You think he's good-looking?'

'Yes. And his wife is beautiful. They seem like a happy family.'

He smiled. 'Her name is Laurel.'

'Do you know everyone? She was very down-to-earth. She admired my necklace and he pulled me to one side to ask me for the details. He's going to surprise her for her birthday.'

'If Skylar sells a piece of jewellery to a Ferrara I can assure you she's made. They move in the highest circles.'

'Laurel wants an invitation to her exhibition in London. I have plugged Skylar's jewellery to at least ten *very* wealthy people. I hope you're not angry.'

He curved her against him in a possessive gesture. 'You are welcome to be as shameless as you wish. In fact I'm willing to make a few specific suggestions about how you could direct that shameless behaviour.'

A few heads turned in their direction.

'Thank you for telling this room full of strangers that I'm a sex maniac. Are you sure you don't want to dance with someone else?'

His eyes were half shut, his gaze focused entirely on her. 'Why would I want to dance with anyone else?'

'Because there are a lot of women in this room and they're looking at you hopefully. Me, they look as if they'd like to kill. They're wondering why you're with me.'

'None of the men are wondering that,' he drawled. 'Trust me on that.'

'Can I tell you something?'

'That depends. Is it going to be a deeply emotional confession that is going to send me running from the room?'

'You can't run anywhere because your father is about to make a speech and—oh—' she frowned '—Diandra looks stressed.' Taking his hand, she tugged him across the crowded dance floor towards Diandra, who appeared to be arguing with Kostas.

'Wait five minutes,' Kostas urged in a low tone. 'You cannot abandon our guests.'

'But she needs me,' Diandra said firmly and Lily intervened.

'Is this about Chloe?'

'She's woken up. I can't bear to think of her upset with people she doesn't know. It's already hard enough on her to have been left here by her mother.'

'Nik and I will go to her,' Lily said immediately and saw Nik frown.

'I don't think—'

'We'll be fine. Make your speech and then come and find us.' Without letting go of Nik's hand, Lily made for the stairs. 'I assume you know where the nursery is or should we use GPS?'

'I really don't think—'

'Cut the excuses, Zervakis. Your little sister needs you.'

'She doesn't know me. I don't see how my sudden

appearance in her life can do anything but make things a thousand times worse.'

'Children are sometimes reassured by a strong presence. But stop glaring.' She paused at the top of the stairs. 'Which way?'

He sighed and led the way up another flight of stairs to a suite of rooms and pushed open the door.

A young girl stood there jiggling a red-faced crying toddler. Relief spread across her features when she saw reinforcements.

'She's been like this for twenty minutes. I can't stop her crying.'

Nik took one look at the abject misery on his half-sister's face and took her from the girl, but, instead of her being comforted by the reassuring strength in those arms, Chloe's howls intensified.

Sending Lily a look that said 'I told you so', he immediately handed her over.

'Perhaps you can do a better job than I can.'

She was about to point out that he was a stranger and that Chloe's response was no reflection on him when the toddler flopped onto her shoulder, exhausted.

'You poor thing,' Lily soothed. 'Did you wake and not know where you were? Was it noisy downstairs?' She continued to talk, murmuring soothing nothings and stroking the child's back until the child's eyelids drifted closed. She felt blonde curls tickle her chin. 'There, that's better, you must be exhausted. Are you thirsty? Would you like a drink?' She glanced across the room and saw Nik watching her, his expression inscrutable. 'Say something.'

'What do you want me to say?'

'Something. Anything. You look as if someone has released a tiger from a cage and you're expected to bag it single-handed.'

There was a tension in his shoulders that hadn't been there a few moments earlier and suddenly she wondered if his response to the child was mixed up with his feelings for Callie.

It was obvious he'd disliked his father's third wife, but surely he wouldn't allow those feelings to extend to the child?

And then she realised he wasn't looking at Chloe, he was looking at her.

He lifted his hand and loosened his tie with a few flicks of those long, bronzed fingers. 'You love children.'

'Well I don't love *all* children, obviously, but at this age they're pretty easy to love.' She waited for him to walk across the room and take his sister from her, but he didn't move. Instead he leaned against the doorway, watching her, and then finally eased himself upright.

'You seem to have this under control.' His voice was level. 'I'll see you downstairs when you're ready.'

'No! Nik, wait—' She shifted Chloe onto her other hip and walked across to him, intending to hand over the wriggling toddler so that he could form a bond with her, but he took a step back, his face a frozen mask.

'I'll send Diandra up as soon as she's finished with the speeches.' With that he turned and strode out of the room leaving her holding the baby.

CHAPTER EIGHT

NIK MADE HIS way through the guests, out onto the terrace and down past the cascading water feature that ended in a beautiful pool. Children cried for a million reasons, he knew that, but that didn't stop him wondering if deep down Chloe knew her mother had abandoned her. The fact that he'd been unable to offer comfort had done nothing for his elevated stress levels, but the real source of his tension had been the look on Lily's face.

He could see now he'd made a huge mistake bringing her here. *Cristos*, who was he kidding? The mistake had been taking her back to his place from the restaurant that night, instead of dropping her safely at her apartment and telling her to lock the door behind her.

She was completely, totally wrong for him and he was completely, totally wrong for her.

Cursing under his breath, he yanked off his tie and ran his hand over his jaw.

'Nik?'

Her voice came from behind him and he turned to find her standing there, her sapphire eyes gleaming bright in the romantic light of the pool area. The turquoise dress hugged the lush lines of her body and her blonde hair, twisted into Grecian braids, glowed like a halo. The jewel he'd given her sat at the base of her throat and suddenly all he wanted to do was rip it off and replace it with his mouth. There wasn't a man in the room who hadn't taken a second glance at her and he was willing to bet she hadn't noticed. He'd always considered jealousy to be a pointless and ugly emotion but tonight he'd experienced it in spades. He should have given her a dress of shapeless black, although he had a feeling that would have made no difference to the way he felt. It was a shock to discover that will power alone wasn't enough to hold back the brutal arousal.

'I thought you were with Chloe. Is she asleep?'

'Diandra came to take over. And you shouldn't have walked away from her.' She was stiff. Furious, displaying none of the softness and gentleness he'd witnessed in the nursery.

The wind had picked up and he frowned as he saw her shiver and run her hands over her arms. 'Are you cold? Crete often experiences high winds.'

'I'm not cold. I'm being heated from the inside out because I'm boiling mad, Nik. I don't think it's exactly fair of you to take your feelings for her mother out on a child, that's all.'

Nik took a deep breath, wondering how honest to be. 'That is not what is happening here.'

'No? Well there has to be some reason why you looked at Chloe as if she was a dangerous animal.'

'This is not about Chloe.'

'What then?'

There was a long, throbbing pause. 'It's about you.'

'Me?' She stared at him blankly and he cursed under his breath.

'You are the sort of woman who cannot pass a baby without wanting to pick it up. You see sunshine in a thunderstorm, happy endings everywhere you look and you believe family is the answer to every problem in the world.'

She stared at him with a total lack of comprehension. 'I do like babies, that's true, and I don't see any reason to apologise for the fact I'd like a family one day. I don't see sunshine in every thunderstorm, but I do try and see the positive rather than the negative because that's how I prefer to live my life. I put up an umbrella instead of standing there and getting wet. Sometimes life can be crap, I know that but I've learned not to focus on the crap and I won't apologise for that. But I don't see what that has to do with the situation. None of that explains why you behaved the way you did in that room. You looked as if you'd been hit round the head with a plank of wood and then you walked out. And you say it was about me, but how can it possibly—?'

Her expression changed, the shards of anger in her eyes changing to wariness. 'Oh. I get it. You're worried that because I want a family one day, that because I like babies, it makes me a dangerous person to have sex with, is that right?' She spoke slowly, feeling it out, watching his face the whole time and she must have seen something there that confirmed her suspicions because she made a derisive sound and turned away.

'Lily—'

'No! Don't make excuses or find a tactful way to express how you feel. It's sprayed over you like graffiti.' She hitched up her dress and started to walk away from him and he gritted his teeth because he could see she was truly upset.

'Wait. You can't walk back in those shoes—'

'Of course I can. What do you think I usually do when I'm out? I'd never been in a limo in my life before I met you. I walk everywhere because it's cheaper.' She hurled the words over her shoulder and he strode after her, wondering how to intervene and prevent a broken ankle without stoking her wrath.

'We should talk about this—'

'There is nothing to talk about.' She didn't slacken her pace. 'I cuddled your baby sister and you're afraid that somehow changed our relationship. You're worried that this isn't about sex any more, and that I've suddenly fallen in love with you. Your arrogance is shocking.'

He kept pace with her, ready to catch her if she twisted her ankle in those shoes. 'It is not arrogance. But that incident upstairs reinforced how different we are.'

'Yes, we're different. That's why I picked you for my rebound guy. It's true I want children one day, but believe me you're the last man on earth I'd want to share that with. I don't want a guy who describes a crying child as an "incident".'

'That is not—*Cristos,* will you *stop* for a moment?' He caught her arm and she shrugged him off, turning to face him.

'Believe me, Nik, I have never been *less* likely to fall in love with you than I am right at this moment. A little girl was distressed and all you could think about was how to extract yourself from a relationship you're not even having! That doesn't make you a great catch in my eyes so you're perfectly safe. I understand now why you have emotionless relationships. You're brilliant at the mechanics of sex, but that's it. I'd get as much emotional comfort from a laptop. Seriously, you should stick to your technology, or your investments or whatever it is you do—' She tugged her arm from his grip and carried on walking down the path, her distress evident in each furious tap of her heels.

He stared after her, stunned into silence by her unexpected attack and shaken by his own feelings. In emotional terms, he kept women at a distance. He'd never aspired to a deeper attachment and when his relationships ended he invariably felt nothing. He had no interest in marriage and didn't care about long-term commitment.

But he really, really cared that Lily was upset.

The feeling was uncomfortable, like having a stone in his shoe.

He followed at a safe distance, relieved when she reached the terrace and ripped off her shoes. She dumped them unceremoniously on a sunlounger and carried on walking. The braids of her Grecian goddess hairstyle had been loosened by the wind, and her hair slithered in tumbled curls over her bare shoulders.

A man with a sense of self-preservation would have left her to cool down.

Nik carried on walking. He walked right into the bedroom, narrowly avoiding a black eye as she swung the door closed behind her.

He caught it on the flat of his hand, strode through and slammed it shut behind him.

She turned, her eyes a furious blaze of blue. 'Get out, Nik.'

He shrugged off his jacket and slung it over the nearest chair. 'No.'

'You should, because the way I feel right now I might punch you. No, wait a minute, I know exactly how to make you back out of that door.' She tilted her head and her mouth curved into a smile that didn't reach her eyes. 'You should leave, Nik, because I'm—oh, seconds away from falling in love with your irresistible self.' Her sarcasm made him smile and that smile was like throwing petrol on flame. 'Are you laughing at me?'

'No, I'm smiling because you're cute when you're angry.'

'I'm not cute. I'm fearsome and terrifying.'

What was fearsome and terrifying was how much he wanted her but he kept that thought to himself as he strolled towards her. 'Can we start this conversation again?'

'There is nothing more to say. Stop right there, Nik. Don't take another step.'

He kept walking. 'I should not have left you with Chloe. I behaved like an idiot, I admit it,' he breathed, 'but I'm not used to having a relationship with a woman like you.'

'And you're afraid I don't understand the rules? Trust me, I not only understand them but I applaud them. I wouldn't *want* to fall in love with someone like you. You make Neanderthal man look progressive and I've studied Neanderthal man. And stop looking at me like that because there is no way I can have sex with you when I'm this angry. It's not happening, Nik. Forget it.'

He stopped toe to toe with her, slid his hand into her hair and tilted her face to his. 'You've never had angry sex?'

'Of course not! Until you, I've only ever had "in love" sex. Angry sex sounds horrible. Sex should be loving and gentle. Who on earth would want to—?' Her words died as he silenced her with his mouth.

He cupped her face, feeling the softness of her skin beneath his fingers and the frantic beat of her pulse. He took her mouth with a hunger bordering on aggression and felt her melt against him. Her arms sneaked round his neck and he explored the sweet heat of her mouth, so aroused he was ready to rip off her dress and play out any one of the explicit scenarios running through his brain.

He had no idea what it was about her that attracted him so much, but right now he wouldn't have cared if she was holding an armful of babies and singing the wedding march, he still would have wanted to get her naked.

Without lifting his mouth from hers, he hauled her dress up to her waist and slid his fingers inside the lace of her panties. He heard her moan, felt her slippery hot and ready for him, and then her hands were on his zip, fumbling as she tried desperately to free him. As her cool fingers closed around him his mind blanked. He powered her back against the wall, slid his hands under her thighs and lifted her easily, wrapping her legs around his hips.

'Nik—' She sobbed his name against his mouth, dug her nails into his shoulders and he anchored her writhing hips with his hands and thrust deep. Gripped by tight, velvet softness, he felt his vision blur. Control was so far from his reach he abandoned hope of ever meeting up again and simply surrendered to the out-of-control desire that seemed to happen whenever he was near this woman.

He withdrew and thrust again, bringing thick waves of pleasure cascading down on both of them. From that moment on there was nothing but the wildness of it. He felt her nails digging into his shoulders and the frantic shifting of her hips. He tried to slow things down, to still those sensuous movements, but they were both out of control and he felt the first powerful ripples of her body clenching his shaft.

'Cristo—' He gave a deep, throaty groan and tried to hold back but there was no holding back and he surrendered to a raw explosive climax that wiped his mind of everything except this woman.

It was only when he lowered her unsteadily to the floor that he realised he was still dressed.

He couldn't remember when he'd last had sex fully clothed.

Usually he had more finesse, but finesse hadn't been invited to this party.

He felt her sway slightly and curved a protective arm around her, supporting her against him. His cheek was on her hair and he could feel the rise and fall of her chest as she struggled for air.

Finally she locked her hand in the front of his shirt and lifted her head. Her mouth was softly swollen and pink from his kisses, her eyes dazed. 'That was angry sex?'

Nik was too stunned to answer and she gave a faint smile and gingerly let go of the front of his shirt, as if testing her ability to stand unsupported.

'Angry sex is good. I don't feel angry any more. You've taught me a whole new way of solving a row.' She swayed like Bambi and he caught her before she could slide to the floor.

'*Theé mou*, you are *not* going to use sex to solve a row.' The thought of her doing with anyone else what she'd done with him sent his stress levels soaring.

'You did. It worked. I'm not saying I like you, but all my adrenaline was channelled in a different direction so I'm feeling a lot calmer. My karma is calmer.'

Nik was far from calm. 'Lily—'

'I know this whole thing is difficult for you,' she said, 'and you don't need to make the situation more difficult by worrying about me falling in love with you. That is never going to happen. And next time your little sister is upset, don't hand her to someone else. I know you don't like tears, but I think you could make an exception for a distressed two-year-old. Man up.'

Nik, who had never before in his life had his manhood questioned, struggled for a response. 'She needed comfort and I have zero experience with babies.' He spoke through his teeth. 'My approach to all problems is to delegate tasks to whichever person has the superior qualifications—in this instance it was you. She liked you. She was calmer with you. With me, she cried.'

She gave him a look that was blisteringly unsympathetic. 'Every expert started as a beginner. Get over yourself. Next time, pick her up and learn how to comfort her. Who knows, one day you might even be able to extend those skills to grown-ups. If you didn't find it so hard to communicate you might not have gone so long without seeing your father. He adores you, Nik, and he's so proud of you. I know you didn't like Callie, but couldn't you have swallowed your dislike of her for the occasional visit? Would that really have been so hard?'

Nik froze. 'You know nothing about the situation.'

Unaccustomed to explaining his actions to anyone, he took a deep breath. 'I did *not* stay away from my father because of my feelings about Callie.'

'What then?'

He was silent for a long moment because it was a topic he had never discussed with anyone. 'I stayed away from him because of her feelings for me.'

'That's what I'm saying! Because the two of you didn't get along, he suffered.'

'Not because I didn't like her. Because she liked me—a little too much.' He spoke with raw emphasis and saw the moment her expression changed and understanding dawned. 'That's right. My stepmother took her desire to be "close" to me to disturbing extremes.'

Lily's expression moved through a spectrum encompassing confusion, disbelief and finally horror. 'Oh, *no*, your poor father—does he know?'

'I sincerely hope not. I stayed away to avoid there ever being any chance he would witness something that might cause him distress. Despite my personal views on Callie I did not wish to see his marriage ended and I certainly didn't want to be considered the cause of it, because that would have created a rift that never would have healed.'

'So you stayed away to prevent a rift between you, but it caused a rift anyway and he doesn't even know the reason. Do you think you should have told him?'

'I asked myself that question over and over again, but I decided not to.' He hesitated. 'She was unfaithful several times during their short marriage and my father knew. There was nothing to be gained by revealing the truth and I didn't want to add to my father's pain.'

'Of course you didn't.' Lily's eyes filled. 'And all this time I was thinking it was because of your stubborn pride, because you didn't like the woman and were determined to punish him. I was *so wrong*. I'm sorry. Please forgive me.'

More unsettled by the tears than he was by her anger, Nik backed away. 'Don't cry. And there is nothing to forgive you for.'

'I misjudged you. I leaped to conclusions and I try never to do that.'

'It doesn't matter.'

'It does to me. You said that she had affairs—' Her eyes widened. 'Do you think that Chloe might not be—?'

He tensed because it was a possibility that had crossed his mind. 'I don't know, but it makes no difference now. My father's lawyers are taking steps to make sure it's a legal adoption.'

'But if she isn't and your father ever finds out—'

'It would make no difference to the way he feels about Chloe. Despite everything, I actually do believe she is my father's child. For a start she has certain physical characteristics that are particular to my family, and then there is the fact that Callie did everything in her power to keep her from him.'

'You really think she used her child as currency?'

'Yes.' Nik didn't hesitate and he saw the distress in her eyes.

'I think I dislike her almost as much as you do.'

'I doubt that.'

'I'm starting to see why you were worried about your father marrying again. Is Callie the reason you don't believe love exists?'

'No.' His voice didn't sound like his own. 'I formed that conclusion long before Callie.'

He waited for her to question him further but instead she leaned forward and hugged him tightly.

Unaccustomed to any physical contact that wasn't sexual, he tensed. 'What's that for?'

'Because you were put in a hideous, *horrible* position with Callie and the only choice you had was to stay away from your father. I think you're a very honourable person.'

He breathed deeply. 'Lily—'

'And because you were let down by a woman at a very vulnerable age. But I know you don't want to talk about that so I won't mention it again. And now why don't we go to bed and have apology sex? That's one we haven't tried before, but I'm willing to give it my all.'

Hours later they lay on top of the bed, wrapped around each other while the night breeze cooled their heated flesh.

Lily thought he was asleep, but then he stirred and tightened his grip.

'Thank you for helping with Chloe. You were very good with her.'

'One day I'd love to have children of my own, but it isn't something I usually admit to out loud. When people ask about your aspirations, they want to hear about your career. Wanting a family isn't a valid life choice. And I'm happy and interested in my job, but I don't want it to be all there is in my life.'

'Why did you choose archaeology?'

'I suppose I'm fascinated by the way people lived in the past. It tells us a lot about where we come from. Maybe it's because I don't know where I come from that it always interested me.'

There was a long silence. 'You know nothing about your mother?'

'Very little. I like to think she loved me, but she wasn't able to care for me. We assume she was a teenager. What I always wonder is why no one helped her. She obviously didn't feel she could even tell anyone she was pregnant. I think about that more than anything and I feel horrible that there wasn't anyone special in her life she could trust. She must have been so lonely and frightened.'

'Have you tried to trace her?'

'The police tried to trace her at the time but they had no success. They thought she was probably from somewhere outside London.' It was something she hadn't discussed with anyone before and she wondered why she was doing so now, with him. Maybe because he, too, had been abandoned by his mother, even though the circumstances were different. Or maybe because his honesty made him surprisingly easy to talk to. He didn't sugar-coat his views on life, nor did he lie. After the brutal shock of discovering how wrong she'd been about David Ashurst, it was a relief to be with someone who was exactly who he seemed to be. And although she'd accused Nik of arrogance, part of her could understand how watching her with Chloe might have unsettled him. That moment had highlighted their basic differences and the truth was that his extreme reaction to her 'baby moment' had been driven more by his reluctance to mislead her, than arrogance.

It was obvious that his issues with love and marriage had been cemented early in life.

What psychological damage had his mother caused

when she'd walked out leaving her young son watching from the hallway?

What message had that sent to him? That relationships didn't last? If a mother could leave her child, what did that say to a young boy about the enduring quality of love?

He'd been let down by the one person he should have been able to depend on, his childhood rocked by insecurity and lack of trust. Everything that had followed had cemented his belief that relationships were a transitory thing with no substance.

'We're not so different, you and I, Nik Zervakis.' She spoke softly. 'We're each a product of our pasts, except that it sent us in different directions. You ceased to believe true love existed, whereas I was determined to find it. It's why we're both bad at relationships.'

'I'm not bad at relationships.'

'You don't have relationships, Nik. You have sex.'

'Sex is a type of relationship.'

'Not really. It's superficial.'

'Why are we talking about me? Tell me why you think you're bad at relationships.'

'Because I care too much. I try too hard.'

'You want the fairy tale.'

'Not really. When you describe it that way it makes it sound silly and unachievable and I don't think what I want is unrealistic.'

'What do you want?'

There was a faint splash from beyond the open doors as a tiny bird skimmed across the pool.

'I want to be special to someone.' She spoke softly, saying the words aloud for the first time in her life. 'Not just special. I'm going to tell you something, and if you laugh you will be sorry—'

'I promise not to laugh.'

'I want to be someone's favourite person.'

There was a long silence and then his arms tightened. 'I'm sure you're special to a lot of people.'

'Not really.' She felt the hot sting of tears and was relieved it was dark. 'My life has been like a car park. People come and go. No one stays around for long. I have friends. Good friends, but it's not the same as being someone's favourite person. I want to be someone's dream come true. I want to be the person they call when they're happy or sad. The one they want to wake up next to and grow old with.' She wondered why she was telling him this, when his ambitions were diametrically opposed to hers. 'You think I'm crazy.'

'That isn't what I think.' His voice was husky and she turned her head to look at him but his features were indistinct in the darkness.

'Thank you for listening.' She felt sleep descend and suppressed a yawn. 'I know you don't think love exists, but I hope that one day you find a favourite person.'

'In bed, you are definitely my favourite person. Does that count?' He pulled the sheet up over her body, but didn't release her. 'Now get some sleep.'

The next couple of days passed in a whirl of social events. Helicopters and boats came and went, although tucked away on the far side of the idyllic island Lily was barely aware of the existence of other people. For her, it was all about Nik.

There had been a subtle shift in their relationship,

although she had a feeling that the shift was all on her side. Now, instead of believing him to be cold and aloof, she saw that he was guarded. Instead of controlling, she saw him as someone determined to be in charge of his own destiny.

In between socialising, she lounged by the pool and spent time on the small private beach next to Camomile Villa.

She loved swimming in the sea and more than once Nik had to extract her with minutes to spare before she was expected to accompany him to another lunch or dinner.

He was absent a lot of the time and she was aware that he'd been spending that time with his father and, judging from the more harmonious atmosphere, that time had been well spent.

After that first awkward lunch, he'd stopped firing questions at Diandra and if he wasn't completely warm in his interactions with her, he was at least civil.

To avoid the madness of the wedding preparations, Nik was determined to show Lily the island.

The day before the wedding he pulled her from bed just before sunrise.

'What time do you call this?' Sleepy and fuzzy-headed after a night that had consisted of more sex than sleep, she grumbled her way to the bathroom and whimpered a protest when he thrust her under cold water. 'You're a sadist.'

'You are going to thank me. Wear sturdy shoes.'

'The Prince never said that to Cinderella and I am never going to thank you for anything.' But she dragged on her shorts and a pair of running shoes, smothering a yawn as she followed him out of the villa. She stopped when she saw the vintage Vespa by the gates. 'I hate to be the one to tell you this but something weird happened to your limo overnight.'

'When I was a teenager this was my favourite way of getting round the island.' He swung his leg over the bike with fluid predatory grace and she laughed.

'You are too tall for this thing.' But her heart gave a little bump as she slid behind him and wrapped her arms round hard male muscle. 'Shouldn't I have a helmet or a seat belt or something?'

'Hold onto me.'

They wound their way along dusty roads, past rocky coves and beautiful beaches and up to the crumbling ruins of the Venetian fort where they abandoned the scooter and walked the rest of the way. He took her hand and they scrambled to the top as dawn was breaking.

The view was breathtaking, and she sat next to him, her thigh brushing his as they watched the sun slowly wake and stretch out fingers of dazzling light across the surface of the sea.

'I could live here,' she said simply. 'There's something about the light, the warmth, the people—London seems so grey in comparison. I can't believe you grew up here. You're so lucky. Not that you know that of course—you take it all for granted.'

'Not all.'

He'd brought a flask of strong Greek coffee and some of the sweet pastries she adored and she nibbled the corner and licked her fingers.

'I don't believe you made those.'

'Diandra made both the coffee and the pastries.'

'Diandra.' She grinned and nudged him with her shoulder. 'Confess. You're starting to like her.'

'She is an excellent cook.'

'And a good person. You're starting to like her.'

'I admit that what I took for a guilty conscience appears to be shyness.'

'You like her.'

His eyes gleamed. 'Maybe. A little.'

'There, you said it and it didn't kill you. I'll make a romantic of you yet.' She finished the pastry, contemplated another and decided she wouldn't get into the dress she'd brought to wear at the wedding. 'That was the perfect start to the day.'

'Worth waking up for?' His voice was husky and she turned her head, met his sleepy, sexy gaze and felt her tummy tumble.

'Yes. Of course, it would be easier to wake up if you'd let me sleep at night.'

He lowered his forehead to hers. 'Do you want to sleep, *erota mou*?' He curved his hand behind her head and kissed her with lingering purpose. 'I could take you back to bed right now if that is what you want.'

Her heart was pounding. She had to keep telling herself that this was about sex and nothing else. 'What's the alternative?'

'There are Minoan remains west of here if you want to extend the trip.'

'There are Minoan remains all over Crete,' she said weakly, telling herself that she could spend the rest of her life digging around in Minoan remains, but after this trip was over she'd never again get the chance to spend time with Nik Zervakis. 'Bed sounds good to me.'

CHAPTER NINE

THE CREAM OF Europe's great and good turned up to witness the wedding of Kostas Zervakis and Diandra.

'It's busier than Paris in fashion week,' Lily observed as they gathered for the actual wedding.

Nik was looking supremely handsome in a dark suit and whatever reservations he had about witnessing yet another marriage of his parent he managed to hide behind layers of sophisticated charm.

'You're doing well,' Lily murmured, reaching down to rescue the small posy of flowers that Chloe had managed to drop twice already. 'I'm proud of you. No frowning. All you have to do is keep it up for another few hours and you're done.'

He curved his arm round her waist. 'What's my reward for not frowning?'

'Angry sex.'

There was laughter in his eyes. 'Angry sex?'

'Yes. I like that sort. It's good to see you out of control.'

'I'm never out of control.'

'You were totally out of control, Mr Zervakis, and you hate that.' She hooked her finger into the front of his shirt and saw his eyes darken. 'You are used to being in control of everything. The people around you, your work environment, your emotions—angry sex is the only time I've ever seen you lose it. It felt good knowing I was the one responsible for breaking down that iron self-control of yours. Now, stop talking and focus. This is Diandra's moment.'

The wedding went perfectly, Chloe managed to hold onto the posy and after witnessing the ceremony Lily was left in no doubt that the love between Kostas and Diandra was genuine.

'She's his favourite person,' she whispered in a choked voice and Nik turned to her, wry humour in his eyes.

'Of course she is. She cooks for him, takes care of his child and generally makes his life run smoothly.'

'That isn't what makes this special. He could pay someone to do that.'

'He *is* paying her.'

'Don't start.' She refused to let him spoil the moment. 'Have you seen the way he looks at her? He doesn't see anyone else, Nik. The rest of us could all disappear.'

'That's the best idea I've heard in a long time. Let's do it.'

'No. I don't go to many weddings and this one is perfect.' Teasing him, she leaned closer. 'One day that is going to be you.'

He gave her a warning look. 'Lily—'

'I know, I know.' She shrugged. 'It's a wedding. Everyone dreams at weddings. Today, I want everyone to be happy.'

'Good. Let's sneak away and make each other happy.' His eyes dropped to her mouth. 'Wait here. There's one thing I have to do before we leave.' Leaving Lily standing in the shade, he walked across to his new stepmother and took her hands in his.

Lily watched, a lump in her throat, as he drew her to one side.

She couldn't hear what was said but she saw Diandra visibly relax as they talked and laughed together. And then they were joined by Kostas, who evidently didn't want to be parted from his new bride.

The whole event left Lily with a warm feeling and a genuine belief that this family really might live happily. Oh, there would be challenges of course, but a strong family weathered those together and she was sure that, no matter what had gone before, Kostas and Diandra were a strong family.

Just one dark cloud hovered on the horizon, shadowing her happiness. Now that the wedding was over, they'd both be returning to the reality of their lives.

And Nik Zervakis had no place in the reality of her life.

Still, they had one more night and she wasn't going to spoil today by worrying about tomorrow. She was lost in a private and very erotic fantasy about what the night might bring when Kostas drew her to one side.

'I have an enormous favour to ask of you.'

'Of course.' Her mind elsewhere, Lily wondered if it was time to be a bit more bold and inventive in the bedroom. Nik brought a seemingly never-ending source of energy, creativity and sexual expertise to every encounter and she wondered if it was time she took the initiative. Planning ways to give him a night he'd never forget, she remembered Kostas was talking and forced herself to concentrate.

'Would you take Chloe for us tonight? I am thrilled

she is with us, but I want this one night with Diandra. Chloe likes you. You have a way with children.'

Lily's plans for an erotic night that Nik would remember for ever evaporated.

How could she refuse when her relationship with Nik was a transitory thing and this one was for ever?

'Of course.' She hid her disappointment beneath a smile, and decided that the news that they were sharing Camomile Villa with a toddler was probably best broken when it was too late for Nik to do anything about it, so instead of enlisting his help to transport Chloe's gear across to the villa, she did it herself, sending a message via Diandra to tell him she was tired and to meet her back there when he was ready.

She'd settled a sleepy Chloe into her bed at the villa when she heard his footsteps on the terrace.

'You should have waited for me.' Nik stopped in the doorway as she put her finger to her lips.

'Shh—she's sleeping.'

'*Who* is sleeping?'

'Chloe.' She pointed to where Chloe lay, splayed like a starfish in the middle of the bed. 'It's their wedding night, Nik. They don't want to have to think about getting up to a toddler. And in case you're thinking you don't want to get up to a toddler either, you don't have to. I'll do it.'

He removed his tie and disposed of his jacket. 'She is going to sleep in the bed?'

'Yes. I thought we could babysit her together.' She eyed him, unsure how he'd react. 'I know this is going to ruin our last night. Are you angry?'

'No.' He undid the buttons on his shirt and sighed. 'It was the right thing to do. I should have thought of it.'

'She might keep us awake all night.'

His eyes gleamed with faint mockery. 'We've had plenty of practice.' He looked at the child on the bed. 'Tell me what you want me to do. This should be my responsibility, not yours. And I want to do the right thing. It's important to me that she feels secure and loved.'

Her insides melted. 'You don't have to "do" anything. And if you'd rather go to bed, that's fine.'

'I have a better idea. We have a drink on the terrace. Open the doors. That way we'll hear her if she wakes up and she won't be able to escape without us seeing.'

'She's a child, not a wild animal.' But his determination to give his half-sister the security she deserved touched her, and Lily stood on tiptoe and kissed him on the cheek. 'And a drink is a good idea. I didn't drink anything at the wedding because I was so nervous that something might go wrong.'

'I know the feeling.' He slid his hand behind her head and tilted her face to his. 'Thank you for coming with me. I have no doubt at all that the wedding was a happier experience for everyone involved because you were there.' His gaze dropped to her mouth and lingered there and her heart started to pound.

All day, she'd been aware of him. Of the leashed power concealed beneath the perfect cut of his suit, of the raw sexuality framed by spectacular good looks.

A cry from the bedroom shattered the moment and she eased away regretfully. 'Could you pick her up while I fetch her a drink? Diandra says she usually has a drink of warm milk before she goes to sleep and I'm sure today was unsettling for her.'

'It was unsettling for all of us,' he drawled and she smiled.

'Do you want warm milk, too? Because I could fix that.'

'I was thinking more of chilled champagne.' He glanced towards the bedroom and gave a resigned sigh. 'I will go to her, but don't blame me when I make it a thousand times worse.'

Perhaps because he was so blisteringly self-assured in every other aspect of his life, she found his lack of confidence strangely endearing. 'You won't make it worse.'

She walked quickly through to the kitchen and warmed milk, tension spreading across her shoulders as she heard Chloe's cries. Knowing that all that howling would simply ensure that Nik didn't offer to help a second time, she moved as quickly as she could. As she left the kitchen, the cries ceased and she paused in the doorway of the bedroom, transfixed by the sight of Nik holding his little sister against his shoulder, one strong, bronzed hand against her back as he supported her on his arm. As she watched, she saw the little girl lift her hand and rub the roughness of his jaw.

He caught that hand in his fingers, speaking to her in Greek, his voice deep and soothing.

Lily had no idea what he was saying, but whatever it was seemed to be working because Chloe's eyes drifted shut and her head thudded onto his broad shoulder as she fell asleep, her blonde curls a vivid contrast to the dark shadow of his strong jaw.

Nik stood still, as if he wasn't sure what to do now, and then caught sight of Lily in the doorway. He gave her a rueful smile at his own expense and she smiled.

'Try putting her back down on the bed.'

As careful as if he'd been handling delicate Venetian glass, Nik lowered the child to the bed but instantly she whimpered and tightened her grip around his neck like a barnacle refusing to be chipped away from a rock.

He kept his hand securely on her back and cast Lily a questioning look. 'Now what?'

'Er—sit down in the chair with her in your lap and give her some milk,' Lily suggested, and he strolled onto the terrace, sat on one of the comfortable sunloungers and let the toddler snuggle against him.

'When I said I wanted to spend the evening on the terrace with a woman this wasn't exactly what I had in mind.'

'Two women.' Laughing, she sat down next to him and offered Chloe the milk. 'Here you go, sweetheart. Cow juice.'

Nik raised his eyebrows. 'Cow juice?'

'One of my friends used to call it that because whenever she said "milk" her child used to go demented.' Seeing that the child was sleepy, Lily tried to keep her hold on the cup but small fingers grabbed it, sloshing a fair proportion of the contents over Nik's trousers.

To give him his due, he didn't shift. Simply looked at her with an expression that told her she was going to pay later.

'Thanks to you I now have "cow juice" on my suit.'

'Sorry.' She was trying not to laugh because she didn't want to rouse the sleepy, milk-guzzling toddler. 'I'll have it cleaned.'

'Let me.' He covered Chloe's small fingers with his large hand, holding the cup while she drank.

Lily swallowed. 'You see? You have a natural talent.'

His gaze flickered to hers. 'Take that look off your face. This is a one-time crisis-management situation, never to be repeated.'

'Right. Because she isn't the most adorable thing you've ever seen.'

Nik glanced down at the blonde curls rioting against the crisp white of his shirt. 'I have a fair amount of experience with women and I can tell you that this one is going to be high maintenance.'

'What gave you that idea? The fact that she wouldn't stay in her bed or the fact that she spilled her drink over you?'

'For my father's sake I hope that isn't a foreshadowing of her teenage years.' Gently, he removed the empty cup from Chloe's limp fingers and handed it back to Lily. 'She's fast asleep. Now it's my turn. Champagne. Ice. You.' His gaze met hers and she saw humour and promise under layers of potent sex appeal.

Her stomach dropped and she reached and took Chloe from him. 'I'll tuck her in.'

He rose to his feet, dwarfing her. 'I'll get the champagne.'

Wondering if the intense sexual charge ever diminished when you were with a man like him, Lily tiptoed through to the bedroom and tucked Chloe carefully into the middle of the enormous bed.

This time the child didn't stir.

Lily brushed her hand lightly over those blonde curls and stared down at her for a long moment, a lump in her throat. When she grew up was she going to wonder about her mother? Did Callie intend to be in her life or had she moved on to the next thing?

Closing the doors of the bedroom, Lily took the cup back to the kitchen. By the time she returned Nik was standing on the terrace wearing casual trousers and a shirt.

'You changed.'

'It didn't feel right to be drinking champagne in wet trousers.' He handed her a glass. 'She's asleep?'

'For now. I don't think she'll wake up. She's exhausted.' She sipped the champagne. 'It was a lovely wedding. For what it's worth, I like Diandra a lot.'

'So do I.'

She lowered the glass. 'Do you believe she loves him?'

'I'm not qualified to judge emotions, but they seem happy together. And I'm impressed by how willingly she has welcomed Chloe.'

She slipped off her shoes and sat on the sunlounger. 'I think Chloe will have a loving and stable home.'

He sat down next to her, his thigh brushing against hers. 'You didn't have that.'

She stared at the floodlit pool. 'No. I was a really sickly child. Trust me, you don't want the details, but as a result of that I moved from foster home to foster home because I was a lot of trouble to take care of. When you face the possibility of having to spend half the night in a hospital with a sick kid when you already have others at home, you take the easier option. I was never the easy option.'

He covered her hand with his. 'Was adoption never considered?'

'Older children aren't easy to place. Especially not sickly older children. Every time I arrived somewhere new I used to hope this might be permanent, but it never was. Anyway, enough of that. I've already told you far more than you ever wanted to know about me. You hate talking about family and personal things.'

'With you I do things I don't do with other people. Like attend weddings.' He turned her face to his and kissed her. 'You had a very unstable, unpredictable childhood and yet still you believe that something else is possible.'

'Because you haven't experienced something personally, doesn't mean it doesn't exist. I've never been to the moon but I know it's there.'

'So despite your disastrous relationships you still believe there is an elusive happy ending waiting for you somewhere.'

'Being happy doesn't have to be about relationships. I'm happy now. I've had a great time.' She gave a faint smile. 'Have I scared you?'

He didn't answer. Instead he lowered his head to hers again and she melted under the heat of his kiss, wishing she could freeze time and make this moment last for ever.

When she finally pulled away, she felt shaky. 'I've never met anyone like you before.'

'Cold and ruthlessly detached? Wasn't that what you said to me on that first night?'

'I was wrong.'

'You weren't wrong.'

'You reserve that side of you for the people you don't know very well and people who are trying to take advantage. I wish I were more like you. You're very analytical. There's another side of you that you don't often show to the world, but don't worry—it's our secret.'

His expression shifted from amused to guarded. 'Lily—'

'Don't panic. I still don't love you or anything. But I don't think you're quite the cold-hearted machine I did a week ago.'

I still don't love you.

She'd said the words so many times during their short relationship and they'd always been a joke. It was a code that acted as a reminder that this relationship was all about fun and sex and nothing deeper. Until now. She realised with a lurch of horror that it was no longer true.

She wasn't sure at what point her feelings had changed, but she knew they had and the irony of it was painful.

She'd conducted all her relationships with the same careful, studied approach to compatibility. David Ashurst had seemed perfect on the surface but had proved to be disturbingly imperfect on closer inspection whereas Nik, who had failed to score a single point on her checklist at first glance, had turned out to be perfect in every way when she'd got to know him better.

He'd proved himself to be both honest and unwaveringly loyal to his family.

It was that honesty that had made him hesitate before finally agreeing to take her home that night and that honesty was part of the reason she loved him.

She wanted to stay here with him for ever, breathing in the sea breeze and the scent of wild thyme, living this life of barefoot bliss.

But he didn't want that and he never would.

The following morning, Nik left Lily to pack while he returned Chloe to his father and Diandra, who were enjoying breakfast on the sunny terrace overlooking the sea.

Diandra took Chloe indoors for a change of clothes and Nik joined his father.

'I was wrong,' he said softly. 'I like Diandra. I like her a great deal.'

'And she likes you. I'm glad you came to the wedding. It's been wonderful having you here. I hope you visit again soon.' His father paused. 'We both love Lily. She's a ray of sunshine.'

Nik usually had no interest in the long-term aspirations of the women he dated, but in this case he couldn't stop thinking about what she'd told him.

I want to be someone's favourite person.

She said she didn't want a fairy tale, but in his opinion expecting a relationship to last for a lifetime was the biggest fairy tale of all. His mouth tightened as he contemplated the brutal wake-up call that awaited her. He doubted there was a man out there who was capable of fulfilling Lily's shiny dream and the thought of the severe bruising that awaited her made him want to string safety nets between the trees to cushion her fall.

'She is ridiculously idealistic.'

'You think so?' His father poured honey onto a bowl of fresh yoghurt. 'I disagree. I think she is remarkably clear-sighted about many things. She's a smart young woman.'

Nik frowned. 'She is smart, but when it comes to relationships she has poor judgement just like—' He broke off and his father glanced at him with a smile.

'Just like me. Wasn't that what you were going to say?' He poured Nik a cup of coffee and pushed it towards him. 'You think I haven't learned my lesson, but every relationship I've had has taught me something. The one thing it hasn't taught me is to give up on love. Which is good, because this twisty, turning, sometimes stony path led me to Diandra. Without those other relationships, I wouldn't be here now.' He sat back, relaxed and visibly happy while Nik stared at him.

'You're seriously trying to convince me that if you

could put the clock back, you wouldn't change things? Try and undo the mistakes?'

'I wouldn't change anything. And I don't see them as mistakes. Life is full of ups and downs. All the decisions I made were right at the time and each one of them led to other things, some good, some bad.'

Nik looked at him in disbelief. 'When my mother left you were a broken man. I was scared you wouldn't recover. How can you say you don't regret it?'

'Because for a while we were happy, and even when it fell apart I had you.' His father sipped his coffee. 'I wish I'd understood at the time how badly you were scarred by it all and I certainly wish I could undo some of the damage it did to you.'

'So if you had your time again, you'd still marry her?'

'Without hesitation.'

'And Maria and Callie?'

'The same. There are no guarantees with love, that's true, but it's the one thing in life worth striving to find.'

'I don't see it that way.'

His father gave him a long look. 'When you were building your business from the ground and you hit a stumbling block, did you give up?'

'No, but—'

'When you lost a deal, did you think to yourself that there was no point in going after the next one?'

Nik sighed. 'It is *not* the same. In my business I never make decisions based on emotions.'

'And that,' his father said softly, 'is your problem, Niklaus.'

CHAPTER TEN

THE JOURNEY BACK to Crete was torture. As the boat sped across the waves, Lily looked over her shoulder at Camomile Villa, knowing she'd never see it again.

Nik was unusually quiet.

She wondered if he'd had enough of being with her.

No doubt he was ready to move on to someone else. Another woman with whom he could share a satisfying physical relationship, never dipping deeper. The thought of him with another woman made her feel ill and Lily gripped the side of the boat, a gesture that earned her a concerned frown.

'Are you sea sick?'

She was about to deny that, but realised to do so would mean providing an alternative explanation for her inertia so she gave a little nod and instantly he slowed the boat.

That demonstration of thoughtfulness simply made everything worse.

It had been so much easier to stay detached when she'd thought he was the selfish, ruthless money-making machine everyone else believed him to be.

Now she knew differently.

The drive between the little jetty and his villa should have been blissful. The sun beamed down on them and the scent of lavender and thyme filled the air, but as they grew closer to their destination she grew more and more miserable.

She was lost in her own deep pit of gloom, and it was only when he stopped at the large iron gates that sealed his villa off from the rest of the world that she realised his mistake.

She stirred. 'You forgot to drop me home.'

'I didn't forget.' He turned to look at her. 'I'll take you home if that's what you want, or you can spend the night here with me.'

Her heart started to pound. 'I thought—' She'd assumed he'd drop her home and that would be the end of it. 'I'd like to stay.'

The look in his eyes made everything inside her tighten in delicious anticipation.

He muttered something under his breath in Greek and then turned his head and focused on the driving, a task that seemed to cost him in terms of effort.

She knew he was aroused and her mood lifted and flew. He might not love her, but he wanted her. That was enough for now.

It wasn't one night.

They'd already had so much more than that.

He shifted gears and then reached across and took her hand and she looked down, at those long, strong fingers holding tightly to hers.

Her body felt hot and heavy and she stole a glance at his taut profile and knew he was as aroused as she was. In the short time they'd been together she'd learned to recognise the signs. The darkening of his eyes, the tightening of his mouth and the brief sideways glance loaded with sexual promise.

He wore a casual shirt that exposed the bronzed skin at the base of his throat and she had an almost over-whelming temptation to lean across and trace that part of him with her tongue. To tease when he wasn't in a position to retaliate.

'Don't you dare.' He spoke through his teeth. 'I'll crash the car.'

'How did you know what I was thinking?'

'Because I was thinking the same thing.'

It amazed her that they could be so in tune with each other, when they were so fundamentally different in every way.

'You need a villa with a shorter drive.'

He gave a laugh that was entirely at his own expense, and then cursed as his phone rang as he pulled up in front of the villa.

'Answer it.' She said it lightly, somehow managing to keep the swell of disappointment hidden inside.

'I'll get rid of them.' He spoke with his usual arro-gant assurance before hitting a button on his phone and taking the call.

He switched between Greek and English and Lily was lost in a dream world, imagining the night that lay ahead, when she heard him talking about taking the private jet to New York.

He was flying to New York?

The phone call woke her up from her dream.

What was she doing?

Why was she hanging around like stale fish when

this relationship was only ever going to be something transitory?

Was part of her really hoping that she might be the one that changed his mind?

The happiness drained out of her like air from an inflatable mattress.

She never should have come back here. She should have asked him to drop her at her flat and made her exit with dignity.

Taking advantage of the fact he was still on the phone, she grabbed her small bag and slid out of the car.

'Thanks for the lift, Nik,' she whispered. 'See you soon.'

Except she knew she wouldn't.

She wouldn't see him ever again.

He turned his head and frowned. 'Wait—'

'Carry on with your call—I'll grab a cab,' she said hastily, and then proceeded to walk as fast as she could back up his drive in the baking heat.

Why did his drive have to be so *long*?

She told herself it was for the best. It wasn't his fault that her feelings had changed, and his hadn't. Their deal had been rebound sex without emotion. She was the one who'd brought emotion into it. And she'd take those emotions home with her, as she always did, and heal them herself.

Her eyes stung. She told herself it was because the sun was bright and scrabbled in her bag for sunglasses as a car came towards her down the drive. She recognised the sleek lines of the car that had driven her and Nik to the museum opening that night. It slowed down and Vassilis rolled down the window.

He took one look at her face and the suitcase and his mouth tightened. 'It's too hot to walk in this heat, *kyria*. Get in the car. I'll take you home.'

Too choked to argue, Lily slid into the back of the car. The air conditioning cooled her heated skin and she tried not to think about the last time she'd been in this car.

She was about to give Vassilis the address of her apartment, when her phone beeped.

It was a text from Brittany.

Fell on site, broke my stupid wrist and knocked myself out. In hospital. Can you bring clothes?

Horrified, Lily leaned forward. 'Vassilis, could you take me straight to the hospital please? It's urgent.'

Without asking questions, he turned the car and drove fast in the direction of the hospital, glancing at her in his mirror.

'Can I do anything?'

She gave him a watery smile and shook her head. At least worrying about Brittany gave her something else to think about. 'You're already doing it, thank you.'

'Where do you want me to drop you?'

'Emergency Department.'

'Does the boss know you're here?'

'No. And he doesn't need to.' She was glad she'd kept the sunglasses on. 'It was a bit of fun, Vassilis, that's all.' Impulsively she leaned forward and kissed him on the cheek. 'Thank you for the lift. You're a sweetheart.'

Scarlet, he handed her a card. 'My number. Call me when you're ready for a lift home.'

Lily located Brittany in a ward attached to the emergency department. She was sitting, pale and disconsolate, in a room where she was the only occupant. Her face was bruised and her wrist was in plaster and she had a smear of mud on her cheek.

Putting aside her own misery, Lily gave a murmur of sympathy. 'Can I hug you?'

'No, because I'm dangerous. I'm in a filthy mood. It's my right hand, Lil! The hand I dig with, type with, write with, feed myself with, punch with— Ugh. I'm so *mad* with myself. And I'm mad with Spy.'

'Why? What did he do?'

'He made me laugh! I was laughing so hard I wasn't looking where I was putting my feet. I tripped and fell down the damn hole, put my hand out to save myself and smashed my head on a pot we'd dug up earlier. It would be funny if it wasn't so tragic.'

'Why isn't Spy here with you?'

'He was. I sent him away.' Brittany slumped. 'I'm not good company and I couldn't exactly send him to pack my underwear.'

'What's going to happen? Are they keeping you in?'

'Yes, because I banged my head and they're worried my brain might be damaged.' Brittany looked so frustrated Lily almost felt like smiling.

'Your brain seems fine to me, but I'm glad they're treating you with care.'

'I want to go home!'

'To our cramped, airless apartment? Brittany, it will be horribly uncomfortable.'

'I don't mean home to the apartment. I mean home to Puffin Island. There is no point in being here now

I can't dig. If I've got to sit and brood somewhere, I'd rather do it at Castaway Cottage.'

'I thought you said a friend was using the cottage.'

'Emily is there, but there's room for two. In fact it will be three, because—' She broke off and shook her head dismissively, as if realising she'd said something she shouldn't. 'Long story. My friends and I lurch from one crisis to another and it looks as if it's my turn. Can you do me a favour, Lil?'

'Anything.'

'Can you book me a flight to Boston? I'll sort out the transfer from there, but if you could get me back home, that would be great. The doctor said I can fly tomorrow if I feel well enough. My credit card is back in the apartment.' She lay back and closed her eyes, her cheeks pale against the polished oak of her hair.

'Have they given you something for the pain?'

'Yes, but it didn't do much. I don't suppose you have a bottle of tequila on your person? That would do it. Crap, I am so selfish—I haven't even asked about you.' She opened her eyes. 'You look terrible. What happened? How was the wedding?'

'It was great.' She made a huge effort to be cheerful. 'I had a wonderful time.'

Brittany's eyes narrowed. 'How wonderful?'

'Blissful. Mind-blowing.' She told herself that all the damage was internal. No one was going to guess that she was stumbling round with a haemorrhaging wound inside her.

'I want details. Lots of them.' Brittany's eyes widened as she saw the necklace at Lily's throat. 'Wow. That's—'

SARAH MORGAN   461

'It's one of Skylar's, from her *Mediterranean Sky* collection.'

'I know. I'm drooling with envy. He *bought* you that?'

'Yes.' She touched her fingers to the smooth stone, knowing she'd always remember the night he'd given it to her. 'He had one of her pots in his villa—do you remember the large blue one? She called it *Modern Minoan* I think. I recognised it and when he found out I knew Skylar, he thought I might like this.'

'So just like that he bought it for you? How the other half lives. That necklace you're wearing cost—'

'Don't tell me,' Lily said quickly, 'or I'll feel I have to give it back.' She'd intended to, but it was all she had to remind her of her time with him.

'Don't you dare give it back. You're supporting Sky. Her business is really taking off. It's thrilling for her. In my opinion she needs to ditch the guy she's dating because he can't handle her success, but apart from that she has a glittering future. That is one serious gift you're wearing, Lily. So when are you seeing him again?'

'I'm not. This was rebound sex, remember?' She said it in a light-hearted tone but Brittany's smile turned to a scowl.

'He hurt you, didn't he? I'm going to kill him. Right after I put a deep gouge in his Ferrari, I'm going to dig out his damn heart.'

Lily gave up the exhausting pretence that everything was fine. 'It's my fault. Everything I did was my choice. It's not his fault I fell in love. I still don't understand how it happened because he is *so* wrong for me.' She sank onto the edge of the bed. 'I thought he didn't fit any of the criteria on my list, and then after a while I realised he did. That's the worst thing about it. I've realised there are no rules I can follow.'

'You're in love with him? Lily—' Brittany groaned '—a man like that doesn't *do* love.'

'Actually you're wrong. He loves his father deeply. He doesn't show it in a touchy-feely way, but the bond between them is very strong. It's romantic love he doesn't believe in. He doesn't trust the emotion.' And she understood why. He'd been deeply hurt and that hurt had bedded itself deep inside him and influenced the way he lived his life. His security had been wrenched away from him at an age when it should have been the one thing he could depend on, so he'd chosen a different sort of security—one he could control. He'd made sure he could never be hurt again.

She ached for him.

And she ached for herself.

Brittany took her hand. 'Forget him. He's a rat bastard.'

'No.' Lily sprang to his defence. 'He isn't. He's honest about what he wants. He would never mislead someone the way David did.'

'Not good enough. He should have seen what sort of person you were on that very first night and driven you home.'

'He did see, and he tried to.' Lily swallowed painfully. 'He spelled out exactly what he was offering but I didn't listen. I made my choice.'

'Do you regret it, Lil?'

'No! It was the most perfect time of my life. I can't stop wishing the ending was different, but—' She took a deep breath and pressed her hand to her heart. 'I'm going to stop doing that fairy-tale thing and be a bit more realistic about life. I'm going to "wise up" as you'd say, and try and be a bit more like Nik. Protect myself, as he does. That way when someone like David comes into my life, I'll be less likely to make a mistake.'

'What about your checklist?'

'I'm throwing it out. In the end it didn't prove very reliable.' And deep down she knew there was no chance of her making a mistake again. No chance of her falling in love again.

'Does he know how you feel?'

'I hope not. That would be truly embarrassing. Now let's forget that. You're the important one.' Summoning the last threads of her will power, Lily stood up and picked up her bag. 'I'm going to go back to our apartment, pack you a case of clothes and book you on the first flight out of here.'

'Come with me. You'd love Puffin Island. Sea, sand and sailing. It's a gorgeous place. There's nothing keeping you here, Lily. Your project is finished and you can't spend August travelling Greece on your own.'

Right now she couldn't imagine travelling anywhere. She wanted to lie down in a dark room until she stopped hurting.

Brittany reached out and took her hand. 'Castaway Cottage is the most special place on earth. We may not have Greek weather, but right now living here is like being in a range cooker so you might be grateful for that. When I'm home, I sleep with the windows open and I can hear the birds and the crash of the sea. I wake up and look out of the window and the sea is smooth and flat as a mirror. You have to come. My grandmother thought the cottage had healing properties, remember? And it looks as if you need to heal.'

Was healing possible? 'Thanks. I'll think about it.' She gave her friend a gentle hug. 'Don't laugh at any jokes while I'm gone.'

She took a cab home and tried not to think about Nik.

Sweltering in their tiny, airless bedroom, she hunted for a top or a dress that could easily be pulled over a plaster cast.

It was ridiculous to feel this low. Right from the start, there had only been one ending.

She'd be fine as long as she kept busy.

But would he?

The next woman he dated wouldn't know about his past, because he didn't share it.

They wouldn't understand him.

They wouldn't be able to find a way through the steely layers of protection he put between himself and the world and they'd retreat, leaving him alone.

And he didn't deserve to be alone.

He deserved to be loved.

Through the window of her apartment she could see couples walking hand in hand along the street on their way to the nearest beach. Families with small children, the nice gay couple who owned Brittany's favourite bar. Everyone was in pairs. It was like living in Noah's ark, she thought gloomily, two by two.

She resisted the urge to lie down on the narrow bed and sob until her head ached. Brittany needed her. She didn't have time for self-indulgent misery, especially when this whole thing was her own fault.

She found a shirt that buttoned down the front and was folding it carefully when she heard a commotion in the street outside.

Lily felt a flicker of panic. The cab couldn't be here already, surely?

She was about to lean out of the window and ask him to wait when someone pounded on the door.

'Lily?' Nik's voice thundered through the woodwork. 'Open the door.'

The ground shifted beneath her feet and for a moment she thought there had been a minor earthquake. Then she realised it was her knees that were trembling, not the floor.

What was he doing here?

Dragging herself to the door, she opened it cautiously. 'Stop banging. These apartments aren't very well built. A cupboard fell off the wall last week.' She took in his rumpled appearance and the tension in his handsome face and felt a stab of concern. 'Is something the matter? You look terrible. Was your phone call bad news?'

'Are you ill?' He spoke in a roughened tone and she looked at him in astonishment.

'What makes you think I'm ill?'

'Vassilis told me he took you to the emergency department. You *were* very pale on the boat. You should have told me you were feeling so unwell.'

He thought she'd gone to the hospital for herself? 'Brittany is the one in hospital. She had a fall. I'm on my way there now with some stuff. I really need to finish packing. The cab will be here soon.' Knowing she couldn't keep this up for much longer, she turned away but he caught her arm in a tight grip.

'Why did you walk away from me? I thought we agreed you were going to stay another night.'

'I didn't walk. I bounded. That's what happens after rebound sex. You bound.' She kept it light and heard him curse softly under his breath.

'You didn't need to leave.'

'Yes, I did.' Aware that her neighbours were probably enjoying the show, she reached past him and closed the door. 'I shouldn't have agreed to stay in the first place. I wasn't playing by the rules. And as it happened Brittany needed me, so your phone call was perfect timing.'

'It was terrible timing.'

Discovering that being in the same room as him was even harder than not being in the same room as him, Lily walked back to the bedroom and finished packing. 'So you're flying back to New York? That sounds exciting.'

'Business demands I fly back to the US, but I have things to settle here first.'

She wondered if she was one of the things he had to settle.

He was trying to find a tactful way of reminding her their relationship hadn't been serious.

The ache inside grew worse. She tried to think of something to say that would make it easy for him. 'I have to get to the hospital. Brittany fell on site and fractured her wrist. She's waiting for me to bring her clothes and things and then I have to arrange a flight for her back to Maine because she can't stay here. She has invited me to spend August with her. I'm going to say yes.'

'Is that what you want?'

Of course it wasn't what she wanted. 'It will be fantastic.' Her control was close to snapping. 'Did you want something, Nik? Because I have to ring a cab, take some clothes to Brittany at the hospital and then battle with the stupid Wi-Fi to book a ticket and it's a nightmare. I did some research before the Internet crashed and at best it's a nineteen-hour journey with two changes. She's going to have to fly to Athens, then to Munich where she can get a direct flight to Boston. I still have to research how she gets from Boston to Puffin Island, but I can guarantee that by the time she arrives home she'll be half dead. I'm going to fly with her because she can't do it on her own, but I hadn't exactly budgeted for a ticket to the US so I'm having to do a bit of financial juggling.'

'What if I want to change the rules?'

'Sorry?'

'You said you weren't playing by the rules.' His gaze was steady on her face. 'What if I want to change the rules?'

'The way I feel right now, I'd have to say no.'

'How do you feel?'

She was absolutely sure that was one question he didn't want answered. 'My cab is going to be here in a minute and I have to book flights—'

'I'll give you a lift to the hospital and arrange for her to use the Gulfstream. We can fly direct to Boston and she can lie down all the way if she wants to,' he said. 'And I know a commercial pilot who flies between the islands, so that problem is also solved. Now tell me how you feel.'

'Wait a minute.' Lily looked at him, dazed. 'You're offering to transport Brittany home on a private jet? You can't do that. When I told you I was going to have to do some financial juggling I wasn't fishing for a donation.'

'I know. It sounds as if Brittany's in trouble and I'm always happy to help a friend in trouble.'

It confirmed everything she already knew about him but instead of cheering her up, it made her feel worse. 'But she's my friend, not yours.'

He drew in a breath. 'I'm hoping your friends will soon be my friends. And on that topic, *please* can we focus on us for a moment?'

Her heart gave an uneven bump and she looked at him warily. 'Us?'

'If you won't talk about your feelings then I'll talk about mine. Before we left the island this morning, I had a long conversation with my father.'

Lily softened. 'I'm pleased.'

'I'd always believed his three marriages were mistakes, something he regretted, and it wasn't until today that I realised he regretted nothing. Far from seeing them as mistakes, he sees them as a normal part of life, which delivers a mix of good and bad to everyone. Yes, there was pain and hurt, but he never once faltered in his belief that love existed. I confess that came as a surprise to me. I'd assumed if he could have put the clock back and done things differently, he would have done.'

Lily gave a murmur of sympathy. 'Perhaps it was worse for you being on the outside. You only had half the story.'

'When my mother left I saw what it did to him, how vulnerable he was, and it terrified me.' His honesty touched her but she resisted the temptation to fling her arms round him and hug him until he begged for mercy.

'You don't have to tell me this. I know you hate talking about it.'

'I want to. It's important that you understand.'

'I do understand. Your mother walked away from you. That was the one relationship you should have been able to depend on. It's not surprising you didn't believe in love. Why would you? You had no evidence that it existed.'

'Neither did you,' he breathed, 'and yet you never ceased to believe in it.'

She gave a half-smile. 'Maybe I'm stupid.'

'No. You are the brightest, funniest, sexiest woman I've met in my whole life and there is no way, *no way*,' he said in a raw tone, 'I am letting you walk out of my life.'

'Nik—'

'You asked me why I was here. I'm here because I want to renegotiate the terms of our relationship.'

She almost smiled at that. Only Nik could make it sound like a business deal. 'Is this because you know I have feelings for you and you feel sorry for me? Because, honestly, I'm going to be fine. I'll get over you, Nik. At some point I'll get out there again.' She hoped she sounded more convincing than she felt.

'I don't want you to get over me. And I don't want to think of you "out there", a pushover for anyone who decides to take advantage of you.'

'I can take care of myself. I've learned a lot from you. I'm Kevlar.'

'You are marshmallow-coated sunshine,' he drawled, 'and you need someone with a less shiny view on life to watch out for you. I don't want this to be a rebound relationship, Lily. I want more.'

Suddenly she found it difficult to breathe. 'What exactly are we talking about here? How much more?'

'All of it.' He stroked her hair back from her face with gentle hands. 'You've made me believe in something I never thought existed.'

'Fairy tales?'

'Love,' he said softly. 'You've made me believe in love.'

'Nik—'

'I love you.' He paused and drew breath. 'And unless my reading of this situation is completely wrong, I believe you love me back. Which is probably more than I deserve, but I'm selfish enough not to care about that. When it comes to you, I'll take whatever I can get.'

'Oh.' She felt a constriction in her chest. Her eyes filled and she covered her mouth with her hand. 'I'm going to cry, and you hate that. I'm really sorry. You'd better run.'

'I hate it when you cry, that's true. I don't ever want to see you cry. But I'm not running. Why would I run when the one thing in life that is special to me is right here?'

A lump wedged itself in her throat. She was so afraid of misinterpreting what he said, she was afraid to speak. 'You love me. So y-you're saying you'd like to see me again? Date?'

'No, that's not what I'm saying.' Usually so articulate, this time he stumbled over the words. 'I'm saying that you're my favourite person, Lily. And I apologise for proposing to you in a cramped airless room with no air conditioning but, as you know, I'm very goal orientated and as my goal is to persuade you to marry me then the first step is to ask you.' He reached into his pocket and pulled out a box. 'Skylar doesn't make engagement rings but I hope you'll like this.'

'You want to marry me?' Feeling as if she were running to catch up, she stared at the box. 'I'm your favourite person?'

'Yes. And when you find your favourite person it's important to hold onto them and not let them go.'

'You love me? You're sure?' She blinked as he opened the box and removed a diamond ring. 'Nik, that's *huge*.'

'I thought it would slow you down and make it harder for you to escape from me.' He slid it onto her finger and she stared at it, dazzled as the diamond caught the sun's rays.

'I'm starting to believe in fairy tales after all. I love you, too.' It was her turn to stumble. 'I knew I was in love with you, but I wasn't going to tell you. It didn't seem fair on you. You were clear about the rules right from the beginning and I broke them. That was my fault.'

With a groan, he pulled her against him. 'I knew how you felt. I was going to force you to talk to me, but then I had to take that phone call and you vanished.'

'I didn't want to make it awkward for you by hanging around,' she muttered and he said something in Greek and eased her away from him.

'What about you?' His expression was serious. 'This isn't a first for you. You've fallen in love before.'

'That's the weird thing—' she lifted her hand to take another look at her ring, just to make sure she hadn't imagined it '—I thought I had, but then I spent time with you and told you all those things and I realised that with you it was different. I think I was in love with the idea of love. I thought I knew exactly what qualities I wanted in a person. But you can't use a checklist to fall in love. With you, I wasn't trying and it happened anyway. I need to change. I need to find a new way to protect myself.'

'I don't want you to change. I want you to stay exactly the way you are. And I can be that layer of protection that you don't seem to be able to cultivate for yourself.'

'You're volunteering to be my armour?'

'If that means spending the rest of my life plastered against you that sounds good to me.' His mouth was on hers, his hands in her hair and it occurred to her that this level of happiness was something she'd dreamed about.

'I was going to spend August on Puffin Island with Brittany.'

'Spend it with me. I have to go to New York next week, but we can fly Brittany to Maine first. I have friends in Bar Harbor. That's close to Puffin Island. While I'm at my meeting in New York you could visit Skylar. Then we can fly to San Francisco and take some time to plan our life together. I can't promise you a fairy tale, but I can promise the best version of reality I can give you.'

'You want me to go with you to San Francisco? What job would I do there?'

'Well, they have museums, but I was thinking about

that.' He brushed away salty tears from her cheeks. 'How would you feel about spending more time on your ceramics?'

'I can't afford it.'

'You can now, because what's mine is yours.'

'I couldn't do that. I don't ever want our relationship to be about money.' She flushed awkwardly. 'It's important I keep custody of my rusty bike so I'm going to need you to sign one of those pre-nuptial agreement things so I'm protected in case you try and snatch everything I own.'

He was smiling. 'Pre-nuptial agreements are for people whose relationships aren't going to last and ours will last, *theé mou*.' Those words and the sincerity in his voice finally convinced her that he meant it, but even that wasn't enough to convince her this was really happening.

'But seriously, what do I bring to this relationship?'

'You bring optimism and a sunny outlook on life that no amount of money can buy. You're an inspiration, Lily. You're willing to trust, despite having been hurt. You have never known a stable family, and yet that hasn't stopped you believing that such a thing is possible for you. You live the life you believe in and I want to live that life with you.'

'So I bring a smile and you bring a private jet? I'm not sure that's an equitable deal. Not that I know much about deals. That's your area of expertise.'

'It is, and I can tell you I'm definitely the winner in this particular deal.' He kissed her again. 'The money is going to mean I can spoil you, and I intend to do that so you'd better get used to it. I thought being an artist would fit nicely round having babies. We'll split our time between the US and Greece. Several times a year we'll come back here and stay in Camomile Villa so we can see Diandra and Chloe and you can have your fill of Minoan remains.'

'Wait. You're moving too quickly for me. You have to understand I'm still getting used to the idea that I've gone from owning a bicycle, to having part ownership of a private jet.'

'And five homes.'

'I have real-estate whiplash. But at least I know how to clean them!' But it was something else he'd said that had really caught her attention. 'A moment ago—did you mention babies?'

'Have I misunderstood what you want? Am I sounding too traditional? Right now my Greek DNA is winning out,' he groaned, 'but what I'm trying to say is you can do anything you like. Make any choices you like, as long as I'm one of them.'

'You'd want babies?' She flung her arms round him. 'You haven't misunderstood. Having babies is my dream.'

His mouth was on hers. 'How do you feel about starting right away? I used to consider myself progressive, but all I can think about is how cute you're going to look when you're pregnant so I have a feeling I may have regressed to Neanderthal man. Does that bother you?'

'I've already told you I studied *homo neanderthalensis*,' Lily said happily. 'I'm an expert.'

'You have no idea how relieved I am to hear that.' Ignoring the heat, the size of the room and the width of the bed, he pulled her into his arms and Lily discovered it was possible to kiss and cry at the same time.

'We've had fun sex, athletic sex and angry sex—what sort of sex is this? Baby sex?'

'Love sex,' he said against her mouth. 'This is love sex. And it's going to be better than anything that's gone before.'

* * * * *